SEVEN FOR A SECRET

Rumer Haven

OMNIFIC PUBLISHING
LOS ANGELES

Omnific Publishing
1901 Avenue of the Stars, 2nd floor
Los Angeles, CA 90067
www.omnificpublishing.com

First Omnific eBook edition, August 2014
First Omnific trade paperback edition, August 2014

The characters and events in this book are fictitious.
Any similarity to real persons, living or dead,
is coincidental and not intended by the author.

Quotation used from *The Phantom of the Opera*. Directed by Rupert Julian.
United States: Universal Pictures, 1925. Silent film.

Library of Congress Cataloguing-in-Publication Data

Haven, Rumer.
    Seven for a Secret / Rumer Haven – 1st ed.
    ISBN: 978-1-623421-09-0
    1. Romance — Fiction. 2. 1920s — Fiction.
    3. Ghost — Fiction. 4. Chicago — Fiction. I. Title

10 9 8 7 6 5 4 3 2 1

Cover Design by Micha Stone and Amy Brokaw
Interior Book Design by Coreen Montagna

Printed in the United States of America

To Chi-Town and the people I love there.

One for sorrow
Two for mirth
Three for a wedding
Four for a birth
Five for silver
Six for gold
Seven for a secret
never to be told
Eight for heaven
Nine for hell
And ten for the Devil himself

(Traditional children's nursery rhyme)

One for Sorrow

June 2000

The pavement bore no traces of the body that had burst against it six months ago on New Year's Eve.

Young Kate Pembroke stepped around that spot all the same as she toured Camden Court Apartments. Leo, one of the residents and her guide, had just explained how The Leaper — as neighbors now called the dead man — had led a solitary life, as far as anyone could tell. And in a place like this, he said, anyone *could* tell. Quite a lot, in fact. At least the ones who'd stuck around long enough.

Kate was just about to learn The Leaper's real name when a shrill scream sounded from above.

"You all right up there, Vera?" Leo cried, shading his pale eyes from the noon sun with a vein-gnarled hand. Though he stood tall and appeared able-bodied enough, Kate estimated that he was in his eighties.

"Oh! You *scoundrel!*" the raspy voice seethed, just before a head peeped out over a fourth-floor window ledge. Short blond curls with silver roots formed a bright halo around a face darkened against the sky.

"Vera?" Leo asked again. "What did you just call me?"

"Not you, ya coot. You would never *believe* what that old bat allowed to happen in here. My word!" The golden head withdrew from sight.

Kate looked to Leo with a raised brow and timid smile. He merely shrugged and shooed the upper window away with his hand. "That's Vera, another neighbor," was all he said.

"So I figured." Kate grinned and scanned the courtyard as though any further questions she had about the building might be hidden in its hedges. Just then, she heard the fourth-floor window grind open wider in its frame.

"Just look at this, will you?"

A sprinkling of drops anointed Kate's forehead as she squinted up at Vera, who was spastically shaking something over the window ledge. Something small, dark, dangling.

Kate screamed this time.

"Man alive, Vera!" Leo shouted. "What in God's name are you doin'? Nice way to greet our new neighbor. This is Kate."

"Gracious," Vera cried. "You're not to live *here*, are you, hon? In this apartment, I mean?"

"Yeah. As of July."

"My word." Vera crossed herself with the dead mouse still hanging from her fingers by its tail.

Leo winced. "If you wanna drop that down here, I'll bury it for ya."

She spun the rodent like a helicopter propeller before flinging it clear across the courtyard. It smacked against the opposite brick wall with a sickening wet slap and dropped into a rosebush.

"God's sake, woman," Leo muttered, then raised his voice to ask her, "Where'd you come across that wet thing anyhow? The drain?"

"The kettle!" Vera bellowed before slamming the window closed.

Kate had yet to find her tongue. She watched the old man lumber across the yard, yanking a white handkerchief from his pocket. If he was to offer the rodent proper funeral rites beneath the morning glories, it wasn't going to happen right then; he just dug a shallow divot with his heel, laid the mouse carcass inside, covered it with the hankie, and kicked some loose dirt over it.

As he walked back, scuffing his palms against the thighs of his denim overalls, Kate had enough time to retrieve her voice. "So, uh. That's, um, that *is* my place, isn't it?"

"'Fraid so," Leo said. "But don't you mind what Vera says. That woman needs to watch less television and stop inventin' these damned soap operas in her head." The scowl left his countenance and his mild, gray-eyed gaze met Kate's directly. "Don't you mind, now. The place is a little tired, that's all, in need of some sprucin' up. The, eh, the previous tenant had lived there over seventy years, if you can believe it."

Seventy years. That was almost triple the time Kate had lived—period—let alone in one place.

"But don't worry. That place'll be whipped into tip-top shape before you move in. Cable- and Internet-ready. I'll see to that personally."

Kate mulled over the man's soft-sell. Unorthodox, for sure. Suicides and dead rodents weren't the stuff of *Better Homes and Gardens*, yet the man's nervous attempts to impress her all morning cast an endearing—if not morbid—amusement to the situation.

She extended her hand to meet his firm handshake. "Thank you, Leo. I'm excited about living in Lincoln Park. This is an awesome location by the park and lake, and it cuts down my commute to the Adler."

"The Adler Planetarium? You an astronomer or somethin'?"

Kate laughed. "Not quite. I supervise learning activities for the visitors. Anyway, thanks again." She made to turn but caught herself. "Oh, and where's the nearest bus stop?"

"Just around the block there, at Wrightwood and Clark."

"Great. And when do you think I could view the actual apartment? I know the layout's identical to yours, but—"

"You're already lookin' to move in July first, right?"

"Right."

"Tuesday all right with yeh, then?" He rubbed the back of his neck, and before Kate could answer, he said, "You know, I'm sure if you're not happy with the unit upstairs, another will be on the market soon enough…"

Kate thought she heard him mutter, "at this rate," but it was buried too deeply beneath his breath to know for sure.

"Tuesday's fantastic. Thanks again, Leo."

7

Tuesday had come and gone, as had the remainder of June, and Kate had moved into her new residence at Camden Court Apartments. A studio. All to herself.

It was July first, a Saturday. At her bathroom sink, she ran cool, slick hands over her brow bone and cheeks, then patted her palms dry on her khaki shorts.

Mental note: Unpack towels next.

As she made to leave, the smooth knob of the door's antique glass and brass handle slipped in Kate's damp palm. She ran her hand along her bare thigh with more determination and grabbed the clear glass knob again with a tighter grip, turned it, and pulled. The door wouldn't give.

She gave another little tug.

Nothing.

Blowing frustration out of her nose, Kate grasped with both hands and gave a solid yank. The knob finally did move toward her. The door, unfortunately, did not.

"Shit."

Kate looked down at the knob in her hand, gleaming like a giant gemstone. A big, gaudy, worthless gemstone that she dropped to the tiles before resting her fingertips at the gaping space where the knob should have stayed. With delicacy, she pinched the thin metal rod poking through from the other side and gave it a little twist—to no avail.

She squeezed it harder and twisted and jiggled it more until she only succeeded in causing the knob on the opposite side of the door to fall out as well.

"Shit. Oh, shit!"

Kate pawed at the hole in the door and tried sticking a pinkie finger through it. Bending down, she peeked through and saw only the cavernous dark of her doorless closet across the hall.

Had Leo said he'd be checking in some time that day?

"Shit."

No, that was tomorrow. But surely Dex would come over that night, eager as he was to check out her new bachelorette pad—and probably test the springs of the college futon she'd resurrected from her parents' basement for her first unfurnished apartment. Not exactly giving her the breathing room she'd asked for, but she'd welcome his doting on this occasion. Could she survive until evening? It was time to appraise her desert island scenario:

She had water; that was key. She could live on water for a while. And she had access to the toilet, which was a nice feature—no need to lose her civility and *Lord-of-the-Flies* her way through this one. She hadn't unpacked her toiletries yet, but she could still shower without soap. That had to count for something.

The shower—there was a window in the shower!

She flung the clear plastic curtain aside and bounded into the tub toward the small window overlooking the courtyard. The window that *would* have overlooked the courtyard, rather, if it hadn't been for the privacy glass textured all over with little retro sunbursts.

Kate gripped the handle to lift the pane upward. Nothing. She tried again. And again. Sealed shut with paint. Or maybe just locked. So she went to unlatch it and found that at least a decade's worth of paint had sealed it in place for eternity.

"Oh, my God, if it was locked when they painted over it…"

Kate stumbled backward out of the tub and, sitting on the toilet lid, did her best to slow her breathing. She tried to keep down the flutter of panic thudding against her breastbone as the double-edged sword of Living on Her Own now pointed at her jugular. She'd known it was too good to be true, that she'd been too smug as she'd woven through her cityscape of moving boxes like Godzilla and descended on her dishware. Reveled a little too much as she'd set to unpacking her plates—*hers*, her own. Not Dexter's. Not for now.

She eyed the rusted valve of her bathroom radiator. If she made it out of here alive, these vintage features would be something to get used to after the newer-build condo she'd shared with Dex. The one with floor-to-ceiling windows overlooking Lake Michigan and the stream of traffic on Lake Shore Drive—no reflection on *their* means. Dex had simply gotten lucky with a wealthy uncle who had no other use for it once he was past the real estate phase of his mid-life crisis. And Kate had lived there all of three months before she'd freaked out that things were moving too fast.

Poor Dex, she thought. *He's been patient.*

They'd been dating exclusively for close to a year-and-a-half now and had been friends and colleagues for longer than that. Both on staff in the Adler Planetarium's education department, they'd had an instant, kismet connection over their shared nerdy love of the universe and bringing it down to earth for the public through demonstrations and workshops. They had good chemistry as co-teachers, but Dex also made her laugh and feel like the most attractive, interesting being on the planet; his kind eyes and tall, lean swimmer's build hadn't hurt his chances with her either. But more than that, he just felt like…home. Kate couldn't describe it, only knew that his simple presence put her at ease.

Until it hadn't. After the initial passion, Kate worried that maybe her feeling of "home" around Dex was becoming a sisterly affection more than anything. She'd thought living together would reignite the spark by shaking things up a little, forcing her out of her comfort zone and causing some fights over toothpaste or dirty laundry that would lead to great, kitchen-counter make-up sex afterward or something.

Instead—nothing. The fights happened—on her end, anyway—but he'd always been quick to apologize and defuse the situation. She'd moved *into* the comfort zone, and he'd made it easy. Too easy. And Kate wasn't resigned to settling down like a couple of old folks just yet—she was only in her mid-twenties! She loved Dexter and they were still boyfriend-girlfriend by definition, but in moving out, she wanted to shake things up again for their own good. Wasn't it enough that they saw each other all day at the Adler? Didn't they need some absence to make the heart grow fonder and all that jazz?

Kate sighed, and another minute of finding patterns in the little white hexagonal floor tiles had calmed her enough to return to the matter at hand. She stood a fifty-fifty chance that the bathroom window was unlatched under that gob of paint.

She stepped back into the tub. With all her might, she braced one foot behind her on the side of the bath for leverage and, with both palms against the window frame, heaved upward.

Nothing. Her breath quickened even more, and her heart thumped as the room closed in on her. "Please," she whimpered.

On the count of three, she summoned all the adrenaline coursing through her and pushed again so hard she thought her face might pop. Her arms and thighs trembled under the force until, with a tearing sound and then a louder crack, the windowpane shoved upward. Fresh air and sunlight hit Kate's face.

"Oh!" With hands still manning their positions at the raised frame, she arched her back and looked to the ceiling in exaltation, then hunched to rest her forehead against the window handle.

And that's when she saw it.

A gathering of sorts in the courtyard below. Tables were arranged in a U-shape with a bunch of old-timers milling about piles of wares and clothing. Above the polite-sounding banter rose Vera's squawk as she appeared to run whatever show was going on.

Kate saw her building door open, too, just in time to catch a thick mass of wavy dark brown hair walk outside. She watched as the young, fit, masculine body beneath it exited through the courtyard gate to the street, escaping without a word.

Ah well, she'd have been too embarrassed to beseech a hot stranger for help anyway.

"Vera! Hello?" she called down at last. The golden helmet-head swiveled this way and that before looking up. "Vera! Hey!" She attempted a feeble *yoo-hoo!*-type whistle. "Up here!"

When their gazes met, Kate saw Vera's little body give a start and throw a hand to her forehead to shield her eyes from the sun. The woman slumped with an obvious exhale, as if relieved to see it was Kate and not whoever she'd thought it was.

"Hey, dear girl!" she called up. "Why don't you come down here and join us?"

"I would with pleasure, but uh…" There was just no cool way to explain her predicament in front of all those people. "Actually, would you mind coming up here for a second?"

"I can't leave things here, dear. Just come down!"

"Ah, well…" Kate looked around at a birdlike little lady stroking a ceramic poodle as an older gentleman inspected the bindings of a stack of faded hardcover books. A tortoiseshell tabby cat sunned itself in the grass at Vera's feet. "I will, but could you please, for one quick second—"

"Nonsense! I'll see ya when you come down."

"Oh, Vera, please! Just really quick."

A cloud came across the old woman's expression, and she stood a little taller. "Are you all right?" she asked, dismissing the Poodle Lady who had just asked her whether there was a shade to go with the rooster lamp. "Has something happened?"

"Yeah, unfortunately, and I could really use your help."

With no further questions or even a word of notice to anyone else at her little garden party, Vera scooped the cat up from its splendor in the grass and made a beeline for the door to Kate's wing of the building. Kate assumed—hoped—the woman was making her way up the stairwell, so she stepped out of the tub to sit patiently on the toilet seat.

Within a minute, she heard Vera shouting and knocking at her unit door. "Kate? Kate!" The knocking grew more urgent.

Kate stood and pressed her face to a panel in the bathroom door. "Come in, Vera!" She bent down and yelled again through the hole, "Door's unlocked! Come inside!"

She heard the unit door creak open and the shuffle of Vera's quick footsteps. "Kate? Where are you, Kate!" Vera shouted, as if that was necessary in such a tiny apartment.

Vera's voice traveled down the hall, and Kate banged on the bathroom door. "In here!"

"Gracious!" she heard as Vera scraped up and down the other side of the door. The next sound was the jostling of the doorknob rod back through the hole. And there it was, jiggling and twisting again under an unseen force until the door yawned open and Kate could breathe again.

She thanked Vera profusely, spilling out of the bathroom and inviting her neighbor to have a seat. Seeing the woman purse her lips as her eyes appeared to scan the chaos of unpacking limbo, Kate shoved aside a giant wardrobe box to reveal a portion of her futon not piled with shoes and clothes and pointed to it. Tightrope-walking her way through the clutter to a small wooden folding chair, Kate kicked aside a cardboard box labeled *Bedroom* and had a seat.

Bedroom. That was a laugh. In this studio apartment, "bedroom" would have to equal "living room," just like "bed" and "sofa" would equal "futon."

The dumbbell shape of the studio gave her some semblance of a proper apartment, at least. A small hallway connected the room where they sat to the kitchen, which was set off at the opposite end as its own separate room, complete with a glass-paneled mahogany door to reinforce the illusion of space. In her mind, Kate was already calling the kitchen the West Wing, as though a library and conservatory could also be found behind that door if one looked hard enough.

Kate's gaze roamed the living room/bedroom during what had grown into an awkward silence with Vera. Midday natural light pierced through the two large windows facing the courtyard, obstructed only by a grimy pair of cheap plastic blinds and a loudly humming air conditioning unit. Avoiding eye contact with her neighbor, Kate looked around at the fuzzy lines of gray already accumulating on the rectangular wall moldings, which had only just been painted a couple days ago.

The apartment painting had nearly set her move-in date back, in fact. Leo had supervised the work and phoned her with much regret to inform her that, no matter how many coats they'd applied, the yellow stains of neglect kept seeping through in spots. She'd assured him it wasn't a problem, so the painters had ceased and desisted.

She could see some of that jaundice now on the wall behind Vera. Unable to avoid her visitor any longer, Kate looked the woman in the eye. On closer inspection, Vera was older but not elderly. From her upright posture, relatively smooth skin, and sheer spunk, she looked to be in her early seventies.

Vera narrowed an eye and finally spoke. "If you haven't noticed, I'm not getting any younger. You gonna tell me what in heckfire happened, or what?"

Picking at her fingernails, Kate swallowed, cleared her throat, and began her tale of The Bathroom Incident. Her train of thought was occasionally interrupted, though, every time she glanced at the torbie cat, which jumped and spun incessantly in the corner by the unit door. Something on the ceiling seemed to draw its attention, so Kate glanced up but saw not so much as a fly or moving reflection of light. Now and then Vera would twist to look as well.

By the time Kate had finished explaining, the old woman's widened eyes had settled into a squint. They homed in on Kate, though occasionally twitching in the direction of that crazy, dancing cat.

Under the intimidation of Vera's concentrated gaze, Kate gave in to the distraction and watched the torbie leap and twirl in the air, pawing at nothing. And then it stopped and just sat on its hind legs in front of the door, shifting its head side to side as if watching a tennis match on the ceiling.

"So, yeah," Kate spoke up as she dragged her attention from the cat back to Vera's squinting assessment. "Anyway, that's what happened with the bathroom door."

She waited for some sweet grandmotherly nurturing, but all she got was, "Well, that was a damn stupid thing to do." Vera stood and looked around at Kate's lack of progress in unpacking, then back at the cat in the doorway. "Now come on down to the sale, Kate. Get out of here awhile and make yourself useful."

"Thanks, Leo. I hope you didn't strain anything."

"No, no. Keeps me young, this does. It's all right there in the corner?"

Kate had lasted all of two minutes down at the rummage sale when she'd spied a fantastic vintage wingback chair. It was a little dingy, with some of its wine-colored velour a bit threadbare in patches, but that could always be reupholstered. Vera hadn't looked pleased when Kate approached her to buy it, darting annoyed glances at Leo when he'd offered to deliver it to Kate's unit. Maybe Kate had irked her in buying merchandise when she was supposed to sell it.

"That corner's perfect," Kate said. "I'm going to put my floor lamp there and would like to buy a bookshelf to hide that extra closet door."

An unexpected feature of her studio was its walk-in closet, a luxury not exactly in keeping with such cramped space. And Kate didn't understand why the closet had two entrances. There was the open doorway off the hall—across from the bathroom—as well as a solid paneled door off the main living space, painted white to match the walls and mirroring the unit door on the opposite side. In comparison to the unit door, though, the closet entrance was substantially larger.

"What's that for, by the way?" she asked. "Why's it so huge?"

Leo had his hands on his hips, breathing heavily after hauling the chair up four flights. His perspiration heightened his spicy, musty scent, like aged newspapers sprinkled with cumin. And like a magician doing the scarf trick, he produced another white handkerchief from his denim pocket — or at least Kate hoped it wasn't the same one he'd mummified the mouse in.

"Ah, well, that was for a Murphy bed, ya see. You'd open the door like so, and the mattress and frame would come down."

"Ahh…" Kate gave a slow, exaggerated nod. "So I'm not much more primitive here with my futon."

"Oh no, not at all. N'fact, no one years ago would've brought many furnishin's into this place. More of a residential hotel, you see."

"Hotel?"

"Built in the twenties. Common for young bachelors just startin' out, tryin' to make it in the big city. It was a tough place to afford more. Still is, I reckon. Anyway…"

"A nineteen-twenties hotel, wow." Kate looked all around with new appreciation. "Sounds so transient, when now residents seem to stay here…a long time."

She hoped Leo would elaborate on the previous tenant. Yet if he'd picked up on her cue, he didn't show it.

Kate stood by her new, old chair and laid a hand on one of its wings, stroking its plush burgundy surface. She decided to press her luck. "Was there rent control here? Or do some people own their units? It just seems there are some — with all due respect — *older* occupants who must be living on social security. And I know all too well the rent's not cheap." She was barely making a go of it herself on her not-for-profit salary.

"Ah, yep, I see. Well, I, for instance, get a little knocked off my rent for helpin' round here. The maintenance and repair work and all that. And why sure, think there've been some special arrangements made over the years. 'Grandfathered in,' to use an appropriate term, though one I never thought would apply to *me*." Leo gave a gruff chuckle. "At least where age goes. Never had a family of my own to get grandkids, but…"

He held his grin as he shook his head and looked down to the floor, but Kate thought she saw sadness, regret maybe, in his raised brows. The way he clenched his teeth made him look almost in physical pain.

"Well, I don't feel any older inside," he continued. "Just my body that forces me to keep up." That gravelly little laugh again.

Kate, willingly catering to the instinctive youthful illusion of It Will Never Happen to Me, just hummed in sympathy and nodded with a dopey half-grin as if to say, *That's the way it goes.*

"Well," Leo said abruptly. "I'd best be leaving you to your privacy. Last thing you need when you're gettin' all settled in is an old codger nosin' around."

"Oh, Leo, you're always welcome here," Kate reassured. She liked imagining he was the grandpa she'd barely had, having lost one when she was young and the other before she was even born. Vera, too, would make a fun and feisty grandma to complement her more reserved ones now both living permanently in Florida. Which reminded Kate: "Actually, I'm going to follow you on my way out. I promised Vera I'd stop back at the sale to start packing things up."

"Great stuff, these sales, eh? Nice to see things still in good condition find new use. There wasn't much of that though in this lot, I tell ya. Which is amazing considerin' *all* the *stuff* that was piled up. Man alive, all the stuff. And it's funny, ya know, 'cause when I was movin' that chair outta' here last month, I'da never thought I'd be bringin' it right back."

Kate was slow to process what he meant. "Back where, in here? Oh my God, was that the tenant's who lived *here?*" When Leo nodded, she cupped a hand to her mouth. "Oh no, I'm so sorry! I feel like such a jackass. I didn't know."

Leo just chuckled. "Not your fault we took it out! I mean, of course we had to. They don't rent these places furnished, and no tellin' whether the next tenant would like it anyhoo. But you do, so there you go." He paused, and his eyes circled around the studio. "It must belong here…so just enjoy it with our blessings. No charge."

"No way!"

"Proceeds just go to the building's maintenance. She had no survivin' relations, see. Vera and I were the closest she got."

"So then the woman who lived here, she's —"

"We'd best be gettin' back to Vera. I don't want her hollerin' after me."

Out of the building and into the courtyard, the pair rejoined the little crowd that had amassed around the tables of what Kate now realized was a posthumous estate sale. More age groups were represented by this time; sun-tanned twenty- and thirty-somethings with beach bags and bicycles appeared to have returned from a day at the lakefront.

"There you are," Vera said. Seated at a table, she counted money with a pencil poking out of her tightened lips. Age lines circled her mouth like eyelashes. "Thought Leo might've used your toilet and fallen in." She lurched with a jovial *humph*.

"God sakes," Leo muttered.

"Anyway," Vera said, "I was thinking now that most of the kitschy crap's gone, we can rearrange some of the nicer accessories in a more appealing way. Attract the young folks. This stuff all comes back, doesn't it? You kids think everything you do is new and original, but us old farts have seen these things come, go, and come back again." She set to refolding a stack of handkerchiefs, and Kate sat in a lawn chair beside her.

"So, uh," Kate began as soon as Leo had wandered to the far table of record albums, "Leo told me this stuff belonged to the woman who lived in my place?"

Vera kept folding.

"She was elderly, right? So she's…"

"Dead? You betcha. In her sleep, God bless her." She started smoothing some doilies. "It was three days before we found her in there, right in the middle of that heat wave, and — " Vera looked up and seemed to register the expression contorting Kate's face. "Oh, well, I needn't get into the details. Let's just say heat doesn't do a body good."

Kate lost her tongue in Vera's presence all over again; the little lady was sure worth her weight in shock value. Meanwhile, a woman standing opposite Kate's table poked through dishtowels and aprons. Her frizzy brown hair, streaked with gray, was cut in a bob and had a plastic barrette haphazardly affixed to one side. Kate guessed she was in her early fifties and fixed a grin to her face in case they made eye contact. But the woman only shot looks out the corner of her eye toward the next table, where a sun-kissed blonde wearing nothing more than a bikini top and Daisy Dukes ran a finger along the fringe trim of a lampshade, giggling at anything the young man standing next to her said.

"It seems a lonely life, doesn't it," Vera said, "to stay cooped up in a place like this. At an older age, anyway. Maisie over there is on her way to it, too." She nodded toward the frizzy-haired woman, and Kate considered her name fitting for someone so mousy. Appearing lost in her own thoughts, Vera combed the tassels of a velour scarf with her fingers. "You kids probably think us old coots should be in a home by now. But some of us are stronger than that. Some of us have to be."

Kate watched Vera's face for an expression that would give something away, the unsaid she felt so sure was there. The only change in that poker face, though, was Vera rolling a sidelong glance toward Kate's legs. Kate wasn't sure if it was in disapproval of her short-shorts or avoidance of her eyes.

"Have you, eh," Vera said, "been okay in that apartment so far? Nothing…in need of attention?"

"No, Leo and his crew were very thorough."

"Nothing peculiar?"

"There's a wall that's still a little stained, but whatever. I'm not high-maintenance." When Vera didn't comment right away, Kate noticed the torbie cat under the table. Bending over to pet it, she added, "Your cat seems to like it. My apartment, I mean. Did she know, uh, the deceased?"

"Olive. The deceased was Olive."

"Cute!" Kate replied with perhaps too much enthusiasm.

"But yes, the cat knew her. It was hers, after all."

Kate stopped stroking the dead woman's cat and sat up.

"That's how we found Olive. Little Agatha here was mewing and scratching at the door. A neighbor knocked and tried the knob, but the door was locked. Just in case the cat was left alone with no food out, he'd grabbed some bologna from his fridge and knelt down to feed it through the big gap beneath Olive's door. That's when he caught a whiff of the stench inside and called down to the office immediately. The landlord sent Leo, who brought me in tow."

"You three were all friends?"

"You could say so. We looked out for each other, anyway. Olive got too weak to take the stairs anymore, but she refused to move, so Leo and I would tend to what she needed. Groceries and cat food and such."

"That's really nice. And so…you took on Agatha after Olive died?"

"She's company."

"Nice," Kate lamely said again for lack of other words, until she remembered, "So that explains why Agatha was acting so weird by my door, right? She, like, remembers or something?"

Vera bent to pick Agatha up and set her on her lap. She leaned toward the cat's head and hummed a single note into its fur before saying, "Something." Her frown turned into a wicked smile as she scratched at the cat's throat. "Aggie here might still smell somethin' in there, huh, Aggie."

Kate's stomach dropped. And though Vera's teasing smile grew as she burrowed it into Agatha's head and giggled away gruffly like a schoolgirl who chain-smoked, Kate whispered to herself, "You can't be serious." She stood to rummage about the remaining goods and showcase them better to end that conversation.

Plucking away an array of silky, filmy headscarves — with a clear plastic rain bonnet thrown in the mix — Kate felt sacrilegious rifling through it, like she might as well have been grave-robbing and twisting rings off the fingers of corpses. Until something sparkling caught the light and darkly dazzled her eyes.

"Oo-ooh!" she exclaimed. "*What* is *this?*" She lifted a little black beaded evening bag from the scarf pile.

Vera raised her brows. "Oh! That was in that mess, was it? Huh." She stroked Agatha with an intensity that clearly annoyed the torbie. "And you fancy that, huh?"

"It's *diviiine*," Kate cooed, holding it up by its inch-thick beaded strap and twirling it this way and that to watch it glitter in the low-angled sunlight.

Tiny obsidian beads covered the entire surface of the purse in swirling rows. It looked rectangular from straight on, but from above Kate could see the bag was actually an oblong hexagon, with a lid sloping down from the back like a roof and clasping in the front with a concealed snap. She popped it open to finger its black silk interior — fully intact, no rips or worn patches. Beneath the lid, she noticed the reflective backing of a mirror that had lost its glass. That was its only flaw; in Kate's eyes, it was otherwise a perfect black gem.

"Sold," she said.

"Huh?"

"Sold, Vera. I have to have this. How much?"

"You sure you wanna be taking more of this stuff back into that apartment? The point of the sale was to clear that out. Exorcise it."

"This little thing takes up no space, and I needed the chair anyway. What do I owe you for both?"

"I-I'm not sure that it's right that I—" Vera leaned to look past her. "Leo?"

He glanced up from the Artie Shaw record album he'd been affectionately gazing at.

"Leo, ah, Kate is interested in buying a purse now. She wants something else."

"Oh?" was all he said. The muscles holding up his smile visually steeled beneath his skin.

"Yes," Kate said, looking from one to the other like they were senile. Perhaps they were. "I want to buy this purse also. That all right?" She looked to Vera and softened her tone. "Sorry. I mean, did you want this for yourself? Did you set it out on accident?" Maybe that was why Vera had looked surprised to see it in Kate's hands to begin with.

"Nooo!" Vera answered in an octave higher than normal. "I just wanted to check with Leo on the price. We took turns tagging items, you see, and I don't believe that purse has one."

Kate rotated it around in the air by its strap again. Nope, no tag. She shifted her lips into a smirk. "Oh, I see. So *Leo* is the best one to price a little beaded evening bag?" Chuckling, she turned to him. "Okay, sir, name your price. You know, in light of the going-rate for women's purses like this. What do you see out there on the market?" She, in all fairness, tried to stifle her laugh when she saw Leo's farmer tan turn noticeably redder around his cheeks and ears.

"Eh, just like I said with the chair: free of charge. Yer helpin' us here, so that's payment enough."

After some polite protest, Kate finally accepted his terms and planned a generous tip for the building's maintenance crew at Christmas. For the time being, though, she helped Leo and Vera pack up the estate sale and braced herself for returning home to what for three days had been a dead woman's tomb.

From the confusion of cardboard, bubble-wrap, and crumpled newspaper, Kate rose with the one IKEA pot she owned and walked to the kitchen sink to rinse both it and her ink-stained hands.

As the gray smudges congealed and streamed off her skin, she eyeballed the stove to her left. It was part of a freestanding oven, a smaller-than-average appliance that might not even fit a full-size pan inside or her giant pot on top. But that wasn't what disturbed Kate as she inspected the rusty black stove burners.

"The drain?" Leo's voice echoed in her head.

"The kettle!"

"Bleh!" Kate shuddered, staring at her own kettle on the stove. "How the hell could a mouse even get in there?" She opted to hold off on that tea she'd wanted to brew and filled her pot with water instead.

Screw tea anyway. It was happy hour. She plopped the pot on a burner, and while she waited for it to boil, she unpacked her dual-cassette/CD player and fed it her new Macy Gray disc. Next was a treasure hunt for her corkscrew and wine glasses. After scavenging through five boxes failed to deliver the glasses, she just poured herself a hearty coffee mug of wine. The water on the stove now roiled in a frenzy; a couple handfuls of penne pasta calmed its rapids with some sizzle and steam.

Mug of wine in one hand and wooden spoon in the other, Kate rubbed against the stove knobs as she swayed her hips and sang about getting choked up as she said goodbye and walked away from her man.

Well, not *her*, of course. It was only lyrics to Macy Gray's "I Try" playing in the other room. By the ripe old age of twenty-four, Kate herself had said goodbye to and walked away from plenty of guys with no issue. She was a pro at the clean break.

Dex was the exception, though. Her goodbye and walking away from him had literally been saying the word and repeatedly moving one foot in front of the other in a direction that was not toward his condo. But, figuratively speaking, she hadn't so much *walked away* as taken a step back. Moving out was not breaking up; she only wanted some space.

In fact, she'd ended up calling Dex from the rummage sale that afternoon to ask if he could hold off on coming over until later that evening. She had dinner plans. With herself. Maybe she would have her new purse pull up a chair, too. The kitchen was too hot for comfortably eating at her little bistro table, though, so sitting on her futon and leaning over her resale coffee table in the living room would have to do. The purse could sit on Olive's old burgundy wingback.

It took Kate all of thirty seconds to conclude how pathetic her freedom already was.

After straining her *al dente* pasta and stirring in some pesto, she took her mug and plate to the living room, sank onto her futon, and kicked her feet to the stereo's mellow beat. She did not invite the purse to join her. She just meditated on the gloriousness that *should* be Living on Her Own.

Before long, though, sounds of scratching and rhythmic bumping interrupted her peace. It came from behind her, from the apartment next door.

And there was something else—was it music? Kate pressed her ear to the shared wall. Yes, the faint jazzy strains of the neighbor's music were vibrating through the yellowed wall.

Kate shrugged and returned her attention to Macy and merlot. But after eating a little and drinking a lot, she noticed it had become like a meat locker in there. Getting up to turn the AC down, she powered off the stereo as well—all the better to hear the music next door. She likewise clicked off the sconce lighting that Jaundice the Yellow Wall wore like a pair of earrings.

Settling onto her futon under a chenille throw, she bent one knee upward and rocked it side to side to the dreamy big-band jazz melody; it was faint but unmistakable. Undoubtedly another senior citizen lived next door. They were probably playing it on a phonograph, too.

And yet hadn't Kate seen a gorgeous brunet walk out of her building block that afternoon—or at least the gorgeous *backside* of a brunet? He could have just been visiting a friend, she figured. A girlfriend, maybe, or a boyfriend. But he *could* be straight and single and live in Camden Court. In a studio and alone, like her. And if so, there were only so many apartments in her wing of the U-shaped building. Maybe four to a floor, for four floors, which would make sixteen units. A lot to choose from, but still…there was a twenty-five percent chance he could live on her floor. Kate liked those odds.

Swinging her knee to the rhythm, she imagined how terribly attractive it would be for a guy like that to be listening to music like this. *That might just about be perfection.* Closing her eyes, she encouraged the fantasy. Where should she begin…oh, yes:

No longer fully clothed on the futon but reclining on the hot neighbor's soft leather sofa, wrapped in a cashmere blanket and wearing nothing underneath it…

She stopped rocking her knee and spread it out to the side.

Hot Neighbor's face is difficult to see in the flickering candlelight as he approaches the sofa. Once he's close enough for me to almost make out his features, he immediately drops his head to my neck, sucking and lapping at my skin like it's cream. He moves his way down, peeling away the cashmere while he does so. I draw my chin to my chest to watch his thick mass of wavy dark brown hair dust over my breasts and zigzag across my stomach as the flesh there yields to the press of his lips.

For a moment, Kate considered getting up to fetch her vibrator. Good ol' Dickie Greenleaf—which was indeed green and indulged Kate's obsession with Jude Law in *The Talented Mr. Ripley*. But Dickie couldn't happen tonight. Even in her stupor, Kate remembered Dex was due to arrive at some point. She'd left the door unlocked for him, so he could easily catch her in the act, and getting up now to lock it would ruin the moment. As would getting up to fetch the vibrator.

"No matter," Kate whispered, willing to take the matter into her own expert hands. "Carry on, lover." Hidden beneath the chenille blanket, her fingers ducked under the waist of her shorts, then the elastic band of her panties at the same time Hot Neighbor's mouth moved south.

His strong, smooth hands reach up to circle and squeeze my breasts, then descend to massage the small of my waist. I still can't see his face, but oh, what a marvelous mouth he has as he takes his time and gradually, so delicately, homes in between my thighs and skillfully uses his tongue to part my—

Lips brushed against hers. Without opening her eyes, Kate slowly and quietly pulled her hand from her shorts and lifted the other to clasp short, straight hair. She clutched it so she couldn't feel the fine texture anymore and pulled the face more firmly onto hers, parting the lips with her tongue and hearing not jazz notes but the thuds of dropped plastic shopping bags.

A few seconds later, the other mouth detached to say, "Been a while since you kissed like *that*. Glad I didn't scare—"

"Shhh…No talking." Keeping her eyelids firmly clenched, she blocked out the familiar voice to just feel the body swivel from the side of the futon to a position parallel above her.

They carried on kissing for a while, but the voice reemerged between lip smacks: "Didn't mean to—sneak in—sounded so—quiet from the hall—didn't want to—wake you—if you were—slee—"

Kate jammed her tongue into Dex's mouth to wrestle his down. He gave a soft moan that communicated he was pleased enough getting to second base like this. But Kate wasn't. Still feeling the tingling tickle of that wavy-haired head between her thighs, she impatiently pulled off her T-shirt, unclasped her bra, then flipped Dex's shirt inside out above his head and off his arms.

Flies couldn't be undone quickly enough as they grabbed and tugged and fiddled with one another's shorts, deciphering the logistics of fashion in the dark and finally cracking the code. Kate felt the sensation of a man's weight on her again, and she thrilled at the friction of his chest and navel hair along her skin as he slid over and eased into her.

"Wow, you're already really—"

She clapped her hand over his mouth. He licked and sucked at her palm in what she supposed he thought was an erotic fashion, and she continued to arch into him and ebb with his flow.

But the spell had already been broken. Kate just went through the motions, mirroring his rise and fall. And when she sensed Dex about to withdraw to prolong his own pleasure, she gripped and held his hips to hers, picking up her speed and urging him to follow through on what not even she was mean enough to say out loud.

And five seconds later, the infamous Getting it Over With was complete—to his apparent satisfaction, if not hers.

The aftermath consisted of an hour of spooning and pillow talk while they sipped some Chianti Dex had brought over. He'd also brought a movie rental of *The Sixth Sense* and the Ben & Jerry's ice cream now melting on the floor. They had a good laugh over Kate's bathroom incident, too, but right after that, Kate rolled him out of bed under the pretense of feeling disorganized and claustrophobic with her apartment still in shambles. It would simply be easier if he went home and let her get an early start the next day.

"Just come back to our place to sleep," he replied, his light brown hair still tousled from their romp.

"*Your* place."

"My place. Fine. But just sleep in a real bed to get good rest for attacking all this shit tomorrow. I'll help you."

"To sleep or unpack?"

"Both. Well, maybe not so much sleep," he said with a nudge.

"Thanks, but I can do both just fine on my own. Now, please. I'm begging you. It's been a really, really long day."

He left with dejection shading his deep aqua eyes but holding fast to a rain check for that video — before it was due back at Blockbuster and he'd get charged a late fee.

Shutting the door behind him, Kate flicked the switch to turn the sconces back on and kill the atmosphere entirely. It couldn't be a good thing for reality to so consistently fall short of fantasy. She needed to confront things as they were, see them plain as day and learn to be satisfied with that.

Starting with those scratches on her front door. Slapping a couple of layers of fresh white paint on there couldn't hide the fact that Agatha had clawed a sizable strip out of it. Kate looked around the room and wondered where Olive's body had lain when they'd found it. Perhaps where she and Dex just were, over against the yellow wall. Shimmying her shoulders in disgust, she thought of all the people who had lived — and maybe died — in this building before her.

The music next door had stopped, perhaps already had some time ago while she and Dex had been…what? Making love? Just passing the time? What was it that she'd really wanted when she'd walked out of that Lake Shore condo? Suddenly, she couldn't breathe as the responsibility for Dexter's heart crushed down on her own. Absence was only making things foggier so far.

Blowing her long, toffee-colored bangs out of her eyes, Kate wasn't in the mood to analyze the state of "them" just now. Instead, she looked to the evening bag still sitting on the floor where she'd left it after the estate sale. With a smile, she walked over to play with it again, thinking of when she could first use it and what she'd wear.

Holding it up by its strap, her eyes focused in on the beaded detail. It was like staring into the night sky, a private observatory of her own. As she zoned in on the twinkling and tried to find constellations in its pattern, her ears filled with what sounded like water running. She checked her bathroom, just to be sure, and figured it must be a neighbor. Just the pipes and strange acoustics in the old building.

The volume and intensity of the water increased, though, until it seemed all around her. She could almost feel drops streaming down, then beading on her skin. The blood cascaded through her veins with a new coolness, and an overwhelming scent of lilac dizzied her.

As the sound of running water surged in her ears, Kate gripped the purse tightly. She swept open its dazzling lid and stared into the remnants of the old mirror at her dilated brown eyes, at her flushed and pale skin.

In a flicker—there, then gone—she saw something else.

A pair of fogged green eyes, glaring back.

Two for Mirth

July 1925

Cheap glasses of booze chimed like fine crystal by the time Lon drained the last of his third dry martini. It was the evening of the Hughes gala, but he'd wanted to prime himself at a North Chicago gin mill first. Muffle his ears against the boorish self-congratulations to come; blur his sight to the shiny coifs and sparkling gems that could pierce one's eyes straight into a migraine.

It was a choice society to which Lon belonged, a glittering circle of good old boys swilling brandy and solving all the world's problems in someone's smoky, walnut-paneled study, while their svelte wives and mistresses reclined elegantly on parlor furniture like house cats.

Yes, Lon was a lucky man to have grown up among all this, lucky to die among it as well, if he so chose. Why blister one's hands and muss one's hair when Ancestor or Father or perhaps Uncle Who Never Had Children of His Own has done all the hard work for you? That's why the self-made generations made themselves, wasn't it? To leave a legacy of inherited wealth for future generations? Pad the little boys and girls in velvet-lined cedar cases to preserve their pretty faces?

Leaning against the wooden bar, Lon set down his drink. He stood to arch his back and spread his shoulders, claustrophobic inside his velvet-lined case as it felt increasingly like a silk-ruched coffin. Settling his hands back down on the bar, his fingers tapped out the rhythm of a jazz tune caught in his head.

Brace yourself, he thought as he ran a hand over his slickened hair, then slapped the wood with conviction before he could change his mind.

"Cheers, fellows!" He tipped his hat and bid adieu to his barfly pals, whom he'd never met before in his life and would probably never see again.

They raised their whiskeys and bourbons with a communal "Aaayy!"

Lon saluted then exited onto Belden Avenue from what, to the outside world, appeared to be a vacant and boarded-up building. He sauntered through the leafy residential streets, the heavy cuffs of his wide-legged Oxford Bags flopping against his ankles. Eventually cutting over onto Wrightwood Avenue and crossing east of Clark Street, he felt the breeze off Lake Michigan. It sobered him too quickly.

But before Lon could turn around, the great gray Hughes mansion loomed ahead, with some Choice Society stragglers milling around its steps and shimmering like fireflies in the dark. The music of a piano and string quartet floated on the air to greet him as ladies' giggles popped like bubbles above the notes.

"You there! I say, come on over!" a jubilant male voice called out, to be met with hoots from the surrounding crowd.

All turned and looked in Lon's direction. There was now no escaping if he'd still held any hope of it. When he stepped too near the party lights for his hat brim to shade his face any longer, he affected a tight grin.

"Lon? Lonnie! It *is* you, isn't it!" cried a nasally blonde bedecked in amber beading. She shot up an arm to punctuate her "Darling!" and her lit cigarette dropped from its holder in the process.

Lon stiffly approached the petite yet buxom gal. He resisted offering her another cigarette from his silver case and just kept his hands in the pockets of his trousers. Her face fell at his reserve. Still, she held arms outstretched, empty, waiting.

Like a statue of an ancient woman, Lon thought, *who should be holding a tall urn.*

Indeed, she appeared a clumsy imitation of the half-robed caryatids just behind her, which stood on either side of the Hughes's main entrance and held the balcony above it.

Pursing her deep red lips together in a smirk that best brought out her dimples, the girl held her pose and said, "Tell me you don't recognize me. Come now, you cad."

Lon frowned, squinted, and made a show of leaning over and inspecting her face closely. The blonde held her smile but tentatively drew in her arms, her hands still raised but slack on limp wrists as the empty cigarette holder dangled between two fingers. Scanning her face, he detected a sparkle of genuine anxiety in her eyes, but the smirk twitching at one corner of her lips gave away the evident pleasure she took in his gaze. He mirrored her expression and eased his face past hers to barely touch his lips to her neck.

Rather than plant a delicate kiss there—as she surely expected—Lon merely whispered, "Yes, Effie. I know *you* all right," before withdrawing away to a more respectable distance.

With a wink and a bow, he suavely sidestepped and glided past the group at the black iron gate, leaving Effie to her blushes and the others to their eager inquiries as he ascended the stone steps to the Hughes's limestone palace.

Lon strode through the oak doors without hesitation or ceremony. His smooth gait hiccupped, however, at the sound of a throat clearing to his right.

"Sir?" a butler haughtily implored from the corner of the foyer, raising his brows and looking pointedly at Lon's gray fedora.

"Ah." Lon removed the hat and handed it over to him—but not without playfully rolling it up and down the length of his arm first.

"Yes, well," the butler muttered with a *tut-tut* as he shuffled away.

Lon laughed quietly and weighed the options of heading left or right beyond the entryway.

Left was a garishly opulent sitting room ornamented in white and gold. Its white sofas were draped with gem-encrusted women tittering at younger men in tuxedos. At a small table in one corner, a few folks played their hand at cards. In the opposite corner, a couple fell giggling into a potted tree after dancing to the glaringly amateur fiddler and pianist performing "Chopsticks" in the adjoining music room.

Right was a dim library of sorts with deep turquoise-papered walls. A haze hung in the air there, dulling the chandelier's lights into fuzzy white dandelions against the narrow painted panels of an ornate wooden ceiling. Dark bookcases lined either side of a crackling fireplace, and the center of the room was clogged with black bow ties. It was the usual stodgy scene Lon had expected: ruddy-faced businessmen boasting their pompous tales of stock prices and motor cars or speaking out against Bolshevism, with chests puffed and cigars turning soggy in their jabbering mouths.

Disenchanted with his options, Lon decided to turn neither left nor right but to walk straight ahead through the golden foyer. Passing between a pair of cream marble columns, he admired the grand oak staircase to one side. To the other stood a fireplace painted in gold leaf, a sizable mirror worthy of Versailles mounted above the mantel.

Staring down at the floor as he strode deeper down the corridor, Lon lost his focus in observation of the intricate mosaic design, step after colorfully tiled step—until his wingtips stubbed against a marble lip rising about an inch from the floor. He looked up to meet the life-sized stone likeness of a courtier wooing a fair maiden above a fountain. The couple was white as purity and forever frozen mere inches from embrace.

"The thrill of the chase," Lon murmured. "The only thrill there is."

He sidestepped them to peer through yet another doorway. It led into a dining room paneled in rich, dark wood and with lofty, arched beams above—a room fit for a king, not the clutter of crushed flowers and stained table linens it actually contained. People milled around the chairs rather than sitting on them, and a couple of young ladies in tawdry dresses looked one glass of champagne away from using the long table as their stage like the party-crashing chorus girls they probably were.

Lon ducked away just in time for a servant to scurry from behind him and into the dining room with a silver tray of crystal coupe glasses. The glasses brimmed with the sparkling nectar of the gods that had been forbidden fruit for years, and he kicked himself for not having been quicker to snatch one. Whooping ensued in the dining room, and he watched the servant disappear with an emptied tray through a different door at the back, presumably into the kitchen.

Bemoaning his luck, Lon stepped back out and wandered toward the oak staircase. He heard the band playing outside and briefly considered strolling out the side door by the stairs, but the garden ran alongside the house and met the street. Through the iron fence, he'd be visible to Effie and the other folks he'd narrowly escaped on the sidewalk—not any more desirable than his other options so far.

Another servant darted by from the dining room on his way to the library, and the cacophony of voices and laughter and clinking glasses in the neighboring rooms and garden began to close in and pound on Lon's brain. Stale smoke, sweat, and floral fragrance congealed in the thick air to stifle him. This time, as the platter whirred across the foyer from the library to the front parlor, Lon managed to snag a champagne coupe.

Sipping from the shallow glass before it could drip any of its golden bubbly, he marched over to the staircase for lack of anywhere else to go. It was the imperial sort that had a central flight of stairs leading up to a half-landing, from which a pair of parallel flights then angled in the opposite direction to the second floor. Taking a couple of steps up the first flight, Lon gave a long, low whistle at the massive stained glass window looming above the landing. He gawked at it up to its full height and nearly fell backward.

Holding on to the banister with one hand to steady himself, he twisted and raised his glass to toast the marble lovers below:

> *"Bold Lover, never, never canst thou kiss,*
> *Though winning near the goal—yet, do not grieve;*
> *She cannot fade, though thou hast not thy bliss,*
> *For ever wilt thou love, and she be fair!"*

He took a swig of his champagne and sneered. *"More happy love! More happy, happy love!"* He cackled into his glass as he drank, nearly spitting his sip onto the wooden steps when another voice spoke from on high:

> *"For ever warm and still to be enjoy'd."*

Lon looked above him but saw no one and couldn't tell from the acoustics where the voice came from. It belonged to a female, though. He drained the last of his champagne and carried on up the first flight toward the broad mezzanine beneath the window.

The voice continued to speak with silky emphasis:

> *"For ever panting, and for ever young…"*

The sweet articulation flowed through him, and he stroked his thumb over the champagne glass's curve as he slowly proceeded up the steps.

"All breathing human passion far above," he muttered back as, gradually, he looked above his left shoulder to where he'd distinctly heard the voice. Through the filigreed iron baluster there, he saw fluid emerald fabric cascading its way down the steps. *"That leaves a heart high-sorrowful and cloy'd."*

His gaze trailed up the fall of green to see an alabaster elbow peeking through the swirling black and gold-gilded iron. Then, on approaching the landing, he saw a shoulder, a protruding clavicle…a jaw…and a face, turned away from him.

A face from which purred, with a hint of malice, "*A burning forehead, and a parching tongue.*"

Lon stepped onto the landing and walked to the next flight of steps where the woman sat.

He contemplated her with a curious grin and a hand in his pocket. Tapping his empty champagne coupe against the stained glass with casual irreverence, he dropped his gaze to his feet before lifting it again. He could now see her face in profile.

From her fine, straight-edged nose to her pointed chin, he panned his sight up to an elfin earlobe adorned only with a single pearl. Glossy, deep brown finger-waves were bobbed to reveal her swan-like neck; angling down from her neatly trimmed nape, the curling tip of her hair hugged a well-defined cheekbone.

The woman gradually turned to him with a raised brow but no hint of a smile. "*Who are these coming to the sacrifice?*" she quoted.

"Indeed," Lon replied. "*To what green altar, O mysterious priest*-ess?"

She leveled her gaze on him. "'Priestess?' I believe you take liberty with your Keats."

Lon smirked. "Is that so?"

"Why? Have you, too, come to worship at my feet?" She'd said it haughtily, but Lon detected a trace of the theatrical.

"I didn't realize I had to wait in line." He planted one foot a couple of steps up from the landing and smugly lunged toward her. Then, leaning his forearms on his bent knee, he looked down the stairs leading to the empty foyer.

Though she still faced him, Lon watched her catlike eyes roll toward the banister to peer below as he'd done. She tugged at the string of pearls wrapped snugly around her neck. One corner of her lip curled upward as she twirled the beads about her fine-boned fingers. But she said nothing.

Looking more closely at her eyes, Lon observed how the vibrant green irises that perfectly matched her dress were framed with red veins. She rapidly looked to her lap then back at the banister. Twisting toward it, she clutched the railings with both hands.

"Well," she grunted as she hoisted herself and all her finery up from the step. "I suppose if they don't come to me in droves, then I'll just go to them." She stood and kicked one silver-slippered foot out from beneath her silk gown as if ensuring she wouldn't trip over it, only for her next step to catch the fabric regardless.

On instinct, Lon dropped his glass and caught her by her shoulders as she fell. Her hands gripped his elbows.

She and Lon stood frozen, inches apart, eyes darting over each other's faces for several seconds. Lon felt the warm, soft press of her anxious breath against his face and her light squeeze that pulsed at his elbows like a fluttering heart.

She'd been standing rigidly as she recovered from the near-fall, but after a time, Lon felt her go limp; the pads of his fingers sank deeper into her creamy skin as marble thawed into pillows of satin. He took one step upward to close their distance, to further steady her in case her slackening posture meant she might faint. Easing his hands from her shoulders down the backside of her arms, he secured his palms at her elbows in the same way she grasped him. He then pulled his face away to better focus on her eyes, to gauge her alertness.

She really is a beautiful creature, isn't she, he couldn't help but think. Taller than what he normally had, smaller-breasted and perhaps a little too bony. A rather thin upper lip that accentuated the pout of her fuller lower one. *She'd look more attractive if she offered a proper smile.* Otherwise there was no doubt about it: she was exquisite. Lon knew this not to be a matter of his opinion, but a fact. This beauty had nothing to do with which eye beheld it. It was there, filling all eyes in the same way, no more, no less. *She is for everyone.*

As these thoughts ran through his mind, he noticed her reddened eyes squint and fix him in a sharper glare. They burned with a jade green he'd once seen in a great bonfire, the hottest of flames devouring all they came into contact with. Had he offended? Had he dared to leave his hands on her this long?

But despite whatever animosity seemed to well inside her, her body did not tense. She only slackened more with the same fluidity as the gown that practically dripped from her. She was like an ethereal nymph, newly emerged from the sea foam yet sure to soon melt back into it, giving him no choice but to let her go.

And he *should* let go. What held him there, caught so dumbstruck in the mischievous gleam of her cat eyes? Paralyzed from going back down those stairs to join the merriment of everyone else when instead all he could do was look beyond her face to the upper landing and wonder which of those second-floor doors would lead to a suitable bedroom. He couldn't pretend now, after all, that he hadn't noticed the enormous emerald winking at him from her ring finger — the promise of another man that ordered Lon to find another woman.

But wasn't that all part of the allure? Wasn't that supposed to make her that much more unattainable? His gaze fixed on a mirrored door to the right of the upstairs landing.

Having made his choice, he looked back at the woman in his arms to see her thin upper lip drawn into a tantalizing sneer. She gripped his elbows tighter and pressed her torso against his; he could actually feel the bones of her slim hips just beneath his. Her shoulders fell, and she stretched her long neck to the side, moving her face past his to brush her ruby lips along his neck. Slowly, softly, Lon felt her mouth glide up to his earlobe, at which she darted out her tongue to lick.

Lon closed his eyes and skimmed his palms up and down the woman's arms a couple of times before sliding them back up and along her shoulders. His fingers roamed up the delicate flesh of her neck and tickled at the base of her chocolate waves. There was something so cool and clean and fresh about her; her scent reminded him of linens drying in crisp autumn breezes, or of a frozen Wisconsin lake, with a sweet undercurrent of vanilla mingling with an almost masculine musk.

All the while, the woman gently lapped at his ear like a house cat grooming its paws, her body undulating against his in a continuous, playful motion.

Lon felt himself swelling, and he ran his hands from the nape of her neck down over her shoulder blades, feeling the smooth skin exposed through the rear cutouts of her gown, all the way down to the small of her back, where he settled his hot palms and pulled her closer. At this, the woman wasted no time bringing her face around to look at him, and she thrust her lips against his.

Molding his mouth to her own, she sucked on his lower lip with a teasing bite. Lon lifted one of his feet a step higher and leaned his lanky frame down against the temptress as though he might take her right there. He knew he shouldn't attempt this with all the revelry — and probably her fiancé — downstairs, but that mirrored door was suddenly so terribly far away. Especially now that she was purring against his neck as she nipped at it again and pulled him to lie down.

Their panting turned shallower, and they both seemed to hold their breath as they concentrated on silently stretching out along the flight of stairs.

The woman released her arms to scratch against the wall with one hand and clench the iron baluster with the other as she eased herself back down to where he'd first found her. Lon hastily loosened his tie and unbuttoned his gray suit coat to be one less layer of fabric away from her skin. He balanced on top, careful not to crush her against the steps.

She grabbed the lapels of his open jacket and swept it off his shoulders and down to his elbows, where she used it to sharply tug him toward her.

"Careful there, girl." But Lon's smile betrayed how much he indeed liked her roughness.

The woman yanked his jacket again and then jerked her knee up between his thighs.

"Say!" Lon exclaimed, his smile gone. "What's the idea?"

She hadn't kicked him, but she'd come threateningly close—presumably as a caution. Tied up as he was in a straightjacket of her making, he could do nothing but heed that warning.

L on froze, immediately aware of how awkward and unattractive his
position must look with his legs a couple steps apart and his arms
pinned to his sides. It was only a matter of time before his balance
would falter, but he did what he could to lift more of his weight onto
his knees and off of the woman in green.

Releasing him, she lowered her offending knee and rose up to
a seated position where she could look him levelly in the eye. Lon
prepared himself for the daggers her eyes or lips would launch at him
as part of whatever game she was playing.

To his surprise, the woman threw her head back and laughed—not
wickedly, but in almost childlike delight. She helped him straighten
his tie and put his coat back, sweeping her palms across his chest to
smooth the lapels down. He freed a leg from around her and spun
to sit beside her on the step, sheepish. Glancing around the stairwell, the figures in its stained glass window and golden *toile de jouy*
wallpaper mocked him.

"Oh, look," the woman said in a rich, almost musical tone, "I'm
sorry, old boy. I shouldn't have done that."

Lon stared at her with as little expression as he could muster
while he tried to slow his breathing. Her chest, too, still rose and fell
heavily as she continued to catch her breath in laughter. He knit his
brows, waiting for some sort of explanation and preparing himself
for it to never come.

She merely adjusted her posture and smoothed out the length of her gown. Eventually, she dabbed the pad of her middle finger at the corners of her lips, tucked errant strands of hair behind her ears, then fanned her face with her hands as she again let out an exhausted laugh.

"Look, Lon, I just wanted to—"

"Pardon?"

"I said I just wanted to—"

"Sorry, but how do you know me?" Lon grabbed his lapels and hoisted the collar of his jacket higher against the back of his neck.

She tilted her face and grinned with an amusement he found patronizing. "Who doesn't know you? Well, *of* you, anyway. You can wear common day clothes to a formal evening soirée as often as you like, old boy, but there's no faking you don't have money. I could practically *taste* it on you."

Lon's cheeks burned like when he'd come indoors from sledding as a boy, direct from the snow hill to the mouth of a tall stone fireplace. He'd always feared the grand hearth would gobble him up if the rest of his cavernous family home wouldn't first.

"You look younger in person," the woman continued. "There's a freshness about you. I wouldn't have guessed you a day over twenty."

"That so?" Lon played along. "And so you know how old I am as well?"

"An old and wise twenty-five," she said.

"And you?"

"Nineteen."

"A baby."

"Woman *enough*, apparently."

Lon huffed a single chuckle. "Apparently," he said, nodding. She wasn't radiating the hot-and-cold vixen anymore but something milder and warm—sincere, Lon judged at his own risk. He allowed himself to let a bit of his guard down. "And just as apparent, perhaps, is that I'm not *man* enough." When she didn't comment right away, he added, "Wouldn't you say?"

"I'm sorry I had to do that," she finally said, "or felt I had to. It was impulsive, I know."

Lon sucked in a breath that he trapped inside his billowing lips as he simply nodded again.

"I'm sorry," she repeated. "Sorrier still that I had to cheat you of your thrill."

"What's that?"

"Well, I've cheated you of your thrill, you see, by cheating you of the chase first."

"I'm not sure that I follow."

She propped her feet on the step below the one she sat on, folded her arms, and rested them on her knees. Tilting her face in that curiously condescending way she had, she looked him square in the eye. "I didn't give you a chase. Therefore, by *your* logic, I didn't give you a thrill. It isn't as fun when a woman just throws herself at you, now is it? Not as much as when she plays coy? Hard to get?"

Lon's mouth had been hanging open as he squinted through her explanation, but when his own words essentially slapped him in the face, he closed his eyes and clamped his teeth with a click. He held a pained smile for a moment.

"Well," the woman continued, "I'm not painted on a Grecian urn for men to write poetry about. Nor am I sculpted of marble. Or did I seem made of stone just then?" She raised her brows and again became the seductive kitten of a few minutes earlier, if not for the irony in her voice.

Lon cleared his throat. "You didn't exactly remove *all* of the chase, you know." He pointed to her emerald ring.

She looked at it and frowned, then polished it against the fabric at her breast. Holding her hand away from her, she contemplated it with evident distaste, like it betrayed her by wearing the ring. "All that glitters is not gold."

"So I've heard. But it sure does dazzle, doesn't it?"

"I suppose. Dazzles to blindness at times. At the most critical of times." She broke her stare from the gemstone and looked back at Lon before giving him an utterly disarming smile.

He'd known she had it in her.

"Lon Ashby," she said softly, "my name is Eva, Eva Hughes. For the time being." She extended her fine-boned hand to him, the one free of any jewelry, which Lon accepted and shook.

"Hughes, eh? So this is your old shack." He hadn't yet released her hand, only ran his thumb across it. "For the time being."

Eva smiled shyly.

"And what will one day replace 'Hughes'?"

"Redcliffe."

"Ah. Would that be Finlay, then? I thought I might have recognized him in the study."

Eva gave a slight nod. "You know him?"

"I know *of* him. His family. Well done, you." Lon still rubbed his thumb against her knuckles nervously but didn't let go until he'd raised them to his lips for a light kiss. Eva held her smile, but some thought hidden behind her green eyes turned them to glass.

"Tell me, Eva," he ventured, trying to ignore the trembling in her lips, "is there somewhere I can escort you? Where you can grace this lovely night with your lovely presence? It seems a shame to waste you on the staircase. Shall I take you to your fiancé?"

She squinted one eye in thought, then parted her lips as if to respond when a click upstairs drew their attention to the second floor. A thin sprite of a thing in a long white nightdress emerged from behind the mirrored door Lon had eyed earlier. She raised a pale hand to her mouth to stifle a yawn.

"Why, Ollie!" Eva cried, starting to her feet at once and bustling her gown up to her knees to ascend the steps. "Ollie, my dear girl, why are you still awake?"

Ollie pouted and rubbed her eyes. "It's too loud." After thoroughly scrubbing her closed lids with her fists, she blinked her eyes into wide alertness. They were green, like her sister's, though much paler in comparison.

"Oh, I'm sorry, my love, but do try to go back to sleep," Eva said.

Quite awake now, Ollie smiled with a sideways glance at the banister. "I want to go down *there!*" She pointed a skinny arm with coltish awkwardness.

"Ah, ha-ha. Nice try, little one, but it's not like the royal balls you see in fairy tales. We're going back to bed this instant." Eva clasped her sister's shoulders and redirected the gangling girl back to her mirrored door. Looking over her own shoulder, she gave a nod for Lon to follow.

He met them upstairs at the foot of a four-poster bed, which swallowed the girl in clouds of pillows and bedcovers once Eva had her tucked neatly back inside. Precious china dolls lined multiple tiers of shelving, and the intricate molding running around the ceiling was bordered with hand-painted characters from every nursery rhyme imaginable. The room did indeed appear more of a nursery than the sleeping quarters of a budding adolescent.

Eva sat beside Ollie and smoothed down her straight, dark blond locks; the girl's face appeared flushed, and Eva touched the back of her hand to her forehead.

"Your temperature's all right. You sure you're feeling fine?"

Staring at Lon out the corner of her eyes, Ollie nodded vigorously.

Eva narrowed one eye again and gave the girl her signature head-tilt. "How long have you been awake? Were you only up just now?"

"Uh huh," she said, looking to Eva but still nodding large and fast. "There was a loud bump downstairs, right below me. Then everyone started singing to beat the band, which is also so bothersome outside my window." She pouted.

Eva leaned back with an exhale. "I see. And did you hear anything… else?"

Lon masked a laugh by coughing into his hand.

The girl glanced back at him, and with just as exaggerated a motion as her nods, shook her head no. She then stretched with a lion-like yawn.

"Okay, then," Eva said. "I can't stop the music just yet, nor can I promise there won't be noise down below as our guests perform impromptu vaudeville routines all over Mommy and Daddy's furniture, but do your best to dream through it. Shall I tell you a story first? Would that help?"

Though the girl was clearly several years younger than Eva, Lon still thought her too old for such a routine. He waited for Ollie to balk at the idea in juvenile fashion as she rubbed her eyes again, but she nodded in consent.

"All right," Eva said. "Let's see…"

Lon stood silent with his hands in his pockets as he listened to Eva recite "Wynken, Blynken, and Nod" by heart. As she whispered the sweet words, she rested her head on one hand at the top of Ollie's pillow and traced the other along her sister's fingertips.

> *"All night long their nets they threw*
> *To the stars in the twinkling foam…"*

Looking around at the shelves of dolls, Lon observed some were babies in pale christening gowns and patterned jumpers while others were young girls in grown-up dress reflecting all sorts of nationalities, time periods, colors, and fine fabrics. Some had eyes and hair that were painted on whereas others had lifelike glass eyes peering from underneath long, black lashes. And from beneath large bows or hats hung tendrils of every shade of blond, brown, and red. All sat impeccably straight and were impeccably cared for.

Lon looked back to the living doll tucked in the bedcovers, watching Ollie's heavy lids flutter then fall in defeat beneath Eva's cooing tone. He smiled and leaned against one of the bed posters as Eva sent his own consciousness to the skies:

> *"So shut your eyes while mother sings*
> *Of wonderful sights that be,*
> *And you shall see the beautiful things*
> *As you rock in the misty sea,*
> *Where the old shoe rocked the fishermen three:*
> *Wynken, Blynken, and Nod."*

When she finished, Eva leaned down to delicately kiss Ollie's forehead, then displayed great care in getting up without disturbing her slumber. She looked to Lon, pointing an index finger against her smile, and he followed her lead in tiptoeing out the bedroom door. He turned back to gently pull it closed, catching his reflection in it as he did so. Confronting his pale blue, liquor-reddened eyes, he admonished himself for the fancies he'd had of ravishing Eva behind that same door only minutes earlier.

She stood waiting for him on the landing, her hand resting on the newel post. "Thank you, Lon," she said. "I apologize for that."

"Not at all," Lon assured her. "Thank you for the bedtime story. I'm sure to have sweet dreams now."

Eva looked to her feet as she smiled. "To answer your question, from before..."

Lon straightened his posture to a soldier's stance and offered her his arm. "Milady? Your destination, please."

She looked up and scratched her nails on the newel cap. "A moment," she said, before lightly prancing toward another mirrored door and disappearing behind it. When she re-emerged, sheer ivory fabric embroidered in black beading draped from her arm, and a little black beaded bag hung from her opposite hand, with which she quietly shut the door. She wrapped her bare shoulders in the shawl and snaked her free hand through Lon's upheld arm.

"Please, sir. As the poem says, let's sail *'on a river of crystal light, into a sea of dew.'* Take me to the stars."

Infinite points of light winked down at Lon and Eva as they sat side by side on a stone bench beneath the open sky. Now and then, the soft grumble of a lion vibrated through the nighttime sounds of crickets in the grasses and waves off the lakeshore.

When Eva had proven so marvelously successful at sneaking them both out of the Hughes mansion unobserved—and snagging a bottle of champagne from the kitchen at that—it had hardly surprised Lon when she'd ushered him into the Lincoln Park Zoo thereafter. They'd only had a couple of blocks to walk arm-in-arm beneath the starry summer sky, taking turns chugging from the bottle's mouth in the shadows, before they'd each removed their shoes to stealthily ease their way inside zoo boundaries and patter by the Lion House, giggling all the way to where they presently sat.

"Ready?" Eva asked. "On the count of three. One…two…"

Three. Together they threw their arms out with flourish to cast an imaginary net into the sea of stars above.

"Hold on tight, now," Lon said. "Don't let go."

"Never." Eva smiled and pantomimed holding fast to a rope's end and keeping the slack.

They sat a few minutes in silence like this, just staring at the night sky. Eva did, at any rate. Most of the time Lon sat staring at *her* staring at the sky, trying to see the stars reflected in her eyes and watching how they twinkled as much as the little purse she held in her lap. He lifted the champagne bottle from the pavement and brought it to his lips for a swig, then handed it to her. She followed suit and returned the bubbly to him without a word.

Daring to break the meditative hush, Lon eventually asked, "Do you come here often? At night like this?"

He saw her smile in profile, how one corner of it stretched all the way back to the dark brown curl of hair kissing her cheek.

"I do," she replied. "Not as often as I'd like. But I do."

Lon scanned the moonlit clearing and tried to focus on the tall black silhouette at its center. He thought he saw butterfly wings extending from it. "What am I looking at, exactly?"

She hummed a whimsical tune before answering, "She's the Dream Lady. She watches over the little ones as they sleep, brings them dreams. I like to think she watches over us big ones, too."

Lon set the bottle back down on the ground and stood to approach the structure. Feeling around its base, he noted the drowsy bronze heads of two sleeping children at the winged woman's feet. Then he walked around the Dream Lady, running his hand along the carved relief of the long rectangular pediment on which she stood.

Looking up to watch how the stars circled around the angelic head as he walked, he asked, "Is this a tomb of some kind? Is someone buried here?"

"No. It's only a monument."

"A monument to dreams?"

"To a mortal maker of them. I've been reading Eugene Field's poems to Ollie ever since she was born, like the one tonight."

"How old is she?"

"Ollie? Thirteen, if you can believe it. Going on fourteen. Time is truly a frighteningly fast beast."

"I'll say." Lon returned to her side on the bench, thinking time may have been moving rather *slowly* for Ollie, but he didn't find it his place to remark on it. "You're a devoted sister, a mother almost. She's lucky."

Eva chuckled. "She's lucky I have a sense of humor. She *is* trying at times. Don't let her cherub cheeks fool you otherwise."

"Naughty?"

"Mm, smart. She's rather quiet, but you can always see her calculating before she says a word or makes a move. Frankly, I worry about her."

"Why?"

"It may be my own doing, sadly. She's clearly gotten too old for bedtime stories, and yet I encourage her to dream. She's becoming a woman, I know, yet she's such a child. I coddle her while I still can. But I can't pretend I don't see that glimmer of adult wishes in her eyes every now and then, without yet understanding what it means to be 'adult.' I think I humor myself that *I* know."

Eva breathed in heavily and released the air in a long, meditative flow.

"So," she said, "I worry I may have vicariously padded her too much in fancy to know the difference, to know that sometimes life simply is what it is, and, when faced with real decisions, we must grow up and make practical choices. Life isn't always just about ourselves, is it? So perhaps it requires sacrifice of one's own dreams to fulfill those of others."

Lon shifted uncomfortably on the bench. Eva's words hit closer to home than he was prepared for, a gentle slap on the wrist for no longer giving in to such sacrifice. He rested his elbows on his knees and wiped his palms against each other in slow strokes as he frowned at them.

"Oh, but I'm probably sounding corny," Eva said. "Speaking in clichés."

"No," Lon finally said. "I seem to be a living and breathing cliché, as it were. Or am I confusing them with lies?"

"Oh, Lon. Why would you say that?"

"You know, Eva, you haven't yet explained to me why you were so intent to cheat me of my thrill. Why me?"

Her tongue clucked against the roof of her mouth as she seemed to measure her next words.

"Oh, it's not that I wanted to deprive you of a thrill, old boy. In fact, I do hope I gave you *some*."

Lon hummed in the affirmative.

"Why you, indeed." She tapped her nails against the stone bench. "I watched you from the balcony tonight, the one above the front door. I was standing there just inside the doorframe, hidden enough from sight, but I could see you walking along the avenue. I watched you as you arrived and greeted everyone."

The way she'd said "greeted" made Lon curse the day he'd ever laid eyes on Effie.

"You seemed quite familiar with that girl. And yet it also seemed quite the charade. You had *her* fooled, certainly, but you didn't fool me. You can't move in the circles we do and not know something or other about each other's stories. Surely you know something of mine?"

"Of your father's, yes. Of course. His business, rather. I largely ignore all that talk, however. That and gossip. I try my best to stay above it."

"But you don't stay out of it, unfortunately. There's quite a lot of talk about you, you know."

Lon only rubbed his palms together with greater pressure.

"I'm sorry," Eva said. "I don't believe a lot of it anyway. Or at least I don't take it to mean what most of those silly girls do. I think I know what you're up to."

"Hm."

"Don't worry, old boy, it happens to us all. There's a lot floating out there about me, too, so you're not so special." Eva elbowed him in his ribs.

Lon stopped rubbing his hands and just clasped them together. "Well, my brother the war hero and future lord of lumber helps take the attention away as well, so don't think all the limelight is for you," he chided.

"Please. Look who my father is. Daddy soaks up quite enough himself. In fact, I rather enjoy the dark he displaces me into."

"He seems to still do well these days. Weathering everything all right? Staying on the level?" Lon added this last part in jest, though he was, in truth, curious.

"Oh yes, Father's doing all right, I suppose. Divested some of his branch properties but is keeping the bulk of the plants warm by producing that ghastly near-beer. And malt syrup. You know, so Prohibition doesn't impede anyone's *baking*, heaven forbid."

"Ah yes, I'm sure these days no one is up to anything besides baking up sheets and sheets of cookies in the privacy of their kitchens."

"And bathtubs." Eva chuckled. "Father's also made some shrewd investments, making the gamble, of course, that all this will run its course soon enough. He's determined to outlast it and be poised to pick up right where he left off when he does so.

"It's an understandable concern," she went on. "Nothing these days is guaranteed, so it does make sense, doesn't it, that he'd want to hedge his bets by other means, too? Unlike you, we're but the poor *nouveau riche* whose fortunes can tumble as quickly as they've been built. Mother might pretend each afternoon she's sipping her tea in an Old World palace, but the fact remains this is Chicago, USA, and that neo-Baroque monstrosity we live in is barely a quarter of a century old."

Lon felt her eyes on him as he nodded toward his lap. "Money is fleeting for us all, no matter when or how fortunes are made."

He didn't know whether Eva had heard what he'd said when she continued, "And though men believe building empires should be left all to them, isn't it funny how it can take a woman to uphold them."

In the pregnant silence which followed, Lon sensed she wanted to say more, so he waited. All Eva did, however, was cough politely into the back of her hand and pull her shawl more tightly around her.

"Well," he said, "Finlay certainly does all right. Speaking of, I still can't help but wonder why on earth…It's just that you've yet to answer my question. Let's have it, old girl."

Eva relaxed her grip on her shawl, and the gauzy fabric slipped off one shoulder. "Lon, I know you didn't always carry on the way you do with all these women. I know this because you were once engaged, weren't you? And you've refused to take another woman seriously ever since."

He leaned back on his palms and crossed one leg over the other without response.

"I also know," Eva proceeded, "that you try so hard to affect the air of the middle class, if not the lower. That you've had words with your father and all but disinherited yourself from the family, which is why your fiancée called everything off, isn't it? Well, now let me tell you what I *think*. I *think* you act detached and above everyone and everything. But I *don't* think you actually take yourself all that seriously. I also think you aren't immune to commitment. It's only that you were hurt and now you can't trust. And that's the real reason why you philander among women like some sort of revenge."

Lon snorted, subtly shaking his head at her bold conjectures.

"Write it off as batty women's intuition if you must," she said. "But I think if you're not interested in genuinely romantic relationships right now and not interested in our social milieu altogether, then that makes you just about perfection to me."

Lon unclenched teeth and cleared his throat. "To what purpose?"

"Oh, don't make it sound like I had this all premeditated, old boy. I admit I knew of you before and my interest was piqued, but it wasn't until I actually saw you right out there on the street—and then on the stairway—that I conceived just how ideal you are. Someone unattached yet unavailable and indifferent and yet…*earnest*. Principled. Someone who's so perfect to be…" Eva looked down at her lap and wrung her hands. "Well, that is, if you're willing to be—" she looked up and directly into his eyes "—I suppose my confidant? My friend? I've really needed someone like you, Lon. You cannot possibly imagine how much. Or can you?" Her eyes searched his face.

Lon sat up and wiped the grit of the stone bench from his hands as he mulled over her words.

"Anyway," she said, "that's why I needed to get your thrill out of the way. Seeing you with Effie…" She twisted her emerald ring and pulled it on and off her finger. "I didn't want to risk becoming the object of another of your chases had I remained too aloof or wasted precious time flirting."

The presumptuous little thing, Lon thought, but he let her keep talking.

"Flirtation is such a frivolous waste of time. I know I'm still young, but, well, I think life's too short to waste time *chasing*, don't you agree? And what's romance but fleeting once one is caught. I'm through being hunted and snared. I may have put one concern to rest through engagement, but I'm still free to confide in anyone I please. But these women are tattling hens, and the men are wolves." At last, she left the ring on her finger but spun the emerald around it instead.

"Look," Eva persisted, "maybe I've got you all wrong. Maybe what happens in the evening underground doesn't all quite make it to the afternoon parlor. But I simply don't think that you are. A wolf, that is. Not once the chase is out of the way." She shifted in her seat. "I've got you right, haven't I? That you're different from most men? Your motives—they're different?"

She pivoted toward him on the bench, still wringing her hands. Lon stopped wiping his own and faced her. In the bright moonlight, he saw more than stars twinkling at the bottom of her eyes, more than comets streaking down her cheeks. He wiped one of the falling stars from her face and lowered his hand onto hers to still them.

"Will you, Lon?" Eva sniffed. "I know I must have offended you so greatly just now, and I understand if you don't want to clutter your life with one more poor little rich girl. But, will you? *Be* here for me? I'd very much like to be here for you, too, if ever you would need me."

He wrapped an arm around her shoulders. Cupping her head in his hand, he brought it to his shoulder.

Eva nuzzled against the lapel of his gray suit coat, sniffling into it. Lon rested his chin on the molasses waves of her hair and caressed his fingers through them. The scent of icy cool wind wafting off frozen waters briefly came back to him, but it just as soon thawed into fields of lilies of the valley, and there again was the masculine musk that Eva's skin had since sweetened to jasmine and rose.

The crickets orchestrated a droning lullaby; the lions purred themselves to sleep. And the whispering tide smoothed over ripples of sand for the Dream Lady to sprinkle in everyone's eyes.

Three for a Wedding

July 2000

"Ow!" Kate yanked her head away from her coffee mug and sucked on her burned tongue.

Leaving the latest frozen, over-syruped and sized-in-foreign-terminology coffee drink craze to the Lincoln Park Trixies, Kate preferred to play it old-school—hot and black. Even on a warm, sticky day.

But it was pleasant in the shade where she sat. A mild breeze whispered across the leafy front patio of an independent café modestly tucked off Fullerton Avenue, Kate's oasis for a Saturday afternoon of solitude. Her apartment had come to feel oppressive after a while, and she just needed to get some air.

"Well, well!" she heard, and she lifted her face from her book. Moseying up the avenue was Vera with a big smile beneath rhinestone horn-rimmed sunglasses. "Fancy meeting you here, dear girl. It's been a while!"

"Yeah," Kate said. "I got your note at my door. Sorry I didn't respond, just been so busy at work and getting my place situated. You know."

"Mm hm. I figured so much." She looked at the café exterior with a smile. "Ah! Bourgeois Pig," she pronounced with care. "You know, I've never been here." She brought a hand to her heart with a laugh. "We old farts like to mingle at the Panera on Diversey. Just a block from the building, you know."

Kate smiled politely.

"But everything's been okay?" Vera asked.

For the last week, Kate had been reluctant to broach the subject with someone else, yet she'd known that Vera was the likeliest candidate. She wasn't sure why, but somehow she knew nothing would surprise the old gal. Even if Vera didn't believe what Kate had to say, she wouldn't judge. And if she did judge—so what?

"Actually, Vera, if you've got a second."

Vera frowned and immediately tugged a wrought iron chair out from under Kate's table with a nails-on-chalkboard scrape against the cement patio. She abruptly sat down and said, "Spill it."

"Well, do you ever feel like something's a little…*off* in our building? Strange sounds you can't explain, a general heaviness in the air, and…"

"Ye-es," Vera said hesitantly, observing Kate with a round, bulging eye.

"You have?"

"*You* have?" Vera asked back, making Kate question whether Vera's "Yes" before had been an answer or just a cue for Kate to say more. Vera's next words didn't help clarify. "Sounds such as what, dear?"

"Like rushing water in all directions. And the cat—"

"Cat?"

"Agatha. She must've gotten back inside my apartment block somehow. Someone always seems to be moving in or out of my stairwell, and they leave the main door propped open. I found her scratching at my door one night after work and wanted to return her to you but didn't know which unit is yours. I banked on her being savvy enough to find her way home, I mean, assuming it's normal for her to roam around outside like that?"

"That damn thing has always lived on a long leash, and *I'm* not about to become her keeper. So don't mind her, dear. You were right not to."

"The thing is, she was staring upward again like something was on my door or the stairwell ceiling. She jumped up on her hind legs and hopped just like she did inside my place that one day."

"Cats'll do that, you know. And Aggie lived there for quite a long time."

"Okay. But *do* you sense something about the building, too?"

"Old buildings are just like that. They have a memory. Cling on to everything."

Kate widened her eyes, picturing residual spirits waltzing in circles inside every studio.

Vera shrugged. "Oh, I just mean dust and crumbs compress into the spaces between the floorboards. Mildew in the tiles, mold in the walls. It just sits and collects, like me and the other old residents, heh!" Her gruff laugh became a cough. "I'm sure what you hear, dear, is just the dead weight of that big old mausoleum settling. Mice running around in the rafters. And the ventilation gets poor. That's probably why the air feels, eh, 'heavy,' as you say."

Kate furrowed her brows but gave a conceding nod. "I guess you're right. And I'm sure the thing with the purse—" she half said it to herself as she spoke down to her mug "—was just too much wine that night." She shook her head up and down with growing conviction that Vera was right and took a comforting sip of her coffee, which had finally reached a non-scalding temperature.

"Something with the *purse*, did you say?" Vera drummed her closely trimmed nails on the tabletop's metal grating.

Kate's "Mm hm" echoed inside her giant coffee mug as she took another sip.

"Your new one? As in, Olive's *old* one?"

"Uh huh. But it was stupid, never mind."

"If there's something wrong with it, I'll gladly take it back, dear. There's always Goodwill or Amvets to donate to."

"No, no, I love it! I really do. I think it was just weird lighting, and I was tired, and the mirror is kinda warped."

"Oh! Well, you should have a purse with a proper mirror. Let me just take that right back and refund your money." Vera reached out eagerly as if Kate could produce the merchandise on the spot.

"Oh, stop. I didn't even pay for it. And I do still want it. Sorry, I didn't mean to sound like I was complaining."

Vera settled her hands back down and resumed her thrumming on the tabletop. "Something odd with the purse's mirror, then?" she said casually as she looked across the street at Children's Memorial Hospital with suspiciously sudden disinterest.

Kate waved her hand as if she could brush the topic out of the air. She was too young to let herself come off as the more senile of the two.

"Kaaate?" The raised inflection at the end of the name sounded like a parent demanding answers after a broken curfew.

Kate took a gulp of coffee and felt the jitters of her caffeine rush. It wasn't helping her keep composure. "Fine. Whatever. I looked at the mirror and my eyes looked green, and I thought it was weird. That's all."

"Green?" Vera leaned forward and squinted. "Huh, your eyes are brown."

"Hence why I thought it was strange. But you know what? Honestly? The mirror's glass is missing and parts of the reflective backing are scratched away and scuffed up, so my reflection probably looked faded. Look, don't worry about it, seriously. It was nothing, and I feel so dumb for even bringing it up."

Vera didn't say anything, just screwed her mouth to the side as she bit the inside of her cheek. Her eyes were scrutinizing but, as Kate had counted on, not appearing to judge.

Kate took to nibbling the inside of her own mouth during the brief silence until Vera finally said, "Oh, well, that makes sense, dear. I can see how that would give a fright, though. Anyway…"

"Yeah, it was a kind of an aggravating night as it was. I had a lot on my mind and don't think I paid much close attention to anything, especially not Dex." She laughed at her lap.

"Dex?"

"Yeah," Kate said with endearment. The same way she might for a pet guinea pig, though not necessarily how she'd dreamed of referring to a lover. "Dexter. He's my boyfriend."

"Boyfriend!" Vera gave a single clap of her hands. "Now you're getting interesting."

"Well, I don't know how interesting it is, but he's a good guy. We first met at work and have been dating for just over a year now."

Her neighbor winked as she asked, "So, it's serious?"

"Oh, well. We're exclusive but not really looking to move things forward yet. At least I'm not. We tried living together, but what's the rush? We're young. We have time."

"Time." Vera appeared to consider the word carefully. "I don't doubt its existence, but it sure isn't something any of us can *have*. You'll see. The older you get, the faster time'll flap away from you." For all her cynicism, a new gleam came into her eyes. "But the time you do have can be for moving forward—or not." She raised her brows and pouted her lips as she shook her head. "Who's to say what we single gals do with our lives? Right?" She winked again and leaned to nudge Kate's arm with her elbow in a gesture of camaraderie.

"Did you ever marry, Vera?"

"Me?" She brought a hand to her heart in exaggerated offense. "Heavens, no! But I was proposed to several times."

"Reeeally," Kate replied with a big grin. "Now *you're* getting interesting."

"You know, I look at you and swear I can see myself."

Kate forced the muscles of her face to keep holding up her smile. "Reeeally," she repeated through her clenched teeth as enthusiastically as she could.

"Yes, I can," Vera sang. "I even had the same hair color, as Nature originally intended it—until She tooketh away." She pumped her palm against the bottom of her well-sculpted and sprayed hairdo, which held up miraculously well in the humidity. "As it is, I don't find it true that blondes have more fun, but darker shades just don't work on me ever since I had to start drawing my eyebrows back on."

Kate smiled with an air of pity. How lucky she was to be in her twenties and how sad for those who were not.

"In any case," Vera said, "rest assured, you and I are a lot alike. Two peas in a pod. We're independent, our own people! That's right, my girl. Always the chase, always the thrill. Never lose sight of that, dear."

"So these proposals you were talking about…"

From Vera's wicked giggle, Kate could tell all the men were lining up in the woman's mind. She was probably barking orders at them in her imagination, too, prodding them with a stick.

"Yes. Oh, I dated some fine-looking men. Good prospects, too. Most of them were introduced to me by my parents. I received the pick of the litter in our community, you know." She rested her chin on her fist. "Yes, they would parade before me at the house, then take me out on dates. I would let some kiss me, and others I didn't give the time of day. Time was on my side then, too, girl. But even though I realize now it's not and never was, I don't have a single regret." That gleam of mischief reentered her eyes. "I just couldn't tie myself down to one man. My *entire* life, right there and then spoken for me? No sir, I didn't want that. See, you're a lot like me. Hats off to you."

Kate faked a grin and took two long sips of her coffee. *Not on your life, sister*, she thought, knowing that, for her, things would be different.

But something inside her had sparked out, and Kate no longer felt the contentment of a pretty sunny day out-and-about by her lonesome. She thought of Dex and wondered if she should have taken him up on his offer to take a long bike ride down the lakefront path to Hyde Park and grab breakfast — Medici's fresh-squeezed orange juice alone was worth the journey.

Is this how it starts? Choosing a day by yourself turns into choosing a life by yourself?

She looked at Vera as the spirited old gal spun off on a story about her "Panera Pack" from the other day at lunch. Something about one of the men loudly breaking wind because his hearing-aid battery had gone out. If he couldn't hear it, it didn't exist.

Kate periodically paid attention, smiling and nodding through Vera's tales, but was unable to get Dex or any of the guys she'd dated out of her head. The fact was, Kate very much wanted to get married someday, when she was ready and the guy was without a doubt The One. She thought Dex could be Him, but she'd always assumed that she'd *know*. Lightning would strike and obliterate any reasonable doubt. Maybe she was meant to persist through trial and error, then; keep seeing other people. The guys had definitely gotten better over the years as she honed her selection process into a science.

Yet whenever she was *just* about to get more practical about it all — write up her lists of pros and cons and see how Dex or any other guy weighed in on paper — Kate would get this vision of herself standing in the doorway of a church, a bridesmaid bouquet in her hand. As she'd look down forlornly, in her peripheral vision she'd notice guests' cars driving away, only to look up and see Jake Ryan from *Sixteen Candles* in his sweater vest, his button-down shirt rolled to his elbows. He'd be leaning against his red sports car, smiling and waving at…her?

Me?

And then she'd meet him halfway as he jogged across the street to her.

Fuck, Kate thought as Vera's gritty voice dulled into background noise. *John Hughes, you've ruined me for all men.*

As Vera had only been out walking and didn't want to order anything at the café, Kate felt bad keeping her there. So she promptly finished her coffee and Dream Man thoughts and offered to walk Vera home.

It was slow-going eastward, but by the time they crossed Clark Street on Wrightwood Avenue and were about to hang a left onto Camden Court, Kate remarked how obsessed she'd become with the pale gray stone mansion on the corner there.

"I mean, it's *gorgeous!* You just don't see stuff like this in Illinois. It reminds me so much of backpacking through Europe after graduation. I haven't been able to walk by a single time without trying to see inside the windows." She slowed her stride once they'd reached the mansion steps and pointed to the front door and the two caryatids flanking it. "Look at that — using statues as columns. Architecture used to be so thoughtful."

When she didn't hear a response, Kate looked over to see whether Vera was even paying attention or had kept walking toward their building. But Vera was standing there beside her, looking at the house, too.

"Sorry," Kate said. "We didn't have to stop. I'm just fascinated. It's such a romantic surprise, tucked away here in the middle of the city."

"No," Vera said, "you're right to be intrigued. This house is just over a century old. An official Chicago landmark, in fact. Not many of its day still stand, and none of them that ever did came close to matching it. It *is* a romantic place."

Kate thought she heard Vera actually sigh at the end of her sentence, but she figured the woman must have only been catching her breath after their walk. Sighing as she spoke of something "romantic" did not strike Kate as something Vera was biologically capable of.

When her neighbor said nothing more, just stared intently at the house, Kate took the liberty of rounding the corner to peek up into a large side window. "Oh!"

"You all right?"

"Vera, have you seen the ceiling in this room?"

Vera hobbled around to where Kate stood.

"*Look* at it," Kate said breathlessly. "There's actually a painting in the center of the ceiling! It's like the Sistine Chapel or something." She pointed her fingertip in loop-the-loops at the intricate plaster sculpting around the mural. "It's just dripping in flowers and garlands and cupids."

Beside her, Vera nodded in agreement. Still looking at the window, she said, "But, you know, when it comes down to it, it's still just a house. And it's still just people who lived inside it. Same as you and me, in more ways than they might've been different."

"Does anyone live here now?"

"No. It's commercially owned. Rented out for private parties. You'll see wedding receptions in the garden most every weekend, just wait."

"Oh," Kate cooed. "I want my wedding here."

She took one last good ogle before she motioned to Vera that they could resume walking home. Even as they did, though, Kate wasn't entirely willing to let it go. "So, who did live there? Originally. Do you know?"

"That was the Hughes house," Vera replied. "Built just before the turn of the century for a wealthy brewer. Warren Hughes was his name. And he obviously had a taste for the Old World. Some of the fixtures in there were brought over here from Europe to make sure it was just right. An avid traveler, he was. In love with Bavaria and King Ludwig's palaces."

The old woman had done so well keeping her energy up all that afternoon, but now Kate noticed how Vera had begun to trudge, hanging her head wearily toward the sidewalk. Kate was glad they were now only a few yards away from their apartment building.

"I'd think a descendant would have held on to that place. Why get rid of it? Or did Warren not have anyone to leave the legacy to?" Once inside the little brick enclosure of their courtyard gate, Kate stopped to hold the iron door open. She studied Vera as she walked through it.

"Had two daughters," Vera said, her face looking saddened. "One was an exceptional beauty, so they say, the other plain in comparison but nice-looking. Quite a few years apart from each other but supposedly thick as thieves until one of them just disappeared into thin air. Only a teenager, yet never seen again. And the other, I guess she died tragically not too long after. This was all back in the late twenties, before the stock market crash, and the story goes that, after such great loss of life, Hughes and his wife moved West before they lost their money, too. I don't believe anyone lived there again until maybe the forties, fifties. Eh, well. People come and go. That's what happens when you live long enough."

Kate walked Vera to a building entrance that was on the same side as hers but farther back in the corner, adjacent to the base of the U-shaped building. She asked if Vera needed assistance up the stairs.

"Naw," Vera said, exhaustion apparently not making her any less stubborn. "I'll do all right." She reached for the banister and started up the first two steps, then turned back to Kate. "Oh, and if you find Aggie over at your door again, just throw her into the courtyard. She'll do fine enough out there on her own."

Kate left Vera's stairwell, but she didn't go back to her apartment. Instead, she walked out the door and cut over to the next one that led inside the base of the building's U. She knocked at the door of a first-floor apartment there. It smelled of baked beans on the outside, and on the inside, Kate thought she heard the rustling of papers and shuffle of footsteps on the wooden floor.

Leo's face was twisted with anxiety when he initially opened his door, but after a couple of seconds focusing on Kate, he broke into a warm smile. "Well, hello, little lady!" he said cheerfully, backing away from the door as a signal for her to enter and make herself at home.

"Hi, Leo!" She was surprised how pleased she actually was to see the old man.

"Can I get ya somethin'?" He helped Kate navigate around piles of newspapers on the floor. "Anythin' to drink?"

"Oh, no, I'm fine."

"Ya sure? An ice-cold Coca-Cola maybe?" He wore a boyish expression that made Kate worry refusing his hospitality would offend him.

"Sure."

He returned from the kitchen and handed her a can that really did feel ice cold. It burned her palm, so she set it on the side table next to his sofa, where she sat after brushing off a couple of peanuts.

Leo crossed the room toward his threadbare recliner, its old cushion sunken like it already bore his weight. He hesitated a moment, just staring down at the chair. Kate worried he was having a stroke or a bowel movement until he cleared his throat and, after a few seconds, sat.

It was her first time inside Leo's home since he'd toured her through it as a model for her own. At that time, she'd felt a little wary of the building given the sparse and scattered appearance of its supposed "show property"; the twin bed shoved in his kitchen made it look even less appealing. But now that she knew Leo better, she found the dated sixties furnishings and minimal décor of his predominantly brown and green bachelor pad endearing. It could have been pulled off in a trendy retro way but *so* wasn't, which was *so* Leo. He wasn't trying to recreate an era out of fad; he was still living in it out of habit.

"So how's your weekend?" Leo asked. "What brings you by?"

"So far the weekend's so-so. I ran into Vera at the coffee shop, and we had a nice long talk and walk together afterward. I just dropped her off. She looked like she could use a rest."

"Ah." Leo grinned. "Yep, that's what happens to us old-timers. Our batteries don't last as long before they need recharging again."

"Yeah," Kate said. "You know, I'm sorry to barge in on you like this. I'm not even sure why I did. I guess I just have some questions."

"Questions?"

"About this place. This area."

"Hm. Well, all right. Shoot."

"Vera was telling me about the Hughes mansion on the corner? About the family that lived there? I love that house, and she sucked me into its story, but then she was tired and didn't seem to know much beyond the basics. I thought since I was over here I'd ask if you happen to know more about it." *More like* exactly *what she knows that would make her so upset — the stuff I won't find on the Internet.*

Kate thought she saw a twinkle of amusement in Leo's eye; perhaps he was glad for a chance to show off knowledge superior to Vera's. In the little while she'd known them, the two always seemed engaged in a friendly private battle.

"Well, it just so happens that, yes, I do know a little somethin' about that."

He hoisted himself up and Kate waited quietly as he disappeared into his walk-in closet. She heard drawers opening and closing and the crackle of papers.

Looking straight ahead of her, down the hallway to his kitchen — it was all an exact replica of her own studio — Kate then heard something skid to her left. She looked to her side, but all was still. Searching for what it could have been, she noticed her Coke can standing right up to the edge of the side table, inches from where she'd set it and with a visible trail of water in between.

Kate held her breath a few seconds before rationalizing that the condensation must have dripped down the can and made it hydroplane across the table. The floor probably sloped in this old building, or maybe the legs of the table were uneven. Yeah, that must have been it.

Leo emerged from his closet with a shoebox and set it down on the coffee table in front of Kate. He'd removed its lid, so she saw right away how it was stuffed with newspaper clippings and photographs.

"I tell ya, kiddo," Leo said, "it's ridiculous the stuff you accumulate as you get older. Stuff you should just throw out but don't." He batted a hand at the air as though shooing away a fly. "And then it gets to where you start keepin' other people's junk because they start dyin' all around ya."

Kate bit her lips between her teeth, unable to fathom a world without family and friends around her. If living a long life meant possibly having to outlive everyone else you cared about, why did everyone seem to want that so badly? Why grow old?

"Anyway," he said, "I got this box from an acquaintance who's passed on. Been meanin' to go through it and see if there isn't somethin' worth saving. Maybe track down a relation who would want it." He paused and coughed into his hand.

"Have you found anyone yet?"

Leo coughed again. "Well, findin' the relation is one thing, but them wantin' anything to do with it is another. It opens a whole other can o' worms sometimes and leaves me wonderin' why bother to begin with. Anyway," he said, "doesn't hurt using it to benefit your curiosity, I guess. If you really take an interest." He sat back down and kicked back with his feet up on his recliner.

She had already begun rummaging through the box, peeling one fragile news clipping from another and scanning the faces that smiled or frowned back from them. "So there's something about the Hugheses in here?"

"Haven't gone through it all yet, but I reckon there would be. I s'pose you could say the collector was an amateur local archivist."

When her excavation revealed a big article with a large yellowed and faded photograph, Kate caught her breath. "So lovely."

Leo pulled his chair lever and, after releasing the footrest down, leaned toward the coffee table. She watched his wrinkled lips pucker as he strained to make out the photo she held out to him. "Oh yes," he said. "A wedding announcement."

Kate brought the clipping back closer to her face. "'The marriage of Miss Evelyn Hughes of Chicago —'" she shot her face up to look at Leo in excitement "'—and Finlay Redcliffe of Lake Forest took place Sunday, October fourth, at nine o'clock at Saint Clement Church.' Wow. Is that the St. Clement's just over there on Deming?"

"Prob'ly."

"Wow," Kate said again. "Look at her veil. Oh, she's stunning. It takes my breath away." She looked up at Leo for an agreeable response, but he was no longer staring at her or the clipping but out the window in the direction of where Vera's block stuck out at a ninety-degree angle from his. Kate thought he could be looking up at Vera's floor.

She didn't want Leo to catch her watching him, so she looked back to the wedding announcement in mute concentration. Beneath it was a fashion column reviewing Evelyn's fine attire for the event, which stated her age as nineteen. *Only a teenager*, Kate thought. *How in hell did they get it together at such young ages back then?* Vera's words also echoed in her mind, and Kate pondered whether Evelyn had been the Hughes daughter who'd run away or died tragically.

In the silence, Leo spoke up. "Sure is beautiful." A long pause. "Beauty like hers, though —" he nodded at the press clipping and met Kate's gaze "— can be a blessing and a curse, I reckon."

Kate drew her brows into a huddle and dropped her smile. She lowered the article to her lap.

"You have your beauty on the outside that attracts one type of man, ya see," Leo told her, "and you've got your beauty on the inside that attracts another. If you've got both types of beauty, then you attract both types of men. And at a time like that, well, there were a lotta' types of men that didn't give a girl much choice. That was a time when a lotta' gals instead just started up-n-choosin' for themselves. It was a turnin' point in the right direction, ya see, but it didn't come easy. Not for everyone." Leo looked away from Kate and back out the window.

She laid the announcement inside the shoebox with care and replaced the other clippings she'd removed. "Thanks for sharing this with me. Maybe I can drop by again sometime and look through more. Whenever it's not a hassle."

His morose face softened into his usual grin. "Anytime, little lady." Kate moved to stand, and he likewise got up with a grunt and escorted her to the door like a gentleman. "Don't forget your soda pop."

"Nope." Kate smiled.

When she swooped the slippery can up from the table, she glimpsed a sepia wedding photo behind it, mounted inside a beveled pewter frame. The picture appeared to be a casual snapshot rather than a formal portrait, one taken by a wedding guest, perhaps, that seemed to have caught the couple in a candid moment of embrace before they'd quickly smiled for the camera. She thought to comment on it while in the mood to wax nostalgic about romantic days gone by, until she noticed how very much the young groom resembled Leo. How very happy he looked with his arms wrapped around his round-faced bride with the bashful smile. How very much that expression of his contrasted with the one he'd just worn when looking out the window.

Kate spun around from the table and kissed Leo on the cheek before walking out his door and into the sun.

"Yes, I'm sure, Dex, just go without me. Have fun."

As Kate hung up her phone, she only felt mild regret blowing Dexter off twice in one day. He'd invited her out to early evening volleyball at North Beach, but he'd be with his buddies there, enjoying the weather and drinking plenty of beer, so she didn't feel she'd disappointed him too much.

Cracking open Leo's cold can of Coke, she swigged the sweet fizz and fell back onto her futon, which was folded up in sofa-form. She laid her head back and propped her feet on the coffee table's wooden frame, flapping her knees in and out restlessly. Rolling her head to the side, she glanced at her ugly air conditioner, then looked out the window next to it at the apartments across the courtyard. She didn't think painting these rentals was allowed, but a third-floor apartment across the way had deep red walls, except for white moldings and chair railings.

"That'll be a bitch to paint over when she moves," Kate said to herself, until she remembered where she lived — if people weren't moving out right away, they seemed to stay forever to die on the spot.

As it was, the woman across the way was home. Kate recognized her as Maisie, the mousy middle-aged lady from the estate sale. At night when the lights were on inside, Kate often saw the woman pace back and forth across the length of her studio, bouncing a little bundle in her arms. Or she'd be sitting on her sofa, holding a baby's little hands as she sang to it and smiled. Kate never noticed anyone else over there, though. Given the woman's apparent age, it would seem she was a nanny or maybe even a very young grandmother. Maybe she'd adopted, or maybe she'd just narrowly made it before her biological clock slammed her fertility window closed.

Whatever her speculations, Kate had fun playing her game of *Rear Window*. All she needed was a state-of-the-art camera lens like Jimmy Stewart had and she'd be set to sniff herself out a murder mystery in this old 1920s hotel.

What was with her and "mystery" these days? Peeking through windows and probing into stranger's lives? Had Living on Her Own become that boring already? Kate was consumed enough with getting her own life started, as twenty-somethings must do. Preoccupied with teaching at the planetarium, brainstorming new make-and-takes for the Adler kids to color and construct and hoping they learned something. That she wasn't just sending them home with a piece of crap-on-a-stick to clutter their parents' fridge. Or she'd be coordinating museum overnights with the local Girl and Boy Scout troops, training new volunteers and helping at special events like the winter Celestial Ball. Hell, she even subbed for Vicki's volunteers sometimes.

For as little as it paid, her job could really swallow her life. Not because she was forced to work long hours or invest so much of her mind and heart into it, but because that's what being an educator — a *good* one — demanded. An average one could phone it in, but that wasn't Kate. She cared about doing right by those kids and that learning institution. The drawback was that it didn't often leave her with much mental or emotional energy for anything else.

Or anyone else. She did phone it in with Dex; she knew that. She'd been increasingly treating her boyfriend like a friend with benefits, and now the benefits were trailing off, too. Maybe she'd become drawn to the misfortunes of others lately just to feel better about herself. To know that even the young and rich could lose it all. Kate didn't have so much to lose, did she, if she took some risks? She still had time to answer the big questions about love, settling down, and creating a future that was about more than just her—much more time than Mousy Maisie across the way, for sure. Yeah, that *was* reassuring.

Kate exhaled heavily and rolled her face away from the window. Opting not to analyze too much on a deserved day off alone, she started to sing some Macy Gray out loud. Once she reached the refrain, a series of knocks sounded right behind her head. It came from the apartment on the other side of Jaundice, the yellow wall.

Uh oh, am I annoying Hot Neighbor?

She went quiet and listened for anything else. Some more faint tapping followed, but it sounded quick and playful, not like a complaint.

Tap tap, tap tap-tap, tap tap.

The longer it lasted, the more she identified a rhythm to it, something on the order of the old "Shave and a Haircut" knock yet different, and she sat forward to tap out the same beat on the glass pane of her tabletop. When she stopped, it was silent next door.

Until it started again—*tap tap, tap tap-tap, tap tap*—then stopped. In the silence, a chill gripped Kate's spine, and her ears filled with an ambient echo as though listening to seashells. She set down her soda and, after rubbing her hands to warm them, again mimicked the rhythm on her table. As if in response, the knocking started again. Kate tapped it out once more and hummed a tune to accompany it.

When the tapping next door seemed to echo her new melody, Kate stopped to bite the tip of her index finger, feeling her heart rate quicken and cheeks burn. Was it just coincidence, or had she just tapped her way into communication with Hot Neighbor?

Suddenly shy and anxious about what might happen next, she turned to press her palm against the wall behind her. It felt warm, a soothing contrast to her room that had just turned so cold. She imagined Hot Neighbor sitting there with his hand against the wall, too, directly opposite her. What if he'd noticed her before and wanted to get her attention? Maybe seen her around sometime, even if just out his window, and then followed the sound of her footsteps and door slams to trace her to this unit? Kind of stalkerish but awfully flattering, Kate thought. After all, she was doing the same thing with him.

After a span of silence, she drummed out the original rhythm again with the pads of her fingers, figuring it would be too quiet to hear through the wall anyway. Immediately she heard and felt the vibration of a soft knocking directly against where her palm lay on the wall.

Tap tap, tap tap-tap, tap tap.

Kate joined in, and ever so gradually, their raps fell into perfect time with actual music playing with increasing volume from next door. The sweet yet somber melody crackled into mellow, austere piano chords, and Kate shivered when a soulful voice rang out and pierced her heart. It sounded so passionate, so mournful, as raw and present as an open vein.

She stood to shut off her overactive air conditioner, close the blinds, and draw her velvety green drapes, preferring silence and darkness. Returning to the futon, she kneeled on it and leaned toward the wall until her face pressed against it. Slowly, she sank to sit on her heels, then settled on the cushion.

Closing her eyes and losing herself to the seductive melody, she didn't even need Dickie Greenleaf. She simply eased her hand—still warm from the wall—down past her waist, between her thighs, and let the fantasy begin.

October 1925

Lon turned the invitation over and over in his hand before stuffing it into the interior pocket of his morning coat. It was half-past eight in the morning on October fourth, and he knew he should commence his ten-minute walk to the church if he wanted to arrive respectably early.

He stood from his desk chair, stepped around his Murphy bed, and walked to the wall mirror opposite his windows. The reflection of light gave an impression of space contrary to what the room actually offered. He'd also begun painting a landscape on one of the walls to offer more color and depth, the hotel's restrictions be damned; he wasn't living anywhere else anytime soon. Straightening his bow tie and smoothing down his lapels, Lon deemed himself ready to go.

As he strode down Camden Court and approached Wrightwood, he saw the fanfare in and around the Hughes house on the corner.

Damn it.

He should have known not to walk so openly on their block so close to show time. If anyone asked, he would say he'd made much better time driving into the city than anticipated and let the chauffeur handle the car while Lon took a stroll through the park.

A cream Rolls Royce waited at the base of the home's front steps. Behind it was parked an identical car but with black trim around the fenders and footboard. Women in eggshell white tulle milled about it, and an anxious Mrs. Hughes pranced up and down the steps between the car and the main entrance in a fluttering attempt to manage everyone involved.

But not all were in their places. Lon knew at least one wasn't there yet.

Counting on their distraction and the muted camouflage of his black tails and gray trousers, he removed his top hat and used it to cover the right side of his face as he jogged across the avenue and to the side of the mansion. He tucked behind a protruding bay window and looked around for any other pedestrians or motor traffic. Fortunately, it was a quiet Sunday morning with many attending services or sleeping off hangovers if they weren't already clustering at the foot of St. Clement's for an exclusive peek at the society event of the year.

Pressing his back against the pale gray limestone like a cat burglar, Lon looked up to the second-floor bay window, then moved along the house's exterior to get a better view. But he couldn't see into the second-floor room from this angle, only the little nook at the window.

Please, Eva, just let me see you.

Through the first-floor windows just above his head, he could hear footsteps and other commotion inside the dining and music rooms. Outside—and through the front door, presumably—he heard, "Eee-VAH!" in Mrs. Hughes's chirpy falsetto. "Darling, it's time!"

Please, Eva, let me see you this once. You alone, old girl. You as you are now, not as you will be.

As though in answer, he saw a curtain quiver at the edge of the second-floor window. He held his breath. "Please," he whispered.

Long, pale fingers wrapped around the curtain just then, and she stepped into view. She appeared statuesque, dressed in ivory lace from the Juliet cap crowning her head to the sleeves trailing down over her bony wrists, from the V-neck baring her clavicle to the layers draping beneath a silk sash at the gown's dropped waist.

Releasing her hand from the curtain, the bride folded it above the one at her stomach, and Lon watched her delicate breastbone heave up and down in measured breaths. Her face appeared stoic. The bride drew her chin down to her neck and unfolded her hands, only to re-clasp them with their fingers entwined as though in prayer, then closed her eyes.

"Eva," he whispered.

Her eyes flew open as if she felt his presence—as Lon liked to think she did—and she turned her face gradually toward the side window panel and looked right down at him.

He flinched when their eyes met, only as a reflex of getting caught, which he'd been trying so hard to avoid until then. He readily relaxed his posture, however, in the safety of her gaze. She touched her fingertips against the glass as she unceasingly smiled down on him. In that moment, the bridal attire disintegrated away and she became only Eva.

His confidante. His friend. The one he'd been there for all summer, the one who'd been there for him.

The morning sun rose over the lake in the east, beaming in through the bay window to bathe her in an angelic glow. There she stood above him, surreal yet real, fantasy yet flesh.

The Dream Lady.

On impulse, Lon mouthed the few words he suddenly needed to say, and Eva nodded back. She brought one hand to her lips to kiss the pads of her fingertips and replaced them on the windowpane, sprinkling the glittering sands of what dreams Lon still grasped on to down into his eyes. He instinctively raised the back of a hand to his forehead, like he had to shield his eyes from her light.

Or was it to shield her from his dark.

"Eee-VAH!"

The apparition of Eva vanished, and Lon knew the bride was marching her way down the grand imperial staircase to the door, and from there to her new life as Mrs. Redcliffe.

"Lon! Hey, Lonnie!"

Lon looked up from the twig he'd been scraping along the hedges that bordered the church property. His glum face broke into a smile.

"Hey there, Ollie!" he replied. "Why, just look at you! You could be a little bride yourself."

Ollie blushed and looked to the sidewalk as she ground one patent-leather toe into the gravelly surface.

"I mean it, Ollie. Someday a lucky young man is going to whisk you away as his wife. All in good time, though. I don't want you to grow up too quickly."

"I'm fourteen years old now, Lonnie. I'm practically a lady. Just you wait."

Lon chuckled. "All right, then."

"Really, Lonnie? You'll wait for me?"

He laughed louder. "I'll still be your friend, if that's what you mean."

"When I'm a lady in furs and pearls, you'll take me to dinner?"

"Oh, Ollie. When that time comes, sure. Dinner."

For a moment, she stared at him with an intensity that said, *I'll hold you to that.*

Then she grinned in evident self-satisfaction and held her chin higher. "It was a *most* lovely ceremony, didn't you think?" She laid her lace-gloved hand at her chest with ladylike delicacy.

"I suppose it was," he said. "I regret to say I had a bit of car trouble driving in. I didn't want to make a spectacle of myself by entering late, so I've just bided my time out here. It's a beautiful morning."

"Oh." Ollie's face dropped to a slight pout. "So you didn't see me walk down the aisle?"

"I'm afraid I missed out, my dear. Care to show me now how you did it?" Lon swept his arm to indicate the length of the sidewalk not yet mobbed by guests or onlookers.

She perked up and raised her chin once again with a serious—adult-like, she probably supposed—expression as she dramatically took one step, brought her feet together, took another step, brought her feet together, and so forth. Lon noticed fluctuations in her height as she walked on the balls of her feet as if wearing a higher heel than the blocky ones she'd been granted.

She continued on this way to the corner, where her hand was taken right away by a member of the party, sweeping her back to the church before she could hardly give Lon one last girlish grin and wave goodbye.

Lon stood there with his hands in his pockets, chuckling quietly to himself, before walking in the other direction down Orchard Street and onward to his hotel.

It was true that he hadn't attended the ceremony despite having been well on time. He'd been too restless after seeing Eva in that private window ceremony of their own to do anything but wander the neighborhood. It was inevitable, however, that his feet would take him to the church—just outside of it but near enough to her. He'd kept mainly to the Orchard side of the building, standing parallel to where she kneeled at the altar.

He didn't mind being seen by the rest of the wedding-goers afterward, though; in fact, it would help him with his alibi that, yes, of course, he'd been there all along as any faithful friend would be. Getting lost in the shuffle at the reception afterward would be easy enough if he really *were* to be there, so he'd merely say that he was, should anyone inquire later.

He took a longer way around as he made his way back to Camden Court Hotel, keeping to alleyways and side streets to avoid discovery. A preposterous farce, he well knew, but one he'd been able to maintain with surprising success for a couple of months now. Keeping a low profile, he'd pretend to be in from the country on weekends and wear his worker's clothes and cap on weekdays. His "higher" class acquaintances wouldn't recognize him in that get-up even if they did condescend to look him in the eye when passing in the street.

He stepped through the gates to his courtyard and climbed the steps to his suite, which he rented by the month. Once inside, he removed his coat, vest, and shoes, untied his bowtie, unfastened the top buttons of his shirt, and walked to his kitchenette to pour himself a whiskey. Walking sluggishly back into his living area with his glass, he placed a vinyl of Bessie Smith's "Chicago Bound Blues" on his Victrola in the corner.

He crossed the room to sit and slouch on top of his Murphy bed, then reclined onto his side. Propped on one of his elbows, he raised his glass and took another burning swig of whiskey and grimaced. Lon lay on his back and balanced the glass tumbler on his chest, tapping the melancholy tune against it as he closed his eyes and let the fantasy end.

Four for a Birth

July 2000

"Shit! Oh, shit! This cannot be fucking happening *again!*"

It was late Sunday morning and Kate pounded against her bathroom door in fury. She tried to wiggle her pinkie finger through the hole left by the glass doorknob that had just fallen off.

"God*damn* it!"

If she'd only let Dexter stay over the night before, she could've been saved by now, but no…

Without wasting any more time, she leaped to the shower window and hauled it open.

"Fuck, fuck, fuck, fuck, fuck," she muttered, biting at her lower lip like a beaver while she rested her arms on the window ledge and waited for anyone to appear in the courtyard below. Her eyes immediately went to the open third-floor window across the way, recognizing the familiar dark red walls. Miss Mousy was home, bouncing lightly with her baby and walking circles in her kitchen.

Kate craned her neck and squinted, trying to get a better look at the baby itself, but Mousy had it so swaddled, it just looked like a big cotton cocoon.

"Ew." The day was already sweltering and none of Mousy's windows had an air conditioning unit; there was only a large square fan propped inside the frame of one of the open windows in her living room.

Absorbed in voyeurism, Kate didn't look away until she heard the courtyard gate grind open on its hinges. She glanced down to see the wavy brown locks of Hot Neighbor walking out through it.

Pride be damned.

"*Hey!*" she screamed at him. "*Help!*"

Too late. She watched him walk out onto the sidewalk and turn left toward Diversey, his face obscured by his left arm as he scratched his head. She was just beginning to wonder if she could still find him attractive if he had dandruff when she heard an answer to her plea.

"Hello?" came a voice across the courtyard.

Kate turned to look and realized it more precisely came from the open third-floor window. Miss Mousy stood right in the center of it, looking up at her.

Kate nearly lost her footing in the slick tub.

Mousy nodded with a timid smile. "Are…are you okay?" she said at a normal speaking volume that the courtyard's acoustics somehow enabled Kate to hear.

"Well, not exactly!" she yelled. "I'm sorta locked in my bathroom on accident!"

Miss Mousy gestured with an index finger. She carried the baby into her living room and deposited it into an oddly small crib that Kate hadn't noticed before. A matter of seconds later, Mousy's frizzy brown nest of hair bounced into the courtyard toward Kate's side. Today it was parted down the middle with the sides on top held back by two barrettes, and she held what looked like a white cordless phone in her hand.

"Sorry," she called up once standing below Kate's window. "I just wanted to put the baby down." She held up and pointed to what Kate now saw was a baby monitor.

"No, that's okay! I hope I didn't wake it!"

Mousy grinned with a sweep of her hand. "Can…can I help you?"

"I'm in 4C, but my unit door is also locked! Can you see if the building manager or Leo is around?" She presumed everyone knew Leo, given all his work around the place.

Her assumption wasn't in vain. With another smile, nod, and *just-a-minute* gesture, Miss Mousy skittered toward Leo's apartment.

A few minutes later, she was back outside with Leo behind her. Leo pointed at Kate, a signal to give him a moment as he shuffled quickly out the gate and around to the management office. Soon enough, he was back in the courtyard with a loaded key ring.

Miss Mousy evidently still felt responsible for Kate's rescue, because she stuck by Leo's side as he entered the south wing. Within the minute Kate could hear them both inside her unit, and like déjà vu, she was released into her own hallway with the greatest sense of relief.

"Oh, bless you two. My God, I don't know why I keep closing that door when I'm alone!"

Leo and Mousy shared in Kate's self-deprecating laughter. Mousy shyly looked at Kate, but Leo kept his eyes to the floor and jingled his keys, rocking slightly side-to-side as though he could do with a bathroom himself.

"Thank you so much," Kate reiterated, but Leo simply would not look her in the eye. His ears flushed beet red.

"Well," he said, "glad to help. I'll see about gettin' that fixed for ya. Meantime, you enjoy the rest of your mornin', now." He abruptly turned and jangled out of her unit and down the stairs.

Kate pouted. "Have I bothered him?" she asked Mousy. "Was he in the middle of something or not feeling well or—"

"I think he was embarrassed to have interrupted *you*," Mousy quietly interjected with a kind smile but staring pointedly below Kate's eye line.

Kate looked down at herself and clutched together the lapels of her pink terrycloth robe to conceal her dewy chest. With her other hand, she tugged at the front hem that hung only a few inches below her lady parts. "Oh! The poor guy."

"I wouldn't feel too sorry for him," Mousy ventured before leaning in conspiratorially. "I bet you just made his day."

The bubbly quality of Mousy's laugh did little to help Kate relax into the idea of having given an old man his jollies for the first time in probably a long while. She ran a hand over her wet hair and walked in front of her air conditioner to cool off from both the humid bathroom and sheer mortification. She breathed in deeply, then excused herself for a couple minutes while she disappeared into her walk-in closet to make herself decent.

When she stepped back out in a loose cotton sundress and flip-flops, Mousy was standing at the living room window, looking across the way toward her own apartment.

"I'm sorry to have taken you away from your little one," Kate said. "Do you need to get back to it?"

"Her," Mousy said without turning around. "It's okay. She's asleep, and I've got the monitor if anything happens."

With Miss Mousy partially blocking the air conditioner, Kate could smell her stale sweat in the cold air blowing into the room. The apartment was freezing again, which confirmed for Kate that something was off with her AC. *Mental note: Replace archaic window unit.*

She rocked on her feet and twiddled her fingers. "Well…can I fix you some coffee or tea? Or maybe you'd like something cold?"

Mousy turned on her heel to face Kate. She ducked her head with a knit brow as if to ask, *Did I hear you right?*

"As a thank-you for your help?" Kate added.

"You're inviting me to stay?"

Kate nodded, confirming, to her own chagrin, that this was indeed what she was doing.

Her guest's eyes lit from within. "I'd love some tea, thank you."

"Iced?"

"Hot is fine."

"Okay, let me just check what I have and make yourself at home. My name's Kate, by the way. It's nice to meet you, though I'm sorry it's under these circumstances."

Mousy gave her a meek nod-smile combo. "I'm Maisie. Pleased to meet you, too."

Retreating into her kitchen and rummaging through her spice cabinet, Kate called out, "Looks like I've got, uh, chamomile, jasmine, aaaand…green tea."

"Chamomile, please. Thank you."

Kate filled her kettle and plonked it onto a burner. Trying to seem occupied so she could stay alone in the kitchen awhile longer, she shuffled in front of her sink and opened and closed a cabinet and drawer here and there. Behind the kitchen wall, from the other unit off her back stairwell, she heard her neighbor's bird chirp like mad.

"*Shut up!*" screamed the neighbor.

Chirp!

"*Shut up!*"

Chirp-chirp!

"*Shut! Up!*"

Kate laughed to herself. This was the usual comedy routine occurring on this end of her studio — pretty different from her experience with Hot Neighbor at the east end.

She pulled two clean mugs from one cabinet and leaned over to call down the hall, "Let me just wash some mugs for us, and I'll be right out!" As she did so, she saw Mousy circling slowly in place, staring at the walls as she fumbled with the baby monitor in her hands. She didn't look at Kate, who took the cue to stall a little longer.

She was just toweling the second mug off when she started at a soft voice by her side.

"Can I help with anything?"

Catching her breath, "No, it's all good," Kate replied, then relented. "But you can have a seat in here if you like. Then we can talk as we wait."

In an entranced way, Mousy panned her sight along the kitchen before sitting at Kate's bistro table in front of the window.

"Your place is nice," she said. "I heard it left something to be desired. Before, I mean. With the last lady who lived here."

"Oh," Kate laughed out. "Olive. Yes, so I heard, too." Steaming bubbles gurgled inside the kettle as its red metal started to sweat, and she willed it to just whistle already. "I think this is ready. No need to wait and hurt our hearing." She chuckled again lamely and yanked the kettle from the stove.

After placing a chamomile sachet into one mug and jasmine one in the other, she filled each with hot water, replaced the kettle on the stove, and carried the tea to the table, where Mousy sat with a tight-lipped grin and blank look in her pea-green eyes. Kate took a seat opposite her neighbor.

Noticing how her guest still gripped the baby monitor, she remarked with as much cheer as she could muster, "She's a very quiet sleeper. I haven't heard a peep this whole time!"

Looking to the monitor in her hands, Mousy's tired eyes welled with a new emotion, and she smiled as she placed the device onto the black marble table and cupped her steaming mug between her hands. "Yes," she said. "She's a good child. I'm so blessed."

"How old is she?"

"Nine, ten weeks. That's how long I've had her, anyway."

"Wow," was all Kate said, yet that was evidently enough to prompt Mousy to elaborate.

"She's adopted." She removed a hand from her cup to stroke the baby monitor. "But I couldn't possibly love her more if she really were my own."

"That's wonderful." Kate looked to her mug as she held her tea sachet by the string and bobbed it in the water to steep. Its sweet springtime essence tickled at the edges of her nostrils, deodorizing in part the stench of Mousy's saturated polyester blouse. "So did you use an adoption agency, or did you know the parents, or—"

"If I told you, you would never believe it." Her lips pressed into a line and her eyes hardened as she looked Kate up and down as if reluctant yet desperate to tell the story.

Kate gave her the nudge she seemed to ask for. "Try me."

Fingertips patting the side of her monitor, Mousy moved her gaze to her lap. "I…" She swallowed, still looking down, and took a sip of her tea using her free hand. "I never knew my mother. Not really. She was on her own, and there were…issues…and I was put in foster care at a very young age." She glanced up at Kate with that tight grin again.

"I'm sorry."

Shaking her head and looking back to her lap, she said, "I'm going to make certain my child knows me, though. I tell her that every day."

Kate hummed encouragingly as she blew on her tea.

"It's amazing, really, how much she matches my coloring. You'd think she really was mine." She rubbed her thumb along the white plastic. "I'll never forget the evening she came to me. It was the middle of the night, and I was asleep."

Kate pinched her eyebrows together but held off questioning what the hell kind of adoption involves middle-of-night home deliveries.

"There was a loud sound that startled me awake. A thump. Then scratching at the kitchen door, and this, this low moan from the back stairwell."

What. The. Fuck.

"I remember," Mousy practically whispered, "I couldn't figure out what on earth it could be, if it even *was* anything of this earth." She bobbed her head at Kate with widened eyes. "When the sounds settled into a shuffling, like fabric, I finally stood and walked toward the door, quietly as I could."

When Mousy seemed to pause for effect, Kate gave an agreeable "Mm hm," but she was too bowled over by the woman's sudden, eerily descriptive chattiness. She wondered what USA *Up All Night* flick it could've come from.

Her neighbor now stared off into space as if seeing the incident play out in Kate's kitchen. "I crept across the room, and as I reached for the doorknob, my heart was bouncing off my breastbone, I tell you. I slid the chain from its latch, twisted the knob, and opened the door to darkness. Pitch black, except for a pale figure below on the floor."

"The baby?" Kate guessed—hoped.

Mousy closed her eyes and nodded.

"But where'd it come from? Was there a note?"

Eyes still closed, Mousy shook her head side to side.

"But who in this day and age leaves a baby on a doorstep?" Kate blurted.

The woman opened her eyes to look at Kate point-blank. "It was an unexpected, most welcome gift."

Kate took the cue to back off. More gently, she asked, "But why *your* door, do you think? Do you think it was someone who knew what a good mother you'd be to it?"

"Her."

"What a good mother you'd be to her?"

Mousy shrugged. "I do believe it wasn't by accident. I was chosen. By someone or something."

"Well…you certainly are someone special."

Seemingly heartened by Kate's words—and obviously missing their sarcasm—Mousy spoke louder, but her voice shook. "You know, it was like after all these years my hopes had brought it into being. Her."

Sobs choked her off from saying anything more. Kate leaned over to give her a couple *there-there* taps on the shoulder and let her cry it out in silence. When Mousy started to wipe her nose on her brown shirt collar, Kate shot up and grabbed a paper towel from the counter.

"Here you go."

"Thank you. I'm so sorry for breaking down like this."

"Don't be. That was a beautiful story." *And you were right—I will never believe it.*

After trumpeting the last of her sniffles into the paper towel, then balling it up and leaving it beside her mug, Mousy looked to her monitor and seized it in apparent alarm. "Oh dear," she said, even though not a single sound had emitted from the speaker. "I'd better be going back."

"Of course."

"I don't even really need this." She held up the monitor as she stood. "She never does fuss or cry."

"Wow. Lucky you. Uh, let me walk you out."

The air had stagnated in the living room despite the AC's heroic attempts to blow away all its Freon. Crossing the room was almost like walking through water. Kate wondered if Maisie felt like that, too, or if the woman had slipped something in Kate's tea when she hadn't been looking.

On reaching the opened door, Mousy flashed a nervous smile. "Thank you for the hospitality, Kate. The tea was delicious."

Kate bobbed her head in farewell even after she'd seen her guest out. She just stood there, feeling suspended in a pack of wet snow as she processed her morning — until a gust of air tickled the hairs of her inner ear. She jumped, and while she swatted away at nothing, she detected the floral notes of what must have been Mousy's fragrance.

Well, that took its sweet time to join us.

Vera and Leo were going to get an earful of questions the next time Kate saw them.

Kate didn't have long to linger after Maisie's departure. She had to hightail it if she was going to meet Dex for lunch around the corner in fifteen minutes, so she shook out of her stupor and got back in motion. Her hair would have to air dry, and her makeup-less face was a lost cause.

Although…She'd seen Hot Neighbor on his way out that morning, going in the same direction she'd be heading. Maybe he was only running a quick errand. Kate figured she could stand to be a little late if there was a chance she could run into him on his way back.

Half an hour later, she was coiffed in a neat bun, tan-foamed into a "natural" glow, and shoe-horned into a more figure-flattering knee-length strapless dress — black, which made it chic, but cotton, which kept it casual. Wedge sandals also helped her stride the line of daytime whimsy and calf-defining sexy. Affixing her best Holly Golightly shades to her face, she was off to perform her catwalk strut through the courtyard and down the sidewalk.

No one on the way fit Hot Neighbor's specs, though — not along Camden Court, and not when she'd rounded the corner onto Diversey. Feeling a little huffy over the wasted effort, Kate dropped her shoulders and clopped into Panera.

Right away she spotted Dex's tall form. He was studying the sandwich and soup offerings with an intensity normally reserved for his beloved star charts at the planetarium.

As she waited for him to make his monumental decision, Kate glanced over to see if there were decent seats by the windows; the best spot was taken by a group of senior citizens. Armchairs and a sofa surrounded a shared table, and crowding all around it was Chicago's geriatric answer to *Friends*. Kate giggled in her head at the cuteness of it, and right then noticed Vera and Leo were among them. Catching their eye, she waved and pointed to Dex as her excuse not to come over and be introduced.

She moseyed over to Dexter and poked him in his side. Surprise and immediate pleasure infused his face; he was clearly reveling in mistaken flattery that her fancy get-up was for him. Kate met his soft kisses with puckered pecks of her own and patted him on the butt like a baseball teammate, duly noting this unforeseen consequence of her vanity.

"Mm," Dex breathed into her hair as he hugged her. "You are forgiven."

"Excuse me?" She hoped she'd heard him wrong.

"This more than makes up for blowing me off yesterday. And I'll more than make it up to *you* later."

"Whatever. I'm starving." Kate walked to the counter and got in line behind another couple.

Dex scooted behind her, holding her hand while she paid more interest to the great debate between an asiago cheese bagel with sun-dried tomato cream cheese, or a sourdough bread bowl. A startling "Aaayy!" rang into the air, and she turned to see a new cotton-headed senior shuffle through the entrance and over to Vera and her Panera Pack. Laughing, Kate faced forward again to see she was next in line. She flung off Dex's hand as she stepped up.

"For here or to go?" the greasy-faced teen behind the counter asked. The void of enthusiasm in his tone conveyed just how demeaning he found the whole affair of summer employment.

Kate felt a palm slide onto her belly as a wall of heat closed in on her from behind.

"Let's get it to go," Dex whispered in her ear.

She rolled her eyes at the cashier to make him complicit in her annoyance. At the planetarium, she could always count on the teen patrons for their angst-ridden empathy. True to form, he snorted with a dopey grin as he counted her change.

Saluting the Panera Pack on their way out with lunch bags and Dr Pepper bleeding all over the plastic caps of their cups, Kate and Dex walked to her apartment. She forewarned him about her AC being on the fritz, and he said he'd take a look at it after they ate.

Thirty minutes later, though, Dex decided to inspect *Kate's* parts first. His kisses may have tasted of red onion and sugared cherries—and said kisses may have been interrupted now and then by carbonated after-effects—but there on the unfolded futon, in broad daylight, he had Kate's strapless cotton dress bunched into a tube top and her ankles chaffing at his neck as he methodically slid in and out of her.

For her part, Kate let herself enjoy it. She'd dropped over-analysis along with her panties—and this was certainly no "sisterly" affection overtaking her at the moment. She had to give Dex credit where it was due: he couldn't have been a more perfect fit if she'd taken a mold of her lady bits and gone to the store to get him sized.

Eyes clenched, Kate focused on feeling the way Dex glided like a virtuoso violinist easing his bow along her strings and making them hum. She wrapped her legs around his waist, and he settled more of his weight on her stomach. His happy trail rubbed against her navel and his warm breath blew her bangs off her forehead.

And then it happened: she *felt* as much as heard the pulsing rhythm of blues music next door. It wasn't the modern electric Chicago blues found a few blocks away at the Kingston Mines club, but an antiquated, unfiltered melody delivered by the same soulful voice that had penetrated into Kate's urges like nothing else the day before. With its grieving grit, the simple, old-school groove sang in her mind and shot sparks down her center.

Kate reached her arms under Dex's to seize his shoulder blades and pull him closer before flipping him over. Straddling him, she peeled her little dress off over her head. His hands gripped her hips, and she pushed his fingers deeper into her flesh, prompting him to hold her down with more pressure as she picked up the slack for them both.

In tempo with the smoky, lusty strains buzzing through her, Kate quickened her pace, daring Dex to let her ride him into the next plateau as the sultry voice inside her sang, "If You Don't, I Know Who Will."

She was feeling an inner itch now, an anything-but-irritable one that promised so much pleasure if scratched. Keeping Dex's hands planted on her hips, she ground against him as whole notes sped to half notes, *andante* accelerated to *allegro*. Dex curled up off the cushion and licked and sucked at Kate's breasts, releasing one of his hands to tickle up the ivories of her spine and caress the damp skin between her shoulder blades as his other slid around to press firmly at her tailbone.

The itch, that potential for satisfaction, spread like the juicy melodies Kate felt flowing from her and she skidded her torso against Dex's with each breath. Clawing at his neck, she arched into him and bit his ear, whispering, "Keep going, keep going," while that voice in her mind begged to give her what she desired.

Dex carried their tempo from a vivacious *allegro* to an explosive *presto*.

"Yes," Kate whispered.

This was hard, raw sex they'd not experienced with each other, and the spontaneous, mutual momentum propelled them wildly forth. Kate's quiet moans crescendoed as she expended all she had left in her to move only faster, faster, hotter—until she seized Dex's hair and the skin at his neck, tensing the full length of her body in mute ecstasy. She felt her face contort as though crying in pain and, rigid, just clung to him as he followed her climax.

Hot and sweaty, the two held each other for several seconds, catching their breath and relaxing their muscles. Little by little, she eased off of him, and when she reclined on her back by his side, he rolled over to wipe the damp strands from her face.

A waft of lilac drifted past her nose, and she drowsily opened her eyes to Dex. He traced swirls in the shining sweat on Kate's chest as it heaved up and down, and he looked at her with a tender sideways grin. She willed herself to smile back at him, to seal the intimacy they'd shared and affirm that it was a great success for their relationship. Her heart screamed at her to do it.

But instead, she wrapped her fingers around his, forcing them to stop their affectionate scribbles at her breast.

"Dexter," she said softly.

One of his eyebrows twitched as soon as she'd pronounced the second syllable of his name. He bared his teeth in a nervous smile. "Yes, baby?"

"I can't do this."

He held his smile, but his eyelids fluttered. "What?" he whispered, holding her hand tighter.

Kate fought against her trembling lips, struggled to wrestle her voice free as her throat constricted. "I can't. I'm so sorry."

He searched her face, and his thumb stroked her fingers with urgency. Kate said nothing more, only waited to let him process and speak when ready. After several seconds passed, he blinked rapidly again and cleared his throat as he sat up. The instant he did, she felt the cold of his absence.

"Katie," he said. There was a smallness to his voice she hadn't heard before, a fragility to his lean frame she hadn't seen. He seemed to shudder slightly, and Kate also felt a chill as the sweat their joint heat had generated now cooled them. "Fuck." He exhaled, dropping his face into his hand. "Why, why now?" He looked back up. "After we—I mean, wasn't this—?"

"Yes, Dex. It was amazing. *You* are amazing. And I think that's part of the problem. *My* problem."

"That makes no sense. This makes no sense."

Kate remained on her back, but she covered her breaking expression with her palm and turned it away from him and toward the wall. "You ask why now, but it isn't just *now*, Dexter, and you know that."

"You wanted us to take a step back, and we've done that. Christ, Katie, you moved out on me. But I didn't try to stop you. I respected that you wanted space, and I've given it to you. When you want to spend weekends apart or send me home at night, isn't that all you wanted? Isn't that enough? It hasn't even been two weeks. You haven't given it—"

"Time? That's just the thing, Dex. *We have time.*" Still facing the wall, Kate sobbed into her hand.

"I don't understand you. What is it that you want?"

"*Time!*" she yelled. "We've been through this! We're young, Dex. We should enjoy that and sow our oats while we can."

She took her hand from her sopping face and rubbed her goose-bumped arm. Dex stroked her forearm a few times himself, then reached to pick up her chenille throw and drape it over her. Kate pulled its fringed edge up to her mouth and cried harder into it.

"Katie, come on. This is the first time you've asked for that."

"I'm sorry," she sputtered. "I know I've never said it in so many words, but I think it's what I've been wanting. I don't think I even knew it at the time, but I—I mean…I moved out. That should've cued us things would be different. It's my fault. I shouldn't've let us carry on the way we have. There should've been rules for—"

"Fuck rules, Kate! Are you kiddin' me? I fucking *love* you. There aren't fucking rules for that. We take it as it comes, for Christ's sake."

She felt him shift his weight on the futon cushion and then heard the rustle of fabric. Keeping her face partially hidden behind the blanket, she watched him dress. With brisk movements that snapped each article of clothing as he lifted it, Dex layered on his defenses, eventually standing to zip up his cargo shorts. It left Kate feeling vulnerable and whorish, still lying naked beneath the chenille. She held the throw to her breasts and sat up while Dex walked across the room to step into his flip-flops.

"You aren't going, are you?" she asked.

With his back to her, Dex sighed loudly and clapped his hands to his thighs. "Isn't that what you want, Katie?" he replied without turning around. "For me to leave you alone?"

As always, she was caught in the lurch of regretting what she wished for the second she was getting it. She wanted her freedom, but she supposed she didn't want to give Dex his.

If only she could articulate that in a way he would find reasonable. "Dex."

He dropped his head and brought his hands to his hips, still turned away from her. He wasn't going to make this easy, and why should he?

"Dex," Kate implored again.

With another dramatic sigh, he flopped his arms at his sides and spun to face her. Tears glistened off his cheeks.

Reaching around for another corner of the blanket, Kate wrapped herself and curled her legs at her sides. For a few seconds, she couldn't meet his eyes.

"So, what then?" he asked. "Are you breaking up with me?"

"No," she said. "I've told you before, I don't want that." And in that moment, she knew she meant it.

"Okay...So, we're staying together and just continuing to give you space, or we're taking a break, or..."

"I want to continue seeing you, Dexter. I do. It's just that—" Oh, hell, she couldn't keep looking at him. She stared at her cushion and scratched at the faux-suede with a fingernail. "Does it have to be all or nothing? I mean, could we maybe try dating...inclusively?"

"You want to see other people?"

Kate nodded.

"But you still want to see me."

She nodded again, her breath held in her chest.

Dex looked to the floor a few seconds; then, hesitantly, he walked back toward Kate and sat at the edge of the bed. "Is there someone specific you want to see?"

Kate emphatically shook her head. "I haven't met anyone." Which was technically true, even if her body language was false.

Leaning his elbows onto his knees, Dex frowned at the floor. "Do you want to…*sleep* with other people?"

The even tone of his voice and his calm demeanor were not achieved without tremendous effort, Kate knew. Beneath it all, she could see the subtle variation from his usual composure and could have wept over it. She wondered how many others besides her were able to notice such microscopic differences in him; who else had learned the little traits he had like scraping his fingers against his thumbs when he was indecisive or how his body jerked in brief spasms whenever he first fell asleep? If anyone else out there didn't already know these things about him, who would learn someday?

Once again, her double standards trapped her. If this was about having her cake and eating it, too, she didn't want someone else also serving up their desserts to Dex. Kate realized she couldn't kick chicks out of Dex's bed unless she also stayed out of someone else's.

The effort he made to keep calm was all the validation she needed to know that, yes, she needed to keep her clutches on him. As much as she'd tried to blow off the fact, Dex was a good catch.

The problem was that he'd never had to be caught; he always so willingly handed himself over. Like Vera had said, there's something thrilling about the chase.

"Kate?" Dex said. "Answer me. *Do* you want to sleep with other people?"

"I just think we should be able to get to know other people, see if certain qualities make someone a better fit for us or not. It might only confirm that they're assholes and we really do make the most sense together. I don't know. I just think we're young and should take advantage of the time we've got to step away awhile and then come back together if it's what's right for us both. But I think we *do* need rules for that sort of thing, and I think it would be fair to draw the line at sex. Maybe renegotiate if or when it comes to that point. I mean, the initial test would be emotional compatibility anyway, right?"

She expected that answer would make her a hero in his greatly relieved eyes, but all through her spiel, Dex just leaned on his knees and glowered at the floor. The hands he'd clasped in front of him were now separated into white-knuckled fists. The muscle in his jaw pulsed.

After a time, he uncurled his fingers, rubbed them on his knees, and pushed against them to stand. He grabbed his wallet and keys off of the coffee table and walked to the door.

Kate leaped to her feet after him, tightening her blanket securely around her so she could free her arms and grab on to him.

"Dex?"

With a hand gripping the doorknob, he looked at her and gave his verdict:

"Listen, Kate. I want to be with you. I don't want to share you with anyone else."

Her eyes welled at what this would mean.

"But," he said, and a tear streaked down Kate's cheek as she found new hope in that unexpected word alone, "as absolutely stupid as it is, I'd rather share you — with the possibility of one day getting you back to myself — than lose you altogether. I want us both to be happy and will trust that that's what you want, too. That you won't throw it all away unless it's really, really worth it. No cheap thrills." He chewed on his lip as Kate shook her head in promise. "Don't think I don't know this is hands-down the dumbest-ass thing I could agree to, but there it is."

Still holding the doorknob, he slipped his other hand around her waist, and Kate wrapped her arms around his shoulders as he pulled her to him. At first, he simply tilted his head to drop his forehead against hers, rubbing his nose alongside hers and catching the tears stuck in her eyelashes with it. Kate sniffed and tried to clear her nose enough to capture the scent seeping from his pores, Dex's scent, which would still be hers for an undetermined yet reassuringly secured amount of time longer.

When she inclined her face to better smell his skin, he captured her lips with his and pressed into them. Then he abruptly released her and yanked the door open.

"I love you, Kate," he said in a low, quavering voice. "Don't make me hate you."

Scalding, steaming water stabbed at the porcelain under the shower-head as Kate sat naked and curled on the opposite end of the bathtub. She'd turned the water on full pressure and highest heat to drown out sight, sound, and feeling. Hugging her knees, she wept into them to the point of hyperventilation.

At least twenty minutes had passed since she'd successfully converted her tiny bathroom into a steam room. A bulb had burned out in the ugly Jell-O mold light fixture, which gave the atmosphere a dreary, institutional effect.

Taking several deep, quaking inhales and working to moderate the exhales, she made herself calm down. She twisted the faucet to a moderate temperature and pressure, then stood up to finally cleanse herself of Dex.

Maybe she should call her girlfriends afterward, meet just for a drink. Or several drinks and call in sick on Monday.

Which she should do regardless. How on earth could she face Dex so soon in that dark, depressing basement of cubicles? This time, not even the planetarium would help her escape to another galaxy far, far away. As it was, anywhere inside it she'd come closest to the stars had already been christened with Dexter. Even if he quit the next day, she would feel him everywhere.

She loofahed her body head to heels until her skin was red and raw, and still she didn't feel clean.

No, her friends all had work the next day, too, and being with them would mean having to talk about it. All of it. They knew Dex, and they knew Kate too well. Which wasn't necessarily a bad thing if it wasn't for the girls who always acted like they were in perfect relationships, which made their advice patronizing. Her plan for multiple partners would only open her up to their disapproving *tsks*.

At the opposite end of the spectrum were her close friends who hadn't had a serious relationship yet—they tended to be too idealistic. Or, if they'd had one, it had ended badly, so their advice tended to be cynical or founded in nothing; it could easily turn into a bitch-fest against Dex.

As could any conversations with her parents—out of love and loyalty to their only child, one would think, but mostly as another way of expressing disappointment in her choices. Having worked so hard in mid-tier jobs with retirement still too far from sight, they hadn't wanted Kate to saddle herself with a not-for-profit employer, let alone potentially end up marrying someone there. Every phone call led to the mild "suggestion" that she put her education degree to better use in a classroom—more specifically one within an affluent suburban school district. Work toward a pension, receive great benefits, meet a successful single dad, maybe… and then in a few years' time, work toward that doctorate. They'd only awarded Dex a hall pass when that pimped-out condo alerted them he had family money—which had made Kate's announcement about moving out of it all the more tragic for them. Honestly, when it came to Dexter, she couldn't win with her parents either way.

So was this the ideal panel of judges? And did she even feel up to being judged, after Dex had passed his own sentence of shame on her?

Maybe she could just walk to the Irish pub down the block on her own and seek the counsel of Jim Beam. Take the stairs to the subterranean lair, grab a barstool, and pound whiskey slammers. And maybe she could dare to go beyond tapping on Hot Neighbor's wall to knock on his door? Ask him to join her for a casual pint?

Before she could explore that option any further, a sour, almost metallic scent rose with the steam to tickle over her face.

"Ugh," Kate groaned as she dizzied and doubled over. Her stomach had knotted then gone liquid in an instant, but the spell passed just as quickly. The blood in her veins seemed to thrum loudly in her ears, and the water pressure beating against the back of her head became oppressive. Standing upright again, Kate finished rinsing herself, twisted the tap, and yanked the shower curtain aside.

With the water off, the air began to thin, but Kate cracked open the shower window to ventilate it faster.

Stepping out of the tub and toweling off her body, the blood rushed to her head. She became dizzy again, so she twisted the towel into a turban around her hair and leaned forward on the sink. Staring down into the drain as she ballooned her cheeks with a heavy exhale, she could swear she smelled lilacs again. Kate breathed, recovered her equilibrium, and looked up at the mirror.

She jolted backward, slamming into the radiator against the wall. Her naked flesh pressed into it as she huffed in quick, shallow breaths with her eyes fixed on the fogged mirror.

Her countenance was blurred, but her eyes glowed bright white through the mist. They hovered just above a word printed in large capital letters on the mirror's steamed surface:

MINE

Five for Silver

November 1925

Silver spoons clanked against delicate white china as Eva's luncheon party cooled their tea in the secluded Palm Court lobby of the Drake Hotel.

The harpist's flourishing notes helped drown out some of the dull murmuring surrounding her on this All Saint's Day, but it couldn't quite cancel out her own little group: her mother, sister, and mother- and sister-in-law.

Virgie, Finlay's older sister, had a high nasally voice and the terrible tendency to end every laugh with a loud hum, serving as some sort of bridge to return her pitch from high to low. Mrs. Redcliffe — the *other* Mrs. Redcliffe, Finlay's mother — was similarly affected with the need to place emphasis on the fourth word of every sentence she spoke. Eva sat with impeccable posture, stirring her tea and observing the effect her mother-in-law had on Eva's own mother, who'd taken to crafting her responses with emphasis on the *second* word of nearly every sentence.

Ollie, on the other hand, just sat mutely munching through all the cucumber finger sandwiches, back hunched and feet swinging under the table even though she had to lift her knees to keep from skimming the floor. She'd already kicked Virgie once, which Eva hoped was accidental. Nonetheless, Eva touched a white-gloved hand to Ollie's lap now and then as a signal to rein in her spastic limbs.

"I had the *most* divine tea last week at the Walnut Room," Mrs. Redcliffe tittered on. "The cake was *exquisite*. I am positively *certain* the recipe still includes brandy."

"That *does* sound decadent," Mrs. Hughes replied. "We *must* make a point to go down to Marshall Field's this week, Evie, before the masses descend at Christmastime. It's *most* hospitable with its tea rooms."

"*Yes*, Mother," Eva said, playing a private game of stressing the *first* word of her sentences, confident they'd never notice. "*I* agree. *It* is the last word in accommodating gentlewomen in this city. *Positively* charming."

"Indeed, you are *quite* right there," said Mrs. Redcliffe.

"I *couldn't* agree more," said Mrs. Hughes.

"*Quite* unequivocally true," said Eva.

"Ha, ha-ha, ha-ha! Hmmm," giggle-hummed Virgie. "Charles told me the funniest story that happened in the Men's Grill Room there recently…"

Ollie chomped on watercress, mentally checked out of the lofty lounge and, Eva knew, roaming the landscape of her even richer imaginary life.

As Virgie told her story, Eva tapped her spoon at the edge of her teacup, watching it flick creamy drops off its egg-shaped bowl. It reflected the glittering lights of the crystal chandeliers overhead, gleaming just like the silver spoons everyone in that room had held in their mouths since birth. Eva wanted to choke on hers.

Still, she gracefully went through the motions, putting on display the fruits of two decades of attentive grooming and trying desperately to enjoy the spoils of being born into advantage—and of cementing that status by marrying into it as well. Whatever spasms and airless gasps her father's breweries might suffer as the pressure of Prohibition stifled them of breath, the joint venture Eva had formed with Finlay may have been the most strategic in securing her family's place in the social and financial stratosphere. She'd been not-so-mildly entreated to do so, and doing her daughterly duty, had signed her life away on the dotted line.

Eva set her spoon aside and lifted her cup to her lips. She took a polite sip as she looked over its scalloped rim at the routine playing out before her, same as the Sunday before and the Sunday before that, no matter the setting or company.

It was important, though, to promote the camaraderie of the two families in whatever way she could. The better they all got on, the more willing Finlay would be to move to the guest house Eva's father had furbished exclusively for them to inhabit. Constructed of the same gray limestone, roofed in the same black mansard style, and appointed with the same degree of Old World opulence as the primary Hughes mansion, this relatively smaller yet generous space was located directly next door and shared the Hughes's gated garden. And there it sat, waiting for them.

It wasn't that Finlay's sprawling Lake Forest home wasn't handsome or comfortable enough. Indeed, she'd readily found she loved to roam its vast acreage, crunching through the fallen leaves and sweeping them into piles to lie on and watch the sky during autumn when left to herself—which happened often. Yet as soothing an escape the property was from the traffic and noise of the city, today reminded Eva that in this urban bustle pulsed her heart. If she returned to Wrightwood, she could be near Ollie again.

And Lon.

Eva took another sip of tea to warm her against the icy diamond-festooned necklace at her breastbone. It sparkled coldly on skin she would rather adorn with warm dewdrops. The sort that would bead up in the hazy early hours of summer when, almost every night, she and Lon had lain on their backs in the park on the grass, talking until dawn.

She felt herself lying there now, skimming blades of grass with her palms and tickling them with her bare toes. Lon reaching over to hold her dewy hand and tell her they'd best get her home before the servants rose to prepare her family's breakfast. Sneaking in through the back kitchen door to tiptoe upstairs right after hugging Lon goodbye and planting a kiss on his cheek, thanking him for yet another evening of candid conversation.

Losing herself in this imagined space and time, her focus on the Palm Court's central fountain blurred and crisscrossed, putting in motion its golden cupids that galloped atop large fish. She lost sight of the potted palm trees, pastries, and postures of the upper crust exchanging their trifles in low voices around her. Only the rolling swells and plucking of the harp penetrated her consciousness, its melody rippling along her inner strings.

Feeling out of body, Eva did somehow become aware of the teacup and saucer in her hands. She drifted forward to relieve her burden onto the table in front of her, when a crash and peals of high-pitched cries shattered her reverie. Warmth spread beneath her thighs. The women at her table scooted away from the damp mess Eva had made all over the carpeting and her dress when she'd missed setting her saucer on the dark walnut edge. Virgie's laughing hums rose and fell amid the alarm. Ollie ran to the fountain with her cloth napkin, dipped it into the water, and ran back to dab at Eva's layers of ruffles. The girl's swift response impressed Eva, although she figured Ollie had probably been dying for an excuse to dip her hand in that fountain all afternoon.

"It's all right, Ollie, thank you," she assured as she swept off her caplet of matching kelly-green silk crêpe and held it over her lap when she stood. "If you'll excuse me," she said to the rest of her party and made her way to the powder room.

Walking along a row of framed mirrors, Eva paused to look into one and assess the damage. Soon enough, however, she heard the mothers' voices, so she ducked into a water closet with its own sink.

She sighed while she scrubbed at the tea stain, the green ruffles darkening with the water bleeding into them. The color transported her back to Lincoln Park, lying with her Lonnie on a sea of dew.

Tears blurred her sight, and she sank to the toilet seat in heaving sobs.

"Now, now, it's *certain* to come out if treated right away, dear," she heard Mrs. Redcliffe console from outside.

"No *doubt* you've caught it in time, Evie," her mother's voice pitched in. "Chin *up*, my girl."

November 5, 1925

Dearest Friend,

I hope this letter finds you well and hopefully not torturing my kid sister somewhere on the lakefront. Remember, dear, the temperature has dropped since summer, and she could catch cold.

But in all sincerity, thank you for continuing to entertain my little pet on weekends. She and Mother have informed me of such, and it's more than I ever dared wish for, much less expected. I haven't seen or heard from her myself nearly as often as that. She needn't bother with me when she has you, I suppose. I do believe she fancies you. Mother related to me that my sweet sister prizes above everything a doll you gave her for no reason other than she desired it. Such a toy is the last thing I'd have thought she would still choose for herself, but if she found it during one of your adventures, I imagine she would turn nothing down from her dear Lonnie. Oh, how it would break her heart to lose your friendship, so I'm so very pleased my marriage has not caused just that.

I confess I am almost envious. How I enjoyed those Saturday ~~eve~~ afternoons at the zoo, just the ~~two~~ three of us. I am so very curious what has occupied you since. People seem to no longer know much of what you're up to, so no news must be good news, surely? Still no longer cavorting at the dance halls, or I at least hear, so I am glad to know your abstinence from assorted temptations wasn't merely under my supervision. You needn't make such shows, after all, when you can withdraw into your true passion instead.

Perhaps I'm not expressing myself well. No, I'm not at all. What I'm trying to tell you so clumsily is that I couldn't have more respect for — and pride in — what you have pursued these last months — and can only assume (pray) you are yet. You must. Your convictions, Lon, are the most admirable I've seen among anyone I know. Rivaled only by my better half's. And your paintings — my God, your talent brings one to tears! You may feel you need to hide from everyone else's judgment, but I, still your friend, your sister, am one person in this world who would never fault you for forsaking wealth and title for honest work and art. You have nothing to prove to me, so no need for the charades. Although you realize as well I'm certainly not the only one who believes in you, and thank goodness for that.

I have loved my time in the countryside — the new landscape and fresh air does wonders. I have everything a girl could ask for, and yet in the peace there is now and then a homesickness for Chicago and those dear to me there. I returned to the city for my first time only the other day for afternoon tea. So you see, I hope to receive my dose of medicine time to time.

But settling into a new life and duties has been a busy occupation, so rarely do I carve out time for my correspondence. I hope you're inclined to forgive and will write or telephone sooner than this. Ah, but perhaps I should mention you need only contact me at this address this month because, wondrous news! Finlay and I both crave the buzz of the city so have decided to reside there, in the Wrightwood townhouse, for the indefinite future. Preparations will be made to arrive well ahead of Christmas, should all go to plan.

Cordially,

Evelyn

November 14, 1925

My Fondest Friend,

It is a wonder to hear from you! But what is this, no word at all on your time in the Riviera? You will have to enlighten me on this exotic and mysterious honeymoon of yours —to the extent that your own family knew nothing of it! Please do spare no detail of your days abroad —and nights.

Oh, but all my indecency aside, I do hope the escape was invigorating and inspiring. I ought to travel there myself, transfer the region's land and sea to my canvas. No question I would have expatriated to France by now if so many damned people we know were not over there as well. Rest assured, when I do skip across the pond, I will rely on your expert recommendations.

Congratulations, Redcliffes, on your return to Chicago! I hope it will not pollute the peace you have found in the country. And thank you ever so much for expressing that confidence in my pursuits. In all sincerity, I do appreciate that, old girl. You and Aunt Estella are the only ones I fully believe in anymore, for that matter. And Ollie, of course (I wink as I write that—that feisty, funny girl). My darling ladies. Well, Ollie is so young, and I'll have Auntie for her remaining years, but I wonder if I'm to lose you much sooner than that—as an advisor on my art, in view of your newly busy schedule. How I do respect your tasteful eye on the subject, though my new acquaintances have done well guiding a novice's craft in your stead.

You ought to know there are no "charades" committed here. Beyond my "true passion," all I'm doing is broadening my shoulders with the rest of the city, putting in hard work day in and day out, and whiling away my evenings drinking like men of all classes (only in moderation, I promise). The worst I can be branded is eccentric. At best, common. At least I'm no dewdropper sleeping through my days. Where's the worry in that?

I won't pretend it didn't take some time to become comfortable in my new skin, that I did for a while sneak about incognito like an absurd child. But I've found the society I want, and it has accepted me. If I'm ostracized by the old dogs, perhaps I'll wear my worker's clothes into some gentleman's study. Parade my Lowertown set and appall everyone with the scandal of it.

But of course I am only playing with you. Please give my regards to Finlay with my assurance I am too much beneath you to dignify with a response while you are busy planning your impending move. Do contact me when all is said and done, if you remain so inclined.

Yours,
Alonzo

December 1925

"How it *is* good to see you, Lonnie," Eva said with an eager kiss to her friend's cheek. They stood beneath the Biograph Theater marquee, on which Lon Chaney had top billing for the current feature film.

"You are looking very well," Lon Ashby replied with a nod. "It appears marriage suits you."

"Oh…well…Thank you for meeting me at such late notice. I hate to rob you of a day's wages, old boy."

"I suspect I've enough security to allow a matinee this once." He grinned at her from beneath his herringbone newsboy cap.

Eva had likewise kept her appearance modest, wearing an understated gray wool wrapover coat and cloche hat of a darker shade. "Still," she said with a smirk, "we wouldn't want to overstep Auntie's good graces, now would we."

"That's enough, you."

"How about a peace offering." Eva held up two tickets she'd already purchased at the booth. Laying his hand at the small of her back, Lon tipped his hat and invited her to enter the movie house ahead of him.

Selecting discreet seats in the back row of the empty balcony, they settled onto velvety cushions. Eva held the collar of her coat about her neck and tipped her lips into it, waiting for the lights to dim.

"Eva, darling, are you having second thoughts?" came a whisper in her ear.

Her head shot back up. "What?" she rasped back. "What do you mean?"

"I mean—" Lon leaned in further "—being out with me like this. You seem uncomfortable."

"Oh, don't be silly, Lonnie. We've done this dozens of times before."

"Not in a while. Not…in these circumstances."

"Not without our chaperone?" She winked.

"Ah, dear Ollie."

When the lights did fade, Eva dropped her head to her shoulder, rolling it to face him. "Oh, Lonnie, it *is* good to see you. What fun we had sneaking about. Do you still think about those nights?"

"All the time, old girl. All the time." He tapped the underside of her chin with his finger. "I'd imagined *you'd* forgotten."

"Me?"

"Yes, you. Your distance. Your letter."

Eva straightened. "My letter?"

Lon tilted his head, mimicking her usual gesture. "Let's not pretend we weren't appeasing the censors on that one. At least I hope that's all it was. And that I replied well enough in kind."

"Oh." Eva stroked her collar. "Of course. Your letter was lovely." *And I burned it.* "S-So, you've been spending more time with that artist colony?"

"Mm hm. Weekends mostly. They're an amusing and inspiring lot."

"And…you like it there at the hotel, do you?"

"I do. With the park and lake just there, it's the best way to enjoy nature in this city."

"Certainly, but you could enjoy far more of that at your house in the country."

"That's debatable. A bedroom in my *brother's* charming prairie house isn't exactly freedom, and I'm not about to invest in one of my own out there. That commute is far too long. Now I can be taken more seriously at the lumberyards as a real laborer rather than some dandy who slums it once a month as a novel hobby to cure his yawning boredom."

"Ah, but the trains make that easier—seventy miles an hour!"

Lon shook his head, laughing quietly, and looked forward at the film. *The Phantom of the Opera* flickered over his features from the silver screen, masking what emotion she might find there.

"I'm beginning to think you're driving me away, my dear," he eventually whispered, leaning in yet still looking away from her. "I'd hate to be getting in your way, of course, so only say the word."

Eva took her fingers from her neck and laid them on his hand. "You know I won't utter any such thing. If my letter seemed distant, you're of course right in assuming it was out of fear it would be screened, a precaution I had hoped you would recognize as nothing more than just that. A precaution."

"I did."

"I am glad. And I'm sorry." She leaned her head toward his shoulder, her lips close to his ear. "Oh, Lonnie, of course I don't want you to move away, not now that I've just returned. I don't know why I said that. We haven't been together in months, and I suppose I don't know how to act around you anymore."

"By not acting at all. That's how."

She drew in her chin so her forehead pressed to his cheek, then nodded. "I forget that, with you, I don't need to."

"Act, no. Communicate, yes. And truth only."

She eased back in her seat to give his rightful resentment some space.

He turned to look at her, the one side of his face in shadow while the other glowed and swirled with the frightened and prancing ballerinas on-screen. He caressed a finger along her cheek.

"No, my darling," he said, leaning in close again, "you're right to displace me. I know men like Finlay. They don't like to share their toys in the sandbox."

"That's a rude remark to make about my husband. And me, for that matter."

"I apologize. I only mean that surely we both expected our paths would diverge. You've all but said it yourself."

Eva pressed her lips and watched the ballerinas investigate the dungeon-like cellar where the Phantom was known to dwell.

Lon leaned even closer, laying his hand on her lap, and repeated, "I apologize."

Eva swallowed when, with a squeeze, his hand left her knee. "I know someone like me doesn't make sense in the life you've grown into since I went away. But I *am* back now—in every sense, I'd like to think—and I was hoping you might still be here for me?"

"You fool." Lon's visage went dark as the silent film cut to a black frame of dialogue. In a moment it lit up again, and she saw he was smiling. "You silly little fool. You make *most* sense in the life I want. I'm not going anywhere."

The tinny piano music accompanying the film intensified, drawing Lon's attention to the screen. He threw his head back in what appeared a soundless laugh, and he leaned back toward Eva.

"I'm not the one lurking in shadows, you realize." He gestured at the screen. "Living in a lair down in the bowels of society." He patted her hand. "Just let it be, girl, and do finally tell me about the honeymoon. Leave it to my marble goddess to absorb no color from the Mediterranean sun."

Eva sank in her seat, her cheeks prickling with heat as Lon only leaned in further, their faces a breath apart. "Let's watch the movie, shall we?" she whispered. "I am keenly interested in seeing what a Lon actually looks like without his nose. What with all the spiting one's face you've been up to."

She heard Lon cluck his tongue, and that settled the matter for the time being. Eva knew that her little quip hadn't won her the upper hand, though. Who had she been kidding, really, that she could pull off that asinine lie? The moment she'd heard herself project that marvelous fancy of a holiday to Lon during their last night alone before the wedding, she knew she'd be lucky if it bought her a week before he called her out on it. And that wasn't even anticipating he would have remote contact with any mutual acquaintances, let alone continue to play the good brother to Ollie and learn any number of things from Little Sister's loose tongue.

Eva may as well have told Lon herself that she and Finlay weren't to honeymoon further than their own estate. Finlay had needed to remain near his family's textile plants for when duty called—which it had, as often as any given workweek. Yet at the time, Eva had needed to flee the country in her mind, needed to sense the clean break of it. Everyone else had known to allow the newlyweds time alone to settle in; only Lon, the wildcard, had the capacity to break with such decorum. And could she really have risked him appearing outside the window of their country home as well?

She chuckled inwardly. Maybe she should have given Lon more credit than that. And accordingly given herself less, when the real concern had been the opposite. She hadn't wanted to enable herself by calling on Lon when her reliance needed to shift to her betrothed.

Weary of analyzing the situation more, Eva channeled her concentration into the music that had turned majestic as two angels rose into a burst of gray sunlight. Norman Kerry as Raoul looked on from a box seat, captivated by the beauty of Mary Philbin's Christine Daae. Mere moments later, Eva detected Lon adjusting in his seat when Christine spurned Raoul's lovemaking. As the Phantom's shadow made an appearance, Eva, too, felt uneasy.

"*But I warn you,*" he commanded of his young protégé, "*you must forget all worldly things and think only of your career—and your Master!*"

Eva willingly lost herself to the drama unfolding before them, so much so that at the climactic scene in which Christine unmasks the Phantom to behold his disfigured face, Eva herself cried out in terror and automatically twisted to collapse against Lon's chest, her face buried in her hands. He was quick to wrap his arms around her.

"My dear, you haven't fainted, have you?"

She groaned into his lapel. "No, I'm fine. But goodness, that gave me a fright." Yet in the comfort of his arms, her fear dissipated into embarrassment. She now trembled only with a soft giggle.

He stroked her finger-waves. "Don't fret, dear; it's only makeup. Lon's still underneath, nose and all." He punctuated his statement with a kiss on her forehead.

She emitted a pleased sigh into his chest and made no effort to lift her head from it. She'd cautioned herself against allowing her affections to stray, but perhaps she had involved herself in a chase despite her best intentions.

Grasping Lon's lapel, Eva breathed him in. Within the fibers of his tweed coat, the essence of the woods after a rainfall was interwoven with the chemical yet almost nutty and citrusy scent of his oil paints. It all combined to have a sedating effect, and in Lon's warm embrace, she fell asleep to the lullaby of silent-picture music.

When Eva awoke, a mob of Parisians with torches was descending on the Phantom at the riverside. He tried to fend them off with an explosive, though he ultimately called his own bluff and revealed to them his empty hand. With no tricks up his sleeve, he surrendered himself to their fury, and a few tears blazed down Eva's cheeks to anoint Lon's lapel as she watched the villain — the outcast — submerge into the water.

The lights brightened, and she tried to wipe away any signs of sleep and crying from her face. But from the way her eyes stung she knew they must be pink and puffy, and her nose threatened to leak unless she sniffed it. She hoped to at least sit in peace a few minutes longer to collect herself and steal one more scrap of privacy with her friend. Lon hadn't released his hold. He only removed an arm to fish around inside his jacket for a handkerchief, which he brought to her eyes to gently wipe them at their corners.

"I thought you'd slept through the entire thing, old girl. Did you see the ending, then?" he asked.

She nodded and seized the handkerchief to dab at her nose. "If you don't mind, sir."

He chuckled and squeezed her shoulders, kissing her on the forehead as he'd done before she'd fallen asleep. She took the liberty to curl into him again, holding his handkerchief to her face when an usher approached from the aisle. Lon motioned to him they'd be getting along momentarily.

As the usher walked away, Eva closed her eyes against Lon's chest but didn't lower the handkerchief his body had perfumed. He continued to rub her upper arm and shoulder, and then he kissed her head again. At this, she did drop the hankie away, hoping he would keep stroking her and press his lips to her hairline at least once more.

Her patience was rewarded, for he did, and she dared to raise her face slightly. His next kiss fell at her brow. She again lifted her chin incrementally, catching the next kiss at the bridge of her nose. Lon's caress along her arm slowed.

Eva lifted her face again, by just enough.

For the first time since the stairwell in summer, their lips met. Eva pressed into him, brushing the seam of his lips with her tongue.

He reciprocated her advances for a few passionate surges until his mouth just as suddenly broke away. He yanked his arm out from behind her, ran a hand over his closely cropped hair, and affixed his cap, tugging it down over his face. He stood to button his overcoat, then stiffly held a hand out to her.

Eva looked away and bit her lip. Her irritated eyes welled again with warm, salty tears, and her cheeks burned. As she rolled her eyes to the ceiling, blinking rapidly, she double-checked with her fingertips that all the oversized buttons of her wool coat were fastened before accepting Lon's outstretched hand and allowing him to pull her to her feet.

Walking along the row to the aisle, she waited for him to say something—to apologize or admonish, she didn't even care which. Just *something*. But he didn't.

When they'd descended the steps to the lobby, Lon tugged on her sleeve and jerked his head sideways away from the exit doors. He pinched the front tip of his cap between his thumb and index finger and lowered his head covertly. Yet Eva took comfort in the way he laid his hand at her waist like when they'd first entered. She even risked feeling excited about where he might steal her off to instead of just exiting to the street and calling it a day.

Where he led her was a side door to an alley. The moment Eva stepped out, the sky's gray glare pierced her vision from between the cold brick of the buildings on either side. She felt stark and cheap and exposed all of a sudden.

"I'm sorry," Lon said. "I didn't mean—"

Ah, Eva thought. There it was. In that infinitesimal second, she anticipated his next kiss.

"—to shuffle you off into a back alley like some hooker." He looked up and down the alley, everywhere but in her eyes.

A cloud of icy breath rose between them, and Eva rubbed her arms against the chill she felt to her bones.

"It's only that I saw someone in the lobby," he proceeded, "whom I recognized. That might recognize us both, together."

Clenching her teeth so they wouldn't chatter, she rapidly nodded her understanding. Yes, she understood all right where Lon's preferences were. Trying to fantasize otherwise was only going to set her up for disappointment; she'd known that.

"Eva, I'd better go. At the end of the alley, I'll walk that way—"
he pointed "—and you walk that way back toward Lincoln Avenue,
where it'll be a shorter walk for you. You look so cold."

Eva kept nodding dumbly, knowing a ventriloquist's wooden pup-
pet could have found its voice faster. The muscles in her jaw tensed
to the point of pain, and only the hot tears pooling at the corners
of her eyes reminded her that she was a warm-blooded living being.

"Wonderful, old girl," Lon said with a mechanical peck on her
cheek. "We should do this again in the New Year. My treat."

That was the last time Eva would see him until that New Year
had come and gone.

July 2000

"Fucking hell!" Kate tore the bath towel from her hair and used it to grip the knob that, wet with condensation, kept slipping through her fingers. But not without smudging the word off of her mirror first.

Very stupidly, she'd closed the bathroom door again to steam up the room. She prayed she wouldn't regret that as she turned the vintage glass this way and that in a frenzy, panicked it would dislocate again and leave her trapped.

The door unlatched, and Kate fell into the hall and through the open doorway of her closet.

Inside there, she yanked clothing off hangers and out of drawers to dress herself. She slipped her bare feet into a pair of running shoes, then sprinted to her front door and tried the knob to make sure it was locked. It was. She ran to the back door next to her refrigerator. Also locked. Backing against it, Kate spun to scan around her kitchen before creeping back into the living area. She shot glances at her curtains, under her futon, and behind her bookshelf before grabbing her keys from the side table and running out the back kitchen door.

Reaching the basement, she looked around for any movement, any suspicious shadows among the bike racks and dusty wooden storage lockers. She saw nothing but heard the clanking of someone's change tumbling inside a washing machine. The laundry facilities at the other end were better lit, so she unfroze her muscles to walk down there.

The dank air became warmer as Kate neared the washers and dryers. Their whirring grew louder, and she could smell the sterile security of bleach and detergent. The concrete floor vibrated beneath her feet, and she was looking down to kick a fabric softener sheet off her shoe when a scratchy voice said:

"Fancy meeting you here!"

"Oh!" Kate threw her hand to her heart. "Vera, what a relief."

"Didn't mean to frighten you, child. How goes it? Have a seat!"

Vera looked enviably cozy in a bedazzled purple tracksuit, sitting with legs primly crossed on a beat-up old sofa. Agatha was curled in her lap. Kate took a seat next to them.

"Leo's here, too," Vera said, pointing a thumb behind her at the basement's open back door. "He walked me back from Panera soon after you left so I could check on my laundry. Now he's in the lot out back checking for any good furnishings that might've been thrown out this weekend."

Kate suddenly felt so comfortable and happy she could have cried.

"What's the matter, dear?" Vera reached a hand onto Kate's upper arm and gave it a brisk tug.

"Vera," Kate said, her voice shaking, "it's been one hell of a day."

"Ohh…" Vera lifted Aggie and tossed her to the ground, replacing her with Kate in her arms as Kate's tears broke loose. "There, there, honey. I don't want to pry, but if you want to talk about it, I'm told I'm a great listener. Actually, that's not true at all. No one tells me that." She gave a throaty chuckle and succeeded in making Kate laugh as well.

"Another one of them TV stands, but without the inner shelf," Leo proclaimed as he stomped in. "Oh, hi there, Kate! Didn't mean to interrupt your girl talk. I can leave you two be."

Kate sat back from Vera's embrace and looked from one face to the other. Faces that had visibly weathered years of gains and losses, love, hate, and surely everything in between. In the creases carved by decades of laughs and frowns, Kate no longer saw age but *sage*, just what she needed right now. She scooted closer to Vera and patted the cushion on her other side, looking at Leo.

"Not so fast, Mister," she said. "You're not getting out of this that easy."

He raised his brows and pouted his lips as though to say, *Well, excuuuse me!* and circled around the couch, taking a seat on the wide armrest. Kate reached up to pat his shoulder.

"Hey," she said, "that's really cool." The shirtsleeves of his denim button-down were rolled to his elbows, exposing the faded gray-blue tattoo of an anchor on the inside of his opposite forearm. "Navy?"

Leo looked down on it thoughtfully. "Yep. Some days it seems a lifetime ago, but mostly it's very much like yesterday. Doesn't help having this stain to forever remember it by." He picked at the tattoo with his middle fingernail as if he could scratch it off.

"And that right there, Kate," Vera interjected, "is about as much as you'll get him to speak about it."

Kate knew better than to ask why. There was a reason she'd never had the opportunity to meet one of her grandfathers, who would've been around Leo's age had he survived the war. And as for her other grandpa who'd returned home alive but with some shrapnel in his leg, she was told he'd never talked about it either. "Well, thank you for your service. Then and today." She squeezed his shoulder and left it at that.

"Kate's had a bad day," Vera told Leo. "She was about to tell me about it when you barged in like a bull in a china shop. Now, you go ahead, dear."

She slumped down. "Where do I begin? As Leo knows, I got stuck in my freaking bathroom again this morning. I had to shout out the window like last time, and Maisie across the way heard me and got Leo for the keys to my place. Out of gratitude I asked her to stay for tea, which was, uh…interesting." She snorted and twisted her face into a mocking expression she thought Vera would appreciate.

But Vera cleared her throat and stiffly readjusted her posture. Proceeding to brush Aggie's hairs off her velour thighs in long, firm strokes, she darted her gaze all over the basement. "Where did that cat get off to? I hope she didn't crawl into one of the storage spaces. They have such big gaps between those wooden planks."

Kate tried to recover the ball she seemed to have fumbled. "So, uh, got any scoop on Maisie that I should know before I associate with her again?"

Vera looked straight at her. "There are worse people to know." She smoothed her palms along her plush purple thighs.

"Sorry. You're right," Kate dropped her sight to the floor in chagrin, then watched the clothing do cartwheels inside the dryer drum. "It was just that how she adopted her baby and everything was a little…off."

"Ba-by…" Vera nodded in slow motion. "Yes." She patted Kate on the knee, cleared her throat again, and said, "You mustn't be too hard on Maisie. She's been through a lot, and I've tried to do my part to make her feel welcome here and assured someone's there for her if she needs anything. But she's quiet and keeps to herself most of the time, so it really says something that she's reached out to you. I take it you two, ah…talked a little, then, this morning?"

"Yeah, while we had our tea. She was friendly enough. Maybe I should offer to babysit sometime."

"Oh! Well, lucky for you, Maisie never goes out. Reclusive, so I doubt she'd need the help. And she knows I'm around if she does." Vera scratched at her ear and looked out the side of her eye toward the floor. "Nice of you to suggest it, though. Now, about the rest of your day…"

Kate sat up and recounted the conversation with Dex, and though she knew Vera would understand her stance on not committing to just one guy yet, she appreciated the sympathy in Vera's eyes as the old woman patiently listened. Vera didn't moralize when she spoke; all she did say at the end was, "You know best what you're up to giving someone else. It can be as much about the *timing* as the *person*. You'll know when it's right for you."

"That's the truth, Kate," Leo chimed in. "The second you get married, it takes a lot of work. But knowing who to marry is, I think, the easy part. When you know, you know. You kids today analyze the romance out of everythin'. Proddin' and dissectin' each other like frogs instead of diving right in, figurin' it out later. Fallin' in love should be easy; it's nurturin' that love that you've gotta work at. But when you've really fallen, yer willin' to. You don't even question it."

"Why, Leo." Kate slouched back on the couch again. "You old softie, you."

She turned her head to see what eye-rolling Vera was surely doing behind her but was surprised instead to see her neighbor staring at him with a faint smile. "He married the love of his life," Vera said.

With a boyish grin, Leo looked like a bobble-head toy as he wordlessly agreed. Fingering his anchor tattoo again, he said, "The good Lord took her away from me early. But, you know, though I wouldn't have believed it at the time, I wouldn't mind havin' a companion again. Guess it's too late for an old codger like me, but…"

He still grinned at his tattoo, but as Kate looked at his profile, she thought she saw an eye peeking at the other end of the sofa a couple of times. She turned her head to Vera for her reaction.

The old woman wasn't looking at him anymore but around the basement again. "Aggie!" she called out with intermittent *tuh-tuh-tuhs* of her tongue. "Come back here, you stealthy little fur-ball!"

"Well," Leo said, "you're young and have time, I guess."

"How old were you when you married?" Kate asked.

"Twenty."

"Wow. You had about five years on me, then. Well, five and then some considering I'm nowhere close to marriage."

"Yep. But that's how it was in those days. People married young. Got to raisin' families right away. Nowadays, careers come first for both men *and* women. Just the sign of the times, I 'spose. Equality and liberty to make yer own choices is what people have been fightin' for through history, so I can't say I blame young folks in this new millennium wantin' to find themselves and wait till they're older to settle down. So long as you don't miss opportunities when they're right before your eyes. Great love isn't found just every day. You gotta seize it when you find it."

Not in a million years would Kate have expected Leo to be the one dispensing love advice. She knew right then she was staring at a special breed of man, perhaps a dying race of them.

Ah, to be loved like that, by a man who perceives you as his reason for living as much as you do him. Who would stop at nothing until he'd won your heart, then would polish it like silver forever. That, in a nutshell, was the fantasy.

Kate sighed. If only Leo were fifty years younger.

"Mind you," Vera interposed, "he isn't saying you need to hop in bed with the first fella you meet or settle for the one you're with. There's absolutely no need to race to the altar; it only gets harder from there, to be sure. I think in asking Dexter for the opportunity to get to know different gentlemen, there's reason for it. If you feel the least withheld, go with your gut."

"That's what you've always done?" Kate asked.

"That, darlin', is what I've *always* done. And look at me now."

Leo howled, clapping his hand to his thigh. "Man alive." He leaned into Kate as if speaking candidly, though Vera sat well within earshot. "I tell you, that woman is in a category of her own. I will never figure her peculiar species out as long as I live."

"Oh, pooh," Vera grumbled, swiping her hand at him. A second later, Aggie leaped into her lap. "Oh! You'll be the *death* of me, you little stinker. How dare you sneak up on me like that." Yet as much as her words scolded, Vera baby-talked half of them while she scruffed up Aggie's fur and buried her nose in it.

"You've warmed up to her, haven't you," Kate said.

"Well," Vera conceded as she continued to caress the torbie with obvious if reluctant affection, "she's company."

Kate had heard her say that before, which made her wonder if Vera desired companionship every bit as much as Leo. But to actually ask her that could prove the death of *Kate*, so she let it go and moved on to the next part of her singularly hellish day.

"So then, after Dexter, the weirdness really began."

Vera plucked her attention away from the cat to look Kate up, down, and around. "That's right. What brings you down here? I don't see any laundry."

"I didn't know where else to go."

"Huh?" Leo and Vera said at once, then Leo asked, "Uh oh, is there a mouse or somethin'?"

"Something. Do you guys promise not to react like I'm crazy? No matter how crazy it actually is?" She looked side to side and waited for both to nod their heads in promise. "Vera, I told you before about the weird feeling in my apartment. And I swear I wrote it off as of our conversation yesterday. But then today…I was just taking a shower, then I looked at the mirror and saw—" she paused for emphasis, knowing the suspense was killing them "—the word *mine* printed in huge letters across it, smeared in the steam."

She'd dropped her bombshell, and her audience sat speechless for several seconds.

Leo cleared his throat and finally asked, "Was, uh, your front or back door left open?"

"Nope," Kate answered.

Vera clawed at the excess skin of her turkey neck. "Does, ah, Dexter have a key?"

"Nope. I deliberately held off making one."

The silence would have been deafening if not for the laundry churning.

"Was there any sign of breaking and entering?" Leo tried again.

"Nope."

"No one else was in your apartment?" Vera asked.

"Nope."

Aggie rolled onto her back in Vera's lap and purred, the only one to make a sound.

They weren't going to be any help, so Kate outright asked the question she'd wondered before but never believed she'd say out loud: "Is this building haunted?"

There was a sustained pause, and in that space, the dryer fell silent as well. Vera had stopped petting Aggie, and Leo didn't even look like he was breathing.

"Mercy, yes," Vera finally said. She lifted Aggie from her lap, set her beside Kate, and walked toward the dryer. "Ghosts crawling all over the place."

She emptied the contents of the machine into her plastic hamper and began to primly fold her towels.

"I've been rooming with a crotchety old woman for months now," she went on. "I mean one besides myself." She winked, now speaking as casually as if they were discussing the weather. "Sure, all she does is keep quiet in my rocker, and Aggie keeps her company fine enough. But you'd think she could kick in some rent at some point."

"Are you kidding me?" Kate asked, looking to Leo for his two cents. Surely, he would pish at Vera's claims.

But he appeared somber and only licked his lower lip with the underbelly of his tongue.

"There's souls not at rest here," he eventually said. "It's a troubled place, this."

New Year's Eve 1926 / New Year's Day 1927

"Three, two, one…Happy New Year!"

Thousands of revelers buzzing on bootlegged liquor raised their arms in the air at the Aragon Ballroom.

"Wooo!" Effie cried into the cacophony, throwing her arms around her dance partner's neck. "Oh, Lonnie, won't you kiss me Happy New Year? It's bad luck if you don't!" She nuzzled her silver-beaded breasts against his vest and wore a deep garnet, balloon-lipped pout. "Lonnie, you've been giving me the absent treatment all night," she cooed, raising that pout and puckering it as blatantly as a fish.

That's what it is, Lon realized. He leaned back to eye her up and down and had to catch his footing as he almost lost his balance. Squinting through his gin-distorted vision, he confirmed that *that's* what Effie had reminded him of all night in that little dress of overlapping giant sequins and beads: a silvery, scaly fish.

"Ohhh," she moaned into him, tracing her index fingers in symmetrical snakes down his chest. "Come now, darling. Since when are *you* so shy?" She giggled with a hiccup and swayed against him as a trumpet *wah-wahhed* the remainder of the band's jazzy rendition of "Auld Lang Syne."

Scanning the crowd for the other couples they'd arrived with, Lon couldn't make out any familiar faces. The camaraderie he usually shared with just his male companions at the late-night clubs wasn't to be enjoyed this evening. He heard Effie "Mmmm!" at him in pleading and figured, *What the hell.* He joined in her sway as the band's piano began to provocatively plunk out the song "Squeeze Me."

Bending down, Lon practically swallowed Effie's ready lips, penetrating that pucker and unable to care less if an usher tapped his shoulder for indecent public behavior. Passionately groping her hips and bottom thanks to his flask of gin, Lon went for it and waited for the slap across his face.

He had underestimated Effie.

"Mmm," she continued to moan while her fingers tucked into the waist of his trousers at his back and slid around to the front. She gave his fly a tug and detached from his mouth. "Check, please. Let's say we blow this joint and you take me to your hotel." Her eyes were glassed on hooch, but they appeared to focus steadily enough on his.

A mental inventory of his lodgings ran through Lon's reeling mind as he appraised how suitable it was for company. Had he picked up his clothes? Put away his paints and canvas? But perhaps he hadn't been considering the most important question: Did it matter?

"So where are you staying?" Effie asked. "The Drake? Palmer House?"

Lon narrowed his eyes. *Of course. Why should she assume anything less than luxury?*

"Allerton?" she persisted. "Some place real swanky, I'm sure. You *weasel*; I'm *certain* you've been to town sooner than this and haven't called me. Show me where you've been hiding." She grabbed his lapels and looked up at him like an imploring puppy. "Pleeease, Lonnie? Take me where you bring the other girls." Her voice returned to its characteristic nasal whine. A shame; Lon had enjoyed the brief departure. "I'm feeling an edge, and this music's starting to grate on me," she yammered on. "Come, on let's ankle, huh?" She was actually pulling his arm now. "Before my giggle water wears off and gives me a headache."

With Lon rooted firmly in place, Effie kept a hold on him and leaned backward at an otherwise impossible angle. In an effort to motivate him, she released one of her hands to pull up the hem of her dress and reveal her garters.

Not wishing her to fall over, Lon gave in to her tugs, watching this debutante-turned-flapper whom he supposed could be considered a kindred spirit, a renegade of her class — if not for the fact that she was sure to still color inside the lines enough to keep her key to The Club.

She was fodder for gossips, to be sure, but she'd not been branded visibly enough to deny her invitations to all the elite events. She could turn her slang on and off like a light switch, transitioning with ease into the polished Standard English she'd been brought up with on command. And, though twenty-one, her parents still doted on her like an infant. Perhaps they thought it was safer to keep her on an extraordinarily long leash, but a leash nonetheless that would pull taut and tug her back if she ran out the slack. Daddy's Girl, on the perpetual prowl for a Sugar Daddy to support her if ever she did snap that leash.

Back, back, back she pulled him through the crowd of couples springing in lively dancing, their feet drumming against the wooden floor. The surrounding plaster façade of a garish Spanish courtyard closed around Lon like a tunnel, at the end of which he only saw Effie's spread thighs, her garters snapping one by one at the yank of his teeth. Maybe it *was* worth trying to bounce this Sheba off his Murphy bed after all, send them both into oblivion. In his condition at the moment, her hole was good as any.

Effie walked backward, still facing him and bunching the hem of her dress in her fist as she guided him along. The dancing in his peripheral vision appeared to slow, and Lon blinked as his sight blurred and the images converged in front of him. He looked up to the false night sky of the domed ceiling and tried to focus on its artificial twilight. As his hazy vision swam among the painted stars, he saw nothing else, only heard "Squeeze Me" in the very blood rushing to his ears.

A "Whoops!" broke the spell, and Lon found himself pressed against Effie. She'd backed into one of the "palace" columns running the perimeter of the dance floor, leaving Lon to crash into her.

Closing his eyelids to see the stars behind them, he took her lips with his again and plucked at her garter straps as if she were a bass. Effie complied with pleasing sounds for a little while, but it was when Lon crouched, grabbed the backs of her thighs, and hoisted her up against the column that he felt her struggle. "What's the idea!" she cried, holding to him for balance while also trying desperately to keep her dress covering her bottom. "Lonnie, stop it now!" He tried to wedge his body between her legs and wrap them around his sides. "Say, I mean it! Quit it now or I'm really gonna cast a kitten in fronta' all these people!"

Here, kitty-kitty-kitty. Lon laughed to himself as he eased his hands beneath her dress toward her rump. But, with an instinctive sense of decency, he withdrew to let her down — just in time to see two uniformed ballroom attendants make their way toward him. Around them, he heard the disapproving cries of other women, a few of whom appeared to prod their dates to walk over there and knock his lights out.

Lon seized Effie by the wrist and pulled her toward the exit, waving off the men who'd given up their chase but still pointed after him in stern warning.

Out on the sidewalk, she huffed into the frigid air. "You, you're screwy! You didn't even fetch my ermine!" She ran at him and pushed him with surprising might. "The nerve, after dragging me all the way uptown. I'll find myself another ride home, thank you. Don't call on me again. Ever!"

And with that, she stomped her fish scales back inside, leaving Lon teetering on his feet. He hadn't even grabbed his own overcoat, but no matter. The glittering lights of the Green Mill jazz club twinkled in the corner of his eye from the nearest intersection at Broadway.

Rubbing and cupping his bare hands to his face, he blew warm breath into them and set foot to deliver himself from drunk to positively zozzled.

"Three, two, one…Happy New Year!"

Dozens of high society members tipsy on fine champagne raised their coupe glasses in toast throughout the parlor and music room of the Hughes mansion.

"A kiss for good luck, my charming bride," Finlay said, taking Eva's hand and kissing the back of it before pulling her nearer to plant one politely on her lips.

"You call that a kiss?" Eva teased, perhaps two glasses of champagne in excess of her threshold. She coiled her arm around his neck and pressed against him. Her lips roamed over his and traveled down to his neck, then up to his ear.

"Evie, darling." Finlay pulled her arms from their tight squeeze to add a little distance, looking around at the other partygoers and forcing a good-natured chuckle. The Redcliffe influence had tamed Hughes parties quite a bit over the last year. "Ha-ha, yes, perhaps you've imbibed a bit too much," he said loudly for anyone in earshot. "May I walk you to a sofa, or perhaps your old bed upstairs to rest awhile? Collect yourself?"

Eva pulled her arms through his grip and wrapped them instead around his waist beneath his tuxedo jacket. "I think," she purred with a smirk, "you ought to take me home, darling, and lay me on *our* bed."

"Mm, yes," Finlay replied. "Let's do. I'll fetch your mink if you'll say your goodbyes and meet me in the foyer."

Eva tightened her hug and giggled into his neck, "Yes, *master*," with a firm squeeze of his rear beneath his tails.

"Er," Finlay replied and coughed into his hand. "I'll just be retrieving your fur, dear. Why don't you make your way to the door now."

Pressing her lips together in a grin, Eva saluted her husband. She then dropped her hand with such gusto that it swung her around, so she followed its lead and walked in its suggested direction.

Weaving through the merrymakers with a smiling nod, she eventually found herself in the front foyer. She stood on the mosaic tiles between the great columns and swayed to the string ensemble. Fleetingly, she wondered if she ought not quickly run upstairs to check on Ollie, but looking down the golden corridor, she spied the marble lovers above the fountain. Her sister forgotten, the corners of Eva's lips twitched downward, and she softly sang along with everyone else to "Auld Lang Syne."

Her throat tightened, making her voice falter into silence. Yet she still swayed, leaning against the door and frowning.

Seconds later, Finlay descended the grand staircase with her white fur in hand.

"All right, my darling, let's be off."

Compliant, she stood away from the door and allowed the butler — who'd been invisible to her until just then — to open it for her. Humming the song, she clopped down the stone steps, turned an abrupt left at the sidewalk, and marched the short distance to her own home next door. She then took another sharp military turn left up their steps.

Once inside the foyer there, she turned onto Finlay to half-heartedly renew her seduction.

"Mmm, kiss me, darling."

"Of course, dear." Finlay pecked her lips, then her forehead.

"Oh, come now, can't you do better than that?" She fixed a ravenous gaze on him and reached for the fly of his tuxedo pants.

"Eva, my sweet…here…let me just—" And he swept her off her feet and carried her upstairs.

Entering their master bedroom, he laid her on the bedspread and covered her with her white mink, which she promptly snatched off. Crawling onto all fours, she flicked it at him like a whip. "Come here, you."

"Darling, I *must* get back to your father's. There are important men there that I need to speak to, and—"

"Well, if you *must* go, then go!" Eva spat, poised up on her knees. "Here I am throwing myself at you, and you still won't touch me! I am your *wife! I'm* the one you always return to exhausted from your days of commerce or riding or golfing or whatever it is that you do at any given hour with the other Rulers of the World. There's always someone else important to speak to. I fear I don't interest you very much."

"Pardon me, darling, but do I disrespect you? Do I treat you poorly? Deny you any comforts you're used to? After only one year away, you've had to move all but one door down from your childhood home, for goodness sake."

Eva pouted, tears streaming down her face. Why did she always seem to be crying? Ever since 1925, ever since the engagement, and was this how she was to ring in yet another year as well? Another New Year of old tears? A New Woman confined to old ways?

"No," she replied. "You've been a gentleman in every way."

"What then?" he beseeched. "Eva, what can I do to make you happy?"

"Must you really ask? Fine, then. I give up." Hands folded at her lap, she sank onto her heels. "Intimacy, Finlay. I want to feel *intimacy*. I want us to find pleasure in each other, emotionally, physically. I feel all I've accomplished since our wedding is a successful role-play as Wife. My next audition will be for the role of Mother of Your Children. And yet how am I to achieve that when you scarcely lay a finger on me? It's been over a year, and I still simply want to feel like a woman first before becoming a vessel for your seed."

"Don't be vulgar, Eva. It doesn't become you."

"What doesn't? *Modernity?*"

"You know very well."

Eva closed her eyes and mouth at once and concentrated on breathing through her nose.

"Darling, I…" Finlay's voice had softened, and she could hear him approach just before his weight pulled down at the bedside and his smooth hand rested on top of hers. "This isn't how I wanted our evening to end, darling."

Keeping her eyes closed, Eva snorted. "Who ever wants any evening to end like this?"

"Yes, of course, but I only mean to say…I suppose I'm not quite good at being a husband. Not yet. But I swear to you, I'll endeavor every day of my life to try. I've never done this before, Eva. You must be patient."

A tear trapped beneath Eva's eyelid slipped its way to freedom down her cheek. She opened her eyes to look at her husband beside her. "And you think I *have* done this before? Where do you suppose I've stored all my previous husbands? In the cellar?"

Finlay smiled and squeezed her hand.

"I suppose," Eva continued, "*I'm* not much good at being a wife. Yet. I promise to try, too."

"I appreciate that, darling. They always say the first year is difficult. We will work on this second year, together." He kissed her cheek, then leaned further to kiss her lips, not just once but twice, somewhat of a record for Finlay in one sitting. With a double pat of her hand, he rose and straightened his tuxedo jacket. "So then, are you fine to stay here? Or can I escort you back to the party?"

He held his arm out akimbo for her to take. The stance was unsettlingly familiar.

"No," Eva said, staring at his offered arm. "No, thank you. You go on. And please do extend my apologies to everyone for leaving without saying goodbye. As you said, I imbibed too much. I believe I'll sleep it off now."

Finlay patted her head and withdrew to the door. "Happy New Year, darling," he whispered just before closing the door behind him.

Eva lay down on her side and hugged a pillow to her chest, replaying the conversation in her mind and asking herself again if crying was to remain such a regular state of being. Where had her strength evaporated to? Her independence? Her long-ago dreams of becoming a world-traveling journalist? Why did entering into a marriage mean having to check her identity at the door? For being a marriage of convenience, Eva was hard-pressed to identify just what had been so convenient about it.

"I simply want to feel like a woman," played back in her mind. *"We will work on this,"* did as well.

Still practically newlyweds, they were already having to work on it. Eva supposed that was a fair enough reality of commitment, but what she couldn't define quite as precisely was *what* they'd be working for.

At least he was trying. That counted for something when another man in her life had ceased working at even friendship. And from only a block away, if he even still lived at that hotel; Lon could have moved months ago for all she knew. That he remained in Chicago at all was only confirmed through the rumor mill. But Eva couldn't act spiteful of that. She'd brought it on herself and hadn't dared make the effort either. Meeting Lon at the movie house last winter had been a rash misjudgment. And how dreadful to have put him in that position — she'd single-handedly tried to drag him back to his philandering days, after he had been there for her, just as he'd promised.

No, she'd owed Finlay this first year, reserved for just the two of them as they began a new life together. And she owed Lon a chance at his happiness in the way he wanted to seek it. He didn't need a rich married woman cramping his style.

Eva sat up. She didn't need a rich married woman cramping *her* style either.

Striding to her wardrobe, she yanked her hanging dresses along the bar one by one and stopped at a little black knee-length Coco Chanel number she'd bought months ago but never had the right opportunity to wear. Unfastening and peeling off her fern green gown, she stepped into the beaded and fringed black crepe and rummaged around for her favorite black beaded purse, the hexagonal one she'd carried the night she'd first snuck into the Lincoln Park Zoo with Lon. The one that reminded her of the stars, the sea of dew where she could cast her nets and soar with the Dream Lady.

Unfortunately, it wasn't to be found.

"Drat," she muttered, frowning over where she might have misplaced it. Yet not wanting to dawdle any longer than she needed to in the event Finlay returned for her, she plucked up the next best thing — a basic silk clutch — and glided to the door.

She halted. Returning to her wardrobe, she opened a small interior drawer and withdrew from it a little mahogany box lined in black velvet. The winter chill that crept in through the windowpanes had shrunken her fingers enough that her emerald engagement ring and diamond-encrusted platinum wedding band slid off with ease. She tucked them into the velvet's recesses, clapped the case shut, and scavenged through yet another drawer and jewelry box for a plain gold band to wear on her ring finger instead. It wasn't that she didn't wish to look married, just not flashy. She'd forego wearing a fur as well, but the champagne hadn't driven her to complete insanity — it was January in Chicago.

Penning a brief note in her elegant script, she placed it on Finlay's pillow. She affixed a black cloche hat with a low-hanging brim, wrapped herself in an ankle-length black mink, and snuck out to Clark Street where she hailed a taxi to the Green Mill.

Six for Gold

July 2000

"Why on earth didn't you tell me about *ghosts* before?" Kate exclaimed.

"You never asked!" Vera replied.

"Oh, yes I did. I asked point-blank if you'd noticed something a little *off* with this building and then told you about the green eyes in the mirror!"

Vera occupied herself with folding the rest of her laundry.

"Now," Leo interjected in a calm voice of mediation, "go easy on her, Kate. If anyone's to blame here, it's me. I showed you this place and never disclosed anythin' about its paranormal peculiarities or someone dyin' in your apartment right before you moved in."

"And trust me," Kate said, "after the Leaper story, I'd have never guessed there could be anything you wouldn't tell me."

"Truth be told, the phenomena's only been in the last six months. Vera and I, we'd thought we'd seen everythin' before, but when objects started movin' round and people started to appear——"

"I don't believe this." Kate shook her head.

"It's understandably hard to, dear," Vera chimed in, "but please know we didn't conceal it from you with bad intentions. We didn't want you to get spooked in the event nothing at all was wrong with the place. In all fairness, I didn't sense Olive in that space once we got all her possessions out of it. At least not until Aggie jumped around at the door. Olive always spent a lot of time lingering at that door. Really paranoid, she was, always listening for people coming and going. She'd already have that door opened a crack and be peeking out at you by the time you climbed the last flight."

Kate clapped her hands to her mouth, which muffled her voice like a drive-through speaker when she said, "That's why you didn't want to sell me that purse." She dropped her hands. "I'd already bought Olive's chair, and you were worried what might happen if I brought any more of her stuff back in."

Both Vera and Leo nodded solemnly.

"So," Kate said, "you think those were Olive's eyes I saw in the purse mirror? Do you think she's the one who wrote that message on my bathroom one?"

"It's hard to say." Vera dropped the last of her dishtowels into her hamper and clasped her hands together. "She did have green eyes. A very faded, almost gray shade of green."

"And that place didn't have much history before her," Leo said. "Younger than she was at the time, and she was just a teenager."

"How old?"

"Goodness." Vera held a hand to her chin, mashing her lips with a curved finger. "I think she was only about, what, fifteen or so? It was in the late twenties."

"Fifteen! Did she run away from home?"

"Yes, she did. She's *the* one who ran away from home, the one I was telling you about yesterday. The Hughes girl." Vera looked hesitantly at Leo, but Kate didn't see any reaction on his face.

"Oh, my God, seriously? But I thought you said she went missing?"

"So everyone thought."

"Then how did you find out the truth? Did she 'fess up once she figured anyone who would've cared was already dead?"

Vera kept running a firm hand over her lower lip. "No…Olive didn't talk too much about her past, at least not the short bit of her life prior to moving here. Where she came from, if she had any surviving family…" Vera swallowed. "And, well, what have you. But she did have her moments. Not because she was feeling candid but because she'd become rather senile, see. She'd have these little…bursts of clarity, talking about events from years ago as if they'd just happened. It made me…uncomfortable to witness. But it was nothing I could help. You just don't know when something like that is going to happen. She was a ticking time bomb."

Vera's voice had become shaky, and her breathing quickened. Kate looked to Leo again to gauge his response, but he just sat staring down into his lap with a grim expression.

"Imagine her family's unspeakable grief," Vera said. "Believing they might never see her again, might never know if she was even still alive—and here she was, living right down the block from them the entire time."

"How is that even possible?" Kate asked. "How would they not run into her on the streets?"

"Olive underwent quite a transformation at that time. To start, she'd changed her name. You can ask Leo; her name on the lease to that apartment was Stella Parker from the day she first signed to the day she died. But *we* knew her as Olive, didn't we, Leo."

"Time or dementia must've let her guard down at least that much," he said.

"Anyway," Vera continued, "we have to remember that when she ran away, she was a young girl yet, growing into womanhood. She never did get very tall, but given enough time, her body blossomed into new curves no one from her past would have known."

Kate nodded on that point.

"Granted," Vera added, "I imagine it wouldn't have been a far reach to figure out it was her if you had the chance to look at her close up and for long enough. But Olive said she worked very hard to never give anyone that chance. Changed her hair, caked makeup all over her face. I told you before she was always the plain one, which made her a real blank canvas for that clown paint. At a glance and from a distance, you *wouldn't* know."

Kate shook her head. "Fifteen…When she grew up in that beautiful house and must have had every privilege. Why would she leave it all behind to live here? What in her life could have been that bad at so young an age?"

Leaning against the dryer, Vera looked down her hands and wiped them together thoughtfully. "All that glitters is not gold. I told you before that when it comes down to it, that big beautiful mansion is still just a house. And no one standing on the outside can really know what goes on inside a house's four walls. It could have been any number of things: abuse, neglect, teasing at school. A desire to do something different, escape the expectations of one's caste. Who can really say? It was the twenties. Rebellion among young women was the sign of the times. And if it was for love, what wouldn't one do?"

She faltered at the end of that sentence and went quiet. Like the afternoon before, Vera looked tired. She'd since placed her hands behind her on top of the dryer and rested her weight heavily on them. Her downcast expression was an appeal in itself to not be asked anything more on the subject.

But Kate was wildly interested in hearing more of Olive's story and dying to ask why on earth a young girl so desperate to get away would then stay so very near home. But, seeing Vera's state, she resigned herself to ask at a better time and place. Maybe Olive had only been so bold and still wanted the security of home in her reach, just in case she would regret it. Maybe that safety net had been the only way she'd managed to stay away for a lifetime.

Kate did allow herself one more chain of inquiry before she let it rest. "So, Leo, are you saying in all your years living here, the hauntings only first started six months ago? Do you think it has something to do with the suicide?"

"Can't say for sure, but it wasn't lost on me that it was very soon after Tommy's death. Wouldn't you say, Vera? Immediately after, even."

"Mm hm," was all Vera offered.

"Tommy," Kate said. "I didn't know The Leaper's name. Have any others used that roof as a high-dive?"

Leo's face twisted into that pained expression he took on when he seemed to recall. At least that's what Kate hoped; she'd feel awful if her question or choice of words had offended him. Likely not helping his concentration was the metallic drumming of Vera's nails on the front of the dryer she leaned against.

"There've been many deaths in Camden Court over the years," he said. "Some natural, some accidental. Some intentional, be it suicide or homicide. Too many souls attached to it, which I'da thought would've moved on by now if not for Tommy's death seeming to stir 'em all up again."

"Geez, just when ya thought you'd escaped Y2K," Kate joked.

His whiskers scratched against his palm as he rubbed his chin. "But to answer your question, the last jump from the roof of this building on record dates back to nineteen twenty-seven. Or nineteen twenty-eight, you could say, 'cause it was New Year's, see. Stroke of midnight. Another young man around Tommy's age by the name of Alonzo Ashby."

A heavy sigh caught Kate's attention, and she turned to see Vera's head lolling forward. Kate started to her feet.

"Are you all right?" Hooking her arm through both of Vera's, Kate supported her by the armpits. "Did something happen? Are you in pain?"

"I'm sorry, Vera." Leo, too, was at his feet. He stood there looking boyish and useless. "I shouldn't'a—"

"Nonsense," she croaked with her flattened palm upheld to him.

Kate adjusted her hold under Vera's arms. "Let me take you back to your apartment. Leo, if you don't mind following with her laundry—"

"No!" Vera emphasized this by jerkily freeing herself from Kate's arm and walking to the back alley door. "Just leave it."

"Where you goin', hon?" Leo asked after her.

"My blood sugar's low," she snapped. "I'm getting a pop and char dog at the Wiener's Circle. *Don't* follow me."

"I won't," Leo replied, too softly, Kate thought, for Vera to be able to hear him from the distance she'd so quickly put between them. Together, they watched Vera's silhouette pass through the doorway and disappear in a blaze of fury into the low-angling sun.

"Oh, dear," Leo sulked. "I shouldn't'a said anything. The less you know about this place, Kate, the better for everyone, I think."

Whatever blame Leo was assuming, Kate had no idea. He'd only been answering *her* questions.

"God, I'm such an idiot," she said. "You guys obviously didn't want to talk about it, yet here I am dredging it up. I'm so sorry. I'll just stop." She moved closer to Leo and clasped his elbow. "I think I'll need to break my lease, though. Can you help me with that?"

Leo's sunken shoulders hunched forward. Kate thought he looked like a cuddly old teddy bear missing some of its stuffing, which only made her feel worse. But she had to move out of that building. She couldn't stay knowing even what little she did.

"Yeah. Sure, I'll help with that."

With an affectionate squeeze of his elbow, Kate let go and spun on her heel to pick up Vera's hamper. "I'll take this to my place and run it over when she's back. Just let her know."

Leo's sorrowful eyes held fast to the ground. "I'll watch the cat."

With a big inhale, Kate made her way back to the stairwell leading up to her apartment. She was frightened as hell to go back in there yet felt safer knowing Leo and Vera were there for her, living through the same thing as they had for half a year. That would hopefully be enough to keep her from crashing on anyone's sofa anytime soon. And she didn't want fear driving her back to Dexter.

She wasn't certain how long it would take, though, before she could move out, so it occurred to her that in the meantime Olive should become a better-known quantity. Somehow, Kate would need to learn more about her, the life she'd led for over seventy years in that small space, and it seemed doubtful Yahoo's search engine would deliver on a girl gone missing in the 1920s if her own family hadn't known anything. Vera and Leo seemed to be Kate's only hope, but she would obviously need to bide her time with them.

In this case, unfortunately, for the first time in her quarter-century of life, time was something Kate didn't feel she had.

As she rounded the wooden steps onto her last flight, in the dark she barely made out an even darker shadow at the foot of her unit's back door. Then it moved. She would've dropped Vera's laundry if her grip hadn't tightened so hard around the hamper's handles.

Kate held her breath for a few seconds as she listened to the scraping sound up by her door, then blew out a gust of air just when a pair of glowing eyes materialized.

"*Aggie*…Jesus, cat."

Maow! Agatha whined, her reflective eyes turning away from Kate as the cat resumed scratching at the door.

Kate met her at the top of the steps, set down the hamper, and swooped the feline up. It struggled and hissed, which threatened to throw off Kate's balance as she descended the steps again, but the farther she walked the animal away from her unit, the more it calmed. She could hear the shuffles of Leo's footsteps as he poked in and out of the rows of storage spaces, likely looking for the damn cat.

"There's the little bugger," he said as Kate approached to hand over squirming Aggie.

"Yep, she's a pistol, this one. Good luck with that." She gave her biggest smile in desperation to cheer Leo up before sending him home alone.

Giving Agatha a final pat on the head, Kate made to turn when he asked, "I don't suppose ya like stew?"

"Huh?"

"I'm not much of a cook, but I've got some beef and vegetables simmering in the ol' Crock Pot if yer interested in sharin' some."

"Oh." Kate kicked herself for dragging the word out with such reluctance. If anything, she should have been grateful for the excuse not to go back to her apartment yet, so she added, "It's been a while since I've had stew. Yum!"

"Aw, you don't have to act excited about it. Seeing's how it's dinnertime, I just thought I'd offer some eats, but the real reason I'm askin', see, is if you wouldn't maybe be interested in lookin' through more of that box. I didn't tell ya before, but it belonged to Olive."

Kate's smile froze on her face.

The air was heavy with savory meat and potatoes. While Leo clanked around in his kitchen, Kate sat on his sofa, rifling through clippings again as Aggie scampered around by his recliner. Kate respected that Leo had withheld the shoebox owner's identity at first out of good old-fashioned privacy. But now that she knew whom these scraps had really belonged to, she tried to make more sense of them and their connection to each other.

So Evelyn was the older sister, she mused after finding an article likely posted in a society column following the wedding. *If Olive was the one who went missing, then Evelyn must be the one who died soon after.*

There were other articles on the Hughes family, tracking its rise and fall, and Kate felt the cooling blanche of her cheeks when she found an appeal to find the "Missing Hughes Heiress." She shook her head at the senselessness she still saw in the whole affair and dug for more mentions of Evelyn, Olive, or Olive's pseudonym, Stella Parker. She overturned a couple of lipstick-dabbed cocktail napkins with two- and three-digit numbers inked on them. These raised questions, too, but her excavation stopped when a name leaped out from one of the yellowed slips of paper: Alonzo Ashby.

It was a report on a crime scene, dated New Year's Day, 1927. There'd been a skirmish at the Green Mill club in Uptown, and Alonzo Ashby had been charged with assault and battery. Bail had been posted by an anonymous donor.

The address listed for Alonzo was Geneva, Illinois, the primary residence of one Lloyd Ashby, who'd been a decorated soldier in World War I. Kate knew exactly the place. The Frank Lloyd Wright prairie-style home was now a museum, which she'd visited once on a school field trip. The grounds extended on both sides of the Fox River and included elaborate exotic gardens and a pagoda imported from the Orient. Kate vaguely remembered his money coming from lumber and that he'd funded research supporting military intelligence during World War II, but she couldn't recall anything specific about the brother.

At any rate, she knew something about Alonzo now. A couple things, actually.

Leo came down the hall. "Soup's on in a few more minutes, kiddo. How's your research goin'?"

"Good, I think. That Alonzo Ashby you mentioned, there's an article in here about him."

Leo flinched in unmistakable surprise. By now, Kate had seen enough furtive glances and gestures between him and Vera to know that this tidbit of information was something he genuinely hadn't been aware of.

"I'll be damned," he said.

Kate handed him the clipping. He backed away with it toward his recliner, engrossed in the article until he suddenly twisted to look behind him at the chair.

"Beat it," he said, then stood waiting a few seconds, staring at his seat.

"Huh?" Kate asked, wondering if he'd just directed her to leave. Hesitantly, she made a motion to rise.

"Aw—" he swiped the article across the air in front of him "—that pest likes to sit in my chair."

Agatha was presently squirming with a dust bunny in a corner across the room, so looking to Leo's empty seat cushion, Kate pinched her brow and repeated, "Huh?"

Finally, Leo slumped down on it. "Can't see him, but if you pay close attention, you'll notice his weight on it whenever I'm not sittin' there."

She narrowed her eyes, needing a moment for it to register that Leo was talking about his own resident ghost.

"Ah. Does he, by chance, also like to move things around? Stuff sitting on this table, for instance?" She pointed a thumb at the early-American-style side table where she'd set down her can of Coke last time.

"You bet he does. Had to holler at him for the hundredth time to leave my wedding photo alone. I think he has the hots for my wife. Can't say that I blame 'im, but still. I hope he doesn't track her down in the afterlife before I get there."

Looking to that precious candid photo, Kate was surprised she could laugh so casually at Leo's ghost. It wasn't something she wanted to stick around too long and get used to, but the presences her neighbors described sounded benign enough.

All right, I'll play along with this game of it's-no-big-deal. "How do you know it's a 'he'?" she asked.

"With the exception of Vera," he said, "only a man could be so damn stubborn."

She snorted.

"Anyway." Leo returned his attention to the article. "This is most odd, finding mention of Alonzo in here. I wonder if there ain't anythin' more about him in that box. Could Olive have known him?" His face, which had been screwed up in confusion, went wide-eyed as if he'd just answered his own question.

"Do you think she did? Did *Vera* know him, for that matter? Or at least of him? By her reaction, it seemed—"

"Now, Kate, I want you to listen." He pointed the news clipping at her like a warning finger. "I am invitin' you to look through this box because it was Olive's, and I think you have a right to know a little more about the woman who's probably hauntin' ya. I also think it's nice to see young folks take an interest in the history of where they live and learn about the tough lives of those that came before 'em. I'm not sayin' you don't work hard for a livin', but, with all due respect, I assume you've got a college education and that findin' work durin' a boomin' peacetime economy didn't treat you too bad. Everyone's got their story, their challenges, but relatively speakin'—at the risk of soundin' like an ornery old coot—you youngin's have had it pretty darn good. And I think that might make ya pretty naïve."

It was like a yardstick had slapped her wrists, and she didn't understand why. Tears heated up in the corner of her eyes. She blinked quickly as she nodded to Leo in agreement like a child in the principal's office.

"When a person's tellin' tales about someone else's past, it isn't to say sometimes they ain't tellin' their *own* tales. I don't pretend to know the full of it, but Vera's history is tied up in this place somehow. She won't open up to me about it, but whether she likes it or not, no matter how thick the walls she bricks up around her, her heart is right out there on her sleeve when certain things come up and poke a nerve. Sure, she just gets angry and clams up right away, but she has no defense against her reflexes. I've had enough conversations with her over the years to've isolated some'a the buzz words. And for whatever reason, Alonzo Ashby is one of 'em."

Kate dropped her gaze to the shoebox and chewed her bottom lip. "I'm sorry," she said after a time, her voice gritty with the shame lodged in her throat.

"Now, now, I'm not askin' for apologies. I'm just explainin' to you why it was completely stupid of *me* to go tellin' you 'bout it right there in the basement in fronta' her. I should'a known better, and I want to be sure that, if it ever comes up again in her presence, *you'll* know better than to say anythin' about it. You couldn't've known better before, yeh see, but now you do. *Capiche?*"

That was it. The last of the Jenga blocks to be pulled before the whole weight of Kate's awful day came crashing down on her.

Sitting with her hands clasped between her knees, she caved forward in quiet sobs. She squeezed her eyes closed, shutting out Leo, Olive's shoebox, Aggie jumping and pawing at an unseen guest, and the apartment that looked too much like hers. In the darkness she saw Dex, saw the lakeshore she would bike south along the next day to work, saw the hamster maze of cubicles in the Adler basement where she'd have to confront him again.

And behind it all, she saw the flashing golden bulbs of the Green Mill, remembered drinking dirty gin martinis with Dex there every Friday night when she'd lived up north in his condo. Wondered what exactly had happened there on a cold winter night when the calendar flipped from 1926 to 1927.

"Here, child," came Leo's warm grumble. "You'll feel better when you get somethin' warm and hearty in yer stomach."

New Year's Day 1927

Eyes closed, Lon drummed his hands on the table to the bluesy rhythm of "Nobody Knows You When You're Down and Out."

As it turned out, however, someone at the Green Mill had indeed known him in the wee hours of this morning. A few of them, in fact, seated at the half-moon booth nearest the door. They'd recognized Lon as soon as he'd entered and beckoned him to sit. It was a welcome rescue after he'd allowed Effie to slither her silvery, scaly way out of his hands and back into the waters of the mainstream.

The waitress had come over with a coffee cup, into which Lon had emptied his flask. And when that had been drained in two gulps, a generous benefactor within Lon's usual late-night-drinking, early-sunrise-basking clique poured a little moonshine from his hollow cane.

"Panther Piss," his friend had said, wrapping his arm around Lon's shoulder.

As three-sheets-to-the-wind as he was, with every sip, Lon still had to grimace at the drink's special bathtub ingredient.

Feeling the music and keeping his eyes shut, he puckered his lips and bobbed his head in circular motions. The drumsticks beat against his breastbone, and the pianist's fingers tapped along the muscles of his shoulders while the spirit of the homemade hooch spiraled around his closed eyelids in every color he could possibly mix on his painter's palette.

He sat at the end of the booth seat that curved around to face the stage. With his back to the door, icy air briefly rushed against his neck and stood his hairs on end. His skin prickled as it once again warmed, though the chill traveled down his spine and arms.

He opened his eyes.

Slicing through his view of the jazz band, Lon saw the lean, blackened figure that had just entered. His skull wavered on his neck and his undulating vision registered what he believed must be a very thin black bear, come all the way down from his Aunt Estella's wooded Wisconsin estate.

The animal didn't appear to have ears, though. Its head was rather smooth and bell-shaped for a bear, like it was wearing a steel helmet left over from the war.

"Hmm," Lon groaned out loud, jutting out his lower lip and scanning around the booth. His friends looked too lost in song, drink, and necking to perceive the threat of an enemy black bear soldier in their midst.

Lon wasn't, though. He would keep an eye on it and beat it to death with his friend's hollowed-out cane if the animal stepped out of line. The cane still rested within easy reach beside him from when he'd poured his last drink.

That bear was just lucky it had that helmet to protect it.

Lon's pout reclined into a sneer. He took a big swig of panther whiskey from his coffee mug and grasped his companion's cane, waiting and ready.

What he wasn't prepared for, however, was when the bear began to shed its hide.

As the black fur slid from the creature's shoulders, assuming its place was a white swan's neck. An elegant swan in a twinkling black dress. The swan removed its helmet to shake out a bob of wavy dark hair that glinted with bronzy-gold whenever light hit it. Ripples of chocolate stopped at the nape of that long, delicately pale neck.

"My God," he whispered.

"Lon. Ay, Lonnie!" one of his pals bellowed at that precise moment. "We need you to help settle a bet!"

Lon shook his head at the request and begged for the guy not to say another word.

"Lonnie, listen!"

Too late. The swan flicked its head to the side, then rotated its body around to stare Lon straight in the eye.

Eva thought her heart might stop when she heard Lon's name and turned to see him seated there, a mere two strides away from where she stood.

She hadn't at all expected to run into him; she only knew it was a place he'd spoken of with great frequency and fondness. With promises to take her there one day.

They'd never gotten the chance, of course. She'd never expected to, only hoped. Within the sanctity of hopes like that, her dreams could stay alive. Visiting the Green Mill for her first time on this night, she'd only wanted to throw her dreams a little something more to chew on.

She'd already been smiling at the music and the liberation it pulsed through her veins. And when she'd turned around, she only smiled broader on seeing Lon. She beamed liked an idiot, in fact; she knew that. All she would've hoped for in return was a quarter of that dopey grin.

Not the visible recoil she actually received.

Aside from his expression of disgust, Lon didn't look good. Not at all. Time and drink had flushed his face in splotches and given it an unhealthy bloat. His half-mast eyelids looked puffy, and his watery eyes underneath were bloodshot and goggling as he slid out from the table and stood to face her.

He was dressed in one of his finer suits, which Eva assumed meant he'd engaged in special New Year's Eve plans. She automatically looked at the people he'd been sitting with to identify whether he had a date that night. Everyone seated was dressed nicely but with a less polished, eccentric bohemian flair — the Water Tower "Towertown" artists he associated with, likely. The men wore rumpled suit jackets over wool sweaters, and from what Eva could see above the table, the women wore scanty, low-cut dresses.

The group also all appeared coupled off — including Lon and the pretty-faced, ripe-lipped young man who'd had his arm thrown around him. There was an androgynous grace in this man's posture, and his arm seemed to wait for Lon's return as it rested along the top of the booth back, stroking the cushion with his thumb. His eyes didn't meet Eva's but appeared to size her up and down, just as she did to him.

She wondered if perhaps Lon experimented with more than just painting technique with his artist colony. If he hadn't, in fact, confided everything about himself that summer when they'd lain beneath the stars and talked until sunrise. It made perfect if not gutting sense, given the insistent distance he'd kept between them since that first kiss on the stairway. How else could a man resist the closeness they'd shared otherwise? Perhaps it hadn't been willpower, after all — perhaps it had taken more willpower *to* kiss her and keep up certain appearances. She was one to know how far one could be willing to go for that. And perhaps…

Eva wavered on her feet. *Perhaps* he wasn't the only man in her life hiding behind such a mask.

A club patron bumped into her, and she almost lost her footing as the jagged little pieces clicked into place. Looking back to Lon, she scanned him up and down like his companion had to her, noticing for the first time her friend was gripping a cane. She hoped he wasn't injured.

"Lon?" she said, soft enough to avoid shouting, though loud enough to hear over the music.

Lon teetered, despite having the cane at his disposal for balance. His mouth hung open, and his eyes squinted — cruelly, Eva thought.

"Lon?" she asked again, taking a step toward him.

As if on instinct, he lifted the cane and pointed its end at her.

"You *do* know me, Lonnie?" Eva asked.

"Nnoo, I don't," he said thickly. "Ssstay…'way frummy." He waggled the cane in the air. "Don' moovve."

Eva stayed where she was, fiddling with her hat and fur. She shifted her gaze from his cane tip to his friends, silently beseeching them for understanding. She caught the eyes of one man seated in the center of the booth, who right away yelled out, "Hey! Hey, aren't you — ?"

Lon turned on him instantly. "Don' ssayit. Don' thinkit!"

"But, Lonnie, isn't that — ?"

Lon cracked the cane down on the table. "Shiss *nobody*. You hear that? No. Body." He heavily rolled his head back in Eva's direction, ignoring the protests of his group. "Get outta here!" he yelled at her.

Though she felt the burn at the backs of her eyes, Eva refused to cry. Not again this night, not ever if she could help it. "Lonnie, think who you're talking to. It's me, old boy. It's me, E——"

Crack!

"I said scram!"

At the second whip of the cane against the table, the women of Lon's party shrieked and the men reached to seize the stick from him just as the bartender came around to enforce security.

Seeing Lon struggle against them, outnumbered, Eva cried, "No, wait! Please, let him go! Let me speak to him! He's harmless!"

"Baloney, lady!" the bartender bellowed. "Time for the ossified to meet an officer, but not in my joint. You fellas take this guy and gettim outta here. Go on, screw!"

Lon writhed and shouted his entire way out of the establishment, deprived of his weapon at last. Two of his male friends helped a Green Mill employee hold him in place until a taxi or police car would inevitably roll by, whichever came first.

Eva stepped out right behind them, still reaching for their tight grips and imploring them to release him. When no one paid her mind, she circled to stand in front of Lon. She laid her hands on his mottled cheeks.

"Lonnie," she whispered. "It's okay. Please, just be calm, old boy. I'm here with you. I'll see you home."

Lon still glared at her above the blue-veined bags rimming his eyes, but their corners watered, and she couldn't discern whether his lower lip trembled out of anger or remorse.

"Lonnie?" Eva asked, caressing his face with her kidskin-gloved hands and kissing his forehead, then his nose. His breath was harsh, but he quieted and held still. She looked to his companions. "Gentleman, I can take it from here if you'll allow. I can see him home safely and ensure he sleeps this off right away. Please."

The burly bouncer appeared not one iota convinced, but he stood back and folded his arms in a defensive stance. Lon's friends on either side of him looked across at one another and shrugged, loosening their hold on each of his arms.

A green-and-tan Checker taxi slowed as it approached the street-side group, and Eva waved it to stop. "Okay, Lonnie, here we go." She clicked open the back door and stood behind it, waiting for him to follow as she put her black mink coat and hat back on.

At a snail's pace, he dragged his feet one by one toward the car door. He was two steps away when one of his friends—the one Eva had scrutinized earlier—leaned in toward the other and murmured, "I say, fellow, I think you're right. That's Eva Redcliffe."

Having just poised one hand on the edge of the taxi door, Lon spun to wield it in a fist at whichever man stood closest.

Uproar ensued as Lon punched one of his companions in the gut and cracked the other on the jaw before taking a swipe at the bouncer, who caught his fist and twisted it behind Lon's back.

Eva's scream had barely discharged from her throat when the man already had Lon kissing asphalt on Broadway Avenue. Club patrons rushed outside to watch the commotion.

"Call the cops," the bouncer yelled from his wrestler's pose to an assisting employee. "Have 'em pick this guy up at the cemetery, north side."

"Hey, lady!" the taxi driver called out the open door. "You need a ride or what? I'm not gettin' involved in this mess."

"Oh, yes you is," the bouncer shouted up from the street. "You're luggin' this guy down to Graceland. Why don't ya dump 'im at the corner of Montrose and Clark. I don't need the fuzz bustin' this place on New Year's."

"Yeah, yeah," the driver barked back, "like you don't got 'em all in your pockets anyway."

"Hey, pal, it's a chance I don't wanna waste on this guy." He eyed Eva up and down. "This bird'll compensate you handsomely for it, I'm sure."

Eva had been standing with a hand at her lips, paralyzed by the appalling exchange, but she finally lowered it to clench both hands in fists at her sides. She straightened her neck and set her jaw. "If I get in this taxi with him, it'll be to take him home. There will be no undignified dumping at a graveyard, thank you."

"Forget it," the driver asserted. "I'm not chauffeuring that tramp anywhere. And *you* shouldn't either if ya wanna save your neck. You're either in or you're out, lady. I can get you away from this fella in two shakes."

Rubbing her thumbs over her curled fingers, Eva tightened and loosened her fists a few times before lifting one to slam the taxi door shut and wave the driver away. Numb, she staggered to Lon's pathetic figure and kneeled on the pavement to run her fingers through his hair.

So much for not crying in 1927.

"Hey!" She heard among the crowd that had gathered on the sidewalk, "Isn't that Eva Redcliffe?"

XVII

Lon pried his eyelashes apart and rubbed away the crust that had cemented them together. The veins of his temples pounded, and his brain felt shrunken to the size of a walnut. Peeling his dried and rough lips apart, he repeatedly sucked his cottony tongue away from the roof of his mouth in a futile attempt to produce saliva.

Before his fuzzy vision could train on anything in the darkened room, he felt the cool compress of glass against his lips, then water dribbling in between them. He lapped it up in unquestioning relief, and only when he felt the glass leave did he move his head to view the savior beside him—a darkened, twinkling silhouette that reached to brush Lon's hair back from his sweaty forehead.

"Eva," Lon croaked.

"Shhh, Lonnie. It's all right. You're home now."

A patch of dryness twinged in his throat, and he convulsed with a few closed-mouth coughs as he rolled his head to the other side. "Whose home?" he whispered when he'd regained his breathing.

"Mine. I wasn't positive if yours was still Camden Court."

He coughed again and, with a sore arm, rubbed his chin, feeling where it had scraped on the asphalt. "It is. But Finlay…What time is it?"

"It's all right, Lon. It's approaching two o'clock in the afternoon. Finlay knows I'm here with you, and the servants are downstairs, so there's nothing untoward in this. He's gone out for a ride in the country, having luncheon with his parents, and isn't due back until evening. He'll send on my regards and apologies to them with great tact, don't you worry, old boy. Finlay's a gentleman if he's anything."

Squeezing his eyes, Lon huffed as he struggled to sit up on his elbows. He could see that beneath the bedcovers he wore a pair of men's silk pajamas, blue as a robin's egg; he had a vague recollection of someone assisting him into them. A taller man than Finlay, Lon's wrists extended from where the sleeves fell short. "I don't know, I don't un—"

Eva pressed her fingers to his lips and shushed him again. "I said it's all right. I've dealt with it, Lon. That's all you need to know right now."

With a tremor in his chin, he lay back down and ground his fists in his eyes as the hot tears ran. He didn't say anything, just shook in quiet whimpers as he heard the two thuds of Eva's kicked-off shoes and felt the mattress yield to her shifting weight. When the movement stopped, though she was above the cover, he felt the warmth of her body running the full length of his side, and her arm wrapped around his waist as her nose nuzzled just below his ear. When Eva squeezed him, however, it wasn't seduction he sensed. She was merely being there for him, just as she'd promised so many starry nights ago.

And, as he would learn, she'd been at the police station for him as well. Giving her statement as a witness, she'd failed to stir any sympathy for Lon's behavior at the club. Particularly not when another witness—one of Lon's evidently fickle artist friends who, granted, had to testify with a swollen jaw—alerted the police to the fact that Lon had threatened Eva with a cane. Said hollowed and booze-filled cane, however, had been conveniently abandoned just around the corner from the scene of altercation, which might have weakened this friend's story somewhat.

In the end, Lon had been charged, fingerprinted, and made to smile for the camera while, as he also later learned, Eva had contended with another line of questioning.

The police had been notified just past one a.m. that she'd gone missing. One Mr. Finlay Redcliffe had expressed concern when he'd excused himself from New Year's festivities at his in-laws' to check on his wife next door, whom he'd put to bed shortly after midnight. Having had an argument that evening, he'd felt distressed at leaving her alone and wished to properly apologize and encourage her to return to the Hughes party at his side. It was to his great astonishment that he'd found the bed empty and a note left for him on his pillow, which read:

> Darling,
>
> My dear girl Millie Barry has phoned me in distress. I gave my excuses of the late hour, but she simply begged for my company. I must dash, thus, to her parents' residence on Lake View Avenue — only just around the corner, darling — to mend the poor girl's heart. Should it get too late, I shall have accommodation there for the remainder of the evening. Until morning, my love. Do not fret for me. I am so very near and have walked these streets from the very day I could walk at all.
>
> To a Happier New Year,
> Your Evie

Naturally, Finlay had fretted and rang the Barrys at once. When there was no answer, he set off around the corner to walk the few blocks down Lake View Avenue, stopping just shy of Fullerton at the Barry home. No one had answered his rapping at the door. The Barrys had either been out for the evening or away for the holidays; whatever their whereabouts, Eva had not been there.

On his arrival at the station, Finlay had rejoiced at the sight of his wife but just as readily pushed her out of their hug and held her at arm's length as he interrogated.

Every one of her answers had been deemed unsatisfactory — especially how she'd presumed she would justify her black cocktail dress as appropriate attire for a shoulder to cry on after midnight. In truth, Eva's heady champagne state had prevented her from thinking that far ahead.

Nonetheless, by some sense of benevolent grace, Finlay had succumbed to her entreaties to post bail on Lon's behalf and allowed her to bring Lon home with them and put him up in their guest bedroom.

"He's my friend, and he's ill," she'd stated. "He has no one else here to care for him."

All Finlay had requested at that time of Eva, the police, and any remaining witnesses was that the Redcliffe and Hughes names be left out of the entire affair—that, as far as anyone was concerned, Eva had fallen asleep in her own bed after she'd left her parents' party, and no one had seen either her or himself at the Green Mill or police station. Additional "donations" into ready palms helped secure their secrecy.

All this Lon would come to learn soon enough, but lying side by side with Eva on the Redcliffe's guest bed, all he could do was let out the tears and will himself to stay alive against the agony tearing up his insides.

"Phew!" Eva whooped softly in his ear as she wiped his face dry. "Old boy, I do believe you're the most flammable I've known you. Good thing our matches are tucked safely out of reach. Your breath would ignite this entire house."

Lon groaned and hiccupped a pocket of putrid air. "Panther whiskey."

"Lon, are you mad? They use *fusel oil* in that. They say it causes hallucinations and violence. No wonder…" She shook her head and snorted. "Must I stock your icebox with cases of Father's near-beer instead?"

She nudged his arm, to which he groaned even more. Taking his hand in hers, she said, "Oh, look, old boy. I didn't know what all you'd consumed last night, but I never questioned it was anything *but* the liquor talking back there. And I understand what your intentions were, and they were admirable. You were protecting me—not only my reputation but my marriage. And, Lonnie—" she rubbed her nose at his earlobe like a friendly kitten prodding him to play "—I love you for it. Thank you, friend."

Lon lifted his other hand to lay it on hers in turn. While it was a challenge to speak in his strained voice, he paced himself as he scratched out, "Thank *you* for returning me home safely, for taking such risks to do it. I'll pay Finlay every cent of it back." Eva tutted, but Lon squeezed and shook her hand. "Listen. I was a poor friend from the moment I abandoned you in that alleyway and cut you out of my life. No real gentleman would do that. Ah-ah-ah!" he croaked when sounds in Eva's throat signaled more protest.

Lon swallowed, trying to lubricate the rest of his hoarse words. "You're right that my intentions were good. You deserve a chance at happiness, and I think you could find it with Finlay. But when you—" He cleared his throat. "When you kissed me at the theater—" He cleared his throat again. "I wanted to be there for you, Eva, but

I couldn't be your crutch. Forgive me for putting it that way, but I can't be. Not *that* way."

He broke off in a fit of dry coughing, and Eva rose to retrieve the crystal water goblet and bring it back to his lips. Lon likewise sat up, sipping the water as the glass rapidly tapped his lower teeth—Eva's hand was trembling as she held it. He pulled his head away and rolled onto his side, facing her as he leaned on his elbow. Though green was her best color, he felt, she was no less striking in the navy silk dress she wore, its billowing long sleeves tapered into cuffs hugging her slim wrists. She replaced the goblet and returned to his side, her clasped hands seeming to hold themselves still.

"It's the thrill of the chase, can't you see?" he resumed in a clearer though distinctly deeper quality of voice. "Forgive me for flattering myself this much, but I fear you painted me onto an urn that summer. You're good to accept me as I am, but I'm afraid you've perhaps added extra strokes of color and light to my character where you should have shaded. I don't think you'd want me if you had me." He coughed into his hand. "And you *can't* have me, Eva. I do love you, old girl, but I can't in the way I feared you wanted me to."

Eva gave a grave nod, smiling sadly as though he'd only affirmed something she'd already known.

"Not in the way *any* of them have wanted me to," Lon continued, wincing at the memory of Effie. "I tried before, but now I've finally realized I'm done going through the motions with women. I don't know who I've been trying to kid."

Swallowing and bobbing her head once more, Eva picked at the bedcovers. "So what, then? Are you exiling me again? Am I never to see you, just as I haven't when you've only been down the block all this time? Despite how emphatically I just fought my husband for our friendship? Enough that he's allowed you to sleep under our roof and trusts me alone with you all day?"

She cocked her head at him.

"Lon, I erred terribly at the Biograph, and I'll apologize for that until the day I die. I-I clearly presumed too much and took advantage of your kindness. And I'll own that, yes, it was for the reasons you've stated. But it's yet another new year; we get to turn a new leaf and move on." She slapped her hand down on the bed in the narrow space between them. "Besides, old boy, how could I possibly idealize you when you threatened to swat me with a cane, then spit up all over my brand new Chanel on the drive home?"

Lon dropped his head back and slapped his forehead with his palm to the sound of Eva's wicked laughter.

"You're a naughty boy, Lonnie, but you're *my* boy. You've been trying so hard, I know. And now I see that you haven't been able to fully be who you are, have you? And that's sent you spiraling, has it?"

Lon's cheeks burned. He'd underestimated how well Eva could see through him, even if perhaps she'd only suspected the half of it…

"Well," she said, "I'm not about to stand by and simply watch you sink into the vortex. You're stuck with me, for better or for worse, so you'd better start being more honest. With yourself and with me."

Lon moaned again. "Why would you inflict so much work onto yourself?"

"Because with you, old boy, it doesn't feel like work, not really. And even if it does, I'm willing. I don't even question that."

Lon lifted his head and looked into her eyes with the first genuine grin he'd had on his face in months.

"Say," she added, "how about after a little more lying in and a quick lunch, we go pick up Ollie and take her ice skating? The crisp air will do you good, as will falling hard on your bottom a few times. Oh, come, let's do it. Ollie will be over the moon to see you again! I neglected to check on that little rascal last night and don't think she's quite forgiven me for doing whatever she's convinced I'd done to drive you away. Having *me* is apparently little consolation. She's gone quiet this winter, rather withdrawn into hibernation, so I believe the air and exercise will do her tremendous good, too."

Lon grunted his compliance, a bit remorseful that in forsaking Eva a year ago, with all the best of intentions, he'd forsaken Ollie's innocent friendship as well.

Eva lay back down on her side and curled into him. Pulling his elbow out from beneath his weight, Lon extended his arm as a pillow for her neck.

"Lon?"

The question vibrated into his chest.

"Mm?"

"I really do love you, you know."

"I know."

"And Lon?"

"Mhm?"

"You deserve a chance at happiness, too. If there's anything I can do, darling, to bring you closer to it, you only have to ask me once."

Lon kissed the hair just above her ear. In the peace of the moment, it seemed mere seconds before all consciousness dimmed to black.

"Lon? Lon!" Eva shrieked, shaking him awake as if to raise the dead.

"Mm?" He peeked an eye open to see that she was above the bed covers and dressed in a hat, wool coat, and gloves. She smelled of ice, but it wasn't the frozen winds trapped in her bottle of Chanel N°5 this time. On closer inspection, he jolted out of his stupor and seized her biceps in alarm. She was hysterical, shaking, her face red and shining. "Good God, Eva, what's happened?"

"Please, Lon, dress quickly. You must help — must help —" her breath caught as she hyperventilated "— you must help us find Ollie!"

"What!" He was out of the bed and already reaching for his trousers. Eva still breathed spastically, but she got to her feet and carried over to him a clean shirt and outerwear of Finlay's.

"I-I…I woke before you, a-and saw to getting some sandwiches made to-to pack and bring to Ollie. B-But when I went…to fetch her…my parents said they thought she'd gone to find *me* and assumed she was here. But she's not, and she's not there, and, oh, I just can't believe this is happening!"

Looking at her intently, Lon sat to tug on his shoes. "And you're quite sure she's not hiding somewhere about either of the houses?"

"No. My parents have had every member of staff help search. Neighbors, friends, too. Everyone is outside right now combing the park and streets, and Finlay's rushing back. Oh, Lon, what if she's gone skating by herself and fallen through the ice! What if she gets lost and freezes or is kidnapped! Or —"

Lon stood again and buttoned Finlay's overcoat; it fit tightly. He lifted Finlay's fedora and kneaded its brim in his fingers. Darting his sight along the carpet, he forced himself to consider all the scenarios even if they were too dreadful to bear.

"Or, Lon," Eva said, her voice regulated and soft, "what if…what if she ran away."

Something in her tone, in the way she'd stated it more than suggested it, alerted Lon to swiftly put the hat on, approach Eva, and hold her arms again. Ducking his head to her height, he forced her to look him in the eye as he searched hers. "What makes you think that, Eva?"

With a dull, dazed expression, Eva looked down and off to the side, then lowered her head toward her wringing hands. Lon looked down at them, too, and saw the plain gold band she twisted around her ring finger.

"What's that you're wearing?" he asked. "Where's your emerald? Your wedding band?"

Eva's face crumpled, and she shook again. "They've gone missing, too."

July 2000

Tears dried, Kate was about to replace the lid on Olive's old shoebox and join Leo in his kitchen when something shiny twinkled from beneath the newspaper scraps. Reaching in to fish out whatever was tucked down in the box's corner, she felt a little slender object and a thin chain. She raised it into the light.

Suspended from her fingers was a long gold necklace with a tiny golden spoon for a pendant.

"Soup's on, hon!" Leo called from his hallway.

Looking up to him, she asked, "What's this cute thing? Were spoons ever in fashion?"

His lips twisted. "Oh, boy. That doesn't look very good for our Olive, now does it."

"Huh?"

"It's just that, well, I heard a' those sorts of things bein' popular among the flappers. The wilder ones with some money, which young gals like that didn't always come into by the most honest of means."

"Why, because it's gold?"

Scratching his chin, he said, "Because of what it's used for."

"They used these? It's way too tiny for food."

"But small enough for a nostril. They scooped cocaine with 'em." Leo rubbed his chin with more pressure; Kate could again hear his whiskers scratch at his calluses. "I don't know what that Olive got herself into as a youth, but for a teenage runaway who left her family's wealth behind, I just have to wonder…"

Kate finished the sentence he'd left hanging: "By what less than 'honest' means Olive's own money came from."

Seven for a Secret
Never to be Told

July 2000

Acloud of white powder settled into their hair and onto their matching polo shirts. Coughing and waving it out of their eyes, they snorted out air to keep the particles from getting up their noses.

"Well, *that's* not how it was supposed to work," said a young man.

"Back to the drawing board," Kate moaned. "Maybe instead of flour we should use sugar."

"Or white sand."

"Yeah, good idea."

"Okay, I'll see what I can find and I'll make a run to the store if we're out."

Kate saluted her coworker and wheeled the activity cart out of the conference room, down the hall, and parked it outside her cubicle in the dim fluorescent lighting of Adler Planetarium's basement. She hadn't thought simulating moon craters would take up the better part of her Monday morning.

But, like her peaceful meal with Leo the night before, it was a good distraction. She hadn't had to see or think very much about Dex. Or Olive, for that matter, who hadn't made any repeat performances while Kate showered that morning. And between Leo's dinner and the morning, NyQuil had sunken Kate into sweet oblivion.

She sat at her desk, shaking and patting away residual flour, and turned to her computer to check email. Her monitor had barely woken from its planet screensaver when a high-low, "Hiii-ii," invaded her territory. She spun back around toward the aisle.

"Hiii-ii," Kate mimicked. *Fuck off*, she inwardly sang with the same inflection.

"So," said Vicki, the volunteer coordinator, with round eyes and a confidential hush. "I heard. I'm so sorry."

"Heard what?" Kate asked sharply.

"Yoouu-knoow," Vicki replied in that damn high-low pitch. She'd been standing outside Kate's cubicle wall with hands and head peering over it but now took the liberty to step inside. Hunching down, she whispered, "You and Dexter."

"Oh," Kate whispered back, "well, don't worry about it because we're fine."

Vicki pinched her brows together and huffed sharply as her head pushed back on her neck like a chicken's. "That's not what *I* heard."

Placing her elbows on the side-extension of her L-shaped desk, Kate stacked her hands and rested her head on them, looking up at her coworker. "Well, do enlighten me. What happened in *my* private life that you would know better?"

That same huff and another jerk of Vicki's chicken-neck. "Sorry, Kate. I just heard you'd broken up, that's all. That's what Dexter's telling everyone."

Kate opened her mouth to retort but found it empty. She resorted to pishing and narrowed her eyes as she collected her words. "I think you've misunderstood. We're still together."

"Oh," Vicki chirped, not appearing convinced. "Well, that's great. Sorry for the misunderstanding. Myyy-baaad." Her eyes rounded again, and with a plastic grin she said, "Okay, have a good day!" and left to Monday-morning-small-talk somewhere else down the row.

Kate chomped on a pen and swiveled back to her computer. Squeezing the cheap plastic in her teeth, she heard it creak just before another voice sounded behind her.

"Hey."

She knew without turning around who it was. Spitting the pen out onto her keyboard, Kate leaned back and slowly spun back around. "I knooow," she groaned.

"When were you going to tell me?" Her good friend and colleague, Blair, had waltzed in from the cube next door and sat on Kate's side desk, staring her down with fierce amber eyes. Of the friends Kate had considered calling to go out the prior evening, Blair was the closest to thirty and fell in the category of "Perfect Relationship." Subcategory: "Patronizing Advice."

"It *just happened.* I don't know why Dex is already telling everybody."

"First of all, you know Dexter better than that. I doubt he's told *everybody.* More likely Vicki just overheard him talking to one of the guys. Second of all, if a guy that private is telling anyone anything already, it's probably because he's hurt as hell." Blair flicked her dark brown hair behind her shoulder. "You dumped him, didn't you?"

"No, I didn't."

"Buuut?"

"Buuut, we're going to start seeing other people, too. That's nothing out of the ordinary." As it came out of her mouth, Kate realized that last sentence was more for her own assurance than Blair's.

"That's true," Blair said, nodding and pouting out her lower lip. It gave her chin a lumpy texture that, like the rest of her judgmental expression, was an unappealing feature on an otherwise attractive face. "But it works better the other way around, doesn't it? Play the field, *then* narrow it down to just the one?"

"Blair! Look, that's great you found your guy, you've stayed exclusive, and now you're engaged. Hurray for conventional chronology! But it's different for everyone, and I think it'd be worse if I'd asked Dex to take a break. I don't know anyone whose break wasn't a break-up in disguise, do you? Ross and Rachel, *hellooo?* I'm not going to deal with bullshit euphemisms, and I'm not going to deal with bullshit conventions. Dex and I were very straightforward about this, and I think it takes a great deal of emotional maturity to pull it off."

"I guess so. What I don't get, though, is how it works being serious with someone for such a long time and then suddenly dating someone else, too. Rebounding after a break-up is one thing, but how do you do intimacy with more than one at the same time?"

Kate cocked her brow with a saucy smirk. "Chinese finger cuffs?"

"You know what I mean. How will you alternate back and forth between guys like that? At the most basic level, it just doesn't sound sanitary."

"We're not sleeping with other people. That's where we drew the line."

"So? There's plenty else you can do to get around *that* technicality. And intimacy's more than sex." Blair shook her head and looked into the air as if she could see all the possibilities orbiting above them. "If I knew the man I love was out there forging an emotional connection with someone else—I mean, if that were Brad, I would *freak. Out.* And it wouldn't even take that. Even if he just went out on a string of superficial dates. God, that might be worse!"

Kate adjusted in her chair. "Why?"

"*Think* about it, Kate: Dexter taking some other girl out on romantic candlelit dinners, trying too hard to make clever jokes because he's actually nervous about impressing her. And she *will* laugh because she thinks he's cute and wants him to like her. And then he reaches across the table to take her hand and tells her how beautiful she looks, and then before you know it, they're inviting each other to weddings and meeting each other's friends and family, and while they're slow-dancing, Dexter sings along to 'Wonderful Tonight' in her ear, and—"

"Dex would never sing that," Kate said flatly. As that, however, was the only item on Blair's list she could refute with certainty, her stomach quaked.

"Whatever. Are you visualizing the reality of this, Kate? You're seriously cool with him doing the meeting-chicks-drunk-at-bars thing again? Setting his buddies up to play wing-men so he can meet the big-boobed blonde who's smiling at him from across the room?"

Kate maintained her best poker face. "Yes."

"Getting to have butterflies and awkward first-date kisses all over again?"

"Yes."

"With someone *else*. And then coming over the next day and kissing and sleeping with *you*. And maybe feeling less satisfied afterward or not in the mood to do it to begin with because the comparisons are so fresh. Between her, who doesn't criticize him and still dresses up all sexy and Brazilian waxes, and you, who wears sweatpants to bed, picks fights, and probably laughs harder these days at queefs you make in front of him than his corny jokes. You two are cool with that?"

"Yes."

"Well, awesome! Good for you! Let me know how that goes. In the meantime, I'm sure Dexter's pumped knowing that he's not enough for you." Blair hopped down and withdrew her pseudo-optimism from the cubicle to return to her own.

Kate swiveled back toward her computer and picked up her pen. Holding its ends in each hand, she pressed her thumbs against the clear shaft of plastic as a poor substitute for a stress-relief ball. Blair's audacious words and the images they conjured swirled in her head until — *crack!* She'd split the pen in two, and ink bled over her hands and lap.

"Shit." She held her splayed hands out and assessed the damage. Fortunately, she'd paired her blue Adler polo with a black pencil skirt that day for some semblance of workplace chic, so the black ink wouldn't stain that. As for the shirt, she had half a dozen in her closet at home to take its place and could borrow one of the red volunteer shirts for the time being.

"Oh, Kate, I'm sorry," she heard Blair say, and when Kate turned around to see her friend back at her cubicle, the apologetic sentiments changed to "Oh, shit!" once Blair saw Kate's Bic bloodbath.

"Don't worry about it." Kate wheeled back in her chair and got up. "You've done enough for me this morning. Go take it easy. And if anyone asks, I went out to buy marshmallows for the air-pressure demos."

She slid past Blair, not caring whether she inked her friend's outfit on her way by.

After a bathroom break of crying, changing her shirt in the stall, and washing her arms in the sink, Kate speed-walked past her cubicle world, through the security door, and into the blackened lower level of the museum.

Dexter's favorite exhibits in this gallery were the antique star charts and astrolabes. But Kate's had always been off in a corner in the recreated medieval classroom where kids could dress in tunics and sit at wooden desks to learn about early astronomical tools. Tucked away was a display case housing an illuminated stained glass sundial from antiquity. And beside that was a little window seat in the classroom wall where visitors could rest and admire the relic.

Sitting there, Kate focused on the dial's intricate and lovely hand-painted details: the banner of numbers for the hour of day, the signs of the zodiac, and the sun at the top bearing a mild expression on its face as it warmed all below with its mustard-yellow tint. Kate knew the dial had withstood five centuries and could still serve its purpose if set in one of the main windows upstairs. That's perhaps

what she loved most about it; that it was relegated to a hidden corner
to help preserve its integrity—saved as a special secret for only the
lucky to discover.

About ten minutes into her serenity, hushed voices echoed among
the exhibits. Kate straightened up, ready to explain the classroom
and sundial should a member of the public wander in.

Instead, she heard a familiar high-low pitched "III-knooow," followed by a peal of laughter. "It's a way to track the relative *positions*
of *heavenly bodies*."

"Oh, brother," Kate muttered under her breath at Vicki's transparent
double entendres. She must be flirting with one of the volunteers again.

"That's actually correct. Anything else?" came a male voice, less
flirtatious but hugely more unsettling. It was Dexter.

"Weeell," Vicki sang, "more or less. Those *bodies* are always on the
move, you know? Orbiting and *intersecting* and *colliding*—at least as
they appear to the *naked* eye."

"That so?" Dex replied. "But have you ever explained to your
volunteers how an astrolabe works?"

God, Dex. Kate almost pitied how not suave he sounded when
thrown such obvious bait—until she remembered she didn't want
him to be good at this.

Especially not with Vicki the Robot who was good at following
directions and spitting out information fed to her, but not particularly
creative when it came to processing and transforming that information into meaningful knowledge for children. She hadn't shown the
slightest innovation in creating new activities for her volunteers,
instead dumping it onto Kate's department while Vicki treated the
workday as a prolonged happy hour, minus the alcohol (as far as
Kate knew). For the first time, Kate was witnessing Vicki's one true
creative talent in action.

And she had the body to back it. She was the one female in the
office whose hourglass figure actually managed to fill out her standard-
issue polo shirt in a flattering way. Not heavy or thin, just buxom
in all the right places, and her baby-smooth skin and long, thick
auburn hair gave her an almost mystical mermaid quality that just
did not sync with the pallid, earthy atmosphere of the subterranean
Adler workspace. Passion for science, education, and working with
children and the public was what drew employees and volunteers
here. But Vicki...

Apart from relieving the museum of its urgent, last-minute need to fill the position, the only value Vicki added as volunteer coordinator was getting mankind to explore *her* final frontier. The Astro-Overnights for children made for adult sleepovers in her office.

Unable to take Vicki seriously, Dex usually deferred her training requests to Kate and other education staff, but now he'd let the Robot get him out into the gallery. After his outstanding efforts to avoid Kate all morning, he probably just needed distraction, but this was downright desperation.

Kate leaned over just enough to peek through the classroom window at the display case where they stood. They didn't seem to notice.

"Well…" Vicki trilled and pressed her finger to the glass to point at an astrolabe.

Kate *hated* when people smudged the display glass.

"Maybe if you give me a smile for once, I'll tell you."

Dexter shifted on his feet, his shoulders hunched and hands in his pockets. He exhaled as he brought his chin to his chest, but his face did resurface with a tight grin.

Vicki hummed. "That's better, but let's turn that waning crescent into a waxing one."

Dex's shoulders lurched with a chuckle. Never failed: the way to that guy's inner peace was through outer space.

Oh, she's good.

"All right," Dex said, crossing his arms, "so show me you know how to work this tool."

Vicki tittered. "Oh, I know how to work *many* tools."

"C'mon. Tell me what you know about *this* one."

She pouted. "Someone woke up on the dark side of the moon."

Dex tilted his head with a sigh, but smiled and playfully ducked away when she poked him in the belly beneath his folded arms.

Now she knows that he's ticklish. And has good abs. Kate's turn to pout.

"Fine," Vicki said. "Sooo, those circular plates on the astro-*labia*—oops, I mean astrolabe—are al-*tit*-ude circles." As she said it, she dragged her index finger around the entire circumference of one breast.

Oh, gag. As Vicki paused for effect, Kate could tell from Dexter's raised brow that he wasn't buyin' it. She readied for him to shut that shit down and couldn't wait to hear what choice words he'd use.

All he said was, "Go on."

"And the al-*tit*-ude circles—" she traced both index fingers around both breasts, bringing them together at her breastbone "—*converge* on the *zenith*." She drew her hands down her torso, all the way to the fly of her short denim skirt, where they broke away and poised at her cocked hips.

Dex's posture straightened. His hands, thankfully, stayed in his pockets.

"Very impressive." He laughed, but there was an edge to it. It could've just been lingering vitriol toward Kate. But it also sounded suspiciously like the way he'd cheer on Kate's impromptu strip teases or when she'd discreetly rub his crotch at a crowded party as a signal to meet her in the coat closet.

In the beginning, that is…back when Kate *used* to do those things. Back when *she'd* laughed at his bad jokes, didn't criticize, dressed sexy, and bikini-waxed because she'd liked him and wanted him to like her.

Kate thought about the first time she'd heard that laugh: at the after-work happy hour when she'd first given Dex her number. That was the same night he'd also flirted with Vicki. Kate's selective memory—and the gin and tonics she'd drank all that night—had conveniently buried that observation. But the scene playing out before her now brought it all back. Yes, Dex had flirted first with Vicki but moved on to Kate after Vicki had moved on to three other non-Adler men at the bar.

Kate had gotten Dex by default.

She closed her eyes and leaned back, not caring to see what pantomime corresponded with Vicki's next statement, only hoping she was keeping her hands to herself: "The, uh, front side, you see, is a *projection* of a celestial hemisphere with the North *Pole* in the *center*."

That laugh again from Dex. The tragedy of it was that Kate was stuck. She had to sit there and endure the verbal foreplay.

Or did she? She had a right to walk back to the office and do her work. And making her presence known could bring the sordid thing to an end—and possibly mortify Dexter into never looking at or speaking to Vicki ever again. Or it would only delay the inevitable. Vicki wasn't one to miss her target once she'd locked him in the crosshairs.

Kate weighed her other option: staying put and quiet. It would be torture, but it would spare her any open embarrassment. The real beneficiary, though, would be Dexter, who'd be left to Vicki's devices as if Kate had never been there. If that's what he wanted, or just needed to move past the hurt.

In the time that Kate reasoned through these scenarios, Vicki's flirtations had filtered into white noise. She no longer heard the distinct enunciations of bizarrely suggestive astronomical terminology, or their playful giggles. She no longer heard anything, in fact, even when she tried.

The voices had gone.

Kate whipped around to see if they'd discovered her inside the classroom.

No one was in there with her.

Ever so gradually, she leaned to peer back through the window to see if they'd left altogether. If so, then *she* could finally leave.

Confident that was the case, Kate had almost exposed her entire face through the window when she caught the red of Vicki's shirt against the blue of Dex's. Kate shot back into her original position, cupping a hand to her mouth as her heart squeezed and stomach liquefied. When she looked at the glass sundial again, all she could see was the dark scorpion painted at its center, ready to sting.

She thought through her options again—and settled on Door Number Two. She would stay put until they'd finished whatever silent interaction they were having. For the immediate time being, Dex's secret would be safe with her.

Kate biked home from Adler to find Aggie pawing at the entryway of her unit. Scooping the cat up in one arm, she opened the door to a frigid apartment even though the AC hadn't been on all day.

She was now certain Olive had been creating those cold spots and, worse, that nauseating lilac scent. Not inclined to hang with the dead woman at the moment after the day she'd had, Kate dropped the cat and her backpack to hoist her golf bag onto her shoulder instead. She left Agatha in the courtyard to find her way back to Vera, then set off for the Diversey Driving Range. Teeing off from its second story, she imagined every ball in the bucket was one of Dexter's.

She'd never hit so well with her driver.

Exhausted, sore, and running out of excuses, she eventually made her way home at sunset. The humid air and new-paint smell greeting her at the door were most welcome. Kate didn't have much of an appetite, but the growling hollow in her gut nagged her to throw it something after all her exertions — especially since she had a bottle of white wine chilling to help her cope with the living and the dead that haunted her. She grabbed a box of saltine crackers out of the kitchen cabinet and a jar of apricot jam from the fridge.

While she was getting ready to smear the fruit preserve onto the crackers she'd arranged around a large plate, Kate heard a *Chirp!* from behind her kitchen wall. The battle of the species was game-on again next door. Predictably, the bird's owner shouted, *"Shut up!"*

Chirp-chirp!

"Shut! Up!"

"Gawd," Kate groused to herself. "*You* shut up, lady. It's a bird! That's what it's supposed to do!"

As if the bird sensed an ally through the wall, giving it renewed confidence to just go for it, it went on an animalistic rampage.

Chirp-chirp! Chirp-chirp-chirp! Chirp-chirp! Chirp! Chirp-chirp-chirp!

"SHUUUT! UUUP!"

She'd had enough.

Carrying her plate and a wine glass to the living room instead, she uncorked her frosty bottle of Pinot Grigio and played her Big Bad Voodoo Daddy album on the stereo. She didn't want to risk a noise complaint, but she did turn up its volume enough to drown out Bird Nazi Neighbor back at the other side of the apartment and entertain Hot Neighbor at this end. She figured he would like hearing the jazzy sounds of this late nineties swing-revival, the best match to his music she could find in her CD tower. Maybe they'd get into another flirty round of tapping rhythms through the wall.

Two glasses of wine later, Kate forewent the glass altogether and just held the bottle by its neck like a giant wine cooler. Her plan had worked; an infusion of alcohol was just what she'd needed to detoxify her blood of all fear and loathing. She'd even turned her apartment lights low to set a mood and bounced around to the beat of "You and Me and the Bottle Makes Three Tonight."

When bored of that and restless because Hot Neighbor hadn't responded to her music, she also felt a little ballsy.

"Whaaat if," she wondered aloud, "I invite everyone in my stairwell for cocktail hour in my place this Friday. How fun would *that* be!"

Kate rushed with the birth of this brainchild. She would make a theme of it and buy up some Jazz Age and Swing Era tunes, and they could drink wine and martinis and gin fizzes and other classic cocktails. The time frame could be a simple two-hour window — six to eight o'clock, maybe — and that way she could wind it down at eight if it was a bust or keep it raging if it was a success and Hot Neighbor wanted to get in her pants. Leo and Vera could be honorary stairwell neighbors, and she'd ask their advice on whether to invite Mousy Maisie, too. It would be a grand hello and farewell to everyone (ghosts included) before she moved out.

The true brilliance of the plan, Kate knew, lay in the open-invitation concept. However much she'd deluded herself to the contrary, the fact was she still wasn't certain the well-built man with the thick wavy brown hair lived next door to her. Seeing the guy walk out of the building for that second time, though, had raised her confidence that he *did* live somewhere off her stairwell, so this invitation would be the catch-all.

It was also so much less awkward than blindly asking him out — in the event he wasn't available, or he wasn't interested, or he wasn't above taking out restraining orders against young women who relentlessly fantasized about him and stalked him down.

No strings, no pressure, just a friendly mix-n-mingle among neighbors.

Kate raised the wine bottle to her lips and decided it was now or never. With sobriety would come second-guessing, and she couldn't risk that. She fetched her laptop from its carrying case and brought it over to the coffee table. Hovering over it like a hunchbacked evil genius, she dashed out a basic invite.

With a couple dozen flyers in hand, she tiptoed barefoot out into the stairwell to slip them under people's doors. Starting at the bottom, she worked her way up so Hot Neighbor would be the last to receive his and able to catch her back at her place should he want to RSVP in person right away.

The deed done, Kate tossed her extra flyers onto her side table and lingered in the open space near the door like Agatha had. She needed to keep moving, to channel her nervous energy as she waited for the special knock to strike.

She didn't know how to swing dance by herself so decided to do the Charleston.

"How d'ya like this, Olive? This how you used to do it?" Kate twirled around and watched herself dance in the oversized mirror she'd hung above her side table. "Hmm…" It appeared she'd lapsed into the Kid n' Play Kickstep, looking more like a nineties house dancer than a twenties flapper.

Kate corrected her form and really got into it. She wildly swung her arms back and forth as she stepped and kicked one foot forward and stepped and kicked the other foot back. Then she squatted with her hands on her knees, crossing and uncrossing her arms while her legs flapped in and out. Her reflection in the mirror made her laugh out loud.

Straightening up, she fluttered jazz hands in the air as she shimmied around in circles, stopping when she faced the window. All had fallen dark outside but for the apartment windows across the way—including Maisie's.

"What *you* up to tonight, Mousy?"

She bopped her way to the window and scissored two fingers between the blinds to spread their slats apart.

Maisie was sitting on her sofa with her swaddled infant in her arms as usual. Her dark brown blouse appeared unbuttoned most of the way to reveal a nude-colored top underneath. Kate strained her eyes to observe more closely, and saw that—nope, the top was, in fact, the nude skin of one of Maisie's drooping breasts. Kate could briefly make out the large rusty nipple at its tip before Maisie brought the baby's mouth to it.

She didn't know what to make of this. Even if Maisie weren't too old to lactate, she hadn't actually given birth, so her body shouldn't be producing milk. Either way, Kate hoped the new mother had a back-up plan for actually feeding the child. Otherwise that was one sadistic way to finally get that kid to cry.

She was about to cease and desist from her voyeurism when Mousy quickly pulled the baby away, set it in the crack between her thighs, and buttoned her blouse. She then carried it into the kitchen and, releasing an arm, spread out a pastel-colored cloth that had been lying folded on her kitchen table. Once all four corners were stretched out, she walked back and forth to bring what looked like diaper-changing supplies.

Kate kept stepping side-to-side and snapping her fingers to the lively swing music as she watched. She felt disturbed spying like this, but she'd never really seen the baby. Mousy's tale of its arrival had sounded so far-fetched and just, *creepy*. And for that baby to have arrived after the dead had reawakened all around them in this building…

Kate wondered if those presences could have had anything to do with a living child appearing out of thin air. Or if Maisie had experienced any similar hauntings and felt threatened with a child in her home. Or maybe she wasn't even aware of the entities, and her innocent little charge could become a target. The life force of the child could attract a spirit like a magnet.

A wave of urgent protection—or plain morbid curiosity—surged inside Kate.

It was her day job to explain the universe to the public, but over the years all she knew was that the more she learned of it herself, the more she learned how much mankind didn't know about the sweeping cosmos around it. In opening her mind to the possibilities existing in the far reaches of space, it wasn't so big a leap to open herself to the phenomena happening right here in her backyard.

Perhaps, then, it was her duty of neighborly love to keep watch over Mousy and the baby when she could, see for herself any oddities occurring there—both the paranormal and Mousy's potential negligence. The latter was plenty to protect that child against.

"Oh, duh!"

She just remembered a beginner telescope packed away in a brown box labeled "Adler Crap." It was shoved in the corner of her closet and in easy reach. The resin replica of an antique wood and brass telescope was really no stronger than a pair of basic binoculars. She'd only bought it from the planetarium gift shop in spring to watch the Lake Michigan regattas from the amazing vantage of Dex's shoreline condo.

Kate flipped the switch to her living room lights so no one could see her spy. "Boobeddy-boop-boop, da-da-d-da," she scatted as she held the toy telescope horizontal in her hands like a dancer's cane and performed a solo kick-line back to the window. "Ta-ta-ta, pow-wow, OW!" she cried—that last bit of improv was running her shin into the coffee table in the dark.

Back at the window, it appeared Mousy had gotten her supplies sorted, and she was gingerly holding the baby with both hands to lower it to the table. Kate peered through her eyepiece and adjusted the fuzzy lens while Mousy unwrapped the baby's swaddle. Tweaking the scope's shaft a couple more times, Kate brought her circle of sight into focus just in time for the baby's unveiling.

"What. The. *Fuck?*"

She felt like a cartoon character doing it, but she pulled her face away from the telescope and rubbed her eyes with a hand before looking back to make sure she'd seen clearly.

Mousy partially obstructed the view as she reached for her supplies. But the baby was visible. Shining with a dull sheen beneath the overhead lamp. Holding one arm frozen in the air. Lying eerily still. Rocking a little only when Mousy reached past it and bumped into its upraised arm.

Kate snatched the telescope from her face, closed the blinds, and dropped her velvet curtains in front of them. The jazzy music jarred against her new mood, so she turned off the stereo and grabbed the wine bottle on her way to sit in Olive's wingback chair.

In the silence and dark, all she could hear was the *gul-gul-gul* of wine draining through the bottleneck and down her throat, along with a rapid, throbbing pulse in her ears. The hairs at her neck stood on end, and out the side of her eye, an opalescent mist hovered by the door. The moment Kate looked straight at it, it disappeared, leaving a floral trace in its wake.

What was happening right in her backyard was perhaps further beyond her reach than she'd estimated.

March 1927

Rocking back and forth, Eva combed the cornsilk hair of a Victorian doll.

Nursery rhyme characters pranced around on the walls, and the little doll's china hand curved perfectly around Eva's finger as she held it close. Placing the ivory comb aside, she picked at the delicate lace trimming on the collar and bustle of the doll's powder-blue dress and ran a finger along its well-tailored pleating and seams. Then, retrieving the ivory comb and swaying in the rocker at her slow pace, Eva set to stroking the doll's hair again.

Her expression blank, she recited from "Wynken, Blynken, and Nod." When she got to the old moon's question, *"Where are you going, and what do you wish?"* her eyes began to tear.

> *"All night long their nets they threw*
> *To the stars in the twinkling foam —*
> *Then down from the skies came the wooden shoe,*
> *Bringing the fishermen home."*

On the last word, Eva's face broke into sobs and she clutched the frail blond doll to her. Sharply inhaling at its hat then its dress, she could find little trace of the lilac and powder scent of her sister. *This room, her clothes… With every day they lose more of her.*

"We *will* bring her home, Evie, my dear," her mother said from the doorway. "Your father will see to that. Someone will trace that emerald. We're not to give up hope."

"I know, Mother. I do hold on to hope. Every now and then it simply catches up with me, that's all."

Mrs. Hughes nodded at the doll as she entered Ollie's bedroom. "That one's her favorite, isn't it?"

"For a time, it was. It always reminded me of her, too. The sunny color of her hair when she was tiny."

"Mm," Mrs. Hughes agreed, contemplating one of the golden ringlets between her thumb and forefinger. "We liked to dress her in blues, too, didn't we. She never did grow out of that color. How she let us pet her and spoil her." Mrs. Hughes released the curly lock and dropped her face into her hand.

"Oh, Mother, we mustn't blame ourselves. That child wanted for nothing where genuine affection was concerned. We assured her of as much each and every day in some way."

"I know," Mrs. Hughes said hoarsely, her hands primly folded at her waist. "I only wonder if it was too much. Too smothering."

"I never once heard her object. Though I suppose it's our lot to play-act much of the time. Spirited individuality is deviant if not a disgrace." Eva now saw the precious doll in her lap as a marionette with invisible strings attached. She huffed a cynical laugh. But, caressing its silken hair, her smirk eased back down to a frown. "Yet surely Ollie could have opened up to me about something like that? Known I would have understood? Or Lonnie even."

"Has he shared any confidences between them?"

"No, not for lack of desperately wishing he could. I suppose sometimes she mentioned being eager to become a lady, but that's nothing beyond normal fancy for a girl indeed so close to becoming a woman. You would have been introducing her to society only this year, and—"

"*Will* be. We *will* introduce her. She'll be back safely under this roof well before she turns sixteen years of age. That emerald will lead us somewhere."

"That emerald could still be well-hidden on her person, wherever she is. Or cut up and sold through any number of illegal outlets by now. Those thieves could have convinced her it was made of paste, costume jewelry. How could she assert its value without giving away who she is, who she knows. Regardless, if no one's reported it by now, Mother, I—"

"Do *not* say such things. Do *not* speak of Ollie associating with such a filthy underworld. Ever."

"Fine, Mother, but if it was stolen from her, or stolen from me originally by someone else entirely—"

"Would you already have them dredging the lake for her, Eva? You're sitting here crying as though you're already mourning her. I won't have this pessimism in my house." Mrs. Hughes wrung her hands so roughly that they chafed to bright pink around her white knuckles. "I cannot *stand* to have it."

"Don't be so extreme, Mother. That's hardly what I'm saying. I'm only trying to be realistic that we can't hang all hopes on a tiny bit of jewelry. And I am sitting here crying because *I miss my sister*. I am devastated that I can't see her or hold her any given time I want to. You know how it was, living in this big open house and so easily hearing the patter of her light step on the stairs or the trill of her canary-like singing. Well, being just next door, not a day goes by that I'm not also reminded."

"Would you prefer to forget? Snip her out of all memories like, like—"

"Of course not! I only mean—"

"Eva, this…this right now, with you here and, and her not…" Mrs. Hughes waved her hands before her face. "Mussing up her personal effects—"

"Holding *one* doll that I'm perfectly capable of replacing exactly as I found it. I assure you I had nothing to do with that other one, so you need not accuse me of that again. Nor those photographs."

Mrs. Hughes shook her head, and Eva immediately regretted her words. Amplifying the horror of the entire situation, not only had the family discovered that every single photograph and small painted portrait of Ollie had gone missing, but of the family photos that remained, Olive's image had been clipped out of every one.

Eva's wedding album, too, had been massacred to remove Ollie's presence from the bridal party. Not so much as the thumbprint-sized miniature of her remained in her mother's golden locket. The only likeness they'd had on hand to share with the police and detectives was the family portrait hanging above the fireplace in the music room, painted several years prior when Ollie had been a small girl. Beyond that, they'd been left to describe her from memory to sketch artists and research media archives for any features on the family that had included photographs. Their number was few and outdated.

If Ollie had run away on the steam of her own will, it could not have been impetuous but a well-thought-out plan carried out in small, methodical increments unnoticed by anyone until the official alarm had been raised.

Eva stood, brushed off the Victorian doll as though ridding it of contamination for her mother's benefit, and set it back on the shelf. "That doll, by the way—the missing one—was her favorite. The one from Lonnie."

Mrs. Hughes harrumphed.

"So—" Eva elevated one eyebrow at that reaction "—I've no doubt wherever you find that doll, you've found Ollie."

"You are working on my nerves, testing me, and I simply—"

"You simply *what*, Mother."

"Cannot take it. You have always tested me, so please go. Please go home to your husband and set to work producing a family of your own. Then might you know a mother's curse. Then might you know my pain."

"Your pain over a lost daughter that drives you to push your other one away? The one still standing here and hurting alongside you? This is a shame, Mother. I wonder if you don't, in fact, blame yourself or Father but *me*."

Mrs. Hughes didn't protest.

"Yes, I see," Eva said. "Getting tipsy and enjoying myself at the party I had every right to attend rather than sitting upstairs watching my little charge. Carelessly leaving my wedding rings at home as I gallivanted off to a place of sin."

"Putting your marriage in jeopardy all the while. You neglected your duties to both your sister and husband that night, you—"

"And there it is! Ah!" Eva clapped. "Took only ten weeks. Finally, you've come out with it."

"Your sister looked up to you, Evie! She paid such attention to everything. And with you taking up with that, that…"

"*What.*"

"That disgrace. Sure, sure! Of course the doll that disappeared with her was from him. I don't doubt his influence reached farther than any of us can have imagined! Slumming as he does in those putrid clubs, dancing to the wails of savages. Is that the gratitude your generation has for those who've provided you everything? Shucking it away as somehow *beneath* you? When you yourselves couldn't scrape any lower."

The all-inclusive "you" was not lost on Eva.

"And everyone knows now he works at the lumberyard," continued Mrs. Hughes. "I don't know whom he supposes he's fooling or what he's trying to prove other than that he himself is a fool."

"He's not trying to fool anyone by working for his own family's business. He's just living a private life the way he wants without shouting it from the rafters. And what he's proving is to himself that he can know the satisfaction of a modest living well earned!"

Mrs. Hughes continued as if she hadn't heard a word: "And Mrs. Whitworth only just called on the Ashbys the other weekend. They admitted to knowing hardly anything of their young Lonnie's goings-on, that he hadn't slept under his brother's roof in Geneva in well over a year. Hopping from one flapper's bed to another, no doubt. Mrs. Belden's daughter Effie has an axe to grind with him, that's for certain."

Betrayed by the heat in her cheeks, Eva hoped she'd applied enough face powder to mute them.

Her mother pressed on. "Although I wonder if the man's reputation in that respect is merely a clever façade. I wouldn't be surprised if his fiancée found him out and it's the real reason she called off their wedding."

Eva's teeth clamped down on her tongue.

"Finlay had told me, you know," her mother said, "about Lon's companions at the station that evening, the affectations of one in particular. What kind of company is that for a man of his lineage to cavort with?"

Pushed beyond her threshold, Eva finally spat out in disgust, "Oh, *Mother*. What is all this? It doesn't sound like you."

"That sort of lifestyle isn't natural," Mrs. Hughes persisted.

"Really? Tell me — is it 'natural' for a husband not to consummate his marriage in eighteen months?" *Or cannot red herring swim upstream as well as down?*

"That is vile conversation."

"It's the truth."

"Then I'll condescend to it briefly to say this: that husband of yours is a fine man of upstanding reputation. He, too, works for his daily bread, and I'm sure his business keeps him quite busy and pre-occupied. Someone has to keep the world running, keep his family comfortable. If marital…*relations* aren't transpiring, then the wife is to blame. Finlay is doing his duty by day. You need to abide yours by night. Just as I did as a young bride, seeing to it that a husband's home is his haven, keeping the plagues of his day's stress out of mind. You must open your heart to accomplish this, make yourself available to him as a mature woman, not run off to play with friends like a child.

"But if you care at all about your friends, you'll listen: Lon would find it in his best interests to seek a nice *lady* of proper breeding to marry and settle down straight away. Follow the trail his father and brother have blazed for him."

Mrs. Hughes ceased wringing her hands and cupped one around the other into one large fist to shake at Eva.

"And *you*," she said, "would do best to remove yourself with Finlay back to the country. For all its refinements, the sins of this city have tantalized you too much. It's not the place for those of weak character. Go home, Eva. Go to Lake Forest and to your husband. Start your legacy at long last or people really will talk — of what they most assuredly whisper already."

Eva had been pinching the bridge of her nose and squeezing her eyes closed for the majority of the lecture, but at this point she said, "Enough. You aren't yourself, and I do understand why." Drawing a deep breath, she stood tall, straightened her shoulders, and strode to the doorway, where she paused and laid a hand on the molding without turning around. "Nonetheless, just hope that when you do need me, you'll know where to find me. I'm sorry we can't say the same for Ollie."

Her fingers curled and scratched at the molding, and she glanced to the side to see her reflection in the mirrored door. Looking into her vibrant green eyes, she saw only Ollie's.

Eva swallowed under the intensity of their gaze, and before stepping onto the landing and down the imperial stairway, she added, softly, "You may not believe it, but I would give my life for that not to be the case. I'd give my soul."

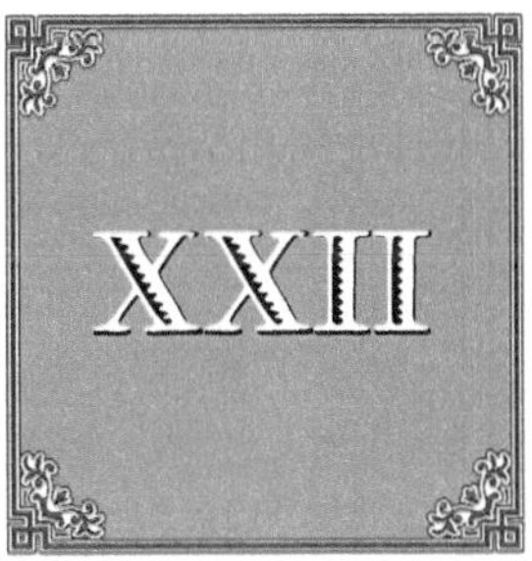

July 2000

"What's that, dear?" Vera asked.

Kate concentrated hard on articulating as she repeated, "Her baby. Iss notta baby."

"I'm afraid I still don't understand."

After too much wine had sloshed the saltines around in her stomach, Kate had snatched up her extra party flyers and walked to Leo's apartment via the basement stairs. Vera had already been visiting him, which killed two old birds with one stone. Now the three tenants were sitting in Leo's living room, the two women seated on the sofa and him in his favorite recliner, displacing his ghost to who knew where.

Yet buzzing as strongly as she was on that bottle of wine, Kate suspected Vera's failure to comprehend her message didn't have anything to do with slurred speech.

"I think you *do*. Thass the mysst'ry, the big secret of Mousiss baby. How sshhe got it."

"Mouses?" Leo asked. "You havin' a rodent problem at your place, Kate? I've got traps here—"

"Nooo!" She felt like she was arguing with her parents. "You aren't liss-ning! Mouse-*ee*, Miss Mousy. Maisie."

"Mm," Vera hummed. "A little nickname you've come up with for her. That's not nice, Kate. She hasn't had the advantages you have."

"Firss of all, you don' know me, not really, to know what advantigges I may or may not uhvad—not-uv—*have* had. And I *do* feel bad for her. I won't call her Mousy ennimore."

"Leo," Vera rasped, "might you fix her a pot of coffee to get her talking sense again? I myself think I've overstayed my welcome here and am retiring for the evening. Good night."

She stood with pops in her hipbone and knees. Kate lamely handed her a flyer for the cocktail hour, at which Vera squinted with a frown.

"Thanks. But *I* don't drink." She flicked her wrist to toss it on Leo's coffee table; it missed and drifted down to his braided rug. "See you in the morning, Leo. I'll order your usual for ya."

Leo hurried to hoist himself from the chair and shuffle past Vera to get the door. "'Bye, now," he said with a modest nod. Kate watched his eyes soften as their gaze followed Vera out.

Shutting the door, he crossed back through the room and into the kitchen in an awkward silence.

Kate scolded herself to get it together, to calm down and not slur in fury next time she said anything to him. She needed to speak clearly, even it meant slowing down to Forrest-Gump speed. And, whatever she did, she had to keep it reverent.

This didn't preclude her from taking another chance, though. Once the black coffee had percolated, Leo returned to his chair, and a few sips in silence helped sober her somewhat.

Zoning in on Leo as he scratched lightly at his threadbare armrests, slunk down in his seat and moping, she finally said, "You really love her, don't you."

His head shot up, and his ears burned beet red. "How ya figure that?"

Kate cocked her wobbling head and grinned as a way of asking who he thought he was kidding. Leo smiled back.

"You two're good t'gether," Kate said. "I used t'think you were total opp-sits and could never get 'long." She paused to mentally script her next words so she'd say them better with her thick tongue, shaping them syllable-by-syllable in her head. "But now I see—" pause "—how that works for you." Concentration. "You complement each other. Per-fect-ly."

Leo's smile closed and slanted to the side, and he looked down at his lap, shaking his head.

"She doesn't know," Kate guessed.

"Nope."

"You scared?"

"Yep."

"Don't be. Love's th'besst compliment. Ever."

"I've been wantin' to say somethin'. But she's not interested in takin' up with anyone. Never has been. Besides, there's this Jerry at Panera who keeps makin' her laugh. A real card, he is. Steals the show every time."

"Oh." Kate flapped her hand at him. "Vera's too feisty for that. They'd juss keep outdoing each other. Thass not love."

"Mm, I s'pose not."

"Leo. *Tell her.*"

"All in good time, hon."

"Life's too short."

"Yes, it is, Kate. Listen to your own advice."

Kate huffed a sad laugh through her nose. "Yeah."

"Look, I will say somethin'. Someday. Maybe. You gotta promise me you'll let me do it in my own time, my own way. Can you keep this secret till then, between you and me?"

"Cross my heart."

"Anyway…" Leo blew into his giant mug lined with the city's distinctive skyline, then took a sip. "I wouldn't take it too personally, Kate. She gets like that, you know."

"I know."

"And look, I haven't, uh, told her anythin' about letting you look through that box. To avoid saddlin' her with all the clutter, we'd divided Olive's effects between us some. Vera's got another one just like this and was askin' for mine right before you got here, actually. Said she was thinking of puttin' together a scrapbook in Olive's memory. Guess we both forgot since she left so sudden. Ah well, I'll run it up to her later. I don't 'spose, though, you'd want to have one last look-through?"

Kate had buried her nose into her just-as-huge Chicago edition Starbucks mug, savoring the steam on her face. She lifted her eyes to look above its rim at Leo and decided not to answer his question until he answered hers.

"Maisie's baby," she said. "I assume Vera knows. But do you? That it's a doll?"

"I don't doubt it's cute."

Kate snorted. "Not as in *adorable*."

"Well, it's nothin' I talk about."

"So you do know it's literally an inanimate toy?"

He rubbed the back of his neck. "Helpin' out with odds-n-ends, you know, with maintenance stuff and everythin', I get inside a lot of these apartments."

Kate nodded in silence, waiting for him to continue and having to prod when he didn't. "Like Maisie's?"

"Well…"

She raised her brows.

"All right. I was fixing Maisie's lock this once, and I saw it lyin' there. In what looked like a toy crib, too." He screwed his face and scratched behind his ear, apparently finished with his story.

"And?"

"Oh…well…Maisie was speakin' in a hushed voice, telling me how the baby was sleepin' so could I please keep the volume down. Now, I could tell where I was standin' that there was nothin' I could possibly wake up. But I didn't know if she could tell that I knew. So I've kept it to myself. It's not our place to know what happens behind closed doors."

If the coffee had partially sobered her, Leo's words finished the job. Kate's wrists stung from getting slapped again.

She frowned down at her hands and picked at her nails. "I've heard of this before. Childless women with such strong maternal instincts, they need to go through the motions. I get it; I'm not judging. It's the baby monitor and the…breastfeeding that throws me more than anything. Like, maybe she's taken it to an unhealthy level. And she could have a ghost over there preying on that, too. I'm concerned."

"Well…"

"I know, none of my business. So I want to go through that box again, but should I? I think Vera wants it back for a reason. Scrapbooking my ass."

Leo chortled. "Now yer startin' to sound like *her*. See how she grows on ya?"

Kate pressed her lips into a tight grin. "Like a fungus."

"Well," Leo tried to say between his wheezy chuckles, "I don't see the harm in letting ya look through the remainder of what's there. Not much left, and Vera has the rest anyway." He grunted as he stood and scuffled in and out of the closet to bring the shoebox to her.

As Kate foraged her way down to where she'd left off, she thought of the crime report she'd discovered last time.

"Hey, Leo? That Alonzo Ashby. Do you know anything more about him?"

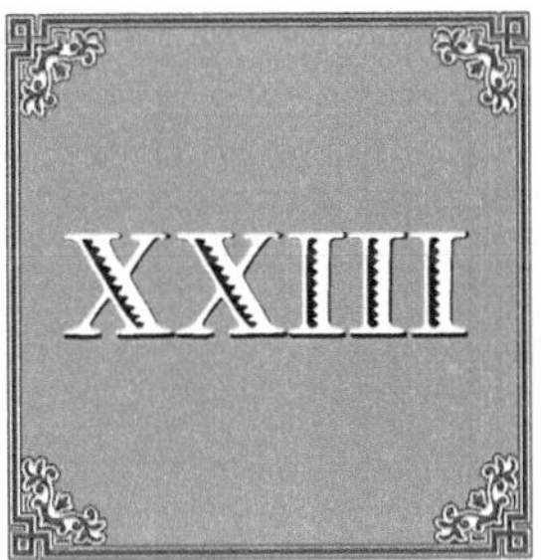

April 1927

Watching from a concealed vantage point, she saw Lon greet a stranger at the hotel's gate.

A young man, it seemed, boyish almost, with a slight build beneath his tweed newsboy cap and dark oversized coat. A rather unseasonably warm-looking scarf was wrapped around his neck and covered the lower part of his face. He seemed of average height, though a few inches shorter than Lon.

As the men stood beneath the entrance's brick archway, they both appeared to glance around at the street and courtyard, perhaps determining whether they could be seen before looking back at each other.

She watched how, with only brief hesitation, Lon took the visitor's face in his bare hands and stroked the cheeks with his thumbs. Bent toward it to connect with a kiss.

Her heart beat rapidly with envy, despair. Should she have ever had reason to suspect as much, to see Lon's secret unfurl before her eyes was aching to bear. She'd always known the obstacles keeping them apart, but not this impossible one.

Yet she didn't walk away. She only watched as long as she could while Lon and his companion pulled apart and walked hand-in-hand up the stone steps before disappearing through the door to his wing of the hotel. Beyond that threshold, their interactions would go unseen.

But not unheard.

She, after all, had a secret of her own.

Eight for Heaven

July 2000

"Some say Ashby was a homosexual," Leo said to Kate in a low voice. "And we're talkin' about a time when you'da never seen something like those rainbow-colored rocket ships on Clark Street just north a' here. You seen them things? Shaped like a, like a…"

"Phallus? In Boystown, you mean? Yeah, so?"

Leo raised his brows and tilted his chin into his chest, rolling his eyes up to look at Kate levelly.

"Oh, God, Leo. Don't get all old-school homophobe on me."

"I'm just sayin'. That sorta openness didn't happen in those days."

Kate huffed. "I don't care what generation you're from. Everyone deserves love."

Leo kept his brows high and held his hands up in surrender. "Hey, I agree with ya. I'm just explainin' how it was and the legends that went round in the gossip rags and this place. Stuff that got passed on considerin' who he was. Busybodies love a good local celebrity death to brag about, and Tommy's suicide got everybody talkin' about it again. Died right on the same spot, those boys did."

Kate saw Leo's eyes flatten, retreating into a distance she couldn't see. After allowing him a moment's pensive silence, he spoke again.

"What a shame; what a shame that was. I can't believe that boy woulda' done it."

"Tommy? The one who died this past New Year's?"

"That's the one."

"You knew him?"

"Not really. But probably better'n most, sadly." He gave a low, melancholy chuckle. "I serviced his maintenance requests, too, see. He assisted me on some jobs, n'fact. Not a real resourceful fella, but ya give him some direction and he'd work hard and follow instructions to a T. He was a real nice boy that way, helpful, smart, but kept to himself a lot. Didn't talk much."

Leo shifted in his chair. "He drove a Checker taxi, ya know. Used to park it right out in front. I always had this impression drivin' that car was his only way to be his own man and by himself all day, yet still have the company of folks glad to order him around."

"Sounds very lonely."

"Well, he lived in the right place, then. To this day, I can't figure out whether this building attracts the lonely or breeds 'em."

"Do you think he haunts it, too?"

"Possibly. Probably. Wherever he is, I hope he's found some real companionship."

Kate stared at Olive's shoebox and chewed her thumbnail in thought. "I wonder," she said, "if Alonzo was lonely, too."

Leo hummed in consideration.

"Do you think Olive was already living here when he died? Do you think she knew him?" The clicking of her thumbnail against her tooth punctured the silence when Leo didn't respond. "And why did he off himself here? Why not his home in Geneva?"

He glanced out the corner of his eye and said, "Fine. You take your turn."

"What?" Kate asked, but Leo said nothing more, just stood and shuffled his slippered feet around the coffee table and to the sofa, where he sat down beside her. She watched the chair cushion he'd been sitting on rise like baked dough once liberated of his weight, only for it to depress again in the center with the unseen force of Leo's "roommate."

"Wow," she said. "That's really hospitable of you."

"Well, feel I oughta give him some comfort in his afterlife. It can't be too fun for him stuck here with me."

"Maybe you can set him up with Vera's lady. Get her out of the rocking chair and keep her better company than Aggie."

"Not a bad idea. Ol' Hattie in your wing's got a ghost that keeps spookin' her canary! She's always hollerin' at the darned thing to shut up."

Kate shook her head at what was really happening behind her kitchen wall. Nothing could surprise her anymore. Maybe she *could* give coexisting with Olive benefit of the doubt. But then again…*Nah*.

"So," she said, "what do you know about Alonzo?"

"Well, for starters, he didn't live in Geneva. He lived here. Made a right mess of himself that night, he did, and he was dressed in worker's clothes, but a neighbor was able to identify him. His family was real well-to-do. Like the Hugheses, except old money. Prob'ly descended from European nobility, but the American Ashbys were royalty by virtue of their lumberyards. Had loads of 'em, here in Illinois and up in Wisconsin."

Leo hiked his pant legs up a little and leaned forward with his elbows on his lap. Kate could tell he was on a roll of some sort by the gleam in his eye.

"An aunt of his, it turns out," he continued, "donated a large sum to this building, first in the year of Alonzo's death and then again in forty-eight when she herself passed. An Estella Ashby. I found the old records in the management office when I was helpin' with some filing."

"Another Stella? Like Olive's alias?"

"Popular name, I s'pose. Though this was *Eh*-stella. A spinster with no children to leave her money to. And looks like plenty of it stayed up in that big ol' family house of hers still standin' there up in the North Woods; a museum now. Guess Estella was a real patron of the arts, an active promoter of literacy, too, with a library right in the house now open to the public. She was born in that house, and she died in that library."

Kate stared at him with her head tilted and mouth dropped open in a stupefied smile. "Huh. That's a lot of information to have at your fingertips. It seems you've known a lot more about Ashby than you've let on."

Leo still looked down at the floor and rubbed the flattened palms of his hands together. "Well…just concerned about Vera, is all. I did some diggin' to see if I might not find out why that name triggers her in such awful ways these last months. Anyway…" He clapped his hands together with a dull pat and met Kate's gaze. "Yes. I know a bit about Alonzo Ashby. Though nothin' that I want to. For as much hoopla as he stirred up after his death, seems a lot was shuffled under the rug. His lifestyle was a real embarrassment to the family."

"Was that why he killed himself?"

"They say if it wasn't family disapproval or a lovers' quarrel, it was the pressure of an intolerant society."

"Because he was gay?"

"The speculation only came up, see, 'cause the residents who recognized him claimed a young man visited him frequently in the night, that they'd carry on real friendly-like sometimes right there in the courtyard. Don't rightly know and don't rightly care. It was his business what he got up to in his own home." After pulling a white hankie from his pocket to trumpet a quick nose-blow into it, he waved a hand in front of his face. "So much hearsay."

"Well—" Kate shrugged "—I suppose it adds to the building lore. Whether it's true or not, people want to feel part of a history."

Leo's joints cracked as he extended his hand into Olive's shoebox and passed his thumb over the edges of the pile of clippings. Then he stopped at one, lifting it slightly for a closer look.

His already ruddy complexion reddened deeper, so Kate glanced in to see what had caught his eye. From her angle, though, she could only see the blackened corner of a newspaper photo, with a stream of yellowed white snaking into it. Evelyn Hughes's bridal veil, if she recalled the image correctly. Leo was so pure, maybe he was merely blushing at a pretty face.

But looking back at him, Kate watched him squint with the same leaden expression she'd seen before when first looking through Olive's archives. If he *was* looking at the bride, it didn't seem that pretty face gave him any pleasure.

"Mm," he grumbled in the back of his throat. "I just don't rightly know."

April 1927

"Heaven. Lonnie, it's truly heaven."

Lon detached his lips from the earlobe he'd been sucking to twist and look upward. The dim candlelight flickered against the ceiling's deep midnight blue, just barely illuminating the speckles of painted constellations. Clouds might have cluttered the night sky outside, but here in Lon's room, the stars were always out, there for the gazing.

"How Michelangelo of you," the voice teased.

Lon looked back down at the slim body reclining beneath him on his Murphy bed and said, "It's for you, you know." He traced his middle fingertip up and down the center of his guest's shirtfront, settling it in the divot of a bare clavicle before daring to undo the top shirt button.

"I know."

Fingers combed their way through his hair to the back of his head and pulled him down where lips could meet and tongues could dance. Lon moaned softly at the feel of the body pressing against him, liberating the one genuine desire he'd been suppressing for so long.

Breaking away from their kiss, his mouth roamed over the chiseled jaw and down the long neck as he undid one button and then another. For each one he unfastened, he replaced it with a kiss to the chest heaving beneath it, his heart aching at the pleasured sighs his touch could command.

She could hear it through the wall. All of it. The whispers, the laughter, the groans of ecstasy.

And that particular voice belonged to someone she knew. Unmistakably.

Suddenly, the situation was so much worse. She would have much preferred the truth be what she'd thought she'd seen through her window, looking down on them in the courtyard like that from her own suite. Had Lon's heart been closed to her all this time by virtue of her gender alone, she could in time come to accept that fate, and move on.

But this…

After everything she'd been through, everything she'd been willing to give up, she was not about to lose Lon to another woman.

Least of all to her sister.

"I'm dreaming, aren't I?" came a whisper at his ear as he next slid suspenders off narrow shoulders. "I'll open my eyes again, and this will all have vanished."

Lon cupped the face beneath his and ran his thumbs over delicate cheeks. "Open your eyes," he whispered back, "and see the sands of dreams you've scattered." He heard the warm breath rising to his face flutter, and he closed his eyelids as he slowly rubbed their noses together. Resting his forehead atop the fine brow-line, he repeated, "Open your eyes. See that you're here with me."

And she did, just as Lon opened his to see his Dream Lady.

He lifted his face to stare deeply into her eyes a long moment before Eva looked once more to the ceiling. Lon felt her legs bend, and her knees rose until her inner thighs settled just above his hips. The action had pushed up the bottom of his untucked shirt, and the coarse wool of her men's trousers stroked at the bare skin of his waist.

Her fingers trailed down the buttons of his shirtfront and snuck underneath to caress the flesh of his warm stomach. She gave a coy grin as she circled a finger around his navel, but soon the smile faded.

Bringing both hands to her chest, she unbuttoned the rest of her shirt and spread it apart to reveal a white cloth binding her already small breasts into a flatter silhouette. She unfastened a pin holding the fabric in place at her side and unwrapped the first layer, then the next. And the next.

Her line of sight still panning along the star-kissed ceiling, she felt her way back to Lon's navel and flattened her palm to his skin. She smoothed her hand against him in a half-circle and slid it down his trail of hair and inside the waistband of his trousers. Lon released a heavy breath and swallowed as she eased her fingers farther.

Eva's eyes closed on the painted ceiling and opened again to meet his gaze.

"Take me, Lonnie," she said. "Take me to the stars."

Seated on her hard wooden floor with an ear pressed to the wall, she listened to the rhythmic creaking of springs, the smacks of lips, the sighs, and Eva's moans.

She raised her hand to her mouth to stifle her own cries, the sobs that shook her as tears streamed down her cheeks no matter how tightly she squeezed her eyes closed. Curling her knees into her chest and rocking, Ollie hugged her baby doll for consolation.

Afterward, Eva watched the golden outline of Lon's svelte nude form as he stepped beside his table. Out of a cluster set there, he raised one candlestick to the cigarette between his lips. Placing the candle back down, he strode back to his bed where Eva lay; he sat on the disheveled sheet and mutely stared at her as he drew in a slow inhale.

Fearing his image would evaporate in the billows of smoke he blew between them, she was relieved to see him still sitting there when it cleared. She sat up a little, feeling one of her tiny breasts escape from beneath the covers as she reached for his cigarette. She plucked it from his lips and inserted it into her own, reclining back on the pillow. They watched each other in silence, Eva puffing soothing vapors into her lungs as Lon reached to caress her bared flesh.

Whispering a phantom-stream of smoke from her lips, she spoke. "Penny for your thoughts, old boy."

Lon palmed her breast. "I was just recalling the night I first met you. On the stairs."

Eva smiled and arched her back to encourage his fondling. It worked; leaving his one hand to its task, Lon bent down to take the freshly unveiled nipple into his mouth. "I remember — thinking —" he said between kisses " — that your beauty — wasn't subjective." He sat up again. "'She is for everyone,' I thought of you then. And, afterward, I forced myself to remember, 'She is for *him*.' But now, I'm not strong enough to believe anything other than you are only for me. Just as I'm only for you."

Eva held the cigarette between her long, elegant fingers and lifted it back to Lon's lips. The corner of her mouth drifted into a vague half-smile.

Pulling on the cigarette, Lon exhaled and said, "I mean it, dear girl. I have never, and *will* never, belong to anyone in this life but you. You have had my heart from the moment you recited that silly Keats poem."

"*You* started it, old boy. I didn't recite alone." Eva broadened her smile.

"That's true. But I did leave you alone, didn't I. To that big, empty house full of people. Only for you to haunt yet another big, empty one."

"Not the way I left you, darling. I gave you no choice but to respect that distance." She arched her back again and propped up on her elbows with feline grace. "Though who'd have known you'd be such a damned gentleman after all, protecting my virtue. I'd certainly hoped you wouldn't."

Lon raised his eyebrows. "Well, I suppose now I'm not. Just the home-wrecking wolf everyone expects of me."

Eva sat up and twisted to snake her arms around Lon's neck. "And just think what that makes *me*, old boy."

"*You're* lovely."

"You're kind."

"I'm honest."

He drew another inhale of his cigarette, and Eva leaned closer with her lips parted. Gently, he exhaled curling wisps of smoke onto her tongue, which she breathed in and blew out toward the starry ceiling in a light-headed reverie. Leaning back, she glided her arms off Lon's shoulders to stretch them over and behind her head as she settled back onto the pillow.

"God," Lon said, appearing to stroke her curves with his gaze. "I'm undone. You destroy me, Eva."

He tugged the bed sheet down a few inches from her waist and laid a hand on her belly, swirling circles around it before sliding his fingers under the covers to lightly massage her there. Eva closed her eyes and squirmed, biting her lower lip.

After a moment, Lon removed his hand and stood, bent down to offer her one last drag from the burned-down cigarette, and walked to stub it out on the candle holder. Before returning to her, he wandered to the Victrola in the corner and placed its needle on a record.

Irving Kaufman crooned "Tonight You Belong to Me," and Lon was back beneath the bedcovers and in Eva's waiting arms.

And as they rose and fell together in tempo with the music, giving and receiving and releasing sounds of mutual satisfaction, a loud thump and shatter of glass next door was all that could have diverted them from their intensity.

Lon and Eva both paused and looked to the shared wall.

"Your neighbor?" Eva panted. "Suppose we're disturbing him?"

Lon looked down at her and smoothed away the short brown strands perspiration had plastered to her forehead. He shrugged and shook his head. "The beauty of this city is that you can live right on top of other people and never have to meet a soul."

Unable to stomach the sounds of their lovemaking, Ollie decided to distract herself with makeup. She walked to her chair and snatched up her black purse—her favorite beaded one, the one she'd stolen from Eva.

She was about to walk into the bathroom when nagging, masochistic curiosity instead brought her back toward Lon.

Resuming her position on the floor with her back against the wall joining their suites, she unsnapped the bag's lid and pulled out her new tube of lipstick. Twisting it until its red column reached its fullest height, she held up the purse by its top flap so she could look into its little mirror and apply the color.

Dabbing the crimson to her lips, Ollie gratefully listened to silence. Had there been any climax to the activity next door, it had passed in the time she'd walked away.

Minutes later, however, low, muffled murmurs began vibrating through the wall again, and Ollie strained her ears to understand their words.

"*— only for me — I'm only for you,*" she heard her Lon say to someone else.

"*I mean it, dear —*"

"*— never will belong to anyone in this life but you —*"

"*— my heart —*"

Ollie dragged the blood-red lipstick side to side first over her top lip, then the bottom one. As if in a trance, she lost focus of herself in the mirror and started coloring outside the lines.

"*You're lovely.*"

She smeared the lipstick over her mouth, then applied it in dark circles at the apples of her cheeks.

"*God, I'm undone. You destroy me, Eva.*"

Wearing the stick's tip to a rounded nub, Ollie dropped it to the wooden floor. She heard the light creak of footsteps, then the scratchy sound of music. Recognizing the tune from all the times she'd heard Lon play it before, Ollie closed her eyes and swayed in time with the cadence. She imagined, like every other time it played, that it was Lon singing it to *her*, that when she was ready to make her presence known to him, show him the woman she'd grown into, he would take her in his arms, and she'd belong to him that night and every night thereafter.

Breathing slowly and spreading her thickly painted lips in a smile at her fantasy, she soon heard the straining springs of Lon's bed again. Heard Eva gasp and cry Lon's name. Lon returned those wails with grunts that picked up in pace and urgency.

And Ollie opened her eyes. Looked back into the mirror at the clown with the baby cheeks. A little girl playing with Mommy's makeup.

She clawed at the mirror, wanting to rip it from the purse's lining. When it did reluctantly detach, the momentum threw her elbow back against the wall. It hurt, but nothing like her heart. She then curled her fingers around the glass to break it in her fist, but it only sliced her palm. She whipped it to the floor, where it splintered into shards.

The creaking ceased next door, and she heard Eva's inquisitive murmur. Clasping her injured hand to her mouth, Ollie scrambled to the bathroom, mixing blood with lipstick to yield the ripe red face she beheld in the mirror above the sink. Standing under the cold gray-white light and holding her hand under the even colder water running from the faucet, Ollie grimaced at her trembling reflection. The onyx black blades of her severely cut and dyed bob hovered over her shoulders like guillotine blades.

"He's mine," she whimpered. "He—he's supposed to be *mine*, all mine!"

Without turning off the water, she sank to her knees and retched toward the tiles. Nothing came out but a spindle of saliva stretching to the little white hexagons stained brown-red by her bloodied hand.

"Mine," she wept into the cold tile.

"That's mine. *This* is yours," Eva said as she grabbed her button-down shirt from Lon's hands and tossed him another one she'd retrieved from the floor.

"Easy mistake." Lon chuckled, easing his arm into the shirt he'd caught with his face. "Though I *would* like to see you in my clothes, old girl. Foremost to get you back out of them. But also so I won't have to see you masquerade in Finlay's."

"These are *my* clothes, thank you very much. Pinched them years ago when helping St. Clement's gather a clothing fund. Someone donated a few pieces their teenage son had outgrown, and, as far they knew, I took them to outfit my young, growing cousin in the country."

"Very clever. And rather uncharitable of you."

"Oh, look, old boy. For anything I took, I compensated for it handsomely."

"So you've made a practice of sneaking around incognito, have you?"

"Sneaking into the zoo more comfortably, to cavort with other animals, yes."

"Fancied the apes, did you?"

"Waited for wolves," Eva purred, tugging at Lon's freshly knotted tie as he buttoned her shirt over her tightly re-wrapped breasts.

Fastening the last button at her neck, he eased her suspenders up onto her shoulders and, with them still in his grip, pulled her closer. He rested his lips at her hairline and exhaled a loud sigh from his nose. "I wish you would stay, darling."

Eva clasped his elbows and nestled her face against his. "I know." She lifted her chin to look him in the eyes. "Someday, I pray that I will. For eternity."

Their eyes searched each other's for a prolonged moment until Lon pressed his lips against Eva's desperately. They both wrapped their arms around one another, squeezing each other close and holding fast as if their lives depended on it.

Lon moved his hands to either side of Eva's face and angled it back to stare at her. His fingers greedily stroked along her cheeks and through her hair, and a wince escaped his throat.

Eva tightened her lips and swallowed as a pair of tears strayed from the corners of her green eyes. "I love you," she said hoarsely. "I can't bear how much I do. The time we've wasted…"

Holding her face firmly, Lon kissed her again with force, then they rested a moment with their foreheads pressed together. "Go, my heart," Lon whispered. "Go now to ensure I can see you again."

With a last, longing look, Eva wrapped herself in her overcoat, placed her cap over her pinned-up hair, and withdrew back into the night.

Watching from the window, Ollie clawed her nails down the pane as she saw Eva furtively cross the courtyard and let herself out the hotel gate.

Strolling toward Wrightwood with hands in her pockets, Eva couldn't contain the smile broadening across her face. She bit her lower lip as she replayed the night in her mind, recalled the heat of Lon's touch and the taste of his tongue. She looked skyward and spotted a patch of stars unhidden by the clouds.

"Heaven," she whispered.

Perhaps they were just another pair of star-crossed lovers. Perhaps no good could possibly come of their union. Eva surely didn't want to relegate her love for Lon to sneaking around and stealing bits of time where they could find it. She wanted to love him openly, belong to him as he belonged to her. Become his wife, the mother of his children. Of course it was all too much to ask for, or even hope for.

Yet one thing she knew: no matter the outcome, she was reckoning with a force she was powerless to fight against. Not anymore.

No more fighting, she thought as the pale limestone of her parents' mansion manifested into view through the budding trees. She raised her eyes to the second floor windows and recalled the horrid words she and her mother had exchanged there in Ollie's old bedroom. For all Eva's grief, her mother's accusations had been the final kick while Eva was already down. She'd practically seen the referee kneel at her side, pounding the seconds into the mat before raising Life's boxing glove in victory to the cheers of millions. Internally beaten and bruised, Eva had had enough.

Finlay had been good to her, however. That much was certain. He'd listened to the filtered version of her conversation with her mother and expressed compassion; he did know what Ollie meant to Eva, that her anguish those weeks had been nothing less than her mothers'.

But he also knew that every measure had been taken to find the young woman—his intervention in the matter had seen to that as two of Chicago's most powerful families joined forces in the effort. He'd earnestly conceded his doubt to Eva, and together, they'd vowed to work toward moving on.

This had not precluded Finlay's diligence in his work, however. His time away on business had only lengthened, keeping him at the city office or country facilities into the late hours of evening. So he claimed, anyway. As far as Eva was concerned, she wasn't. Not when it came to how he spent his separate life from her. Not after tonight. Call them low standards, but she wouldn't set double ones.

When Finlay's pattern had achieved a predictable sense of regularity, Eva had decided she was ready to test it. From the back of her wardrobe, she'd unearthed an inconspicuous leather suitcase filled with young men's clothing. Binding her breasts was probably a needless precaution, but one she'd been willing to take. What if, after all, she bumped into someone on the street in the dark? Giving any of her femininity away was something she hadn't been willing to risk.

Rounding the corner onto Wrightwood Avenue, Eva now saw her own house, and a twinge of nausea ate away at the pit of her stomach. The adrenaline rush of anticipation and the unknown had been so euphoric on departing that place, she'd half-expected she wouldn't return to it ever again. All that had lain ahead of her then was promise of a future different than was carved out for her—or the one, rather, she'd been carved *into*, as if she were a caryatid meant to eternally uphold the houses of Hughes and Redcliffe.

No, on stepping out her front door, she sincerely hadn't thought further than that. Not even as far as what she'd have done if Lon hadn't, in fact, been standing at his gate to meet her as planned.

After their New Year's reunion and Ollie's disappearance, they'd made a proper show of remaining at arm's length. Lon had almost convinced her he'd really meant all he'd said about her not being able to have him. Thrill of the chase and all that nonsense.

But his eyes had betrayed him.

Once clear of the fog of intoxication, her Lonnie's eyes had revealed a larger sin: coveting thy neighbor's wife. It smoldered in every exchanged glance, even those Eva stole when Lon thought she wasn't looking.

For once, Eva had been grateful for all the gaudy golden mirrors adorning both Hughes homes. One evening a week ago, she'd consulted a foyer looking glass to touch up her makeup while Lon had patiently waited by; he was to accompany her and Finlay to dinner at her parents' home that night. Applying her lipstick, Eva had glanced over at Lon's reflection instead, just in time to catch him watching her. It was then she'd fully seen in his face the power and tragedy of the truth.

Her heart leaping out of her chest, it had been at the Hughes's courtly dining table later that evening that she'd slipped a hastily written note into Lon's trouser pocket—detailing the critical where-and-when.

Call it women's intuition or dumb luck, but Eva had taken the gamble. And won.

Passing through the Hughes's wrought iron gate as quietly as she could, Eva now tiptoed across the shared garden and stole into the back door of her house. Unnoticed by the help, who would have already been sleeping, she pranced up the stairs and discarded her men's clothes, replacing them carefully in the leather suitcase and crawling into one of her usual dressing gowns after washing up.

She attempted reading on the chaise longue at the foot of her bed until she saw the garish cupid bedroom clock tick forth into an unreasonable hour. Brows knitted, she stepped into bed and eased beneath the satin sheets, wondering what on earth was keeping Finlay, or if he was to stay the night in the country.

An undefined amount of time later, she came to consciousness to a kiss at her cheek.

"I'm sorry to wake you, darling. I only wanted you to know I'm home safely." Feeling Finlay's hand stroke her hair, then his body sidle behind hers, Eva caught her breath when his arm coiled around her waist. Eyes wide open to the darkness, she felt his breath at her neck as he asked, "Eva, darling, have you been smoking?"

July 2000

Kate sang along with Fred Astaire as he serenaded from her stereo, weaving her way through party guests to refill empty glasses and plates.

So far, her Friday happy hour was a success with nearly a dozen takers. Not all were from the stairwell but had invited friends of their own from elsewhere in Camden Court.

No one had shown the courtesy of RSVPing, however, so she'd had no idea what she was getting into. For moral support, then, she'd invited Blair and her fiancé, Brad. At least then she wouldn't have to drink away her sorrows alone if no one else showed.

Kate stepped over to Blair and bumped hips with her. Both in little black dresses, the two ladies pouted their lips and, for a few beats, strutted side to side in sync with one another in their signature Robert Palmer "Simply Irresistible" dance.

"So," Blair said curtly as her eyes panned the room and Kate topped up her flute of champagne. "Which one is the guy?"

Kate rolled her eyes, knowing full well every eligible man milling about her apartment was gray-haired — and that her friend knew that, too. She scowled at Blair. "He isn't here. Not yet."

"Want me to go knock next door?"

"Hell no, I want you to stay right here where I can see you."

Blair tapped her French-manicured fingernails against her glass and winked across the room at Brad standing tall and lean, boyish yet professorial in his tortoiseshell eyeglasses and linen blazer. He appeared to be in friendly conversation with Leo, who also wore a dress jacket for the occasion — granted, a bit rumpled and tight-fitting, but its faded blue looked rather nice with his wide zig-zaggy necktie.

"You're not kidding about this place," Blair said to Kate. "Geriatric Park."

"I know; they're the only ones that stay. But it's grown on me. They're sweet."

"Them or the people I *can't* see?"

Kate laid a reassuring hand on Blair's arm to ease the thoroughly spooked-out expression twisting her beautiful face. She was the only friend outside Vera and Leo whom Kate had confided in about the paranormal turn of events her recent move had taken, and somehow the more she talked about it, joked about it, and experienced that Olive's presence wasn't a frequent or threatening occurrence, the more at ease she felt biding her time there until she could get out of her lease. Throwing herself into longer hours at work and surrounding herself with people (and booze) when home had sure helped, though.

Kate refilled her own champagne glass and set the bottle down on her side table before catching Vera's eye across the room. The old woman had shown up after all, on Leo's prodding. She hadn't exchanged more than three words with Kate, however; she instead occupied herself with cracking pistachios over by the window next to Miss Mousy, who held her baby monitor to her ear. Periodically, Maisie also ducked to peer across the courtyard at her own place.

Kate expelled a long sigh, feeling a little queasy about the "baby" all over again. Leave it to the living to trump the undead when it came to freak-factor.

"Oh, c'mon, he'll probably be here any minute," Blair said, evidently mistaking what troubled Kate. "But remember, if he isn't, that's okay, too. You'll live."

"Yes, I know. Thanks for giving me so much credit."

"Hey, I'm just saving you from your delusions."

"That so?"

"Yes."

"And *how* so? In what way am I deluded?"

"Well…Have you noticed Dex and Vicki have made it official?"

Kate's stomach plummeted, but she remained poker-faced. "Oh, please. They might be flirting, but nothing's official so long as he's still dating me, too."

"And that situation satisfies you? That's enough for you, Kate? Are you two even speaking anymore? That's how he's still dating you?"

Kate took a substantial swig of her bubbly and crossed her arms with the glass still in hand, looking everywhere else in the room but at Blair. "What makes it so 'official,' anyway?"

"You don't know?"

Kate swallowed and set her jaw. "No, enlighten me."

Her friend hesitated, prompting Kate to look back at her. When Blair held her frank tongue for any number of seconds, it was cause for concern.

"It's okay, you can tell me. I've been so head-down all week, it's better for me to know what I've been ignoring. Just…rip it off like a Band-Aid."

Blair pursed her lips for a few seconds. "She came to work today in the same skirt and shoes as yesterday. And wearing his shirt."

Keeping one arm protectively wrapped around her waist, Kate raised the other to take another swig of her drink. "We all wear the same sad-ass polos."

"Yeah, but she wears the red one in a small, and today she wore what looked to be a blue extra-large." When Kate shook her head and opened her mouth to question that as well, Blair added, "With Dex's nametag still pinned to it. And she kept giggling and flipping up her skirt to show his boxers underneath." As Kate still swiveled her head in doubt, Blair leaned in to whisper, "They were those novelty ones he'd gotten from the office Secret Santa. You know, that say 'Uranus' on the butt. Your favorites?"

Stopped midway to forming a response, Kate's mouth hung open. What her voice couldn't deliver she screamed through her eyes.

Blair laid a hand on Kate's shoulder. "I'm sorry to be the one to tell you, Kate. Vicki's such a conniving bitch, I'd have doubted it meant anything if not for the fact she was wearing all this in front of Dex all day, and it didn't appear to bother him. It's enough that I've seen them coming and going out of her office all week; they could just continue sneaking around like that. But coming into the office in the morning together with her in that getup I'd guess was meant to send the message. Officially."

Kate zoned out at the pattern on her oriental rug. "Loud and clear."

"I'm sorry, Kate," Blair repeated. "But this is what I warned you about. It sucks that it has to be this immediate, but it was only a matter of time before he'd move on. Even if it *is* just a rebound and doesn't mean anything, there's someone in the picture now besides you. It's what you asked for whether you like it or not."

The CD-changer rotated to "Moonlight Serenade" and a loud "Aahhh!" punctured the air. Kate looked to see one of her stairwell neighbors raise her gnarled hands in the air and sway to the music. An aged man in a thick sweater vest took her uplifted hands in his own, and the two began to dance. A few others paired off and followed suit, nudging Kate's coffee table with their legs toward her folded-up futon to make room.

Out of curiosity, Kate looked to Leo to see if he might ask Vera. The old man did appear to dart shy glances over at the object of his affection but didn't make a move.

Brad, too, looked over at Blair, pumping his eyebrows in invitation to the impromptu dance floor. To Kate's immense flattery, Blair smiled but waved him off.

She turned back to Kate. "You said you and Dex drew the line at sex, though, didn't you? That must make you feel a little better?"

Kate leveled a sober gaze at her friend. "Do you find Vicki the type that would honor that?"

Blair screwed her lips and shifted on her feet. "Mm, no. But all that matters is that Dex is the type to honor it, right?"

Squinting back at the floor, Kate was about to agree but caught her voice.

"What is it?" Blair asked. "Don't you trust him?"

"'No cheap thrills,' he said," Kate muttered bitterly. "He actually said that, in warning to *me*, and here's Vicki—Cheap Thrills incarnate." Her vision blurred with moisture, and she screwed her lips until she found her voice again. "I never doubted I could trust him. Dex just isn't that kind of guy. He's decent. But…" She rolled her eyes sideways toward her unit door, which stood propped open as an automatic welcome for guests to enter.

Blair fleetingly followed her line of sight. "But? How exactly did you leave things?"

Kate didn't look away from her door, seeing through the neighbors standing there. "That was the last time we even spoke. He hasn't said a word to me all week, you know that? I guess I can understand. That's fine; it's a transition period. It's just that he'd agreed to stay together. He said it was worth trying if it meant holding on to me. So, not that it went well, but it could've been much worse, you know?"

Frowning sympathetically, Blair nodded. "He's a big boy. He could have turned you down."

"Exactly."

"So then what? Did he storm out? Or did he leave on friendly terms?"

"We were standing there at the door, and he kissed me."

"Huh. Well, that's sweet. I guess."

"But then he warned me not to make him hate me." Kate blinked through her tears. "Like if he did, it would be all my fault and he'd exact some sort of revenge."

"Can you blame him?"

She kept blinking while looking at the door. "But I haven't done anything! I've just been feeling guilty hurting such a good guy when he gave it all of a *day* to move on. And to the office bicycle!" Realizing her raised volume had probably carried through the room, Kate lowered her voice again. "Why didn't he just lay her out on my desk and fuck her right there in front of me?"

Blair grimaced and raised a cautionary hand. "No, no. Don't even go there. I'm still processing the astro-labia."

Kate downed the rest of her champagne and was formulating her next thought when Brad snuck up from behind Blair and tickled his fiancée's waist. Blair lurched in shock and nearly spit out the sip she'd just taken

"Ladies?" Brad flashed an asymmetrical smile. "Can I bring you any drinks? Hors d'ouevres?"

"Is that my cue to get back to hostessing?" Kate asked.

"Not at all, my dear. You've outdone yourself."

Kate shot him a sidelong glance with a raised eyebrow. In the end, she hadn't gotten as fancy with the appetizers as anticipated; she'd been more concerned about getting the liquor right.

"Really! This is great. Thanks for having us."

It was so like Brad to always play the perfect gentleman, and Kate liked testing his ass-kissing ability now and then. Especially at a time like this when she needed it—ass kissing definitely trumped heart stomping.

"Sorry to interrupt you girls," Brad said. "Though, Blair, we really ought to watch the time. Remember, dinner at seven."

Blair nodded. "Don't worry, Kate, it's only the Persian place around the corner. We can leave up-to-the-minute."

"Do what you gotta do." Kate grinned through her disappointment. "And actually, Brad, if you don't mind, I could use a martini. Dry. Gin. Dirty."

"Ah!" Brad's brown eyes lit up, and he rubbed his palms together like a nefarious mastermind. "Leave it to me, milady. *Tout de suite.*"

Blair shook her head and laughed as he walked away to Kate's kitchen. "He's so pretentious."

"Yeah, but you love it."

"Yeah, I do."

Kate smiled beneath a dramatic eye-roll. "God, you two make me want to vomit."

Blair's hand reached out to Kate's shoulder again in solace. "You're gonna find him, Kate. Someday soon, I promise."

As if Blair had then spoken into a walkie-talkie and said, "Cue the hot guy. Entrance One, over," a tall, dark, and handsome young man with thick, wavy brown hair crossed the threshold into Kate's studio.

Kate had only just happened to glance up in time to catch his eye, which triggered a bleached-white smile that nearly melted her into a puddle on the floor. She willed herself to smile back and greet him, but instinctively, she grabbed Blair's arm instead and pulled her into the kitchen to join Brad.

"Oh my God, oh my God, oh my God, oh my God, oh my God." She paced in the small space between her stove and back door, inhibiting Brad's elbow room as he concocted her drink at the counter with the flourish of Tom Cruise in *Cocktail.*

"Kate, breathe," Blair coached.

"You saw him, too? I didn't just imagine it?" Kate asked as she attempted to relax.

"You mean Gaston out there? Uh, *yeah*, couldn't miss him. Are you insane? Get back out there and talk to him! Make him comfortable, Miss Hospitality!"

"Okay, okay, I know. Brad, how's that drink comin' along?"

"I could use some blue cheese—"

"Oh, for God's sake!" Kate reached around him and grabbed the martini glass off the counter just as he was plucking the pimento out of an olive. Taking half the glass down in one swallow, Kate grimaced, choked, then straightened herself. "Could you pour a fresh glass of red wine, please?"

Frowning at his prematurely consumed concoction, Brad obliged, and two-fisting it, Kate stepped around him and into her hallway as Blair silently cheered her on with spirit fingers.

She saw that he was still there. He hadn't turned on his heel just because Crazy Lady in 4C had shunned his smile.

And speaking of crazy ladies, Kate hoped Olive understood she was *not* invited to the party. Especially not at this moment when Kate needed to have major game.

Dismissing the supernatural and smiling broadly, she locked her eyes on Hot Neighbor and let his white teeth beam her in. The faceless enigma that had haunted her fantasies was now here, in the flesh and with a face.

Oh, what a face. She homed in on the dimple in his square chin.

"Do you drink red?" she asked his dimple politely before looking in his eyes and raising the wine glass to him. He stood a good six inches taller than her.

"Indeed, I do," Hot Neighbor replied. At the deep, velvety tone of his voice, Kate unraveled.

Yet she managed to gracefully hand over the glass without spilling or breaking anything, even when the transfer entailed a brief brushing of skin. Gooseflesh spiked all the way down her bare arms and she hoped the low-cut neckline of her dress—and boost of her new bra—would distract him from that.

"Cheers," she said, "to, uh…"

"To new acquaintances," he offered.

"I'll drink to that." Kate clinked his wine glass with her martini and took a sip. In a shy, awkward silence, she just grinned at him and stirred an olive around the shallow gin in what she hoped was a seductive manner. Hot Neighbor smiled back, his hazel eyes piercing through the suddenly charged air between them; Kate could practically see the crackling sparkle of electricity. She popped the olive into her mouth and rolled it over her tongue.

"So," Hot Neighbor finally said, "you're the hostess?"

"Mm hm," Kate answered, sucking on her olive and keeping the conversation in his court. *Keep some mystique, girl.* She tapped on her glass to the rhythm they'd knocked on their shared wall the other day, hoping he'd recognize it. *Tap tap, tap tap-tap, tap tap.*

"You live here, then?" he asked.

Okay, not the sharpest observation for igniting illuminating conversation—and no mention of the tune she'd tapped—but the night was still young. Kate could work with it.

She chewed her olive and nodded. "Yes. Welcome to my humble abode." She gave a mock curtsy. "And you? You live…"

"Here, too, yeah." He gestured back toward the open door. "Thanks for the invitation."

"Thanks for coming."

"Well, thanks for thinking to host something like this. It's nice for, uh—" he glanced around the room with a little laugh "—*neighbors* to get together."

"Yeah, we've got an interesting bunch here, don't we?"

"I only just moved in last month so I don't even know anyone."

And I take it if he's still here, he hasn't met his ghost yet either. "Same here, pretty much. Other than Leo and Vera." Kate searched around her room and pointed them out, catching Vera staring at them a split second before the woman looked away.

"Oh, yeah, I met Leo when he showed me the place," he said.

"Same here. And Vera was hosting that estate sale in the courtyard. I don't know if you—"

"Yeah, I remember. I saw you there working one of the tables. Sorry I didn't stop by to, uh, check out your wares."

Do I detect a bit of saucy in that remark? "You saw me?"

He gave a side grin and stepped back to eye her up and down. "You aren't too hard to notice."

For as well as she maintained her outward composure, Kate swooned from within. Her air conditioner was on its low setting to keep it quiet, and without any Olive AC at the moment, she could feel the late July heat drip sweat down the back of her thighs. Still, she shifted with giddy energy on her open-toed platform heels as she skidded the pad of her middle finger around the rim of her martini glass.

Her face was on fire; she blew her bangs off her forehead for some relief. Looking to the floor, she took the opportunity to inspect Hot Neighbor, from his polished brown dress shoes to the deep indigo running up his long legs. She only got as far as where the denim started to hug a muscular pair of thighs when she heard:

"Sorry if I've made you uncomfortable. Though I wouldn't say it if I didn't mean it."

"N-No," Kate said into her glass as she took a small sip for reinforcement. She peered over it to see where the buttons of his crisp white shirt ended and a sliver of bronzed skin at his chest began. "I've, uh, I've noticed you, too."

"Have you?" Hot Neighbor said in a boyish high-pitch. "No."

"I've only seen you on your way out so haven't had the chance to say hello."

"Well, hello," he said, shifting his wine glass to his left hand to extend his right.

Kate transferred her glass in kind and took his hand. Though he appeared cool and collected enough with sleeves rolled to his elbows, his palm was warm — not clammy like Dexter's could get, but Kate sensed (hoped) he was just as nervous as she was. Daring to rub her thumb slightly over the web of skin between his thumb and index finger, she noted a softness that implied an occupation in keeping with the white collar of his well-pressed shirt.

Their handshake lingered a few seconds, before Hot Neighbor raised Kate's fingers to his lips. As he brushed a light, polite kiss on them, Kate could practically hear the neighing battle cry of the gallant steed he'd surely ridden in on.

It was to her great chagrin when he gave her hand back.

"So, uh, h-how long have you lived here? In Chicago, I mean," she asked.

"Born and bred in Barrington, but I moved to the city for law school."

Kate ticked boxes left and right in her brain. *Affluent suburban upbringing. Check. Lawyer. Check.* "Oh, so you're a student?"

"No, I practice at a firm now." He swept his hands outward in a *ta-da* fashion, indicating his clothes and adding, apparently in explanation, "Casual Friday. But I graduated back in, what was it, ninety-five?"

"Ooh," Kate said again, bringing her fingers to her throat and caressing it through her mental calculations that estimated this sexy beast at close to thirty or older, depending on whether he'd gone to law school straight from undergraduate. Hot damn.

"And you?" he asked.

"About three years now, since undergrad."

He kept his eyes fixed on Kate's as he took a sip of his wine. And just as soon as he'd brought his glass back down, he raised it again and took another, deeper swig.

"Look," he said abruptly after, "I hate to run, but I've got a scheduling conflict tonight, unfortunately. But I wanted to at least run up for a drink on my way from work to dinner, and I'm glad I did. It's nice to know you."

"Oh, w-well, yeah, I agree. Thanks so much for stopping by!" Perhaps trying too hard to mask her disappointment with enthusiasm, Kate actually expedited his departure by retrieving his glass from him. "Here, I'll just take that for you. Have fun tonight!"

She would regret that stupid, gracious hostessing maneuver for the rest of the night.

"Thank you, uh…"

"Kate."

"Thanks, Kate," he said, leaning in to place a hand at her waist and a kiss at her cheek. "Let's do this again sometime soon. Well—" he scanned the other partygoers "—maybe not all *this*, but the two of us. Drinks. Next week some time?"

"Yes, I'd love that, uh…" Kate circled the two glasses around as filler for the Mystery Man's name.

"David."

"David." *Pin him down!* her gut screamed at her. *Commit to a date!* Kate gripped both glass stems to the point she could've snapped them, not believing what boldness she was about to force out her mouth. "How does Wednesday work for you?"

Wednesday would be the weekly staff meeting where she could publicly announce to all, including Dex, that she had to leave early for a date. Yet Kate sort of wished she could suck her sentence back into her mouth like a spaghetti noodle—a Thursday or Friday night probably would've been more expected. Was Wednesday too eager?

Quick, balance it out with something casual. "Fado's, maybe?" she added. That was a typical enough watering hole for the after-work crowd. *Nice touch.*

"Wednesday's perfect," he said, to her relief. "I'll call you in the next few days to confirm plans? Your number's on the flyer, right?"

"Either way, you know where to find me," Kate said. She smacked her forehead from the inside for letting herself sound so available, while simultaneously running through her mind what outfit to wear.

"Excellent. Talk soon, Kate."

All she could do as he walked out and down the stairs was grin moronically and shake her martini glass as a wave goodbye.

"Sooo," she heard in her ear from behind, "how's that grass on the other side. Greener?"

Smiling in a trance, she pivoted on her heels toward Blair. "There is nothing green about that man. Only: Red. Hot. Maturity."

"An experienced one, eh?"

Kate winked. "Let's hope so."

"Okay, Blair, darling," Brad interrupted, finishing off a cocktail wiener. "We'd better get going before we're late."

"And before you kill your appetite," she replied, pointedly eying all the barbeque-saucy toothpicks on his napkin. As he wiped his mouth and hands with a fresh napkin, she hugged Kate goodbye. Before she let go, though, she whispered, "Be careful with Red Hot, Katie. Don't get burned."

Turning to kiss Brad goodbye on the cheek, Kate looked back to Blair as she walked them out. "Enjoy your dinner." She waved them off down the stairs; then, when they'd descended out of sight, she muttered, "Don't burn your judgmental tongue on it."

Lingering at the doorway, she looked from the empty stairwell to the door directly kitty-corner from hers. She leaned against the frame and sighed in expectation of when she and that apartment's resident would next meet, burning in curiosity over what his place looked like on the inside.

She stepped forward a bit, tempted to test the knob in the crazy off-chance it would open, when she felt a heavy energy press in on her, taking her breath away in a very different manner than David had. Rolling her eyes to look all around her, she felt the hairs on her arm stand on end and a cold puff of lilac-scented air at her ear, like breath. With all the music and murmur filling her studio, she could have easily been mistaken, but she thought she heard the word "mine" uttered in a low, almost electronic voice.

She flinched at the sound as if shooing a buzzing mosquito at her ear, and turned around to see Vera standing right behind her. Kate started, clanking the two glasses in her hands together.

"You all right, dear?" Vera asked, her mouth stern. "You look like you might'a just seen a ghost."

"Well, we both know that's more than just an expression round these parts, don't we?" she replied.

Vera puckered her lips and glanced down at Kate's glasses. "Yes, well…I'm on my way out, Kate, but I want to thank you for the invitation. This was a nice get-together for everybody. Ethel and Hank are absolutely having the time of their lives cutting a rug over there. You might have trouble getting them to go home."

She gave a gruff laugh, a sound Kate was grateful to hear again.

"Anyway," Vera said, "I think Maisie enjoyed herself, too. Didn't talk to anyone but me, but that was still very good of you to invite her, get her around other people. I'll be seeing her home now. She's, uh—" Vera looked over her shoulder at the mousy woman straining to bend out the window "—she's, uh, wanting to check on the baby."

Kate smiled and nodded in respect. "Of course. I'm really happy you came, Vera. I'll talk to you soon?"

"I'd like that. Stop on by anytime, dear." She patted Kate's arm and looked back over at Maisie with impatience. "Excuse me," she said and crossed to fetch her companion.

On their way to the door, the two women paused to nod and wave their goodbyes to Leo, who stood motionless with a plate in one hand and a cheese-topped cracker in the other while he chewed. All he seemed able to do was to bob his head and lift his full hands, his eyes wide in innocent discomfort.

"'Bye now, Kate," Maisie said quietly as Vera briskly walked with her arm-in-arm to the door. With her free hand, she clutched the silent baby monitor to her chest. "What a nice party, thank you."

On closer view, Kate noticed she'd affixed a pair of rhinestone barrettes in her frizzy hair, evidently wanting to dress up her brown polyester tracksuit for the occasion. Kate felt oddly flattered.

"So sorry to run out," Maisie said, "but you'll know how it goes one day when you have kids. They're real needy in the early years."

Kate pressed her lips together but made sure to turn them up at their corners. Her hands were still full, so she just backed out of the door and gestured the glasses toward the stairs like an air traffic controller. "'Bye, ladies."

As they made their slow way down, Kate reentered her studio and finally ditched her and David's glasses. Then she made a beeline for Leo.

Artie Shaw's "A Room With a View" played on the stereo. Kate snatched the paper plate of crackers and cookies from Leo's hands, dropped it on her coffee table, and pulled him to the center of her carpet.

"Sorry to interrupt your conversation, Leo, but if you're not going to fill any ladies' dance cards on your own, I've gotta take matters into my own hands."

She beamed up into his bashful face, took his hands after he'd wiped them on his slacks, and assumed the stance, waiting for him to lead.

Which he did. With unexpected grace, Leo guided her through a simple two-step. The remaining party guests formed a little circle around the two, clapping and whooping from the sidelines in a festive dance-hall spirit. Kate looked around at each of the pale, papery faces, doubting there was a full set of real teeth to be found among their smiles.

Yet, as nostalgia twinkled at her from their eyes, Kate felt in true fellowship with their merriment and flashed her pearly whites back, beckoning them all to join her and Leo. It didn't take much arm-twisting. Seconds later, all were paired up and had fun switching up their partners while Artie's hypnotic clarinet played on.

All except Kate and Leo. She wanted to keep that tall drink of water to herself for the time being, at least until she could give him a mild—yet firm—lecture on missed golden opportunities. Blushing to his ears, he nodded like a scolded schoolboy and, grinning, held her closer to spin her around and around.

And there on Cloud Nine, Kate never once felt her feet touch the floor.

Nine for Hell

October 1927

"Happy anniversary, darling."

"Happy anniversary, dear."

Raising crystal water goblets and nodding heads toward one another from across the long expanse of their marble dining table, Finlay and Eva toasted their two years of marriage. The yellow light of midmorning slanted in through the tall windows.

"Are you feeling fine?" Finlay asked.

"Yes," Eva answered.

"No spells today?"

"No spells today."

"You won't miss me this afternoon, then? You're quite sure you're not angry?"

"Not in the least, dear. Duty calls."

"Ah, that's my happy bride."

Finlay folded his morning paper and playfully slapped it down on the corner of the table. Rising to his feet, he strode to Eva's end of the table and gave two swift yet delicate taps to her cheek with his fingertips. She tilted her head up with a little smile and closed her eyes as he bent down and mechanically planted a kiss on the top of her head.

"Until evening, then, darling. So dreadful for an anniversary to fall during a work week."

"Indeed."

"Well, I love you, dearest. I'll rush home as soon as I can."

"Do that, dear thing."

"Right," Finlay said with a crisp smile and exited the dining room.

Eva puffed her cheeks and released a burst of air as soon as she heard the front door open and close. She sank back in her carved wooden chair and, after adjusting the embroidered silk pillow specially placed at her lower back, she pulled the lapels of her burgundy velvet robe together over her tender breasts, willing the nausea to subside.

"Happy anniversary, old girl."

"Happy anniversary, old boy."

Clinking two highball tumblers and pressing lips to one another's as they stretched the length of his bed, Lon and Eva toasted their six-month love affair. The gray cloud cover that had approached by afternoon was blocked out by Lon's heavy draperies.

"Are you feeling all right?" Lon asked, dropping kisses along her neck by candlelight.

"Better now," Eva answered. She took a sip of gin and swallowed it with her chin raised. "Only a bit dizzy. But I blame you and the hooch for that." She tilted her head and smiled at him, nudging his bare thigh with her bare knee.

Lon drank from his glass and, taking Eva's, twisted to set both tumblers onto the wooden floor. Returning his attention to where she lay on her back with an arm thrown over her head, he brushed the backs of his fingers from her breastbone down to her navel and over the slight swell beneath it. Noting the new curvature, he flattened his palm to her belly and rubbed it in elliptical motions.

"Must you be so attentive to my bulgiest bits?" Eva asked. "I blame you for that, too, you know."

"What do you mean, old girl?"

"I mean loving you is making me fat. I've never been so happy, Lonnie, and you've been the best exercise, really, working me into a hearty appetite. I eat like a man now."

Lon continued massaging the soft skin of her stomach, then, trailing his middle fingertip back up to her chest, he traced the curve of a swollen breast.

"I do like where you've allocated this fat of yours," he said.

"Of course you would notice that, too."

Lon cupped her firmly. Eva winced.

"I'm sorry, darling, Have I hurt you?" he asked.

"They're just a bit sensitive, my growing girls. Be gentle, but, whatever you do, don't stop."

Lon eased his grip, circling his palm lightly instead as he kissed and nipped his way down her torso.

"No, indeed," Eva sighed, bending her knees as he passed below her belly. "Don't you dare think about stopping now."

Lon lightly skimmed his fingers over her hips and along her thighs before sinking them into the flesh there and spreading her knees, eliciting a heavy, tremulous breath from her. He heard nails scrape on fabric as Eva clutched the bed sheet on either side of her; her hips rose and fell to the rhythm his mouth played into her. Looking up to Eva's face, he saw only the underside of her fine jaw and admired the new silhouette of her fuller breasts. He listened to her breathe fiercely through her nose and, in time, felt the tremor in her body as she likewise strangled the bedding and practically pulled the sheet out from under him.

Lon hummed, kissing the insides of her thighs before moving his way back up her stomach. "You've added new spice to your flavor, my girl." Eva's new douching practice was no doubt the culprit, a measure she'd taken to reinforce their usual *coitus interruptus*.

Eva panted in the afterglow. "Wha — what are you talking about, silly boy?"

"Only that your recipe is perhaps a little more savory?" he said, peppering kisses up to her neck. With hands planted on either side of her, Lon lifted himself to extend above her and settled the weight of his hips over hers. "Must be this new manly diet of yours, ripping red meat off the bone," he chided, rocking his hips side to side and pressing his lips to hers.

"Hm." Eva breathed into their kiss, then separated. "I suppose I'll have to take your word for it, old boy. I'm not quite the connoisseur you are."

Lon pinched his brow. "Why would you say that?"

Eva huffed out a laugh. "Only that I wouldn't know the difference. How should I?"

"Oh, but I have plenty to compare? Is that what you mean?"

Eva started to inch up onto her elbows, and Lon eased back to allow her room to prop herself up.

"Lon, I have no idea what—" She rubbed a hand over her eyes. "Oh, let's forget that I ever said it. I don't know why I did."

Straddling her, Lon sat back on his heels, frowning.

"It was nonsense, old boy. Just forget it!"

"It was mean-spirited." He rose onto his knees and swung off of her to sit at the edge of the bed. He reached for his glass and downed the rest of his gin.

"Lon…" Eva said softly, sitting up and gathering the sheet to her shoulders. "Why are you being so coarse with me?"

Lon rolled the glass between his palms as he looked to the floor, mute. After a time, he said, low and hoarse, "I have everyone in this world judging me, Eva. I can't take it from you."

"Oh, Lonnie." She crawled to him and curled into his side. "I haven't. And I would never. You know that. You know *me*."

"I know you haven't been altogether yourself lately." He raised his head and turned it to her. "Are you certain it's happiness making you eat? Making you ill? It isn't doubt? Regret?"

Eva slowly shook her head, brushing her lips lightly at his shoulder as she did so. "It's *guilt* that eats me up inside, Lonnie. It's been six months of deceit, sneaking out on a good man."

"Even though he may be doing the same to you."

She ceased swaying her face and looked up at him, taking his chin between her thumb and forefinger. "As for doubt, I have none. As for regret, I'll never feel it."

Lon curled a hand around hers and sank his face into her palm to kiss it. "Never regret it," he whispered.

"Apart from wishing it had only been you first." She rested her head on his shoulder, and they sat in silence awhile.

Lon wondered if Eva might have even nodded off, because after a time she gave a sudden lurch and sat up. She raised a hand to her chest as though feeling her heart beat, breathed long and deeply a couple of times, then stepped out of bed and walked her alabaster form toward her clothing on his chair.

"I'd better go," she said, straightening out her bandaging and commencing to wrap it back around her chest. She grimaced a bit as she wound it tightly.

"My poor, darling girl." Lon rose to help her dress, holding the waistband of her trousers open so she could step into them. He caught her when, balanced on one foot, she wobbled a little. "Can you rest tonight? Beat what's ailing you while Finlay works late?"

Fidgeting with her fly when the button resisted fitting through the hole, Eva gave up and sank to the chair. From her miserable expression, Lon thought she might cry.

"Oh, Lon." She raised drooping, glassy eyes to his. "It's our anniversary as well, remember? Who would have figured it would calculate to this." Biting her lower lip, she shook her head. "He'll be coming home early. Some sort of…celebration will be in order." She fingered the button of her slacks again but made no effort to try fastening it again.

Without a word, Lon reached for his own trousers to pull them on, then descended to his knees to assist Eva with hers where she sat. In silence, he dressed her in her shirt and suspenders as well, then her socks and garters. When they stood, he held out her coat. She walked into it, then stepped into her shoes. She pinned her hair and adjusted her cap as Lon kneeled once more to tie her laces.

When he rose, he pressed his lips together and gave Eva a light punch to her shoulder as he would to a chum. "Congratulations," was all he said.

Looking to the ground as she walked to his door, she spun on her heel before he could open it for her.

"Lonnie?"

"I already know what you're going to ask, and I have your answer: two years is cotton. Perhaps a new handkerchief with his monogram will do." When she didn't smile at his feeble anniversary joke, he nodded for her to go ahead with her real question.

"I…I've decided that I'm giving myself one week to tell him."

Lon's heart leaped to his throat, choking off any words he could attempt to stutter. He watched Eva's eyes dart all over his face, searching for the answer she'd really wanted, and after a few seconds, he allowed his true emotion to break out on his face.

Eva beamed in return. And that time, she did cry. Throwing herself back into his arms, her hat was knocked off her head as she buried her face into his shoulder. "It's really going to happen, isn't it? We'll really be together?"

"Yes, yes, my darling girl!" Lon laughed into her hair.

He clutched her as fervently as she held him while they both shook with excitement and kissed each other frantically all over.

Eventually, Lon seized Eva's face in his hands and stood back a little to ask, "But you know we won't be able to stay on here. We'll have to say goodbye to Chicago, old girl. Start somewhere new, without any connections or prospects or—"

She silenced him with a firm kiss. Detaching with a loud smack of their lips, she exclaimed, "All that matters is we'll be together. Forever, Lonnie. As to whatever else could happen to us, the Devil may care!"

On overhearing their private words, their eager lovers' plans, the little devil next door did care. A great deal.

Listening to the sounds of Eva's departure outside her door, Ollie rolled a tear-stung eye to her window and watched two blackbirds alight on a windowsill across the courtyard.

"*One for sorrow, two for birth,*" she recited from childhood memory, holding her doll for comfort.

Seated cross-legged on the wingback chair she'd found ditched in the back alley, she cradled the baby and picked at a hole in her stockings. Oh, that she could have run away with Wynken, Blynken, and Nod and captured all that glittered from their boat. Instead, the only fishnets she had were on her legs, and all they'd managed to catch were lewd grins and rough hands. But some of the clients could be nice; some paid compliments and tipped her with extra cash or jewelry. At the very least, they bought her liquor at the start of every night, lit her cigarette, or let her take a dip inside their treasure boxes with the little golden spoon she'd also been gifted. It all numbed her from what would then carry on upstairs in rooms reserved by the hour.

Though sometimes she rather liked it. She wasn't one to turn her nose up, after all, at the ancient profession that hadn't discriminated against her age or asked for identification, not the employment that paid her bills after Eva's emerald had bought her freedom. And she particularly didn't mind when a tall, fair-haired and lean young man approached her. In the hazy dim light, she could avoid looking at him too closely, and in the dark, she could imagine he was Lon. She'd unleashed hidden talent that her Parker School education could never provide, and with practice would come perfection when, at last, she'd make her way into her neighbor's bed.

Walking over to the window, she peered out the warped glass in search of more blackbirds and found some. A string of other dark birds lined up along the rooftop ledge. And Ollie continued to count them.

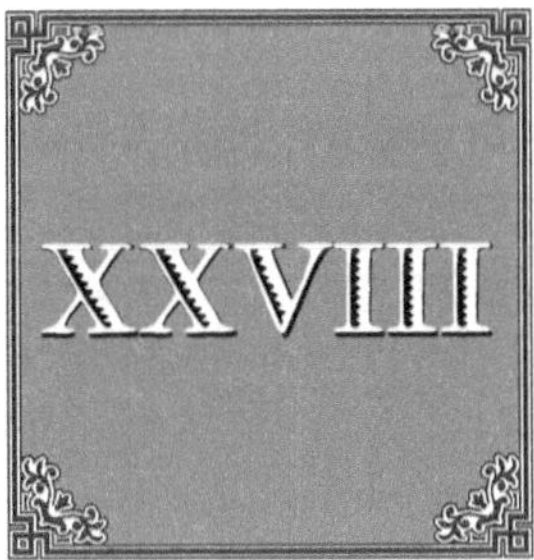

Whistling to the tune of "Everybody Loves My Baby, but My Baby Don't Love Nobody but Me," Lon skipped up the steps to his Aunt Estella's grand white house, dried russet and orange leaves crunching underfoot. He tapped the front door with a twig he'd picked up on the winding drive, and as he waited for an answer, his whistles and hums turned to giddy singing that he was Eva's Sheik. He started to run the stick back and forth along the immaculate side railings of the white porch.

"Stop destroying my property," came a soft-spoken voice that still somehow managed to sound tough as nails. "I put a fresh coat on that this summer."

"Auntie," Lon said with exaggerated affection as he flicked his twig over the side of the railing and walked to the door, arms held out wide to the tall woman. They embraced in a tight hug, and Estella patted his back heartily. Breathing in deeply, he took in her familiar scent of fresh soap and gardenia, which mingled with the smoky spice of burning leaves in the distance. Lon then stood back to take a look at her. "Looking healthy as an ox, my girl. An ox. Time will never age you."

"Oh, pooh." She swiped her hand at him and ushered him inside. "You know you're written into the will already, so you can forget buttering me up."

Lon chuckled as he followed her in with his hands shoved in his pockets. Veering slightly off course, he stepped toward the imposing grandfather clock at the side of the foyer and tried to set his rapidly beating heart to the measured pace of its large pendulum.

Breathe, old boy. She'll never take you seriously if you gush like a smitten schoolboy.

He was so fixated on the ornamental gold tracery of the clock face, swirling about like his thoughts and emotions, he hadn't even noticed the time—so he jumped back in alarm when the old clock scolded him with its quarter-past chime.

He heard short, hissing spurts of air and turned to see his great-aunt standing between the French doors she'd opened to her living room, shaking in quiet laughter at his expense.

"Stop milling about the entryway," she said. "Go on and take a seat in here while I fix us some tea."

Lon smiled with admiration as the aged yet statuesque woman squeezed his arms with affection and made her way to her kitchen in back. How she had kept on all those years caring for herself in that great big house he would never comprehend. Granted, she walked with a cane whenever she ventured outside of it and was already considering moving her bedroom down to the first floor library for convenience, but she could still surmount the stairs when she had to without assistance. With the exception of paying a landscaping service to maintain the extensive grounds outside, from the day she'd inherited the home from Lon's great-grandparents and paid the household staff their severance—enough for each to live a modest, independent retirement on—she had done it all on her own and overseen the Midwest lumberyards at that.

She couldn't go on that way forever, he knew, but for the time being, the woman did all right.

"Here, dear," came that speak-softly-and-carry-a-big-stick voice, and Lon reached for one of two delicate teacups and saucers sitting on the silver tray Estella held out to him.

He settled onto a beige sofa as she propped the tray on a small wooden Queen Anne table and carried her own saucer with her to an adjacent high-backed chair upholstered in rust-colored velvet. Taking a sip too hastily out of nerves, Lon flinched from the heat and caught his aunt's measured eye as she clinked her spoon inside her china cup.

"So," she eventually said on dissolving the remainder of her sugar cube in her tea, "what brings you by, my boy?"

"Well, as I said when I first phoned you, it's been such a long time since I—"

"Level with me, boy." Estella never broke her eye contact with him as she sipped her tea with a grin.

Lon felt his cheeks simmer as he smiled back. "Oh, Auntie. You'll never believe it."

"Try me." She raised her brow. "Is there someone I ought to know? Someone I'll be meeting sometime soon? The someone who puts that new twinkle in your eye and jitter in your hands?" She looked pointedly at the teacup that was rattling against its saucer in Lon's grip.

Feeling like a boy of twelve, he bobbed his head excitedly and set his tea down on the table. "Oh yes, Auntie. I do hope so."

Estella took a prim sip. "And you're in love with—"

"I am, Auntie. I am very, very much in love with her. A beautiful young woman. Tall and elegant like you and just as grounded. But that's only the beginning of her merits."

"And she loves you in return?"

"She does." Lon bobbed his head again but slower, still trying to believe the truth of it himself. "I don't know how a man like me should get so lucky, but she does love me. And, Auntie, she knows everything—everything there is to know about me, things even you only know the half of—and she loves me still. Not in spite of it but *because* of it."

Estella took another sip of her tea and regally sat back in her chair, a smile spread across her finely sculpted face. "She has seen your talent?" She released her cup handle and pointed her long fingers toward a grand portrait on the wall opposite Lon—a richly rendered likeness of herself.

"She has. And she's inspired it." Lon hoped his face did not burn as brightly as it felt when he viewed in his mind the recent masterpiece Eva was posing for. A work in progress.

"And she is also from Chicago."

He nodded tentatively. That was clearly a statement, not a question, and Lon sensed a stream of new understanding flow between their eyes. The pleased look in Estella's told him he wouldn't be enduring a line of questioning on the girl's prospects, her lineage, and so forth. She had somehow already learned all she needed to know.

Estella stood and waved at Lon to remain seated as she bent to also set her teacup and saucer on the table. But instead of sitting back in her chair, she rose, stepped around to sit beside him on the sofa, and wrapped his hands firmly in hers.

"And the lady's name?" She gave his hands a squeeze during a pregnant pause. "Either her maiden or married one will do."

His lungs collapsed of air. His cheeks burst into flame. Folding over as his body deflated in on itself, Lon rested his forehead on his aunt's knuckles, smelling the crisp linen scent of her soap. Estella released one hand to stroke his hair.

"I just need to hear you say it," she sighed.

He squeezed his eyes and kissed her hand before sitting up and recapturing some of his wind. Looking her square in the eye, he said, "Eva. Eva Hughes."

"Or *Missus* Redcliffe, even."

Lon swallowed. "Yes."

Estella raised her brow and smiled at her lap with a high-pitched little hum.

"You…you already knew. Didn't you," he asked. "But how? Have we been so transparent?"

Rubbing his hands in hers, his old aunt chuckled. "No, no, my boy. Only to me. And, well, perhaps to *Mister* Redcliffe."

Lon closed his eyes again.

"Finlay paid the family a visit, you know," Estella continued in his silence. "Me, your parents, your brother. He was paying us respect, you see, by informing us fully on the circumstances of your…arrest." After a brief pause, she then punctured the air with the high pitch of her next word. "*As* well as politely requesting that we mention nothing to anyone of his lovely wife's presence at the…incident." As her nephew groaned, she added, "You, my boy, have diverted everyone's attention in different directions. But I could see through it then, and I see through it now."

Lon bowed his head.

"Tragic about the sister."

He nodded, chin still to his chest.

"No new developments?"

He shook his head where it hung.

"I imagine Mrs. Redcliffe has been in need of great comforting, then."

He said nothing.

"Comforting that her husband has perhaps been unable to give her?"

Silence.

"It's a wonder…"

When Estella's hesitation dragged out long enough, Lon braved a glance at her face.

"…that not all can see what I see. Perhaps when one isn't complicated with one's own love affairs, others' entanglements become all the clearer. Or maybe it's my complicated understanding of them after all."

He searched her face for meaning.

She patted his hand. "It wasn't just my pride and righteousness that couldn't bear continuing to pay John his wages, you know."

"John?"

"You remember him, don't you?" She sat back and chuckled gruffly, shaking her head in seeming self-deprecation. "Oh, perhaps you wouldn't. There I go, humoring myself with age again — it was your *father*. Your *father* was the one John used to tell of the gnomes he'd find while trimming the hedges. They'd set traps for them together when your father and his sister stayed here during their summer holidays. Had them believing in garden gnomes and pixies until your daddy was at least twelve, I think." She giggled like a woman decades younger until her face sobered. "Anyway, he was also the one whose young wife once tended to me as a lady-in-waiting, up to the time she became sickly."

"So John was…" Lon drawled out. "The gardener?"

Nodding in meaningful rhythm with each syllable, Estella added, "And married."

"Aunt?"

"Her sickness was Nature, mind you. No foul play. But I dare say her delicate constitution made circumstances terribly convenient. I was left alone, unobserved in my room. And his duties required he leave her side at the cottage to tend to the house here. Yet in the end, I —" the air audibly caught in her throat, but she powered through the quavering that had entered her tone "— I had to do what was right by her. For both of them."

Estella pressed her lips together as her grasp on Lon's hand firmed. He spoke nothing to break her silent meditation.

"So, you see," she began again, "I know the looks, the tone of voice, the whispers — the stolen moments when love isn't allowed to see the light of day. As you know, it isn't often I come to Illinois and torture myself with social engagements, but you were such a gentleman to escort me to the Everett's summer ball. And, my boy, when you did…I saw you. *Each one* of you. Looking over the shoulders of your dance partners at someone else waltzing in another's arms."

Sensing from her eyes there was more in her words than he could infer, Lon merely asked, "Are you very ashamed of me?"

"I am very moved, Lonnie." She patted his hand again. "And praying you are no more ashamed of me." She sighed wistfully and slowly shook her expression into something more somber. "I'm also very dismayed by your timing. That you two kids couldn't have simply found each other first."

At the echo of Eva's words, Lon lowered his head; blowing out a heavy exhale, he tried to swallow his keen disappointment. Somehow he'd thought in coming here he'd find the answer. His aunt's home had always delivered the best cures for scraped knees and upset stomachs (no matter that her adventurous grounds, bountiful feasts, and open rules were usually the cause of such malady in the first place), and he'd never questioned it could do the same for heartache, too. But adultery? No, he'd been asking for too much there.

"However," Estella said briskly, and she raised his chin with her long finger. Lon blinked through a lens of tears to focus on her intense gray eyes. "We don't enjoy the privilege of choosing who or when we love. What matters, Lonnie, is that you *do* love. Now, it's going to be messy, but that, too, shall pass."

Biting his lower lip, he found in those gray eyes a glimmer of hope. Yet in seeing again the possibility of achieving his impulsive dreams, he just as suddenly saw less and less of a clear, realistic course of action he could follow. Outside of his room, out from beneath his painted canopy of stars and from above Eva's soft skin, Lon saw the objective glare of daylight angling in through Estella's windows. In front of her heavy brocade draperies, flecks of golden dust hung suspended in the rays, ashes returning to ashes in a purgatory he now felt trapped inside.

His chest heaved, and his gut grumbled in agitation. Estella sat watching him process his thoughts, and as if in answer to them if not his very prayers, she slapped her hands to her thighs and said:

"All right. Enough stewing over this. Let's figure out what we're going to do about it. But after lunch. We can feed your heart after that stomach."

Clutching the banister as she slowly ascended the stairs to Lon's residence, Eva fought the trepidation weighing on her heart. Once at his door, she lightly knocked to the beat of "Tonight You Belong to Me":

Tap tap, tap tap-tap, tap tap.

She heard distant shuffling and the creak of floorboards, but he didn't open his door. Knocking out their private code a little louder, signaling to Lon it was her and no one else, Eva pressed her ear to the door and heard more stirring, but not from inside his place. It came from the next room, and she looked to the neighbor's doorway in time to notice a shadow playing at its base.

With a quiet gasp, Eva spun her back to the neighbor's peephole, at the same time remembering Lon wouldn't be back from his aunt's estate until that evening. Keeping her head bowed, she stuck her forefinger and thumb up into her cap and wriggled out a hairpin. Bending it this way and that and trying it in the lock in different ways, she at last found the winning combination and slipped herself through the door, out of her clothes, and into Lon's bed.

Rolling up into fetal position within the security of his sheets, she tried to nap but was disturbed by what sounded like the neighbor's door opening and — were those footsteps padding out onto the landing? Eva held her breath and waited until she soon heard the door close again. Silence followed.

Left alone with her thoughts, she ran a hand over her bare, swollen breasts and stomach and sobbed into Lon's pillow, crying over old memories of Ollie, crying for her own new condition. Crying out of desperation, yet dread for Lon's return as she writhed in her personal hell.

"No, Aunt! You can't mean it?"

"I do, my boy. I want you to have it. For when the time is right."

Seated with him at her noble table that had been carved from the very same white pine tree as the paneling on the dining room walls, Aunt Estella tucked a little black velvet box into Lon's palm and wrapped his fingers around it. She clasped her own hands around his and gave a good shake as if to weld the box into place between his palms.

Lon protested, "Auntie, no." But he could see it was a losing battle.

She steeled her gaze at him. "Listen to me. You see this through. This is your tangible promise to that girl, something she can see and hold on to when it otherwise seems all will be lost. You'll have to wait this out, but stay the course. And when the time comes, I want you to bring your young bride here, where you can weather the rest of the storm. No one will trouble you here if I have anything to do with it."

"But this is—"

"I know full well what it is, and Mother would want you to have it. I've had no use for it, and I've always intended it for you. Read my will if you don't believe me."

"But the imposition on you if we—"

"Nonsense. What's an old gal like me need with this big house? Listen: it's an ideal place to lie low and get your affairs sorted. Get on your feet and pray to come out of all this respectably."

"But—"

"But nothing." Estella let go of him to throw her hands to the air. "Oh, you're going to make me say it out loud, aren't you? Fine. I'm not getting any younger, my boy, so don't think this whole arrangement is solely for your benefit. You two will earn your keep around here, help me out. The only thing happening faster for me these days is slowing down. This old girl isn't what she used to be. I confess it: I'll need you as much as you'll need me."

Lon's shoulders sank, and he looked down at the black box as he popped it open. An old mine-cut sapphire winked at him from its platinum nest of filigree.

Clapping the box shut, he pushed back his heavy wooden chair and rose from the table, but he didn't walk away until first leaning down to kiss his dear aunt's cheek and hug her firmly where she sat.

With another kiss and a fond farewell to the gray woman smiling radiantly up at him, Lon sped out the door, down the winding drive, and into the autumn colors to meet his train and destiny.

July 2000

"Got a date tonight?"

"Yep, with Destiny."

With the pad of her ring finger, Kate smoothed the deep crimson she'd just applied to her lower lip and snapped the cap back onto her tube of lipstick. As she leaned over the bathroom sink to make one last close-up inspection of her pores, she glanced down to make sure ample cleavage showed at that angle — should she, say, drop her napkin and have to pick it up from the floor. Or lean over the table to wipe delectable sauce from the corner of her date's delectable mouth.

"Someone's getting lucky tonight," her coworker Lucy chirped and gave her a high-five on her way out the door. "See you in the conference room in a few. Fabulous bag, by the way."

"Thanks," Kate replied as she picked a clump of fresh mascara off her lashes and touched a finger to her curling iron to be sure it was cool enough to store away.

Stacking what makeup essentials she could into the odd hexagonal shape of her vintage purse, Kate stood up straight and admired her reflection. She'd opted for a black-knit tank top and silver-gray pencil skirt that hugged her curves down to the knee. The classic silhouette said "*Respect me*" while the deep V-neck of the top and side slit of the skirt elaborated on that point with "*But you can still sex me up if you want to.*" Paired with her new strappy high heels and

Olive's stunning black beaded bag—making its twenty-first-century debut—the ensemble was perfect for a date with David.

And a dig at Dexter.

Remaining beauty supplies and dumpy work-gear shoved into her backpack, Kate tossed the bulky bag into one of the volunteer lockers and, after slamming its metal door, practiced her sexy-walk past the maze of cubicles and onward to the conference room for the Wednesday staff meeting. She'd deliberately timed it so she would arrive fashionably late and all eyes would be on her.

She walked through the doorway, flipped her toffee curls back, and playfully hopped onto the side counter since all the chairs were taken. When offered a slice of pizza from the conference table, she declined with a loud, "No, thank you. I have a dinner date in the Gold Coast." David, it so happened, had since upped the ante, upgrading their date from drinks at Fado Irish Pub to dinner at Bistro Margot. Technically, the restaurant was located in Old Town, not the ritzy Gold Coast, but why split hairs with those people when dating David was still already so much more sophisticated than Dexter.

Only once everyone was settled with their paper plates and fizzing cans of soda did Kate finally conduct a proper scan of participants. Everyone could be accounted for except one education staff member and one volunteer coordinator.

Meeting Blair's gaze across the table, her friend pouted and shook her head sympathetically, then cocked it in the direction of the door and rolled her eyes. Kate took it to mean they were either hiding out in Vicki's office or had skipped out of the Adler altogether. She slumped. And there wasn't even any pepperoni left if she wanted to drown her disappointment in little round pools of grease.

No point in sticking around. With a wave to Blair, Kate hopped off the counter and ducked out without further ado. At least that way she'd have plenty of time to commute to Old Town. She could arrive early to spruce up and be cool and collected for David's arrival.

"Sorry I'm late!" Kate cried from nearly a block away after she'd rounded the corner and seen David standing on the sidewalk outside the restaurant, wearing dress slacks but no suit coat and talking on his cell phone.

It was one of those hazy, humid Chicago summer days when the air wrapped around you like a wet down comforter, and Kate felt her limp curls matted to her neck and upper back. As she struggled to ignore the painful blisters bursting and oozing beneath her shoe straps—thanks to her sticky, bloated feet after jogging to and from the "L" train—now and then she caught swampy wafts of her armpits.

David acknowledged her with a quick nod and continued speaking into his phone. He was still talking when Kate approached him and stood patiently waiting for him to finish—and wishing she could evaporate into the misty air in the meantime.

"Hey, beautiful," he said after turning off his phone with a beep and pushing down its antennae. He spread out his arms and moved in for a hug and kiss on the cheek. Kate arched slightly backward as he did so, as if that would prevent him from feeling how much perspiration her soaked knit top had absorbed.

"I'm so sorry I'm late," she said again, pulling away quickly and smoothing the wet hair from her face. "I waited ages for the bus at the museum campus, and then my phone died, so I grabbed a cab, but the traffic wasn't moving, so then I bailed and walked to the nearest 'L' stop, and I'm just so, so sorry."

"No problemo." He smiled broadly, his gleaming white teeth perfectly aligned like Chiclets, and not a crease or sweat stain on his just-as-white shirt. His dark wavy hair was swept back as if he had his own private wind blowing on his face, keeping him poised and dry. "But it's really filled up here, so I just called and got us a table at this fondue place up in our neighborhood, if that works for you? That way we're closer to home, too."

"Oh, yeah. Sure." Kate smiled through her disappointment, as she'd been really looking forward to fine French cuisine at the bistro, not skewering and cooking her own raw meat in boiling, sputtering oil. He hadn't made a reservation in advance? And how was she to interpret the "closer to home" thing—as an easy escape route in case of failure, or shorter way to stumble to one of their beds in case of success? Were either of those good?

Uh, yuh-huh! she had to remind herself as far as the "successful" outcome.

"Great." David raised an arm that was still sans sweat mark, to Kate's deepening embarrassment, and hailed a taxi. When one pulled up to the curb, he opened the door and said, "After you," with a theatrical bow.

The same tone didn't apply to the cabbie once inside, however. When the driver asked for the restaurant's address, David replied, "Shouldn't *you* know?" and explained the route.

He then turned to Kate and said, no doubt loudly enough to hear up front, "You know, in London, they subject taxi drivers to rigorous tests so they know every city block and don't resort to asking their passengers for directions. I don't know what these guys think we pay them for." The driver turned up the radio to blast Santana's "Smooth."

Kate just politely smiled and nodded. In all fairness, the entire drive would amount to not even a mile, so knowing the way shouldn't have been that hard. And, anyway, she was more concerned about raking her fingers through her hair to untangle it as discreetly as possible. She lowered the window a crack and welcomed the breeze on her face—but prayed it wouldn't blow her body odor in David's direction. He now sat at the edge of his seat, chastising the driver through the middle window and over the music.

"Why are you going this way? It's a straight-shot up Wells to Lincoln—"

Kate took advantage of his distraction by grabbing her powder and comb out of her purse. She avoided the mirror remnant inside the purse's top flap—all she needed right now was Olive's glare again—and stuck to the one in her compact case. A powdered face and tamed locks later, she felt so much better she'd almost forgotten what a dick David was being to the cab driver. Almost.

The man was put out of his misery soon enough when they arrived at the curb in front of Geja's Café on Armitage Avenue. Laying a hand at the small of Kate's back, David led her down the steps to subterranean fondue delights. She shivered at his touch despite the summer heat.

The darkness of the interior momentarily blinded her with its abrupt contrast from the blazing outdoors, but with that magical hand still pressed to her back, Kate let her date guide her to an intimate, tucked-away booth.

Hm, not so bad a change in plans after all, she thought as she slid onto the cool upholstery of her seat and rested the purse beside her. *At least the dim light conceals any mussing I've missed.* Smoothing her sateen pencil skirt out on her lap so she didn't feel like such a sweaty stuffed sausage in it, Kate looked back up to see David's face flickering in candlelight, smiling at her.

"Well, *you're* as a beautiful as ever," he said with a strange little upward inflection at the end, as if it were a question for Kate to answer. He looked relaxed, the intensity from the cab gone from his voice. And his words had sounded like he meant them, so Kate breathed slowly to calm her nerves.

Trying to keep her sophisticated shit together as best she could, she smiled demurely back and said, "Thank you." *And so are you, David. So are you.*

He held her gaze intently, and Kate could practically feel the clothes melting off her when something to her right seemed to catch his eye and ignite a smirk; he then raised his chin in a confident reverse-nod.

Kate turned her head to behold a peppy and petite waitress looking adorably geek-chic in thick black-rimmed eyeglasses, a man's white button-down shirt like David's, and a black necktie with a small cameo brooch for a tiepin. Her sleeves were rolled up above bony little Audrey Hepburn elbows. For as dowdy as the effect could have been, she may as well have been showing her ankle in 1850.

Looking up at the young woman only to watch her beam down at David, Kate stole a more full-on sizing-up, eyeing the server from the edgy, angular bob cut of her dark hair to the white and black leather of her spectator oxfords, a cool masculinity that couldn't have made her look more beguilingly feminine. Suddenly aware of the cool compress of air conditioning on a large surface area of her upper body, Kate felt exposed, showing too much skin and leaving too little to the power of a man's imagination.

"Hey, you!" the waitress chirped with a graceful flick of her fingertips at David's shoulder.

"Hey, you," he replied with enthusiasm in his voice and a light in his eyes.

Kate was now closely assessing whether the server's shirt looked David's size. Her cheek muscles strained to hold up her smile as she looked back and forth between presumably old acquaintances so gladly remembering each other for *auld lang syne*. Her upper lip had started to slide down and stick to her dry teeth when someone finally offered an introduction.

"Allie, this is Kate. Kate, this is Allie," David said, and just as Kate felt back in the loop, the waitress broke into giggles and that damn pixie hand was touching his shoulder again. But this time,

Allie leaned into it and made David support her weight. "Like the TV show," she tittered.

"Ha! Yeah," David suavely guffawed back—with too much approval, Kate thought, for such a lame joke.

Sighing, Allie turned toward Kate with a sweet smile and said, "Well, it's very nice to meet you, Kate. I'll just leave you two some time alone with the menus and pop back for your order. But first, are we having wine tonight?" Kate and David nodded to each other and then to Allie in agreement. "Great. The usual?" she asked David.

"Yep. Red's okay, right, Kate?"

"Uh huh."

And with that, Allie skipped away, leaving Kate's imagination racing as to what history those two shared. Especially when David snorted out some residual laughter in Allie's wake, humming and shaking his head at the table, his thoughts clearly not keen on keeping Kate company.

So far, it seemed Destiny made for a pretty crappy date.

Until then, she'd been sitting meekly with her hands folded in her lap, but Kate raised them to the table and shoved away her napkin and silverware to lean onto her elbows. The long, boring workday and the chaotic, overheated start to the evening had caught up; her eyes were dried out, and fatigue's gravity pulled her down.

Soundlessly drumming her fingertips against the tablecloth, she offered a little laugh of her own and asked, as lightly as she could fake, "What's so funny?"

"Hm?" David leaned forward, too, with raised brows and a silly grin.

"You're laughing. Why? Was something funny?" *Careful, Kate. Catty's not a good color on you.*

"Oh," he said, screwing his face into a dismissive expression and sitting back again. "Just the *Kate & Allie* thing. She's hilarious."

A laugh riot. "Yeah." Kate surrendered, giving another chuckle to dull any sarcastic edge that might have leaked out of her tone. "So, you two know each other?"

"Yeah, yeah," he repeated in sync with his bobbing head.

Kate waited another couple of beats for him to elaborate. When he didn't, she broke the silence.

"From where?"

"Oh." This time it was a dismissive wave of his hand. "Just—"

"Here you are!" Allie arrived with wine bottle in hand, which she rested on one forearm to display its label to them. She maneuvered her waiter's corkscrew with skill and flourish. Impressed, Kate wondered how much money David spent on his "usual" until Allie said, "The house red," and just began pouring it into both their glasses without asking if one would like to taste it first. Only then did Kate register the inherent commonness of the word *usual*, the word of The Regular whose dates were each just one in a long line.

"Do you need more time before you place your order?" Allie asked, again addressing only David, who cocked the corner of his mouth into another debonair side-grin.

"Kate?" he asked. "Are you a vegetarian or a carnivore? You okay with meat? Fish?"

She nodded dumbly, wondering if Allie's cute quirkiness translated into crazy in the sack. If peeling off all those layers of clothing made for half the foreplay.

"Any preferences?" he asked again.

Looking down at the menu, with a slight shrug, she finally murmured, "Mm, I don't care…um…maybe chick—"

Turning to Allie, David said, "How 'bout the beef and lobster. And maybe throw in some scallops and tofu." He glanced at Kate. "Does that sound good?"

"Uh, yeah, that's great." Kate shrugged again with a mild smile, despising now that this Allie would know he had a "usual" and let him order combo meals off-menu. No doubt little Allie was how they'd managed to get a last-minute table, too, if not the reason David had changed his mind from the bistro in the first place. What, had he discovered his favorite server *there* was off-duty that night?

"Awesome," Allie said as she finished jotting the order down on her notepad, which she then lightly swatted against David's arm. "Remember the tofu night?" she said quietly with a coy giggle.

Kate returned her hands to her lap and dug the nails of one into the palm of the other.

"It was *so* disgusting, but *so* funny!" Allie continued to Kate this time, so graciously bringing her into their positively *uproarious* inside-joke extravaganza. "Kate, if you've never smeared tofu and tuna on your skin—" She turned to David and doubled over, apparently unable to stand up straight again without laying her hand on his shoulder again for support. "Oh my God!" she squealed. "You washed my hair at least twice by morning and still couldn't get the smell out!"

"Yeah, yeah." David coughed. He was grinning, but seemed uneasy.

Kate didn't doubt her own cheeks had flushed, not inclined to hear what other kinky games those two might have been into during their sleepovers.

Catching her breath, Allie clapped a hand over her mouth then slapped it against her breastbone, the thick silver band on her middle finger clacking against her brooch. "I'm totally interrupting your date. I'll go put your order in." She smiled and walked away.

Allowing a few seconds for Allie to step out of earshot, Kate leaned in toward David. "So, you were saying you know her from where?"

David drew his lips into that dashing side-smile again, but this time it was all for Kate. "Grade school. She was a tomboy back then and actually my best friend for a while."

As Kate retracted her claws from her skin, she watched a boyish glow enter David's eyes. A good look for him. Her face relaxed, yet David went on to answer the question her expression must have been asking.

"We grew apart by high school but ended up at Northwestern together. We lived in the same off-campus housing senior year, and my buddies and I started this battle of the sexes with her and her roommates. One night we snuck tuna into these cupcakes they had baking and just left, leaving them to discover it the hard way." His smile lines deepened, and his eyes remained trained on Kate's as his shoulders shook with a chuckle.

She enjoyed this departure from his earlier asshole-attorney mode. He'd probably just come off a tense workday and, combined with the hot weather, needed some time to decompress. Couldn't fault him there. "So then what?" she asked, laughing with him.

"They stormed our place, all tuna cupcakes blazing, and with these bricks of tofu they must've had in their fridge."

Kate genuinely smiled now. David had just become tremendously more accessible, much more on her dorky level. "We had a war like that with the guys across the hall at U of I. They taped over our aerobics videos with porn."

"And you…"

"Filled their shower with popcorn."

David gave a hearty laugh and inquired into the logistics of that one. As they both reminisced about school, friends, and frat and sorority life, Kate felt the rush of being brought into his past. She was no longer intimidated by all those women who might have had their shot before but weren't the ones with him now, in this romantic, dark, and candlelit setting with all the promise of a full bottle of red wine on the table before them.

Kate asked most of the questions and nodded meaningfully while he spoke, knowing how to stroke a guy's ego. As his chest swelled and posture straightened, he appeared to inflate with the attention and moved their conversation on to more recent undertakings. He looked like he felt really good, and she liked making him feel that way.

David raised his large-bowled wine glass and gestured for her to do the same before clinking his to hers. She watched him take a full sip as she did the same and savored it on her tongue, imagining how David's would feel like velvet against hers and ignoring that, for all her serving theatrics, Allie had corked the wine.

Taking a second swig before setting his glass back down, David slapped his hands at his sides and eased back in his seat, repeating, "*You're* as beautiful as ever," with that same funny little inflection.

Re-energized in the beam of his undivided concentration, Kate leaned forward on her elbows, confident again in what she wore and trying to achieve that optimal angle for cleavage she'd practiced. She ventured, "As 'ever'? You've only seen me once before."

"No." Still smiling, he shook his gorgeous head. "I only *met* you once before. I've *seen* you many times. And each time…" He raised his brows as his eye-line trailed down from her face to her breasts, just as she'd hoped. He sucked a breath through his teeth.

Kate reckoned the look in his eyes alone would set their fondue pot to boil, and she grinned smugly with the affirmation that their attraction was mutual. Sitting up, she arched her back and ran a hand through her hair, foofing it a little at the scalp to regain some of its original volume. With Allie dismissed from the contender list, put back in her place as the hired help, Kate raised her wine to her lips and found she actually looked forward to slipping some hot, oiled beef into her mouth that night.

Their pots and proteins were eventually served, and while they dipped their selections, they laughed and chattered on about their jobs, current events, and things they liked to do around the Windy City. They ordered up a second bottle of wine and even took to feeding each other from the fondue forks. When Allie returned to clear the table and take their dessert order, she wasted no time with further nostalgia. David refilled Kate's glass yet again as they waited for the chocolate fondue.

Warm from the wine, cooking, and recollection that they had somewhat of a history of their own, Kate decided to test Hot Neighbor again with their little "inside" jazz thing—the secret knock they'd beat out in sync through the wall that one weekend afternoon. She slid her palm across the tablecloth and rapped her knuckles against it to that specific rhythm—but only its first part, setting David up to knock out the rest:

Tap tap, tap tap-tap…

Kate scrutinized his face for recognition. All she saw was mild bemusement as his eyebrows twitched together, yet—

Tap tap, he knocked back from his side of the table. With a light chuckle, he shook his head. Kate giggled back and affected a shy shoulder shrug, feeling anything but timid now. It was definitely time for a bathroom-mirror check to ensure all systems were still a go.

Grabbing the thick strap of her beaded purse without breaking eye contact with David, she excused herself and began to slide out of the booth.

"Okay," he replied, "but first you have to kiss me."

Kate stopped her sideways scooting for a couple of seconds to process whether she'd heard him correctly. And then, if she had, how exactly she was expected to execute that request. Lean over the table, meet him in the middle? Step around the table and lean down to him while he, what, sat there puckering up toward her? Or would he stand up and come to her? Were any of these options how she'd pictured their first kiss?

In the time those scenarios instantaneously flashed to her, David must have seen her hesitation and rose to his feet—not to step around the table but stopping short in a sort of hovering squat where he was.

Oh God, it's going to happen leaning over the table.

His grin glowing in the candlelight beneath twinkling, almost devious eyes, David bent over the tabletop with both hands still on the booth seat. It wasn't the sexiest image of him Kate could have (and had) conjured, yet her heart ricocheted against her breastbone at the prospect of fulfilling her fantasy—kind of—before dessert had even been served. To receive this validation so soon…and what it could allow them to fast-forward to later that night…

Oh my God, oh my God, oh my GAWD!

Gripping the strap of her purse, Kate worried its beads between her thumb and fingers like it was a rosary. And then, rising to the same awkward squat, she leaned in and met David in the middle.

On first impact, his lips suctioned to hers in a wet yet polite kiss. On the second wave, the front of his tongue contacted her lips. Then, three times the charm, he thrust it into her mouth full-on.

From there, some voracious, neck-jerking kissing ensued for a few rounds. Kate hoped no one else was watching, yet she waited for David to stop first. He did, eventually, with a loud *snick* and proud grin as he sat back on his seat. And Kate, having thus paid her passage to the gatekeeper, slid out of the booth and executed her supermodel-walk to the bathroom with as much composure as she could still muster.

"Oh my God, oh my God, *Oh. My. Gawd!*" she whispered to her reflection in the bathroom mirror, knowing no one else was in there to hear. Those deep sips of red wine had sparkled their way along her nerves and glittered on the surface of her entire body, pleasantly igniting the sensitivity of her nipples and nether regions, yet numbing her limbs and lips.

Teetering a little on the balls of her feet, she reapplied her lipstick, smoothed down her hair, yanked her skirt and top back into place, and marched out the restroom door to rejoin what was looking more and more like a sure thing.

Sure enough, in under two hours Kate was straddling David on Olive's velour chair. She clutched her fingers into his hair as he ran his hands from the pencil skirt bunched around her waist to her thong-bared butt cheeks.

His jaw seemed to unhinge like a snake's as his tongue assaulted hers and his teeth scraped along the skin of her face. But Kate could barely feel it anymore. It was the not-feeling, in fact, that had her urging him on with growing fire. After that second bottle of David's "usual" and the whiskey nightcap Allie had brought them on-the-house, to get her to feel anything in this state, he was going to have to work for it.

Listening to their animalistic noises as she pulsed her body into his, she wondered if David, a.k.a. Hot Neighbor, had ever heard her and Dex through the wall, if it had turned him on and made him wish it were him. If this, then, was also the fulfillment of a fantasy for him—he who had watched her from afar so many times and anonymously knocked his way into her heart.

And now as his wet kisses trailed down to her neckline, she just wanted him to drop his needle on her vinyl, run it along her grooves as she emitted that soulful music that had come from his place next door. She didn't hear it tonight—obviously because he was there with her instead—but how she wished she could. She tried conjuring it in her head, recapturing any measures of the melody she could, and though she knew her voice couldn't possibly do it justice, there in the dark of her apartment, Kate began to hum the tune aloud.

"Mmm…" David vibrated back into her cleavage, a dissonant tone that broke her harmony.

She attempted to hum the verse again, summoning the singer's sensual bleating so that David would remember and treat her to a sexy serenade.

"Mmmm…" he sounded off in a deeper purr, again totally out of tune with her song, so Kate stopped and just savored that he was so into his task—so into *her*—that his music came secondary.

Clearing her throat and scooting back on her knees until she could gingerly step down onto the floor, Kate stood, unbuttoned her skirt, and slid it off. Stepping out of it, she kicked it away and reached a hand to David. Walking backward, she led him from Olive's chair to the futon.

She knew it was breaking her own rules, but damn it, so had Dexter. When she felt the futon cushion's suede texture at the back of her knees, she sank down on it. She let go of his hand to undo his belt buckle.

Using his toes to slip off his glossy wingtips, he unbuttoned and peeled off his white oxford, then his V-neck undershirt. Kate couldn't fully appreciate the breadth of his tanned chest in the dark, but the courtyard lamplight slicing in through the blinds illuminated the erection looking her in the eye. And she hadn't even gotten his boxers off yet.

As she eased her fingers inside his waistline, David shuffled his black-socked feet a couple of inches closer to the futon, bringing his boner a commensurate degree closer to Kate's face. She smiled up at him and simply resumed the delicate procedure of slipping his boxers off of three limbs, as it were.

She succeeded, but that third "leg" nearly poked her in the eye when David shuffled forward a couple centimeters more. Kate distracted herself by running her hands from his smooth, tight abs down to his thighs.

But as ol' One-Eyed Pete closed in for a closer look at her tonsils, Kate slid back onto the cushion and oriented herself along the length of it so she could lie down. David crept onto it as well, swinging a leg over her so that his knees were planted on either side of her body. He descended and picked up their kissing where they'd left off.

Writhing beneath him, Kate was desperate for—she didn't know what. She just needed to feel…and needed to *hear*…

But it was so silent next door. Maybe they could still take this back to his place, where he could put on his music.

No…they were too far along.

Yet instead of thrilling Kate with the friction of his body, David held his rear in the air. To gauge his intentions—and reinforce her pill with safe sex—she whispered, "Do you have a condom?"

Between kisses, he murmured, "We won't need that just yet."

From his awkward position, it crossed her mind that he might be poising to sit back on his heels and pleasure her first. So he was a giver. At last, Kate could play out that vision of his thick brown hair tickling at her inner thighs. She needed to feel…

David pulled away. On his knees and panting, he scooted toward the head of the bed—toward *Kate's* head, more specifically. She lay there, hesitant, but continued caressing his lean, taut sides to keep the connection going. And clearly David wanted her to keep it going, too, as from between the black silhouette of his thighs protruded the huge, quivering appendage he was only one scooch away from sticking into her mouth.

Oh my God, oh my God, oh my God…That is not the feeling I want!

"David."

"Uh huh," he moaned, slipping a hand behind her head to tip it forward.

But before he could lift her face any closer to say hello to his not-so-little friend, she slipped away through his legs and sat up on the cushion behind him. He was still on all fours when he swung his head around to look back at her.

"David, I'm sorry. I can't do this."

He appeared quietly confused for a moment, but then he turned around and crawled toward her, face-first this time. "Hey, that's all right," he said, stroking her cheek. "We can try something else."

Kate exhaled a laugh. "No, I'm sorry, I—I can't do anything right now."

He reached out both arms now to rub hers tenderly, but it didn't prepare Kate for what he asked next:

"Is it your period? We can work around that. Some say it's even better that wa—"

"No, no! It's not that," she said, shaking her head rapidly. She didn't want to play the prude card, but she had nothing else up her sleeve since she didn't quite understand it all herself. "It's just…I think the wine got me a little carried away. We've only just met, it's only our first date, and—"

"You aren't a virgin, are you?"

The fact that he'd asked it jokingly—and very obviously so—steeled those nerves of hers that had just been glimmering with giddiness. Or perhaps she was still so fueled with that silly sensation of unreality that she couldn't pass up an opportunity for sarcasm when it presented itself.

Fine, what the hell, she thought. *I'll play that game.* So she just sat there and smiled.

"Wait, are you?" His rubbing slowed.

"Well…"

In the blue evening light, Kate saw David's eyes widen, and with his hands still at her upper arms, he pushed her away with a light jolt that told her his psyche had just launched her across the room. "Oh, well," he started to say and let go of her entirely.

"Yeah?"

"Then, no, you probably shouldn't."

Kate cocked her head. "Well, maybe not *now*, anyway. Right?"

"Yeah. Not now." Appearing disoriented, he slowly spun to place his feet on the floor and felt around for his clothes. Kate helped.

When all was said and done, people clothed and awkward, Kate walked him to her unit door.

"At least you don't have far to go," she teased with a soft smile.

David snorted a laugh. "No. Lucky for that."

Something in his tone pricked at her. Fidgeting, Kate apologized again for the turn the evening had taken. "It's just all about timing, you know? It's not you, it's just—well, no, it *is* you, because I like you, and I'd like to take things slower. Get to know you better." She moved her hand to his chest and fingered a gap between the buttons there, suddenly desirous to pluck it all open again and feel that chest hair against her breasts. Easy for her to think now that he was leaving, yet she did want to signal that "not tonight" didn't mean "not ever." She hadn't meant to be a cock-tease.

To drive that point home, she confessed, "I'm not really a virgin, you know." Giggling, she felt so clever that she'd duped him. "I was just yanking your chain after that period comment. God, gross."

David nodded with a little laugh.

She felt like such a jerk now, so she laid her hand at his forearm and gave it a gentle squeeze. "Hey, I had a really nice time tonight. Thank you."

He grinned and patted her hand. "So did I. Let's do this again soon."

"Are you free to maybe do something this weekend?" she asked. "Like Friday or Saturday?"

"Yeah, yeah. I'll call you." Leaning down, David brushed his lips to hers, and Kate took in the leathery musk of his cologne. She already couldn't wait for when she'd smell it again, reeling that this man was actually hers to hold in her arms and, eventually, in her mouth.

Feeling goose bumps rise to her re-sensitized skin surface now that the alcohol'd had a chance to process, Kate bit her lip with a grin and opened the door for him. Her stomach flipped a little at the chance to peek inside his apartment when he would open its door to return home. But David only turned to offer a last wave and a "See you around, Kat," before plunking down the stairwell.

Had he just called her "Kat"? Kate held the confusion in her face at bay until he'd rounded to thunk down to the next landing. Then, stepping out to the railing, she listened to his heavy footfall travel the entire way down and apparently out the building door from the swishing sound of it.

She immediately dashed back inside to her window to watch David, there in full view, exiting the courtyard through its main gate.

Now she'd done it. It was almost too inexplicable to be true. She had told Hot Neighbor she was a virgin, blue-balled him, then sent him randy and ready out into the night. Perhaps if Kate's luck could get any worse, Allie would just be getting off her shift at the restaurant and getting off with David and a brick of tofu by morning.

October 1927

Even from the landing, Lon could smell Eva's musk lingering at his door. She'd been there and, by some grace of fortune, would still be, waiting for him. His future fiancée.

After turning his skeleton key in the lock, he glided the door open. With his curtains drawn closed, it would have been pitch black inside if not for the dim light shining in from the hall. Stepping inside, his legs bumped into the frame of his Murphy bed, which someone other than him had to have lowered from the wall. And by the light of the stairwell, he could just barely discern his little home invader's sleeping, miraculous form.

She stirred only a fraction as he slowly closed the door and removed his overcoat in the dark; he left its precious cargo tucked inside the inner pocket for when Eva would be more alert to receive it — and sound of mind to accept it. Setting the coat on the back of a chair, he proceeded to strip himself of all other clothing. Gently, he felt his way to the mattress and crawled under the sheet beside Eva, who, curled up on her side, roused with a deep inhale as he wrapped his arm around her from behind.

"Darling, is it you?" she asked.

It occurred to Lon she could be confused where she was — which "darling" she was with. The real possibility of that stung, but he knew with all his heart that there with him was where she wanted to be.

It was where she was now, after all. "It's me, old girl. I'm so sorry to have kept you waiting."

"Oh, Lonnie." He felt her roll over, and then her soft lips pressed to his. "I don't even know the time, or how long I've slept for."

He squeezed her tight and kissed her forehead. "It's going on about half-past eight o'clock. Much as I dread to say it, old girl, you ought to return home shortly."

Her delicate fingertips caressed his jaw and the soft underside of his chin before feeling their way to his mouth, where she kissed him once more.

"How is Estella? Did you find her well?"

"Well as a young bull, that woman."

She gave a light chuckle. "I'd expect nothing less of her. It was so good to see her at the gala in June. My, how she dragged you by the top hat and tails to that! She's so spirited and charming, and frighteningly perceptive, I suspect. To look in her eyes is to see the wisdom of centuries looking back at you. I don't know quite how she does it."

"Ah, because she *is* perceptive." Lon poked Eva's nose. "She has a tremendous talent for seeing the world as it ought to be, not how it is. Which is what I need to tell you." He broke off to nuzzle Eva's neck. "Oh, my girl, how I wish we had more time tonight. How I wish I'd caught an earlier train!"

"It's all right, darling. You weren't to know I would come."

"I could have only dreamed you would. However did you get inside? I thought you'd lost the spare key I gave you."

"I did. I swear I haven't seen it since the last I was here, so I picked the lock."

Cuddling her, Lon smiled. "You resourceful thing. But what does bring you by? Risking being here so late?"

"Old boy, I—I need to tell you something as well."

Lon brushed his lips across her brow, running his fingers through the silk of her waves and not caring an instant for the downhearted tone in her voice. Still swaying his mouth across her eyebrow, he asked, "Mm hm?"

"Oh, but…half-past eight o'clock. The timing is dreadful. I really mustn't get into it now."

"If it's important, old girl, I certainly think you'd better."

"But you mentioned you have some news, and it sounded so uplifting as you said it. Please won't you share that with me now, before I go, and I'll save mine for another time?"

Lon pulled away from the side-to-side trance he'd lulled himself into and sat up. "I think you need to tell me now. Are you all right?"

"Yes, of course I'm —"

"Are we all right?"

"Lonnie, my heart, you must never doubt we are. It's only that —"

Lon tore the sheet from his lap and lunged off the bed to light his Tiffany lamp. In the golden glow, he saw Eva's face illuminate into a stricken mess, so unlike the portrait he'd been rendering of her. Her skin was sallow, the whites of her eyes the color of salmon. His instinct was to comfort her, but his brain told him to dress himself before receiving the blow.

Eva shuffled over from his bed and did the same. He feigned to ignore the repeated difficulty she had fastening her trousers, observing it only out of the corner of his eye. He'd coasted back to Illinois that evening on the power of his euphoria alone, yet Eva's evident distress and secrecy was enough to siphon that fairies' fuel.

Watching her affix her cap, he knew she'd be telling him nothing that night. And that was certainly no circumstance under which to share with her what he'd so wanted to. Eyeing the open slit of his inner coat pocket as the garment lay disheveled on his chair, he reached to fold it and better conceal its box-shaped treasure.

He was just bending to set the coat back down on the seat of the chair when he felt a light touch on his hips and at the center of his back. Eva had approached him from behind and was resting against him with her hands at his waist.

"Lonnie, I'll be going now, my love, but we can speak later."

"When?" he asked over his shoulder but looking to the ground.

"Soon. As soon as I can get away. Tomorrow, I hope." When he didn't move, she pleaded, her voice constricted and heavy, "Oh, Lonnie, please let's not leave each other on this note."

Lon turned to face her and saw the tears glistening in eyes that had clearly already cried enough that day. Their thickly matted red veins brought him back to the first night they'd met, when she'd played so cool and coy on the exterior while inside she'd been battling for her soul. Other men had caused that torment. He wouldn't cause her this.

"Shh, no tears, old girl." He held her face in both hands and wiped the moisture away with his thumbs. "We will talk about our news soon, both of ours, and take it as it comes. The good with the bad, if such is the case. I love you. I know you know that, and now you must trust in it. As must I."

Her little chest shuddered as she jerkily nodded her head and appeared to calm her breathing. She laid her hands over his, and looking him square in the eye, uttered in a whisper so soft yet carrying a weight of conviction, "Alonzo Ashby, you are the love of my life. Yes, you *must* trust in that."

With a clean, strong kiss, she departed.

The following day, Lon waited for her knock, but it never came. The day after that brought the same silence. As did the day after that. And the week after that.

Sick with worry, he decided to risk approaching her house. A friend to both families, why couldn't he simply call on the Redcliffes? Eva had warned him about her mother, so being observed at Eva's doorstep wouldn't be the most pleasant discovery, but it shouldn't have been anything scandalous, especially if Finlay was home—

Damn it all, Lon thought. He couldn't possibly learn what he needed from Eva with her husband hanging about. No, he needed to catch her by day during the week when the man of the house was away at work. Being observed by Mrs. Hughes in that circumstance, however, *would* be untoward.

His only option was to position himself somewhere he could see Eva when she stood at a window or walked out her door. Yet unlike her wedding day, he couldn't conceal his spying at the townhouse so easily; he could only look on from across the street.

He went so far as entering one of the sister high-rises on West Wrightwood, the one located directly across Camden Court from the Hughes mansion. Inquiring into any west-facing units available for rent by the day or week, he privately hoped to observe Eva's comings and goings from there. He didn't make it past the lobby.

Dragging his feet back out of the apartment building, Lon wondered how long he could lurk outside in its entryway. With archways opening to both sides of the street corner, the covered entrance gave him a decent vantage. Its nice thick support column at the corner also gave him something to duck behind as necessary. It was only a matter of time, though, when he'd be moved along for loitering; his short-term rental request had already triggered a shade of suspicion in the building manager's eyes. The place was rumored to be a Capone hangout, after all, so Lon imagined they came across a number of shifty sorts at that joint.

For the time he had, though, he figured he'd assert a fella's right to stand around and smoke a cigarette—especially under such inviting shelter when it looked like rain. So, after firing up, he placed his silver lighter back in the pocket of his tweed trousers and left his hand in there as he leaned casually against the building.

Every minute or so, he'd bend forward to peek out toward Eva's home for any sign of life. And in the minutes between, when he wasn't looking back through the brass double doors to check if anyone observed him from inside the lobby, he would examine the stone reliefs decorating the entryway. Each square housed a dragon, sphinx, or some other sort of mythical creature. He was contemplating one of them as he stubbed out his first cigarette and went to light another when a *swish* sounded behind him.

"Sorry, buddy, but it's time you get moving along. No loitering."

Lon turned and raised his hands shoulder-high as if he'd been told, *Stick 'em up*. It was the manager he'd spoken with earlier, who looked non-threatening enough in his gray suit and crooked tie. The guy was only doing his job, so Lon just raised his brows and the hand holding the cigarette.

"All right, one more. But that's it. Then I want you outta here, 'kay? Nothin' personal."

Lon brought his unlit cigarette around to his stomach and gave a small bow of compliance. The manager stepped back into the lobby but remained only a couple paces from the doors.

Point taken, Lon felt uncomfortable with the cold glare jabbing in his back like a pistol, so he stalled only long enough to light his second nicotine-fix and decide where to go next. He brought the lighter to his mouth, and as the flame flickered shadows against the inside of his palm, he looked over his cupped hand at the stone tile he'd been studying. Puffing at his cigarette, he concentrated on the lion-like figure, and it hit him: the zoo.

Eva would be at the zoo. If not this day, someday soon. And Lon would wait there however long it took.

Without another moment's hesitation, he took his smoke on the road as he headed east toward Lincoln Park.

Eva wasn't at the zoo that day, when the skies had opened and drenched Lon where he sat. But she was the next.

On another crisp, overcast autumn afternoon, Lon had been sitting on the stone bench next to the Dream Lady statue when he saw Eva approach. From several yards away, he didn't recognize her at first, bundled as she was in women's outerwear and not the men's he'd grown used to. She wore an olive green barrel-shaped, knee-length overcoat with an exaggerated collar of black fur. But the high collar and black cloche hat weren't enough to camouflage those sweet chocolate curls at her cheeks.

And with a few more strides of that saunter toward the statue, it was unmistakably her. She looked nowhere but at that monument, and Lon hesitated to speak so as not to startle her. There were also a few mothers with their small children scampering about, so he didn't want to draw any attention to either of them.

Gracefully stepping closer to the angel, without breaking her stride and without seeming to recognize Lon sitting there, Eva pivoted to the side and away from him. She then paced in a semicircle around the statue, back and forth, passing right by him at one point but keeping her gaze fixed to the Dream Lady the entire time.

Lon actually preferred keeping his silence, cherishing the solitary meditation his lover engaged in; no doubt Wynken, Blynken, and Nod were sailing her fancies away to *"a river of crystal light"* and *"into a sea of dew."* She had a healthier fullness and color to her face than he'd last seen, and he wouldn't be the one to break her peace, loving the solemn expression she wore and unable to resist ogling her exposed legs. She wore nude hose, and from her lean calves to her dainty feet in their basic ankle-strap heels, nothing so fine could have been carved from stone.

Almost hypnotized by her fluid, circular motion, as if she were the Dream Lady's precious satellite, Lon's reverie snapped as soon as his green-and-black moon spun out of her orbit. Without a moment's pause in her steps, Eva had walked away from the monument and, quickening her speed, appeared to cut a warpath to the southwest. Lon leaped to his feet and began a brisk pursuit, baffled as to why she'd leave so soon. Had she truly not seen him?

He wanted to call out, to run and grab at her arm to stop her, but again, there were too many visitors at the zoo to create a scene. If Eva didn't want to see him and resisted his entreaties, to the general public he'd appear to be accosting the poor woman.

For lack of a better solution, he just followed her, keeping several yards' distance behind. She maintained a steady, swift gait as she curved around the South Pond, then cut west toward the Chicago Academy of Sciences Museum.

Passing the building brought the T-intersection of North Clark and Armitage Avenues into view, and Lon pursued in confusion until Eva turned again to approach and ascend the steps of the museum's front entrance. The next mystery was whether she was meeting someone; in that case, Lon knew he must continue with discretion.

Caught between the flat, glassy stares of great beasts, Eva appeared to only fleetingly scan the cases of taxidermy treasures before raising her gaze to the atrium ceiling. The detailed rectangular panels around its central skylights looked like a lovely arrangement of exotic rugs, but tracing Eva's line of sight, Lon couldn't miss what she was looking at: a giant iron sphere suspended at the museum's south end. She paused only an instant before heading for the stairwell to the next floor. After ducking behind a stuffed moose until he felt sure she wouldn't hear his footsteps, Lon ventured up as well.

Moseying along the open western corridor of the second floor, he watched Eva slow her gait and steady herself with a hand on the railing overlooking the ground floor. She peered over the edge and almost immediately turned away with her other hand to her stomach as though struck with vertigo. Holding this stance, her face twitched ever so minutely back in Lon's direction so that he saw her in profile. But, if she was aware he was there, she didn't face him. She turned to walk the opposite way instead, turning left at the end of the corridor to where the sphere loomed.

Lon kept his distance, peering from behind one of the second-floor columns. A white-haired museum attendant stood guard at the ordinary wooden door to the extraordinary galvanized ball. Eva spoke to him, gesturing toward him and back to herself, first to her stomach, then her throat. She then flattened her palm to her chest and sank her head to the side, shaking it with a grateful smile just before the attendant abandoned his post to head Lon didn't know where—he didn't want to take his eyes from Eva.

Holding her pose a few seconds until the older gentleman had disappeared, Eva lifted her head and turned it to Lon. Looking straight at him, she didn't smile, but she didn't frown either. Her eyes simply remained locked on him as she reached for the sphere's wooden door and let the giant orb swallow her.

Her eye contact had not been coincidence, Lon knew; it was an invitation. He quickly walked to the sphere that, now up close, he estimated to be roughly five yards in diameter. Closing the door behind him and ascending a few steps into the belly of the iron monster, he disappeared into its darkness with Eva. Darkness, until… stars. His eyes adjusted to hundreds of points of light surrounding them like a night sky.

Lon allowed himself to marvel a bit before he heard Eva say, "We don't have much time." Her voice echoed inside the unusual contraption. "He's only just gone to fetch me a glass of water, the dear man."

He followed her sound up the last two steps until he touched a wooden rail surrounding the little platform on which they stood. He felt along it until he found her hand. She didn't resist him taking it.

"You have quite the charisma with men, my darling," Lon said, unable to conceal the edge in his tone. "I don't think he'd have done that for just anyone."

"I suppose I offered a good enough excuse." Her voice was hoarse.

"Well then, let's not waste precious time. Why don't you get to your point. There must be one for you to have led me all the way here." His bitterness resonated in the hollowed metal. "How could you so callously ignore me for so long?"

"I wasn't ignoring you, Lonnie. Only getting you away to where we could speak more privately."

"Privately? Here?"

He heard a heavy exhale as her hand went limp in his. "Please, old boy." She sounded so tired. "I didn't have much time to think. I didn't expect to see you at the zoo, and I couldn't bring you home in open daylight with Finlay gone."

Lon eased his grip on her frail hand, but his throat tightened in its place. "If you didn't expect to see me today, then when? When did you plan to next meet, Eva? Ever again?"

Another exhale. "Oh, darling, it's only been a few days."

"Nearly two weeks, Eva. In over six months, we've never gone that long not seeing each other. Without any word, without—"

"I know," she said, ending with a sob. Lon felt her warm press on his shoulder, and in a thick, broken voice, she continued, "Oh, forgive me, old boy. I would have told you that day had you been home; that's why I went to you. But those hours waiting on my own, all the doubts crept in, and I lost my nerve. I've hated myself for it. So much so. I haven't been able to breathe, haven't wanted to live—"

"You mustn't speak so. Here, shh…" Feeling her tug at the lapels of his overcoat to muffle her weeping, Lon's defenses fell to the floor, and he took her in his arms at once. Removing the hat from her head, he buried his face into her hair's sweet coconut oil scent. Lurching with her as she cried—quietly, yet almost violently—he thought of her words. "Eva…what excuse did you give that man? Surely this exhibit isn't safe to leave unattended just for a glass of water? You can't have only said you were thirsty."

"No." She sniffled into his tweed coat. "No, it wasn't just that." Lon felt her stiffen and straighten her posture away from him. He did not relax his grip. "I, I'm—"

In an instant, the stars were snuffed out, and Lon and Eva looked back to the glaring open doorway behind them. In its center stood the slightly hunched museum attendant, bearing a clear glass of water. Lon instinctively pressed himself as far back against the railing as he could go, leaning back and silently, slowly, raising himself to sit on it and lift his feet out of the light, hopefully before the old man's eyes could adjust to the dark. Eva seemed to follow his lead and stepped forward on the platform to block him.

"I'm sorry, Mrs. Redcliffe," the man said, "but you shouldn't be in the Atwood Sphere alone."

"Oh dear, I am so, so very sorry, sir. I would hate to jeopardize my safety, and your position here for that matter, but I suddenly felt much better and simply could *not* resist a peek! I say," she blathered on, "this is the *most* delightful piece in the entire museum. *Fascinating*, truly! It's an exact replica of the Chicago sky, is it not?"

"Why, yes. You see—"

And as he stepped forward to enter the sphere and no doubt deliver a canned lecture on the stars and constellations, Eva hurried down the steps and interrupted him.

"Oh, no, no. Let me just take that water outside. I'd hate to spill it in here and cause this *marvelous* innovation to rust!"

Perched on the wooden railing, concealed in darkness, Lon watched Eva in action as she stood just outside the exhibit's door with the old gentleman and politely sipped her water and probed him with an assortment of celestial questions, which seemed to please the man.

"Why yes," he expounded, "in fact, Dr. Wallace Atwood designed this in such a way that we can plug and unplug the planet holes to portray their orbit. As for the stars themselves, which remain stationary, you see, there are six hundred ninety-two holes punched into that iron in the precise positions of the brightest of them. A significant contribution to science, this. To think Dr. Atwood built it in nineteen thirteen already. And I think it'll be many years yet before someone can top it."

"Undoubtedly." Eva nodded with such a serious expression, Lon almost lost his balance on the wooden rail in stifled laughter. "Well, like I said, Mister…?"

"Hank, ma'am. Just call me Hank."

"Hank, you charming man. I want to thank you ever so much for going to the trouble of bringing me this water, and—"

"The spell has passed, has it?"

"Er—" she shot a glance into the ball in Lon's general direction "—ah, yes. It has."

"Used to happen to my wife all the time, too. More so for our oldest than the younger ones, but that's nature for yeh. Unpredictable."

Eva appeared to strangle her glass, maintaining a tight smile. "That it is, Hank. That it is. Well, as I was saying before, I would hate to endanger your role here by having so carelessly let myself inside Dr. Atwood's Sphere, but would you mind terribly if I allowed myself a few more minutes? Just on my own? I'm so enchanted by it, and it's the first moment's peace I've found in so long being in my, ah, condition." She sounded out of breath, flustered, and her reddened face had broken a sweat. "Well, I would really appreciate a few minutes more. At least until another patron comes along. Is that all right? I won't tattle that you left me alone with it to fetch this glass in the first place if you won't tell that I went inside unaccompanied."

Ah, Lon thought. *There she's got him.*

"Well, I…well, no, no, that should be just fine, Mrs. Redcliffe. Just watch your step, now."

Eva sighed with that same grateful smile she'd given the man before. "Bless you, Hank. Why don't you just be a darling and return this glass where it won't cause any hazard, and I'll be out of your hair just as soon as you're back, if not before."

"Well, I…"

Eva gave a subtle pout and drooped her green cat eyes into puppy-dog ones as she softly rubbed her belly.

"Well, of course, ma'am. I'll only be a few minutes. Just take care on those stairs and hold on to that rail, please, or I'll never forgive myself."

Without further ado, he walked out of sight, and Lon tiptoed down the stairs to meet her at the door as she closed it. He safely guided her back up the steps and into the night sky, where they carried on in whispers.

"Why didn't you tell me this before, Eva?" Lon almost hissed in his excitement. "Why hide from me that the rabbit died, old girl?"

"What?"

"That you're in a family way, my dear! Oh!" He swept her in his arms and kissed her all over her face as she emitted gasping laughs.

"Oh, Lonnie, it feels so much better having you know."

"But how long have *you* known? Why not tell me immediately? My darling, we're going to be a family!" As he hugged her, Lon felt his warm tears meld with Eva's between their cheeks. In his mind, he could already envision Aunt Estella's reaction to the news, the joy she'd feel in watching another generation grow in her home, commune with her land. "You've made me the happiest man alive."

Both trying to keep so quiet, neither could control their elated giggling as Lon held Eva's face and unleashed a torrent of passionate kisses on her forehead, on her lips, and along her neck. They both laughed when he mockingly spit out the long hairs of her fur collar, and when his lips drifted back up to her earlobe, Eva seized him in her arms in a grip he normally felt only when he'd brought her to rapture between the sheets.

"Oh, Lonnie," she moaned into him. "Never again, darling. I promise I won't ever hurt you again, not after this."

"I can't imagine why you wouldn't have told me, you funny old bird." In jubilation, Lon swayed her side to side in his tight hug, hoping she wouldn't feel the ring box through their thick coats. He didn't want her to know its existence until, in the real privacy of his bedroom, she would be wearing the sapphire on her hand. "Believe me, old girl, I won't let you hurt me again."

Eva became a heavier weight in his arms. Riding along with him less passively, she began to slow their joint momentum. "No," she mumbled into his shoulder, "I promise you that, after *this*, I shall never hurt you again."

Perceiving her repetition, Lon slowed with her, and his movement became more mechanical. "When you say 'this,' you aren't referring to what you've already done, are you, but something you're going to do—" he decelerated to a standstill "—right now?"

A tremor reentered her voice as she said, "Lonnie, I…Oh, damn it all, there is no possible way to say this other than…I don't…I'm not…"

Breathless, Lon waited for her to find the words.

"It's only that I'm not certain…whether…the baby…well, whether it's…"

In that instant, Lon was no longer enclosed by the sphere and encircled by stars but standing in the depths of his own private Hades, the punctures of light now tiny flames preparing to lick at his flesh as the iron ball itself dropped to the pit of his stomach. Its coldness burned and spread from within, fastening him to Eva with its frost.

"Are you," he choked out, "are you questioning whether it's mine? But I'm the only man you've been intimate with, Eva. You've always said I'm the only one, that not even your hus—"

"Finlay consummated our marriage in summer."

The sphere began a sick rotation in Lon's belly, his insides churning with it.

"He—" Eva swallowed thickly. "He'd started to warm toward me in the evenings, in spring. The very night you and I consummated our love was the first I noted it, really. It was as if he knew, yet he never spoke a word implying such, and he seemed only happier with me, not disgusted as he should have been if he knew."

"You're certain he doesn't?"

"No, I don't think he does."

"But I thought that he—that you thought he might be—"

"And I still suspect, but even he could only wait so long if he wants anyone else to believe that we—"

"So he, he's been physically…*with* you."

Another moist click of her throat as she must have swallowed again. "He took it very slowly. For weeks he merely held me in his arms before rolling away to fall asleep. But as time moved on, his embraces lasted longer, and then one late-summer night, he—"

"And you let him." The iron in Lon's gut had heated under the fire of Hades and became white-hot. Melting, it oozed to his extremities, coating his heart first.

"Lon, he's still my husband. How could I have refused him? As his wife, it's expected that I—"

Lon's frozen hold on her thawed, and he broke away. "That you what? Give your body over to a man you don't love? While the smell of me is still on you?"

"Please don't be vulgar. Not about this. You have to understand the position I'm in."

"All I understand is that, in all that time, an unconsummated marriage could have been grounds for divorce. I never wanted to pressure you, but you've for so long had the opportunity at your fingertips to pluck when it was ripe. And instead you let yourself spoil."

"Lonnie, how can you speak of me that way? I'm not—"

"Spoiled," he spat. "You are. You're defiled. Leaping from one man's bed to the next. Once you were mine, you were my only one, and you had said I was yours. Under the open blessings of God, you lied that you'd be faithful to him, but on our own sacred, secret altar, *I* was the one to whom you truly vowed it. But you lied to me, too, Eva. You *lied!*"

His pain echoed with her cries off the curved metal. "Darling, I'm sorry, I'm so sorry!"

"And I suppose you only took precaution with me while you freely gave yourself to him."

"No! Not to the extent I could help it. But can't you see your hypocrisy when I've forgiven you every one of your sins. Every last one, Lonnie. Now, please, can we control our volume before someone overhears."

"'Where we can speak more privately,' she said." Lon gritted his teeth. "Is that why you brought me here? Private enough for us to speak alone but public enough that I'd have to contain my reaction? Was that it? Did you suppose I'd strike you? Have you been flinching from me since the Green Mill?"

"Lon, please, I didn't calculate this. Not any of it. What happened with Finlay…it was passionless, emotionless, as clinical as if he'd been handed a husband's rulebook. No doubt he's been under pressure by his family, too, and…and it was only on a few sparse occasions. In two years of marriage, can you imagine? Only a handful of times! For all you once knew, it could have started on our wedding night, long before you and me."

"But it started after. And it only took one occasion to bring us where we are."

"I've acted so shamefully, I know, but I've been so scared. I couldn't tell you, couldn't hurt you, but at the time I wasn't ready to hurt him either. There's so much at stake, Lon —"

"Right." Lon laughed ruefully. "Family honor. Family fortune."

Eva grasped at his coat fabric, but he wouldn't let her secure a hold.

"Lonnie, please. The child could be yours!"

"But it could also be his. So what's the consequence for our future together?" He gave a sour laugh. Dream as he always might have, he rubbed the sand from his eyes and saw not stars, not flames, but the writing on the wall. "So long as there's a chance Finlay is the father, you wouldn't dare run away with me, not with the Redcliffe heir growing inside you."

Silence, except for hyperventilated breathing.

"No," Lon concluded. "No, you wouldn't, would you." He swallowed. "You've already decided to stay with Finlay, haven't you. And… 'after this,' you intended never to see me again. To spare me further pain, is it?"

He wrapped his fingers around her woolen arms and gently pushed her away from him. Descending the steps one slow, heavy footfall at a time, he paused at the bottom to look back up at Eva's blackened outline against the man-made twilight, presiding over him from her pedestal, still as a statue.

"I could have provided for that child's future, too," he said, his voice cracking. "Whether it was mine or not, we…we could have been happy. We could have been a family, old girl. And now…" Lon looked to the invisible floor as he laid a hand against the door's rough boards. "Now, we're nothing."

He pushed the door open to break the spell of their starry night—much to the surprise of Hank, who stood patiently outside. How long he had been there was anyone's guess.

"Sorry, sir," Lon said. "I'm afraid I may have startled the young woman. I let myself in and didn't realize she was there, and she seems quite upset. But she'll be all right."

As he stepped away, he glanced to see the old man admonishing him with a grave frown.

So Lon raised his hands once again like a criminal caught in the act and added, "Don't worry, sir. I've got no business with her," and kept walking toward the exit.

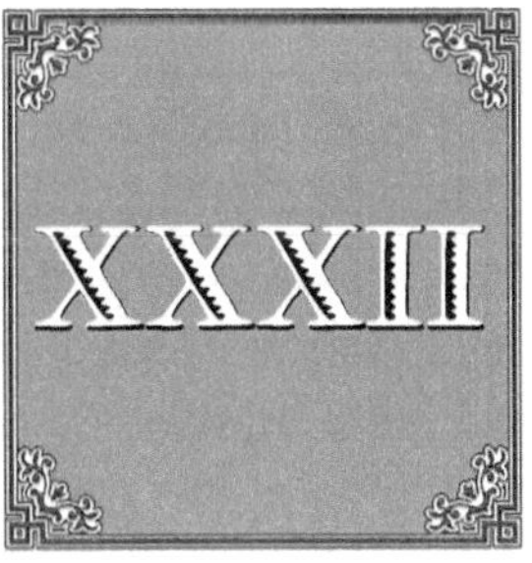

July 2000

"He did not."

"Oh yeah, he did."

"Did not."

"Did, too."

And thus went Kate's mature phone conversation with Blair about the Date with Destiny that had ended with the Big Scooch.

"Ew, Kate. That's nasty one-night-stand stuff, not the foundation of a relationship."

"Oh, c'mon, Blair. We were just drunk, that's all. Having too much fun and got ahead of ourselves. It's chemistry."

"It's *contagious* if you let him stick that thing anywhere inside you without knowing where it's been. That guy sounds like he's been around the block."

"What guy hasn't by his age?" Kate had raised her voice but cautioned herself to lower it so Hot Neighbor David couldn't overhear through the yellowed wall. "C'mon, I only told you because I thought it was funny. I wasn't prepared for it, but, I mean, he's a dude! That's what they do. It's not a deal-breaker or anything."

"Well" — and here came the righteous tone, full force — "just don't let him think you're easy. It's a good sign that you stopped him in his scooching tracks, but you obviously went pretty far to even get to that point. You might think you're projecting this cool, laid-back attitude that guys'll like, but it could be precisely what makes you end up delivering to him exactly what *he* wants. Not necessarily what *you* do."

Kate sighed into the receiver of her cordless phone and heard her breath play back through its earpiece. "I promise, when I see him this weekend, I'll ease up on the booze and keep my clothes on. Mostly." *Damned if I make him think I'm a virgin again.*

She worried whether her sarcasm had backfired so powerfully that David still believed it was true. She'd have thought nailing a virgin would entice him, but if he didn't want the baggage of being someone's first, then what did that say? It was already late Thursday night, and he hadn't called yet to confirm any plans for the weekend.

As if reading her mind, Blair asked, "So when *are* you going to see him?"

"I dunno. Tomorrow or Saturday, probably."

"He hasn't called you, has he."

"God, Blair, it's only been a day! You know the rules of the game. The guy doesn't want to look desperate."

It was Blair's turn to sigh heavily, filling Kate's ears with static. "Kate, trust me. When a guy's genuinely into you, the rules don't apply. Real love isn't a game, and that's how you'll know it when you see it. You'll recognize The One when you aren't over-analyzing him. You'll just…*be*, and it'll play out organically."

"Why do I always feel like Enya should be playing in the background of your advice? I can almost smell herbal incense spraying out of my phone."

"Well, you sound like a cat in heat, so just imagine what's spraying out of mine."

Kate snorted.

"Just listen to what I'm saying," Blair insisted.

"Duly noted and documented."

"And what's that John Hughes mantra we've been working on? Let me hear it."

"*Jake Ryan is a carpenter in real life.*"

"Good girl. Well, hey, if you've got an afternoon free, wanna join me for a trapeze lesson on the lakefront?"

"As long as there's a net, I'll think about it. It might be fun to go to the zoo or something else innocent with David, though. So maybe I should keep my days open until I know what he'd like to do."

"Mm hm. Okay, then have fun this weekend. Whatever you do."

"Thanks, chick. You, too. Say hi to Brad, and I'll talk to you later, okay? 'Bye."

"'Bye."

As she clicked her receiver down, Kate checked both her answering machine and cell phone again for any missed messages from David. None.

Ah, well. There's time yet.

On Friday night, Kate rushed out of work on the dot at five. Not to meet David, because he hadn't phoned yet, but to make sure she was home in case he called her landline or dropped by. He did live just next door, after all. It would be tremendously awkward for him not to contact her soon, given that proximity.

When he hadn't called by seven o'clock, though, Kate's raging stomach demanded food. No doubt David was having end-of-week drinks with colleagues and just grabbing dinner as long as he was out, so she might as well eat, too, and be fortified for any cardiovascular activity with him later.

Yep. Better carb-load.

Within twenty minutes, she was sitting contentedly on her rolled-up futon with an oversized bowl of pasta shells coated in pesto sauce. Curling up to her TiVo recording of the most recent episode of *Sex and the City*, she lost herself to the Carrie-Mr. Big-Aiden love triangle while she waited for a knock on the door or a phone to ring.

By the end of the show and the bottom of her bowl, she'd still heard nothing, but the wall behind her did start to vibrate against the metal frame of her futon. Pressing her palm to Jaundice, Kate saw its yellow flicker a little; she looked up at the copper sconces to see their electric candles brighten then dim a couple of times. Then faintly, just faintly, a sedate jazz tune floated into the air.

So he was home.

Only a matter of time now, Kate thought with confidence. From beneath her unit door, David should have seen that her light was on and heard her TV—ergo, he should realize she was home, too.

But after digesting her way into a food coma—and wrapping up in the safety and warmth of a blanket when Olive dropped the temperature—Kate nodded off to boring summer-hiatus reruns.

Until she started at the sound of a heavy thud.

Oh, God. It's him.

The eerie, futuristic music of *Late Night*'s "In the Year 2000" sketch played in the background. Disoriented, Kate sat up, wiped the drool from her mouth, then combed her hair with her fingers in front of the wall mirror while Conan O'Brien predicted the "future." After a deep breath, she opened her door.

No one was there. And, looking to the neighboring door, she didn't see a light or hear music anymore. Maybe David had tried to catch her on his way out, and she'd missed her opportunity.

Damn.

She slowly closed her door and eased the deadbolt into place so David wouldn't hear it in case he *was* home. It gave her time to reconsider the loud knock and wonder if she'd dreamed it. On further thought, it might've come from the back door. Maybe David was doing laundry in the basement and thought he'd drop by from the back stairwell.

She shuffled into the kitchen to swing the rear door open. No one.

Damn it. Had she made him wait too long while she'd stood at the front door? Made him think she wasn't there? Maybe she could check down in the basement under the pretense of doing laundry, too. *Yeah! Perfect.*

Sliding on some flip-flops, Kate frolicked into her walk-in closet to empty her hamper into her laundry basket. When she stepped to reach for the pull cord, she kicked a small object in the dark.

"What the hell?"

Yanking the string to click on the overhead light, she looked to the floorboards and saw Olive's purse lying there on its side just a few inches from her full-length mirror—possibly the thud she'd heard. She tensed and risked a glance at the floor mirror…

Only to see herself in a tank top and striped pajama bottoms. No green eyes, no creepy messages. Exhaling, she found her breath again and reminded herself her ghost was harmless, her ghost was harmless, her ghost was harmless…

"*Tuh*. Olive, I know I set your purse nicely on the dresser. Come on, now." She picked it up, then set it back where it should have been.

Fetching her laundry necessities, she descended to the basement.

Kate didn't see David doing laundry that Friday. Kate didn't see David the entire weekend, in fact, nor by the next. She also never did fly through the air with the greatest of ease with Blair, but she got every penny out of Dickie Greenleaf, that was for sure.

The sexy, smoky-lounge music next door kept tempting her to just give in and show up at David's door. To go there in person, though, was the line of desperation Kate vowed not to cross.

He's a lawyer. He's important. He's busy. He needs his space. Those were the excuses continually making their rounds in her head. *I'm looking uninterested and therefore more challenging to him every day that passes.*

But that didn't stop her from calling him. She'd busted through that boundary already by the first Saturday. When nine p.m. had rolled around, she'd known it was too late for a proper date but figured that would let her play off the whole matter casually, act like she was meeting friends at a local bar for just a drink or two and simply wondered if David would be keen to walk over with her.

And that's the message she'd left when he hadn't answered her call.

She'd then miraculously waited all the way until Wednesday, when coworkers of hers were grabbing drinks at Fado's. Kate had given fate the chance to deliver David there with his own colleagues, popular happy-hour spot as the Irish pub was, but when it hadn't, she'd phoned him and tried to sound as mellow as possible shouting into his voicemail against the background music and drunken cacophony. By the third time she'd been about to do another lap, Blair had laid a firm hand on her shoulder and shook her head no. To which Kate had sulked and chugged her Guinness.

But she *had* scored an impromptu dinner date that night. A chatty yet friendly accountant she'd met at Fado's invited her and another gal she worked with to Smith & Wollensky with his buddy. It had been an evening of good steak, martinis, and hilarious company, and she was excited about giving the gentleman her number. Until the waiter toured them through the kitchen and her date suctioned to her from behind, his hands roving her body under the pretense of keeping her warm inside the meat locker.

Then there was Thursday night when a group of her college friends had subjected her to karaoke therapy at Trader Todd's, the cheesy tropical-themed bar where the guy who'd played Ogre in *Revenge of the Nerds* always hung out. But neither spotting Ogre in a Hawaiian shirt nor her inexpert renditions of "Total Eclipse of the Heart" and "I've Had the Time of My Life" had been enough to work magic on Kate's mood. However, another piña colada had gotten her to finally flirt back with the lanky redhead who'd been commanding her attention all night. He'd even chased out in the rain after her when she'd tried to bail while he was in the bathroom. The gesture had all the makings of life imitating rom-com art, yet Kate had only reluctantly given him her number. Earning her Viking helmet by drinking an entire ale flight at the Great Beer Palace afterward had only mildly cheered her with a sense of accomplishment.

And there was Friday, when the cute but dull guy who'd hit on her at Gamekeepers sports bar had only proven worthwhile when he and his friend later joined Kate and her single girlfriend for fondue around the corner at Geja's. It had been a spontaneous reconnaissance mission to see if David would be there with another girl and, if so, he could see Kate there with another guy. She'd spotted Allie there, working other tables, but that was all.

By the second Saturday, she'd guiltily listened to all three guys leave their messages on her answering machine with no intention of ever, ever returning any of their calls.

And so, on that Saturday afternoon, there was really nothing she wanted to do more than gnaw on sourdough bread—slumped on a sofa in the middle of none other than the Panera Pack.

"What's the bug up your butt, missy?" Vera asked.

Kate huffed in self-pity as she picked at the soft center of her roll. "Just guys—doesn't matter." She balled up the bread before popping it into her pout.

"'Doesn't matter.' A likely story. Is it Dexter again?"

Kate actually winced at the name. "No. Not only him, anyway. I've met some other people and had an actual date the other night, but I think I blew it." *Well, actually, it's because I* didn't *"blow" it.* "Whatever. I'm giving up on men. It's seems to have worked out all right for you."

Vera gave her deep chuckle. "Well enough, I suppose. But you know, dear, even I have to admit it all depends on finding the right person."

"Since when do you change your tune?"

"Since…Well, just look around you. None of us would be born if some folks didn't pair up and procreate, right?"

Kate worked another bit of sourdough with her fingers as she cocked a brow at the old woman and wondered if Leo was listening—if he was hopefully the reason Vera was turning sentimental, and not that joker in the straw hat seated across the coffee table. The one Leo had jealously spoken of before and who now carried on like he was a regular Johnny Carson.

Vera scoffed, and to Kate's greater amusement, swiped a hand at the guy that said, *Knock it off.* Kate couldn't miss a certain glimmer in Leo's eye at the gesture, too.

That didn't stop Jerry from continuing his monologue a minute later, though, with eyes only for Vera. By then, Kate had diverted Leo with conversation.

"There's really no way out of it?" she asked.

"'Fraid not. Even if there were a clause for breakin' your lease early, these things usually aren't shorter'n six months."

"But all those other tenants who've left?"

"Good timin', as their luck would have it. All their leases were up or close enough that foregoin' the security deposit would do. There's also just the natural turnover of these places among the younger folks."

"Damn it." Kate had been sitting up and at the edge of her seat for a brief while but now sank back down against the pleather cushion.

"She botherin' you a lot lately?"

"No," she said in a juvenile whine. "She's actually saving me money on air conditioning. But the place smells like a funeral parlor."

Vera, who'd been listening in, smiled. "That's our Olive. The woman couldn't bathe to save her soul with that tub filled with newspapers, but Lord, did the woman swear by her perfume."

"A few of those vacated units are still available," Leo offered.

"And bunk up with a new spirit? No, thanks. I'll take my chances with Olive. At least she comes with your glowing references. But she'd better not pull that smoke and mirrors crap again."

"She means no harm, dear," Vera said. "But if you'd like an excuse not to go home to her right away, you can come with me and Leo to the zoo. The walking does us geezers good. And Leo likes the lions." She winked at the man playfully.

"No, but thanks. I'm gonna go into work, I think. Weekends get busy, so there's stuff to do." Swallowing some sharp crust with a bit of pain, Kate added, "And the volunteers can always do with some extra help." *Especially since their coordinator is never on hand for them.*

"Fair 'nough," Leo said. "See yeh round, Kate."

Her stomach sank at the familiar parting words, but at least Leo had gotten her name right.

Kate had thought by the time she'd glided down the lakefront on her bike, she'd have lost herself to the warm breeze fanning her face, and the cloudless blue sky. She'd thought by the time she sank into her desk chair and devised a lesson plan for a telescope activity, she'd have been able to ride the high that was creating and educating.

But not only did none of it detangle her mind from man matters, it had to go and give her a dose of perspective. Stark, unpeeled-from-the-bubble-wrap perspective that wasn't going to cushion her delusions any more.

Jolted from her ruminations by the slam of a volunteer locker and some laughing a few cubicles over, Kate sought privacy to think. The antique sundial had sadly been tarnished for her, and squatting in a bathroom stall bore only slightly more appeal. The conference room was like a fishbowl, and the offices were either occupied or locked — she wouldn't sit anywhere in Vicki's without shining a black light on it first anyway.

Kate mentally toured the museum, navigating all the exhibits for a little nook where she could hide, but it was tough going considering the weekend crowd. All the young families would be filling the theaters, yet there was one area she might be able to hijack for a while.

The Atwood Sphere.

She typed up a quick message, printed out the single sheet of paper, and adhered a piece of tape to it. Then, grabbing her office cardigan off her chair, Kate set off for the lower level exhibit. There, she encountered a petite middle-aged lady standing at its entrance in her red polo and volunteer lanyard. The woman was smiling and waiting for a small group of five people to exit the bulky mining car of sorts that had safely transported them up and down that harrowing height of maybe one meter.

Kate flickered a quick glance at the volunteer's name badge and said with feigned cheer, "Hey, Rita! I'm Kate from the education department. Nice to meet you."

The little woman flashed a big grin and accepted Kate's extended hand. "Pleasure. Is there something I can help you with?"

"Well, yeah, possibly. How busy has it been with the Sphere today?"

"A little slower than last weekend. I've had maybe four groups in the last couple hours, at half capacity." She leaned in with her hand shielding the side of her mouth. "I don't think folks want to pay the extra fee."

Kate laughed. "They never do. Well, it's still probably attracting more than it did five years ago at the Academy of Sciences, so…" She fidgeted with the sheet of paper she'd printed, rolling it into a cylinder. "Anyway, um, we're a little short on volunteers today, so would you mind going down to the office and bringing the UV beads up to the Solar System gallery? The cart's parked right next to my desk at the northeast corner. I can man things here awhile."

"Sure thing," Rita said with a feisty salute, and she walked away with her arms pumping as if marching to war.

Once by herself, Kate hooked a velvet rope across the metal railings where visitors normally waited in line and affixed her piece of paper to it:

EXHIBIT TEMPORARILY CLOSED
We apologize for any inconvenience.
See admission desk for
refund or voucher.

On stepping inside the conveyance, she drove the overkill equipment slowly into the sphere. When the contraption stopped, she sat down in its back row and folded her arms with her cardigan wrapped tightly around her like a security blanket. And there, nesting inside what was essentially a giant shoebox diorama of the Chicago sky, Kate let it all out and cried.

After quaking in silence a few minutes, she sniffed and inhaled a deep breath as she looked for constellations above. Spotting Cassiopeia on her inverted throne, she couldn't help but relate to that feeling of suspension—had her world turned upside down, or was it Kate who had?

The mute darkness and pretty pinpricks of light brought a stillness she hadn't felt in some time. And inside that iron globe, she allowed the perspective she'd gained before to finally fly out of her mind and ricochet all around her where she could see it, face it.

David was never going to call.

And she'd known that. The entire time she'd waited for him to.

Even worse, she'd known she shouldn't have *wanted* him to call. Good on paper—and on the other side of the wall—had been pretty shitty in person. He wasn't the guy.

And who was she kidding? He was a God-awful kisser.

Kate's face crumpled again.

What was she doing? She had been here and done all this before, for years. She didn't need David or any of those jokers to call to know exactly how those dates would've turned out. All she'd proven was that she still had game, which meant very little when she wasn't interested in the players anymore. She may be young, but she was getting too old for this—doomed to repeat history in order to finally learn from it.

She pressed her eyes closed and let her shoulders shake.

A thud and clang vibrated at her feet. Opening her eyes, she saw a dark form climbing into the car. A familiar scent drifted to her nostrils as the figure sidled in next to her on the rear bench. Its warmth pressed against the length of her upper arm.

"What're you doing in here, Katie?"

The kind tone disarmed her, and she shook even harder as she turned and buried her face into her best friend's shoulder and wept. An arm wrapped around her.

When she didn't say anything, the voice continued, "Y'know, the ticket counter is gonna be pissed when all these people come back asking for refunds."

Kate's cries mingled with a weak giggle.

"That's what I like to hear." The arm around her shoulders gave a couple jovial squeezes.

She heaved a large breath in and out. "What are you doing here, Dex? Isn't today your day off?"

"Yeah, and it's yours, too. Could we be bigger losers?"

With her head still on his shoulder, she dared, "Well, I don't know. You seem to score enough these days to win this game."

"Oh, it's not a game, Katie."

"Isn't it?" She shook her head. "Because you've sure been playing at something. Point taken, all right?"

"Kate—"

She sat up and shrugged off his arm. "I've left you alone, haven't I? I could've been a drama queen and made your life a living hell in and out of work, but I haven't, have I?"

"No, you haven't. And maybe that's part of the problem."

She slumped with a heavy exhale. "Why? What have I done wrong now?"

"Nothing. Listen. I'm not proud of what I've done. It hasn't been fair to you, and it hasn't been fair to Vicki. I was just really hurt and angry and wanting you to care—"

"Haven't been fair to *Vicki?* I could give a fuck about her." Her raised voiced echoed inside the globe.

"Me, too, believe me. That makes me feel worse. I've been acting like an asshole, and I couldn't ask you to forgive me."

In the dimness, she heard him suck in a breath after she'd said nothing in response; she looked to him and could make out his dark profile as he cocked his head to stare up at the "sky."

"I'm not saying this like I can honestly earn any Brownie points for it," he said. "I'm not asking for forgiveness or even understanding. I just…" His head swung forward, bringing his chin to his chest. "For what it's worth, *she* pursued *me*, and damn if she isn't relentless. I only gave into it because I felt so fucking sad and alone without you. You have a right to know, though, that I stuck to your rules. I didn't sleep with her."

The air in Kate's lungs eeked out a little at a time.

"I know it definitely looked that way, Katie, and I'm sorry. I'm not going to pretend we didn't mess around a little, because we did. Okay, a lot. But seriously just, like, second base stuff."

This confession shouldn't have made any difference, shouldn't have made her feel any better. Yet it did.

"It was so easy and uncomplicated," he said, "and just took my mind off everything. I felt wanted again, like a man, not some annoying tag-along kid. Until I saw what she was doing. The way she hadn't wasted a minute to pounce and took pleasure in spiting you. That wasn't cool with me, but I'm not gonna lie and say it didn't feel good to hurt you after you'd ripped my heart out and fed it to me."

Kate frowned but let him keep going.

"Sorry," he said. "That's how it felt, but I don't mean to play the victim again with you. I've been acting like a caveman. I just didn't know it until I'd purposely given her my boxers to sleep in. Your favorite ones, too. You know, the—"

"Yeah. Uranus. Got it."

"Anyway, that was a really dick move."

Kate adjusted in her seat and pulled her sweater tighter around her. "The dick move was probably screwing around with someone in our office in the first place. Otherwise, if you really didn't sleep with her, you weren't doing anything I didn't ask for."

"Well, I'm not doing anything with her now. She's pissed, but she'll get over it."

Yeah, by getting under *someone else.*

She heard him shift in seeming agitation. "So, uh," he said, "what about you? Have you been seeing anybody?"

Arms folded, she dug her nails into her elbows. "Mm…" she stalled. "I've only had two real dates."

"Uh huh?"

She could hear the restraint in his throat. "Don't worry. They were disasters."

"Why should I worry? It doesn't concern me, right?"

"Come on, Dex. We both know this was a horrible, horrible idea. Stupid fucking rules. I don't know who I thought was kidding, but I should have respected you more. I should have respected us." She sniffed wetly.

"Are you okay?" he asked. "You hiding out in here, is it because of me?"

"Don't flatter yourself." She elbowed him.

"That other guy, then?"

"Don't flatter him either. I think he does it enough by himself."

"Then what, Katie?" He laid his hand on hers, and she twisted her palm upward to hold it.

Panning her eyes around the white-dotted dome, she said, "You know? This really is an incredible exhibit. Imagine taking the time to drill all those holes, mapping them out just right. All to bring the heavens down to where the public can touch them."

Dexter ran his thumb across her knuckles and looked around the sphere as well. "Honestly. We're so jaded now, but this must have been a marvel back then."

"Until Adler went and ruined it. Poor Atwood, kicked to the curb."

"Stupid Zeiss projector."

"Yeah." Kate laughed, shaking her free hand in a fist at the false sky. "Stupid Carl Zeiss and your advanced technology!"

"Man, the Germans caused all sorts of trouble in those days, didn't they?" Dexter quipped, and as Kate chuckled harder, they adjusted their hands to interlace their fingers together.

She leaned to lay her ear on his shoulder again. "It is a little sad, though, to think of this sitting neglected for so long. It actually feels sad in here, in the quiet with just us two. Poor thing went unloved almost seventy years."

"Practically a lifetime. Nothing should go unloved that long."

Kate nestled her chin against his cotton polo and thought about Leo and Vera. Maisie. All the lonely and unloved occupying her building. All the ghosts enduring the loneliness, too, and for many lifetimes over. Olive, Tommy, Alonzo.

She shivered at the plain truth: Time was on no one's side. *What the hell are we all waiting for, then?*

Dexter hugged her close. "So what happens now?"

"I don't know," she said. "I think I've finally reached the age where I no longer have all the answers."

He turned his head and pressed his lips onto her hair. "Are we still together?"

"Well, we haven't been, have we."

"No, I guess not."

"Then there's our answer."

"Do you think we could be again?" he eventually asked. "If not now, ever?"

Kate felt the waterline of her tears overflow again. As they dripped off her cheeks and probably soaked into his shirt, she replied, "Don't ask like it's up to me. I don't know anything, just that we've hurt each other so badly. More than I ever thought I'd be capable of, let alone someone I care about so much. And you, too, Dex."

"I know."

"I wouldn't have thought you could. With me or anyone."

"Yeah."

"So, what if we bring out the worst in each other? That's not how it should be."

"I know."

"That's not even settling. It's dehumanizing."

"I know. But, Katie—what if the way we work through our worst is how we could bring out our best? Come out of it stronger, better. Together."

She fell silent. Only wrapped an arm around his waist to hug him back.

And together, they looked to the stars for answers.

And Ten for the Devil Himself

November 1927

In the weeks that followed their encounter in the Atwood Sphere, Lon refused to answer the knocks sounding at his door.

Tap tap, tap tap-tap, tap tap.

They never lasted very long, no doubt because Eva was self-conscious of his neighbors, but what took more steel to resist were the silences in between them. The quiet, void of any sound but the low rustle of fabric, the light scratching of nails on the door, the creak of weight against it. And the pitiful whimpers. Lon continued to hear those at all hours, even when Eva couldn't have possibly remained out there. He would shake his head to rid his mind and heart of the madness he seemed to descend into; he didn't dare touch a drop of liquor, knowing how it could spin him into even darker reveries.

When he would finally open his door, it was only to resume work at the lumberyard or other winter jobs where he was needed — fighting the bitter outdoors was fine enough alternative to indoor afternoons with Eva. As he'd step out onto his landing, though, it wasn't her linen and vanilla he could smell, but a sweeter scent tainting it. Something floral that unpleasantly pinched his nostrils.

The only company he'd received in this time was an unprecedented visit from his esteemed aunt. Not one to make house calls, the woman had nonetheless needed to appraise the status of a future on which her own was so inextricably linked. When she hadn't heard from her nephew for weeks after bequeathing him her ring, she'd become concerned the odds stacked against the young couple had indeed toppled over their heads.

Arriving at his door, it was as she'd expected. Lon knew his visible heartache grieved her, yet he couldn't accept her advice to give it more time, to love Eva from afar until answers could more clearly present themselves.

"My dear, what is meant to be will be," Estella told him. "While it isn't always easy to see, we must remind ourselves that all happens for a reason. A *child*, Lon. This has now become bigger than the two of you, and you have to do right by *it*, first, don't you agree?"

Sitting at the edge of the bed with his face in his hands, Lon shook his head violently, and it was clear to both Ashbys that—even in the presence of Estella's infinite wisdom—no answers would be found that day.

On parting, Estella paused at his door. Propping her weight on a silver-handled cane, she looked all around his room with a mild smile but glassy eyes. "It's beautiful, my boy. But you can't torture yourself with this."

"It's my masterpiece, Aunt."

"You can't be taking pleasure from it."

"I'm taking perspective. It's my life story, playing out around the sides of my urn."

"Paint over it, Nephew. Start over on a blank canvas. Leave here and live with me. That offer still stands. This place, it isn't healthy for you. You mustn't cling to it."

Hands in his trouser pockets, he bobbed his head. "I promise, I will be there for you when you need me. But this place holds the ashes of my happiness. I cannot leave. Not yet."

A tremor rippled through the old woman's brow line and around her mouth, and she sighed. "We'll arrange something soon enough."

Patting his cheek with a knobby-knuckled hand, Estella walked out his door and gingerly down the steps to where her driver waited on the street.

August 2000

A summer day, Chicago-style. The sweltering kind when you could literally see the air. Even Midwest-tough Kate had to forego her usual black coffee for a tall iced tea.

The late Saturday morning had found her back at the Bourgeois Pig café, seated outdoors since the kitchen heat inside didn't bring much more relief. Intermittently biting on and sucking through her clear plastic straw, she was closing in on the last four words of her crossword puzzle when a raspy voice broke her concentration.

"Fancy meeting you here, dear!"

Kate raised her head with the straw still clamped between her teeth. She smiled and pulled it out. "Hey, lady!"

"Looking to be alone, are ya? I don't suppose you'd want some company."

With her foot, Kate pushed a heavy iron patio chair out from the table. "Please have a seat, Vera."

The old woman obliged with uncharacteristic modesty; it clashed with her bright teal-and-peach-flowered sun visor and rhinestone sunglasses. And her smile appeared meek somehow, but the puzzle of it didn't distract Kate from the shoebox in the woman's hands. Adjusting for comfort in her seat, Vera set the box on the table.

"What's that you got there?" Kate asked.

"Oh, you might hazard a good guess, huh?"

"Olive's?"

"You've seen Leo's already, I take it."

Kate dropped her eyes to her tea and sipped from the straw. Too soon, she reached the bottom of the glass and loudly sucked between the melting ice cubes in vain.

"I wish he hadn't shown you," Vera said, "but he wasn't to know, the poor fella. And he probably deserves to. That's what I was hoping to talk to you about."

"Oh? You need *my* advice?"

"I reckon so." She primly placed her palms side by side on the box cover and lightly tapped it three times with her fingertips.

To ease her nerves, Kate offered, "Can I get you something from inside? Some cold tea or juice? You look hot."

And she did. Seeing Vera in a loose pink sleeveless top was a first for Kate. Usually the woman wanted to hide the Hi-Bettys of her upper arms; even skinny Vera flapped when she waved. Kate was finally accepting that the same would happen to her one day, just in time for a smug twenty-something to come along and pity *her*.

After eying Kate's empty glass and looking around toward the café window, Vera asked, "They got anything stronger than soft drinks?"

"Mm, I don't think so. But their jasmine tea is nice. I could get them to ice it up for you."

"Oh." Vera knit her brows and bobbed her head, staring down at the box. "Oh. Well, then…"

I thought you didn't drink, Kate mused. But she wasn't in a mood to hold the woman to her word. "On the other hand, I know just the place for a stiff drink. Right around the block on Belden Avenue."

Vera looked up and mirrored Kate's mischievous grin.

"This place—" Vera sipped her Scotch on the rocks "—used to be a speakeasy, you know."

"Seriously?" Kate looked around from where they sat at the deep-stained wooden bar and took another careful taste of her dirty gin martini.

"Yes. They boarded it up to make it look vacant, see."

Taking another salty sip, Kate figured it couldn't have felt much seedier drinking there illegally in the twenties than day-drinking in the new "noughties." John Barleycorn had just opened for the day and was still almost empty; the sunlight glaring through the windows had the same depressing quality as lights-on at closing time.

Yet, somehow, sitting there knocking back hard liquor in the middle of the day with a plucky broad like Vera made Kate feel cool as hell. Retro chic.

Seeing the old woman had already downed one finger of her drink, Kate felt primed to raise the subject. "So. Vera. The box."

"Ah." She nodded and tapped the sides of her tumbler with her fingernails. Then she reached for a cocktail napkin — and a fat red cherry while she was at it, which she promptly popped in her mouth — and wiped the condensation from the bar surface before sliding the shoebox between her and Kate's glasses.

"I want to share the truth with both you and Leo. Starting with you."

Kate took a bigger swig of her martini.

Gingerly lifting the box lid, Vera reached in and pulled her hand back out in a fist. Turning it palm upward, she uncurled her fingers to reveal a handful of roughly oval-shaped scraps, some larger than others, and some blank while others had black-and-white faces.

"Photographs," Kate said, flipping over each blank oval to see they actually all had faces on one side or the other. She also couldn't miss the striking similarity of their features — among each other, but also to Vera. "Are these all portraits of the same person?" *Are they you?*

"Yes," Vera replied with her eyebrows raised but eyes pointed down at the pictures. "They're all of Olive. Or I should say, Aunt Olive."

Now Kate's brows raised. "*Your* Aunt Olive?"

With a broad smile, Vera nodded excitedly. "Yes, yes. It feels very good to finally say that out loud."

"But why couldn't you have said it before?"

Vera sprinkled the photo fragments into the upturned shoebox lid. "Because no one knew. Not even Aunt Olive. Only me. And I believed it was better to keep it that way, because the more I learned about our shared past, the more pain I realized I'd stir up. Auntie was already a very old woman when I first found her, and I felt it best to let her live her remaining life in peace. I was blessed to know her as long as I did."

"Why didn't you take her apartment, then? You could have known her longer, in her afterlife. Do you still want to? I'll trade you."

The old woman laughed. "Dear me, no. I battled against those stairs enough all those years tending to her. I live on a lower story, and I'd like to move to the ground floor if I can."

"You can still come over whenever you want. I don't mind. I'm gone a lot anyway, so I can give you a spare key."

Again, Vera gave one of her rumbling chuckles and, shaking her head, tipped back another drink of her Scotch. "Not to put you off, dear, but Olive was a loon the last years of her life. It's better I don't know what she gets up to now she's dead. I had enough of it cleaning out that place. Gave me the heebie-jeebies. At least my ghost's predictable."

"Thanks a lot."

"Hey, you're young. You're resilient."

Sighing with a hiss through her teeth, Kate drained her martini to the top of her green olive. Pinching the toothpick with her thumb and finger, she stirred the cone of cloudy liquid with it. "Fine. So you didn't want to tell Olive, but why not Leo? You guys seem so close."

Just when sweet, bashful blushes seemed reserved for pretty young things, Kate didn't suppose she'd ever seen anything quite so adorable as the pink flush spreading from Vera's crow's feet to her jowls.

The woman cleared her throat and clinked the ice around in her glass. Kate steadied Vera's hand with her own. "I know how you two feel about each other." She leaned in to make her look her in the eye. "Vera, this is not the time to be stubborn. Don't be independent to a fault. Not when it means missing out on something that could be lovely."

Vera smiled, but the glint in her pale eyes warned Kate not to be fooled. "Speak for yourself. Stand Dexter up for another solo weekend?"

Sitting back and clapping her hands on her thighs, Kate said, "For your information, I'm meeting Dex tonight. He's taking me out for my twenty-fifth birthday."

Vera's smile cracked open to show her gray-yellow teeth. "Well, I'll be. Happy birthday. You've turned the corner on your first quarter-century of life now. There's a wisdom that comes from that. The second half of your twenties can be quite different from the first one, you know."

"As can the second half of your life, Vera, so hop to it."

"Oh, bless it. I'm way past half. I'm closing in on finishing my *third* quarter-century."

"Then you must be a freaking genius by now." Kate winked and nudged Vera's arm with her elbow.

The woman's grin easily took two quarter-centuries off her, but then her face became solemn again. She rattled her tumbler and finished off the second finger of her Scotch. Kate made eye contact with the bartender and spiraled a finger in the air.

"Kate," Vera said more seriously now, "the reason I haven't been able to tell him…about Olive's relationship to me, I mean…is because of who our family is."

Duh! Why hadn't it occurred to Kate before? She practically smacked herself on the head. "Hughes. Are you a Hughes?" That would explain how she'd known so much about their mansion and family tragedies, and yet it didn't explain all she *hadn't* known about what had happened to the brewer and his wife afterward—unless she'd censored herself or simply didn't care. When Vera looked too scared to respond, Kate rambled on, "But Olive never married, right? Did she?"

Vera dropped her eyes and shook her head.

"So then you wouldn't be her niece through marriage, you'd be…" Kate stopped and bit her thumbnail, sorting out the family tree.

"My full name," Vera spoke up, "my *real* one, is Vera Evelyn Redcliffe. My middle name is after my mother, though I was told she mostly went by Eva. She died in childbirth, you see." She reached back into the shoebox and, after fishing around a few seconds, handed a photo and a fragile piece of paper to Kate. "She lost her life while giving me mine."

Evelyn Frances Redcliffe, 1906–1928, read the grave stone, and the death certificate in Kate's other hand went on to confirm what Vera had said was true. Kate expected the emotion in Vera's eyes, but not the tears forming in her own. "She was so young. Younger than me."

Vera patted her hand. "Don't fret, child. It was more common back then, before modern medicine and all. My father, at any rate, went on to marry another woman. Very handsome and affectionate enough, if a little frigid. She didn't bear me any brothers or sisters, and I often wondered whether my parents ever 'did it' at all. Ha! I suppose that's what every child thinks about their parents, opting to believe the stork delivers us. But I—I don't think I was too off the mark on that one." Her stare retreated into the distance.

As Kate received their second round of drinks, she also seized on Vera's silence to articulate a curiosity still burning in her mind. She was about to ask when her neighbor spoke again.

"They weren't going to tell me about my mother, you know. They led me to believe my father's second wife had borne me, and I did grow to love her as my mother. To respect her as such, anyway." She slid aside her empty glass and seized her full one, taking a sip before narrowing her eyes in concentration. "It was just that I didn't *look* like her at all. And I didn't act like her. Not like either of my parents.

"And of course that happens all the time by nature, but once the seed of a doubt got planted in this noggin—" she thumped a finger against her temple "—I started digging. Trust me, stubbornness isn't something I acquired in old age. And when I discovered their wedding certificate in an old chest and saw the year didn't match up to my age, I kicked and screamed that I'd been born out of wedlock. Rather than risk that disgrace, and to pacify my angst, they finally told me the truth."

She paused to drink her Scotch and, presumably, give Kate time to process the information.

By this point, Kate was ready with her first question. "If you were born into all that money, why would you—with all due respect—live in a shithole studio? I mean, why aren't you in a mansion somewhere?"

Vera's widened eyes shone with amusement. "But I was, my dear. I grew up in one in Lake Forest, and I lived a number of my adult years in the one here."

"In Chicago? Where?"

"Wrightwood."

"Not the one by—"

"Indeed, that one. My maternal grandparents transferred ownership to my father before skipping town. My parents opted to stay in what was then still considered 'the country,' but I moved to the big city once I finished school. Only occupied the next-door annex, though. Now and then I'd have a wander and entertain friends in the main house, but it didn't suit me. Beautiful, but too ostentatious for my tastes and too large for my needs, what with no family of my own and all. And cold. Heating that place alone cost a fortune."

Vera pursed her lips and squinted. "No, I was pleased to downsize. The family money isn't what it used to be, so hiring help became a luxury I could no longer afford. Besides, I like taking care of myself. Always have."

"You genuinely didn't know your aunt was already living here?"

"Not a clue. Truly. I moved here for the convenience, nothing more. It was quick and simple for moving what little I kept, and everything else I need was already right here. Nature a block away. The grocers across the street. Hospital around the corner. Retirement home a couple doors down if and when I'm ready. Why else do you think there are so many seniors in this building? Thought you'd admitted yourself into the morgue, did ya?"

She elbowed Kate, who laughed.

"What a shame, though," Vera said, "the years Olive and I lost together, huh? From your point of view, it must seem downright ridiculous."

"Miraculous is what it is. That you came together at all."

"True, true." Vera swigged from her glass. "I am grateful for that. Even if she had no idea."

"Did you *ever* consider telling her?"

She shook her head. "As I said, it would've only confused her more. I didn't want the old gal to keel over in shock. As far as she and anyone else in this building were concerned—Leo included—my name was Vera Finn. Not in law, but in conversation."

"Why? What's so bad about your family history that people can't know? Not to make light of it, but so what if your aunt ran away as a kid? So what if you weren't raised by your biological mother? It's understandable, and these days pretty normal."

Vera raised her eyes to the ceiling. "It's not what I'm hiding but what I'm hiding *from*. Maybe you wouldn't understand, but a pseudonym is a liberating mind-game you can play with yourself. Like Aunt Olive, I just…wanted to feel like someone else for a while. My past may not be an embarrassing or dangerous one, but it's a sad one of mistakes and regret, and not of my making. How ironic that my past should live in the bricks and mortar where I started over. Not so liberating, turns out."

Kate bobbed her head in silence.

"Speaking of past mistakes," Vera said in a lighter tone, "did you find the cocaine spoon? Because I couldn't find it. I know Aunt Olive had one."

"Yeah, that. Yikes."

"Yep. Yikes. Aunt Olive—or should I say Stella Parker—was the quintessential flapper, and I know she turned some tricks to get by in those early years. A young woman like that, selling herself body and soul." At this, Vera's eyes finally did tear up. "Think of how little a person must value herself to cut her face out of every picture she must've ever been in, at least from her old life."

"But how did you know?"

"I told you. She had 'bursts of clarity.' I learned a lot that she didn't realize once the lights would go back out. For instance, how much she was in love with an older man living at Camden Court—a young man, mind, but older than her, which wasn't saying much. Anyway, she called him Lonnie. Lonnie Ashby."

After a gasp, Kate whispered, "Alonzo."

"The one and the same." Vera nodded somberly. "So imagine my surprise when I also learned how much Lonnie was in love with my mother."

"Evelyn."

"The one and the same," Vera repeated.

"So…so that explains why Olive had all those clippings about him in her other shoebox. Makes sense she could have known him if he lived in her building, but—"

"He didn't just live in the building, he lived next door. Only one wall between them."

"Next door? As in next to me? Which side? 4B or D?"

"D, I think."

"God, if it's 4D, the guy living there now is a real douche."

Vera puckered as though she'd sucked a mouthful of lemon juice and not her watered-down whiskey. "He's a what?"

"Nothing. Anyway, I was just going to ask how Alonzo—"

"Lonnie."

"Right, how Lonnie knew Evelyn—"

"Eva."

"Right, Eva. Did he know Olive's true identity, then? Or did *Eva* know she was there and visit her? And then Lonnie met her that way?"

Vera went back to tapping her glass. "It seems they all go farther back than that. My parents uttered nothing about this man, but so many articles I found on business or society events showed a link between all our families. The Redcliffes, Hughes, and Ashbys moved in the same circles, so I can only imagine Lonnie met my mother and aunt one way or another before their respective reversals in fortune. And he clearly knew Auntie when she was young enough to…"

She swallowed. Kate would've thought Vera's saliva was coated in thorns for the look of pain that crossed the woman's face. "To what?"

"To give her a doll, if you can believe it. Not like a collectible, but the sort a child is meant to play with. A baby doll."

"He knew her as a kid, then."

"And she'd treasured that toy until the day she died."

"Wow. He really was an older man. So it was a childhood crush… carried into an obsession? Did she run away to be with him?"

Vera blanched. "It would seem as though. Them both living in that building, it's too coincidental."

"And she brought the doll with her." Kate's next sip may well have been of brine for how unpleasantly the salty gin mixed with the distaste in her mouth. "So did it sell? With the rest of her estate items, I mean? Or did you keep things that were special to her?"

"Some things I kept, yes. But the doll was hers to give, and it so happens she did."

"She gave it to you before she died?"

"No," Vera replied with a thin smile finally warming her face. She laid a hand on Kate's. "She gave it to Maisie, dear."

Kate closed her eyes and exhaled a quiet, "Ohh." Nodding, she reopened her eyes. "That was sweet of her. Really. She must have known Maisie always wanted children."

Vera smiled broader. "Yes. And, yes, it was kind of Aunt Olive to do. It truly astonished me when I saw Maisie carrying that around. I'd have never imagined Olive parting with it. Not for anything. I still don't even know how she managed it. Right before her death. That frail thing, all those stairs."

"Like a last superhuman effort before she could finally rest in peace."

"It really was."

"But why for Maisie? If Olive was going to make a grand gesture, I'd think it'd be for you, or even Leo."

"I couldn't say, dear. Maisie to this day doesn't know she did it, and I don't feel it's for me to tell her if Aunt Olive didn't. She didn't even tell *me*, not really. I only gleaned what had happened from her occasionally muttering about giving away her baby…about climbing up steps, dropping the baby at a door, making things right. No details, no explanations. Just fragments I pieced together and fit to Maisie's story."

"What did she mean, 'making things right'?"

The woman scrunched her shoulders to her neck. "She had little else to do but watch people out her window. She had no television, and while she hoarded newspapers, I don't know that she ever read them." Her throat rumbled with a deep laugh. "Always dog-earing articles to read later. Anyhoo, I think she watched Maisie from across the courtyard and felt for her. It's hard not to. I'm glad you've come to as well." Her hand was still on Kate's, and Vera gave it a squeeze.

"So," Kate said, "would Olive have known Estella Ashby, too, by chance?"

Pinching her face, Vera studied Kate. "I…honestly have no idea. She never mentioned…unless she was talking about Estella and not herself as Stella, but…how did you…"

"Leo told me. He's been researching their family, trying to figure out why Lonnie seems to upset you."

The dull wonder in Vera's eyes sharpened. "Leo's been snooping into my affairs? Behind my back? What gives him the right to —"

Kate waved her hands as though stopping oncoming traffic. "No, no, no! Don't get mad! He's not trying to dig up gold or dirty secrets, Vera. C'mon, you weren't exactly subtle when we talked about Ashby's death in the laundry room. You know Leo cares about you and doesn't like to see you troubled."

"That so? Well, now he's gonna see trouble, that son of a —"

"Stop!" Kate grabbed both of Vera's hands and pinned them down to her polyester lap. "What did I just say to you? Independent to a fault. Try to see it from his good heart's point of view and don't assume the worst. I don't think he's even made any connections yet." She recalled Leo's troubled expression when he'd looked at Eva's wedding photo a few weeks back but decided to bury that little fact. She hadn't been positive it was Eva's picture in the first place, only guessed, and his response could have been indigestion for all Kate knew. Certainly not worth complicating matters with Vera now. "And besides, even if he did, he wouldn't judge you. You know that. You know him."

Vera's pout was insolent, but her lack of response told Kate she was mulling over her words.

The young woman dared go on to say, "So your family history was a living soap opera. So what? It's nothing to be embarrassed of. It's not a reflection on who you are. And you gotta figure Leo spends enough time in that management office to see everyone's records. He probably saw your real name on file ages ago."

From the way the woman pinched her lips, Kate took it to mean she hadn't considered that.

"And it didn't change anything, did it. I don't think he means to go behind your back. I think he wants to take care of you, Vera. But you don't exactly make it easy for him to understand how to do that. He just needs to know where you're coming from, that's all."

After a loaded pause, the little lady did ask, "Well, what exactly did he find out?"

Kate shrugged. "All I know is he traced Lonnie to Estella, and that she lived in a big Wisconsin estate and donated money to our building."

"Our building? Camden Court?"

"Yeah."

"Mercy. Does he have any idea why?"

"Probably some memorial to her nephew. Maybe they were close and she took his suicide hard." As Vera chewed the inside of her mouth, Kate knocked back a little more of her martini. "I wish the guy living next door *now* would take a flying leap," she muttered.

"What's that?"

"Never mind."

Another awkward silence stretched out.

As memories of David tainted her thoughts of all Vera had related, after a few beats, Kate mused aloud, "They were neighbors…he had to have known, then. Lonnie had to have known Olive lived right next door. So why wouldn't he have ratted her out to her family or the police?" She screwed her face. "You don't think they ever…"

Vera raised and dropped her shoulders, a sad glaze to her eyes. "I don't know. Auntie never mentioned it during one of her good spells, but she did…she did seem to recall overhearing her sister next door."

"As in your mom? She and him…might've…?"

"I think so. I think she might've even been the reason he made that jump, heartbroken. If that's the case, then my mother was much better at keeping secrets than my father."

"What do you mean? Like, she kept the affair secret better than he'd kept her maternity secret later on?"

"More like better than he'd kept *his* affair and his *paternity* secret."

"What!" Kate was already three-fourths through her second martini, and she wasn't about to slow down now. Chomping the olive, she urgently twirled her finger in the air at the bartender.

Vera looked to the ceiling and drew in a deep, deep inhale before gesturing the sign of the cross with her right hand and then swigging her Scotch with her left.

"All right…" she began.

New Year's Eve 1927

Approaching Lon's door, Eva was about to tap out her secret knock when she thought, *This is absurd.* They'd been acting like children in a tree house and needed to be adults if they were going to raise a child together.

The many weeks to follow their rendezvous at the museum had been the most miserable yet affirming ones of her life. No, Eva couldn't run with the Redcliffe heir growing inside her, but she could with an Ashby, couldn't she? If she could prove it?

What a coward she'd been, days from telling her husband everything and throwing her reputation to the wind, yet once a baby had become at stake, it had taken her this long to finally confide in her doctor under protection of the Hippocratic Oath. What if it were true, what her physician had told her in the privacy of her bedside? That a blood test could possibly exclude Finlay as the father. Might then she have some sway with a jury when they brought their divorce to court? Perhaps it was hoping for too much, but it was something. Surely worth an effort.

So, after weeks without attempting contact, Eva at last had the nerve to approach Lon this afternoon with new possibility—if, in that remote chance, he would still have her. In hedging her bets, she'd not yet breathed a word of truth to Finlay or anyone else.

Regardless, she refused to treat Lon's home like a speakeasy any longer. Fisting her fingers, Eva raised her arm to rap on his door.

It was past the noon hour, and still Ollie wore her dress and smudged makeup from the prior evening.

Her generous benefactor that night had been "courting" her for some time but hadn't breached the bed boundary. Each encounter, he'd merely keep her glass filled until the wee hours of morning, likewise filling her ears with the fantasies he had of her—those he imagined when returning home to his wife and which he intended to fulfill when the time was right.

Last night, he'd said how he loved her, how he'd rescue her and provide for her as soon as he found a way. Though he meant nothing to her romantically, Ollie was flattered by the monetary value her after-dark companionship held for him.

She *was* fond of the gentleman, though. He seemed older than her usual clients, or at least more refined. When he sat with her in their usual corner booth, his attentions were never diverted by the dazzle and dancing filling the dusty dark space beyond them, his admiration of her curves never distracted by more fashionably slim silhouettes slinking by. Instead, he'd been the one to request she stop binding herself in those dreadful undergarments so that he might reap the rewards of nature's bounty. He would glide his fingertips just above the fringy neckline of the crimson dress he'd paid for, along the exposed pillow of her plump bosom, and then cup her face and gaze at her with a perverse sort of protective, paternal desire. Never had his touch gone further than that.

Ollie sat curled in fetal position on her chair, which she'd pulled to the window so she could watch the birds. On days like these, she couldn't ignore the hollow of having no family. Or, worse, having family so near yet so absent from her life. She could easily run back, she knew that—run home and wash the black from her eyes, the dye from her hair, and be held in the arms of her real father. To have a mother again, even a sister.

But didn't she have enough of those? The other girls, the other lost souls who now understood her better than Eva ever had or could. Her charming sister with her so-called worldly ways. In so short a time, Ollie had already seen a broader, bleaker side of the world than Eva would ever know, the one hidden in shadows, where one flick of a dark angel's wand turned little girls into women.

Rocking lightly back and forth with her doll at her breast, Ollie squinted into the glare of daylight and counted all the blackbirds greeting her that day.

"*Three for a wedding, four for a birth*—" she hiccupped "*—five for silver, six for gold, seven*—" hiccup "*—for a secret never to be told.*"

She sighed when she ran out of birds, then closed her eyes to contemplate the secret she'd wanted to tell for so long. The one she'd been trying to tell ever since hearing Eva's knocks and voice go quiet next door. Something had happened between Lon and her sister, something that had conspired to break them up before Ollie'd had to lift a scarlet-varnished finger to help it.

Since then, on some days when she was still loopy from the night before, she'd tried the secret knock on his door. His refusal to answer would break her heart, and out there on the landing she would sink to the floor, moping in self-pity until gathering herself and returning home to sober up.

He could only ignore Eva's knock for so long, though. Ollie knew that. Because she knew what repressed desire could do to a man, given enough time. She saw it every evening in her nightly gentleman's eyes, a man who'd admitted he was in a sexless marriage and had wanted to save and savor the promise of Ollie, letting the temptation build until he would finally unwrap his sugared little cherry with rapture.

Yes, she'd know just what to look for in Lon's eyes when he did finally answer that door. For when he did, it would be because his starving body yearned for satisfaction; he'd be hungry, carnal. And if Ollie could play it just right, he would devour her, regardless of whether she was or wasn't whom he'd expected. Then, in giving him what he wanted—so skillfully, so ferally, as one who had nothing else to live for—then could she eclipse Eva in his heart. Eva, who had placed too many conditions on their love.

Eva, who had never placed any on her love for her little sister, though. Who, when Ollie had run away, had probably been—

She never let herself dwell on how her disappearance must have affected her family and cursed herself for doing so now. She slowed her rocking, and a tear escaped from beneath her lashes. With a heaviness in her chest, she opened her eyes to blink the moisture away.

Just in time to see three more birds alight on the hotel's roof.

Sniffing, she whispered, "*Eight for heaven, nine for hell, and ten for the De*—"

A soft knocking interrupted her counting. Setting the ball of one bare foot down on the floorboards, Ollie peered around her chair's wing to the door, wondering who could be calling on Lon. The only person in weeks had been his dear great-aunt; perhaps this was the woman returning.

But then Ollie heard Eva's voice:

"Lonnie? Lon? Are you there?"

She held her breath, noticing that her hiccupping had stopped. Ollie also knew that Lon was already out for the day. Soundlessly, she lowered her other foot to the floor.

Pound-pound-pound!

"Lonnie? Old boy, are you home?" Pressing a palm against the door, Eva laid her forehead there as well. "Please, Lon. If you're there, I'll only be a minute, I promise you. I'll—" The door she leaned on was still as a casket, but with a crack and slow scrape, the one to her left announced its opening.

The sudden sound had startled her, but Eva didn't move, only turned her head to the side in a stupor, enough to see the neighboring door stand partially ajar.

She was too tired to hide. And too tired to try anymore, at least that afternoon. Lon was either away or wouldn't see her, and she'd clearly disturbed his neighbor—who hadn't said a word, yet the silence spoke enough. She couldn't very well pick Lon's lock again under this supervision, so Eva decided to leave and try once more tomorrow.

Backing up from his door, she turned to face the stairs and let his neighbor watch her from behind. She rested her pregnant weight on the railing as she felt her way to the newel post beside the top step. Delicately dropping one foot down, she heard the door behind her creak again. Unsure whether it had further opened or closed, Eva let curiosity get the better of her. She looked back.

And into the eyes of Lon's neighbor. First the spidery and clumpy black lashes circling them, then their glaring, pale green centers.

The air leaped into Eva's lungs as she threw a hand to her mouth, simultaneously stepping back in alarm. Missing her footing on the next step, she tumbled down the flight as Ollie's ghost wailed.

August 2000

"And then, oh my God, Dexter. *Get this…*"

Kate was in full-on Animated Drunk mode, a state she hadn't been sure she'd regain after day-drinking with Vera. But a long nap and hot shower — complete with some Olive antics — had energized her for the night.

What surprised her more than stepping out of the tub to see *KEY* shakily scrawled on her steamed mirror was how much it hadn't surprised her. Through the shoeboxes, she'd gotten to know Olive pretty well this summer and felt safe with her. The Phantom Menace she'd detected in early July felt more like the Friendly Ghost by mid-August. Befriending her niece couldn't have hurt getting in the dead woman's good graces either.

And though she couldn't decipher what Olive's new message meant, Kate had decided to at least pay homage by stepping out with the little black beaded purse. She had a sleeveless jersey-knit black dress and killer patent-leather heels to match it.

Her evening out with Dex had kicked off with a rock concert at the Aragon Ballroom in Uptown; he'd surprised her with the tickets at work on Friday. And after ducking out early enough to beat the masses, they'd since foregone plastic cups of beer for glass tumblers of gin and tonic across the street at the Green Mill.

From the back of the intimate space, a jazz quintet *boo-beh-doo-bopped* its way through the mystically charged, yet mellow atmosphere.

It was uncanny how similar that night's act was to the music that played next door — Kate was pleased for the chance to associate it with new and better thoughts. David might be dead to her, but her love of the music would live on. Maybe that had been the real love affair through the wall all along.

The music at the club was loud, so she and Dex had to yell to hear each other. But their booth by the front door — the farthest from the stage — was at least more conducive to relating her day's tale than the Aragon's mosh pit.

She was more than halfway through it when her Animated Drunk hands revved up for the climax. They flew with her words as Dex held their glasses in precaution. "Okay, so he was gay!"

"Huh?"

"*Gay!*"

"What! Finlay?"

"*Yes!*" Kate pumped her fists in the air, then qualified, "Not that there's anything wrong with that!"

"Of course not!"

"But you can see how it complicated things!"

"Totally!"

The band announced its pause for intermission, and Kate welcomed the break. Between drinking all day and shouting all night, her throat was raw.

"So, yeah," she said to Dex at a reduced volume once she had the chance. "Can you imagine how much pressure there must've been to keep up appearances back then? It's bad enough now, and Finlay's family was so prominent. They were constantly in the headlines, Vera said."

"But why does she think her dad was gay?"

"Because he sucked at keeping secrets."

Dex removed his palms from the rims of their tumblers and handed Kate hers. "Bet that's not all he sucked at," he murmured into his glass as he tipped it back for a drink.

Kate swatted his arm. "Ass. Anyway, when her dad died and she sorted his effects, she found this whole stash of love letters. I kid you not. Bundle upon bundle of them dating back to nineteen twenty-five from *another man*."

"Oh, I see. *I'm* the homophobe, but *you* can make a big deal about him getting love letters from a dude."

"Hey, it'd be a big deal if they were from a woman. He cheated on his wife. *Both* of his wives, for *decades*." With finger-quotes, she added, "'Working late' every night, when he really was rendezvousing in a servants' cottage on their Lake Forest estate."

"Okay, but it's not the same thing as if he were straight and stickin' it to another woman. You can't exactly blame him."

"It's still not fair to the wife."

"The unfaithful wife, you mean? I think all's fair in love and wa—ow!"

Kate's palm actually stung from that next smack to his arm. Vicki wasn't a distant enough part of their past for him to embrace perspectives like that.

"You know what I mean," she said. "It's not fair to misrepresent who you are in a relationship. It's fraud."

"But if the other person knows the truth? And still goes along with it?"

"Then I guess it's fair game. Eva had a lot to gain from the marriage. It made them this huge power couple. Saved the family fortune. Her dad owned breweries, so Prohibition must have slammed them. And I'm sure it was marrying up for Vera's stepmom, too. If Finlay was a nice guy who could take care of them, there are worse marriages to be in. But, anyway, Vera doesn't know whether either of them knew the truth."

"Which again begs the question how Vera does. About her dad not being her dad, I mean. Eva may have had her little cabana boy on the side, and Finlay might've batted for the other team, but that doesn't mean they never had sex. And gay dudes aren't sterile, you know."

"This is true. So, moving on…" Kate slid their glasses back a ways on the table in case Crazy Hands flared up again with the juicy bone she had yet to throw. "Vera had proof her stepmom wasn't her real mom, but she also had a hunch about her dad, though she couldn't put her finger on why. So fast-forward to the late eighties when he's on his deathbed and getting all these blood tests. She had his DNA tested."

"You're shitting me. They could do that then?"

"Just started to."

"And it wasn't him?"

"Nope."

"Geez—and here I thought life was simpler in the olden days. Does she have any idea who it was?"

With a smug grin, Kate nodded. "Once she'd found her aunt and made the connection to Ashby, she looked into his blood type."

"Not to burst your or the old lady's bubbles, but matching blood types don't prove anything."

"Well, what's she supposed to do, exhume the freaking body?"

"That'd be awesome."

Kate swatted him again. "Show some respect."

"How about stop hitting me and show some affection." He cowered like a little boy, and she contented him with a big-puckered smooch. "Thanks, sweetie. For that, I'll indulge you. Were the blood types a match?"

"Enough that it couldn't disprove Lonnie was the father."

"Oh, you're on a first-name basis with the dirtbag now?"

"Who says he was a dirtbag?"

"This entire story does."

"No," Kate said in earnest. "I can't explain it, but I get the sense Lonnie was all right. That everyone involved was just an unfortunate victim of unfair pressures, and none of them deserved what they got in the end. If they'd only felt they could be honest with each other and to themselves, it might've bought everyone a lot more time with the people they truly loved."

Wearing a half-grin, Dex reached around Kate's shoulders and cuddled her to him.

"I don't know," she wondered. "I guess I just want to believe that what he and Eva had was real. And that Finlay had found the same. Not the ideal moral at the end of the story with everyone lying and sleeping around on each other, granted, but…it's something. It's more than Olive had. And Vera. Although…"

"Huh?" he asked with a squeeze.

Kate rested her head on his shoulder and smiled. "Well, Vera's still got a shot."

"You know what?" He tipped her chin up so she could look him in the eye. "I think we do, too."

She didn't know if it was the gin, the way Dexter was looking at her, or the intoxication of a clarinet fluttering back to life onstage in the opening measures of "Rhapsody in Blue," but Kate agreed with him. She cupped his cheek and stroked her thumb across it.

"Happy birthday, Katie."

"Yes it is, Dex."

And they kissed as the quintet set notes afloat on the air to dip and dive and rise and roll on a sea that swept behind Kate's closed eyes.

With her lids still lowered, she dreamily sat back and pressed her lips together.

"You all right?" she heard him ask.

"Mm hmm…a bit dizzy, that's all."

"You look flushed. You're sure you're feeling okay?"

She giggled and patted a hand on his knee as she opened her eyes. "Yes, fine. Just boozy." She did feel warm and figured she could do with patting away some perspiration. Propping her vintage evening bag on the table, she popped it open to grab her powder compact. A peek at the mirrored backing beneath the purse lid told her she wasn't alone.

Hello, Olive.

The pale green eyes penetrating hers looked kinder this time, almost twinkling.

Kate snapped the lid closed. "Um, you know, if you don't mind, I'm just going to excuse myself to the ladies' room and…powder my nose."

"Oh, I see, milady." Dex was obviously tickled by her old-fashioned manner. "Perhaps I'll have myself a clean, close shave in the gentlemen's."

Rolling her eyes, she said, "All right, Chuckles. Open Mic Night isn't until Tuesday."

As she slid out from their booth with her sparkling purse hanging from her arm, Dex punctuated the corniness with a quick "Shave and a Haircut" tap on the tabletop. Kate laughed and shook her head as she knocked out the final "Two Bits" from where she stood. Her knuckles had no sooner rapped the second time when the vision of David doing the same at Geja's — the same two knocks, in the same hokey way — replayed in her mind. Her smile froze with the dawn of realization.

"I'll just be right back," she said before she turned and wove through the club patrons to the restrooms in back. The quintet's rhapsody picked up in tempo, and Kate inhaled as much of the warm, moist air as she could to keep alert, stay the course. But her steps stumbled, and she had to grab strangers' shoulders to keep her footing as she navigated back, back, back. The room spun with the music that whirled through her senses like water running down a drain.

Finally through the restroom door, she plopped the purse and her palms onto the counter and stood leaning against it, head hanging. Breathing in and out, in and out, she overcame the prickling little pins and needles that had accosted the surface of her skin. The air was cooler in here and smelled sweet, like…

Lilac.

Kate stood up and blew her bangs off her forehead. Staring into the wall mirror, she watched her rosy color go down, then bent toward the faucet to splash some water on her face. With a last gulp of air, she said, "All right, you," to the purse and brought it with her into the stall.

Sitting on the toilet seat, she snapped open the glittering black lid to face the glassless mirror once more. But Olive wasn't there. The gaze meeting hers was from her own brown eyes, residual tap water creeping down her temples on either side.

What game is this, Olive? What have you been trying to tell me?

Yet no matter how long she looked at it or rubbed it as if it were a genie lamp, the mirror remnant had nothing else to say. But the lining did. She'd only just reached back in for her compact when she felt some of its fabric sticking out.

"Aw," Kate whined as she fingered a loose flap of silk at the bottom. Peeling it back, she smoothed her fingertip over the surface under-neath and brainstormed how to repair it—until she felt a slight give.

Don't tell me the bottom's falling out next.

To inspect the damage, she wedged a fingernail into the narrow crevice she'd discovered between the purse's base and sides and pried the bottom up with it—a false one, it seemed. She pinched its edge and pulled it up as far as she could with her makeup, money, and keys on top. Stowed beneath was a bronze skeleton key.

What it unlocked was a good question, but Kate knew the key was Olive's answer.

XXXVII

New Year's Eve 1927

"Eva!" Ollie screamed, and she dashed down the flight of the steps to where her elegant sister lay crumpled in a black heap of wool and fur. "No, no, no! Wake up, please wake up!"

Frantically, she patted her hands along Eva's heavy coat as she tried to determine her sister's orientation and how best to move her. She carefully removed Eva's hat and registered that she wasn't wearing her pageboy cap or any bit of her male camouflage. That the hat had curved around Eva's head so snugly was likely the only reason it stayed on and had hopefully cushioned her skull from the impact. Her shallow breath rippled the fur beneath her nose, which signaled Eva was alive, though unconscious.

Ollie gently slipped her hands behind Eva's knees and did her best to straighten the slender legs across the landing and roll her sister's body onto its backside. Once lying flat, Eva looked more at peace, like she was only sleeping, which comforted Ollie enough to find her wits and feel the length of Eva's shins and ankles for any noticeable breaks. She then unfastened the front of her big sister's coat so she could inspect there as well.

When Ollie peeled away the bulk of the fur-lined garment, she instantly understood so much: Eva's absence all those weeks. Her urgency this day. And her recklessness in showing up without her disguise—the waistline of those boy's trousers wouldn't have fit her round belly.

Ollie yelped and, through blurring eyes, glanced down in time to see a black-red stain grow along the beige silk lining of Eva's coat.

If anyone in the building block heard her cries, they didn't run to her rescue. All she could rely on was that, though shorter and underfed, she'd become of sturdier stature than her older sibling. That didn't make Eva's extra baby weight less of a challenge, but whether it was adrenaline or the force of love alone, Ollie summoned the strength to carry her sister back upstairs.

It was slow going, and it burned every muscle. And once on the upper landing, Ollie had to lay Eva back down and drag her by the scruff into her apartment. The thickness of her winter coat, enhanced by its decorative bands of fur, absorbed most of the initial bleeding, but as Eva started to hemorrhage even worse, Ollie didn't know what else to do but get her out of the overcoat and into the bathtub.

Panicked, she felt the skin of Eva's sweating, flushed face and wasn't sure how to make the fever subside other than stoppering the tub and running cold water from the tap. Kneeling on the icy tiled floor, she watched in horror as a cloud of pinkish-red billowed in the rising water, the blood discharging from Eva's body and lifting from her dress and stockings. Dipping her hands into the freezing water, Ollie lightly slapped her sister's cheeks and smoothed her brown hair off of her face. She wanted to both fetch a doctor and never leave Eva's side, but as Ollie shivered, shock seized her heart and frosted her skin.

So she just sat there. Numb and frozen. Deafened by the surging water and watching the wet, pink-stained ivory skin of her sister's face turn gray as her vibrant life seemed to drain out.

August 2000

"Keep the change," Kate told the taxi driver who'd delivered her from Uptown to Lincoln Park. She'd tipped him generously, still trying to balance out her cab karma after that rude ride with David last month. "Thank you, and enjoy the rest of your weekend!"

The politeness paid off. She could still hear the engine running the entire time she fumbled through her purse for her keys and let herself in the gate to Camden Court. Sure, the guy could've been ogling or stalking, but when he pulled away as soon as she was safely in, she was pretty sure he'd just been looking out for her.

Chivalry isn't dead.

And neither was Dexter's in sending her home alone. Given their late night, she hadn't expected him to ride all the way south with her when his parents would be visiting first thing in the morning for breakfast. And he hadn't expected her to crash up north with him either, even though it would've been closer to the club. They were in a good place, Kate felt. Still giving each other space yet making time for each other, without any expectation or analysis going into it. They were just *being*, which made being together good and natural again.

As she *clip-clopped* her way to her wing of the building in the wee hours of morning, she noticed a ground-level light on at the end of the courtyard. At Leo's place.

He can't still be awake, she worried. That was the problem with living alone. Lately, Kate had taken to wondering how long it would take someone to find her if she were to drop dead in her studio. How many times someone would have to reach her voicemail; how many days she would have to miss at work; how long until they realized she hadn't replied to an email. She could see it being at least twenty-four to forty-eight hours, and that was with a boyfriend, family, and friends all around her. Not like Olive, who'd had to stink up the place to be found three days later. Not like Leo, who didn't seem to have anyone but Vera—and now not even her, possibly, if she carried this grudge about him investigating her past.

"Shit," Kate said under her breath, and she kicked off her heels. Leaving them where they were, she trotted down the central walkway and around the courtyard fountain to reach the back of the building.

Leo's curtains were only partially drawn, so she crept into the grass and skimmed between the bushes to get a closer look. Pressed against the red brick to the window's side, she slowly leaned toward the center of the pane, detecting the blue flicker of TV light against his walls and scanning along his old sofa until Leo himself slid into view.

Kate gasped and clasped a hand over her mouth.

The old man was seated upright at the end of his avocado-green couch. His head lolled back against the wall at an awkward angle, and his mouth hung wide open as though frozen in a ghoulish scream.

But Kate could see the deep rise and fall of his chest—and Vera's sleeping head rising and falling with it. Leo's arm was wrapped around her shoulder, and while the woman's one arm rested on the little legs she had tucked to her side on the cushion, the other was across Leo's lap, holding his hand.

Even through the insulated windowpane, Kate could hear them sawing logs like champs. *The Andy Griffith Show* played on the TV, so it had been a Nick-at-Nite night-in for them.

Uh oh, you'll be doing the Walk of Shame in the morning, you floozy.

Kate giggled into her palm then flattened it to her heart, cocking her head to the side to just stare at the precious tableau a few seconds longer. Framed as it was in the window, it could've been a Norman Rockwell painting, and she would never forget the sense of goodness and light swelling in her breast right then. She had no idea what all had gone down between now and when she'd dropped Vera off at Panera for a sobering coffee after Barleycorn's. But at this moment, all seemed as it should be.

With a last congratulatory look at the happy couple, Kate quietly bushwhacked her way back to the walkway. Before striding back to the front of her wing, though, she circled where she was for a moment. She skidded the ball of one foot on the coarse pavement and looked down, watching her bare toes rake back along it as though it were sand to draw pictures in.

The concrete still held the heat of the day's sun, and she thought of the extreme difference a few months would make to that. The world had circled more than halfway through the first year of the new millennium, and summer was almost over. Kids were already returning to school in a week, and Kate would have their Adler fieldtrips to prepare for. Then, as the Earth continued its orbit, the leaves would turn and the air would chill. And before anyone knew it, the sun would keep its distance and coat this walkway in ice.

Though thick, warm air wrapped around her, Kate almost shivered at the thought. To be on this pavement on a winter day, on a New Year's night…

She sucked in a breath and rubbed the goose bumps on her forearm, twisting to look up at the roof. The air currents up there would be even colder. Kate almost saw her frosted breath, watched it rise and veil her vision of the rooftop ledge. She imagined the lonely souls up above who had lost their lives here below, and as the hazy image dissipated, the stars sharpened into view.

No Chicago evening was clear enough for a truly wondrous night sky, but Kate appreciated whatever she could see. Were it actually New Year's, she'd have a good view of her favorite star cluster—Pleiades, the Seven Sisters. No use looking for those crazy broads now, though.

Kate felt a crick in her neck, so she brought her sight back to the pavement underfoot. Offering Lonnie and Tommy a moment of silence, she blew a kiss to the ground and walked back toward her door, off-roading onto the soft grass and scooping her shoes up along the way.

As she padded up her stairwell, she thought of how both Olive and Lonnie had trodden this path before. She paused on the last flight. Looking from 4B to 4D on either side of her unit door, she wondered which apartment had for sure belonged to *the* Mr. Ashby, the suicidal adulterer she would never know. The father Vera hadn't known either.

Lingering on each step as she climbed up, she observed David-in-4D's doorknob as if for the first time. It was dull and tarnished with a decorative band circling its front, and its backplate had an arched top and bottom, embellished with ornate scrollwork. The knobs of 4A, B, and C, in contrast, were mounted on plain rectangular plates and of a shinier brass. Backtracking to the landing, Kate verified that 3A through D below had the same kind. The mahogany-stained doors were otherwise identical, but now that she resumed her climb and stared at 4D directly, the difference from the rest was night and day. And yet since its knob and backplate were of the same proportion and color as the rest, Kate couldn't blame herself for having never noticed until now. If ever she'd wistfully looked at 4D before, it had been with keen interest in *David's* knob, not the door's.

But there was more to its distinction than the design: the lock. The lock was a proper old-fashioned keyhole shape—the sort for Peeping Toms, not modern-cut keys.

An old-fashioned keyhole.

The word *KEY* written in fogged glass.

A skeleton key found in an evening bag.

Adrenaline injected into Kate's veins, magnifying the warm rush of alcohol still coursing through her system, and she rifled through her purse to disinter the bronze key from its false-bottom grave. Running her thumb along it, she wondered, just wondered…

Flipping it over, she spied the engraving on the key's oval end. It was shallow and marred by scrapes, yet read clearly enough:

4D.

"Oh my God," she whispered and darted her gaze to the base of David's door. No light was on, and she heard no sound from within. Then again, it was well after two a.m., so it was reasonable he'd be asleep.

What wasn't reasonable at the moment was Kate's sense of judgment after a day and night of gin. That is to say, she knew well enough what would be the right versus wrong thing to do in this situation—she just didn't care. At least not as far as what David would think. Olive had sent her that message and given her this key for a reason, and she'd be damned if Mr. Scooch was going to stop her.

Stop her from what, though? Breaking and entering his apartment? To do what, exactly? Find something? Find what? Lonnie hadn't lived there in over seventy years. What trace of him, Eva, or Olive could possibly still be there?

Olive, for one, could have kept a private stash there if she had access with that key.

Under the floorboards or something. She seems to be a fan of the hidden compartment.

But who knew if the key was even for that door, or any door in the building. The engraving could have been coincidence. And if not, would it even still work? Surely, the locks had to have been changed over time. Why else would all of the other doors' knobs have been replaced? But then why hadn't 4D's?

What's so fucking special about your place, David? she couldn't help but think spitefully. Now she was glad to wake him up. She hoped she would, in fact. *Speak of the fucking devil, and he shall appear.*

Oh, but she really didn't want him to appear. She didn't want to make this about him at all. It was about Olive. She thought it was, anyway. Actually, the more Kate thought about it, the more she realized trying the lock to that door was a very, very bad idea.

She couldn't do it. Not tonight, at least. Maybe in the daytime, when she could be more certain no one was home. She could go into work late one morning, long after David would've left for his law firm. But even then — even if the key worked — by the light of day, could she really picture herself searching through his stuff for God knew what?

No. She wasn't going in there at all. Not ever.

Taking a deep breath of relief that she'd found her resolution, it was time for the Birthday Girl to finally get her beauty sleep. She needed all the help she could get, highly suspecting she was going to look like a tribal shrunken head tomorrow after sucking down a whole salt lick today.

After a good laugh at herself, Kate approached her door and swapped the skeleton key for hers to insert into her lock. It slid in with ease.

But didn't budge when she tried to turn it.

Damn.

She tried again. Nothing. She pulled it out and stuck it back in. Turned it — or tried to, rather, but it wouldn't move.

Yanking the key out again, she took a close look to be sure it was the right one. Undoubtedly, unequivocally, it was.

So work, motherfucker. She stuck it in and couldn't get the damn thing to turn.

"Fuck, fuck, fuck, fuck, fuck, fuck, fuck, fuck," she spat under breath as her giddy buzz took a detour into the Dark Side. "It's my fucking birthday. I do not fucking need this." And of course she didn't have her cell phone on her because Genius hadn't wanted to overstuff her pretty black beaded bag.

There would've been more room in there if it weren't for your fucking little hidden compartment, Olive.

So calling Dexter — or anyone else helpful, for that matter — was out. Sulking, Kate drove her forehead into the door a little harder than she'd meant to.

"Ow."

Leaning there, she figured her only other option was to fetch Leo. He had access to the master key, but…

Oh. She pouted. *I'd hate to wake them and spoil their little evening. They looked so cozy, and I might embarrass them, and…*

No. She'd sooner mortify herself and ask David for help than do any of the above. Standing upright once more, she clenched her fists, then pivoted to face 4D.

Olive, if this is you fucking with me, you are such a fucking bitch.

Taking a moment to steel her will, she finally raised her right fist and lightly knocked at her neighbor's door.

No response.

She knocked again, a little more firmly this time.

Nothing.

Giving it a few seconds more, she tried again, desperate enough to try the special knock she by now understood had been special to no one but her:

Tap tap, tap tap-tap, tap tap.

Not so much as a stir from inside.

She looked around at her other neighbors' doors and contemplated trying one of them instead. In that case, if she was going to wake them anyway, it wouldn't hurt to give David's door one last good, loud rap. She knocked a solid three times.

Nope.

It was possible he was in there, conked out after too many drinks or sticking it to Allie the Waitress. Who knew. But it still seemed odd there would be no sound whatsoever, snoring, humping, or otherwise. At any rate, none of her other neighbors had yelled at her to knock it the fuck off, so there'd be no other witnesses if she did resort to the skeleton key.

Prepping herself with some yoga breathing, she swapped her key back for the bronze one. She hoped against hope it would fit. It would be hugely embarrassing if David was either home or returned home to find her there, but so be it. She'd explain the whole story as best she could. She set Olive's purse on the floor beside her door and returned to her neighbor's.

"Here goes nothing," she whispered.

The key fit into the lock. And it turned.

New Year's Eve 1927

Whistling down the sidewalk on his way home from the yards, Lon blew into his hands and rubbed them together, eager for his radiator. The day had been long and hard, as he'd expected and relished; the work and the elements gave his mind something else to think about. And the evening had delivered him into the camaraderie of an impromptu New Year's celebration, toasting cups of home-brewed hooch within the ephemeral walls of an immigrant's shanty. Lon had shared the gaiety but not the gin, sipping only from a mug of steaming tea with a mild smile and excusing himself with a couple of hours left to midnight.

There was something to the nip in the air that final December day, too, that lifted his spirits. He couldn't pinpoint what could possibly be rejuvenating him almost to the point of cheer. Weather was like that, he supposed. Just as autumn leaves would trigger thoughts of Estella's multicolored acres and cupping hot cider in wool-mittened hands, the smell of snow conjured images of ice skating, the stately Christmas tree presiding over the Walnut Room at Marshall Field's, and that childhood promise of presents, enchanted and secret beneath their wrapping.

But Lon had borne so many unhappy yuletides, and this past one had been no different, just when most of the year had boded otherwise. Perhaps the impending New Year would bring happiness back to him. What a child he'd been, allowing jealousy and insecurity to harden into spite against the one he loved most. Was that love? Was it what love does? To be fair-weathered and self-serving at the cost of putting that wounded look in his lover's eyes? At the cost of the grief it could have fed into an unborn child's veins?

When Eva next knocked, he would open his door to her.

And if she didn't, he would go to her, in broad daylight before God and everyone—"the Devil may care," as she'd said herself.

Skipping up the steps inside his hotel block, he halted at the penultimate landing. He could smell her. Eva had been there. And perhaps was still if she'd let herself inside like the last time so long ago.

Gripping the banister with his heart in his throat, he seemed to momentarily lose the feeling in his legs, feeling simultaneous instincts of fight and flight.

Fly away and help Eva keep good on her promise to never hurt me again. Or fight for us, for what we once had…and give that dear girl every opportunity to hurt me as much as she desires. I will take it. I will have to.

Deliberating a moment, he found his legs again. He lifted one foot, hesitated, then took a step upward. Then another…and another…and then the rest of them in a clambering sprint. The lingering spirit of Eva's perfume was stronger at the top landing, and with stiff, calloused fingers, Lon fumbled with his keys to fit the right one into the lock. With a last, bracing inhale, he opened his door and stepped in.

The room felt lifeless and cold as a tomb. Closing his door then switching on a light, his eager eyes looked around by the dull gold-red glow of his lamp's stained glass shade. His Murphy bed was still flipped up inside the wall. If she had come at all, she hadn't stayed.

Stepping in slow circles on the same spot, he spun until the subject of his masterpiece slid into view. Unable to stomach it, he snuffed his light back out.

As his world went black, the sensation went out from under him again, and Lon sank to his knees on the unyielding floorboards. Clasping his hands together, he folded forward and laid his forehead on them, finally shaking with the tears he'd refused to shed. He rubbed his face side to side against his hands, missing the feel of her soft skin, the warm cushion of her light breath. Pressing his mouth to his thumb knuckles, he lamented their angular hardness, nothing like her petal-smooth lips. And, in a series of tremors, he wept again.

In a dozen or so heartbeats' time, he sniffed with heavy breaths and sat up. His hands still entwined, he concentrated on the wall before him; adjusted to the darkness, his eyes discerning the milky form floating above him. He'd never been a praying man, but there in his private temple, Lon raised his hands to his breastbone and prayed for his goddess to manifest once more.

Tap tap, tap tap-tap, tap tap.

Squeezing his palms together even harder as the breath left his chest, Lon looked to his door. He'd imagined it, surely. The power of wishful thinking. But then—

Tap tap, tap tap-tap, tap tap.

No mistaking it that time. A hand of flesh and bone had knocked on his door, and the sound reverberated on the floorboards. He wasted no time scrambling to his feet.

Whipping the door open to the dim light of the hall, Lon looked into the eyes of—no one. No one stood there at all.

But a frail figure did sit there.

"Eva! Darling!" Horrified, Lon sank to the floor and reached out to her across the threshold, immediately gathering her up in his arms. The lips that had once sneered at him so saucily were chapped and colorless. The waves of chocolate that once tickled against his face were matted and tangled and…damp. A coarse, soiled-looking white sheet draped from her shoulders, and Lon peeled it back enough to see she was naked.

"My God, what's happened to you!"

"Lonnie, I…" she whispered, but appeared capable of no more.

Without any more hesitation, he jumped up to lower his bed from the wall, threw back the covers, then struggled to snake his arms beneath Eva's shoulders and knees so he could lift her and carry her to the mattress. Setting her there as gently as if she were porcelain, he dashed to re-light his lamp and close his door. Returning to her bedside, he swaddled her shoulders more tightly in the sheet she'd arrived in but investigated beneath the flaps of fabric at her waist.

Even in the low lamplight, he could see the pink and red stains smeared all over the sheet's interior and Eva's wan skin on her protruding belly. He laid his hand there to feel for signs of life. The thickened membrane felt firm, still. Sliding his palm over its bulbous contour, he next dragged it to her chest to be sure Eva's heart still beat, that her lungs still breathed…because in that moment, her open eyes looked as glazed as those of the animals inside the Academy's display cases. Her mouth hung open.

"Oh God, oh God, Eva."

Cocooning her in the dirtied sheet, he raised his clean one over it and up to her chin. Running to his wardrobe, he snapped a tennis sweater off the shelf and brought it to his pillow to wrap around her wet, fevered head.

Kneeling on the floor beside his goddess swathed in white, Lon tucked his fingertips into the sweater at her hairline and ran his thumbs across her cheeks, trying to keep them warm and ascertain if she had any feeling of it.

"I'm going to ring a doctor, dear girl. Just stay here with me. Stay awake."

Just as he was about to pull away from her, her head fell to the side, pinning his hand between her face and the pillow. "No, old boy. Don't."

"Now is not the time to be stubborn, my girl. You need attention. Now." His eyes zigzagged along the length of her mummified form. "Good God, the time was hours ago. What's happened? Has someone hurt you, has he—"

"Ollie."

"What?"

"Lon, it's Ollie."

Nausea dripped with a sickening trickle into his stomach. "Don't say such things, Eva."

"But I saw her, Lon. She's here. She's *here*," she croaked out.

His lip trembled at what visions had seized her, what portal she might be escaping through, with the faces of her dearly deceased waiting with open arms. "Shh, shhh. No, no, darling. Don't speak this way. Ollie is still alive and well…somewhere…and right now you're alive and well *here*. With me. On this earth with *me*. You're going nowhere else."

Filling with tears, Eva's eyes closed, and her face broke into a horrible grimace as she sobbed. "The child," she squeaked out.

"Shh," Lon repeated, rubbing his hands on the sides of her arms to warm and soothe her. He wasn't certain if by "child" she referred to Ollie or the little life inside her, whether she was aware if there was a life still there at all. "Eva, sweet, just let me ring someone."

She shook harder in his grasp. "Hol—hold me, please." She wept, her face still twisted so miserably.

Against his better judgment, Lon couldn't will himself to disobey her when she pleaded so pathetically. He swallowed and rose to his feet, sat on the mattress, and eased onto his side. He wrapped his arm around her in a tight embrace as he brought his lips to her cheekbone. Brushing them against the smooth skin there, he marveled that his solitary prayer of minutes ago had been answered so soon. But for fate to deliver her to him like this…

"Eva?"

"Mm?" she hummed, sounding half-conscious.

"Can you tell me what happened? Do you remember?"

She moaned again. "Ollie…She's here…My baby…" The rest was incoherent.

Lon tensed and shook her with his body. "Eva." He propped up on his elbow to look down on her face. "Eva. Don't sleep. Wait for the doctor."

With a flutter, her eyes reopened and seemed to search for him.

"I'm right here, my heart. Lon is with you."

"Lonnie, I…"

"I love you, too, darling, and I'm so very sorry I withheld that love from you. I never shall again. Just stay awake for me and the doctor, okay? Be a good girl and do that?" He resumed his vigorous strokes up and down her arm, and she seemed to come to a little more.

"Mm hm…And when I wake, we'll run away…Raise our baby."

"That's right, old girl. We're going to do all those things we dreamed of. But not when you wake; because you aren't going to sleep right now." He took his hand from her arm to gently pat her cheek instead.

Eva gave a wistful hum then sang the first lines of "Tonight You Belong to Me."

"Come, darling," she said. "Sing it, too."

The backs of Lon's eyes burned, but he continued the tune with its eponymous refrain. Then, together, they sang about dreaming by the light of the moon.

Midway through the next verse, Eva's voice fell off as her eyes looked up at the ceiling. Lon stopped, too, yet she urged him, "Go on, old boy. Sing it."

With a spasm in his lips, he cleared his throat and sang of knowing how she'd no longer be there once the sun rose. But that for now at least, she was still his. When he finished, Eva looked back up at his painted ceiling then to the wall beside her, her eyes far away.

He hugged her close and rocked her shoulders roughly. The cabled sweater slipped from her lolling head. "No, no, Eva. Not yet. Not without me." His voice cracked, and he pressed his mouth to her temple.

"*She cannot fade*," she whispered, quoting Keats like when they'd met. "*For ever wilt thou love—*" she drew in a sharp breath as she shivered "*—and she be fair.*"

Lon felt her eyelashes flutter against his chin until her lids closed. Her breast no longer heaved beneath his arm, and her breath ceased hissing into the air.

"Darling," Lon said, still rocking, "my dear old girl."

His only hope hung on a few fine strands of hair caught in her lips that quivered from the air still escaping in and out. He couldn't bear to leave her like this, but her dreadful sleep was an opportunity to fetch aid without weakening under her feeble sounds of protest.

Muffled voices from the room below infiltrated the stagnant air—there was laughter and gleeful shouting, the clanking of glass and vibration of jazz. A New Year's Eve party, with less than an hour to go until midnight. Ripping apart with indecision, he seized the air through his nostrils and thought through the possibility of summoning one of his neighbors.

His neighbor.

When he'd first found Eva crumpled outside his door, hadn't there been a queer light cast on her, coming from more than just the stairwell sconces? Hadn't she been gilded on one side with yellow light from the room next door—the door that, through the corner of his mind's eye, Lon could now see had been standing…open? The edge of Eva's sheet trailing over the lip of its threshold, as if that's where she'd crawled from?

As gently as he could handle her, Lon eased off the bed and lowered Eva's unconscious head to his pillow. With shaking hands, he lifted the receiver of his phone and dialed the doctor, urging him to at once bring his bag—and an assistant, if possible—to Lon's address.

Then, he strode with quiet yet determined footsteps to his door and opened it. Yes. His neighbor's door *had* been ajar, and still was.

Looking down at the stairs, Lon swung his gaze back to his neighbor's open doorway and crept through it. No one was in the main room or down the hall as far as he could see. He would have checked his audaciousness were it not for the pile of fine clothes strewn on the floor, the fur coat with the monogram "ERF" embroidered in its silken lining, and faint blood stains on the bed.

Quickening his pace, he tiptoed toward the kitchen. On entering the little hallway, he paused to look through the bathroom door. The sharp scent of ammonia hit his nose, subdued only somewhat by a gagging concentration of lilac, and he looked around at the sink and shelving to see makeup and green glass atomizers, hairpins and hair dye, and a pair of hose in need of mending hanging from the radiator.

He marched out of the bathroom and into the closet, where he stood in the middle of a cluttered wardrobe. Sparsely hanging from the bar was cheap fabric and fringe, and on the floor was a scuffed pair of black T-strap heels. The shelves appeared covered in accessories and miscellaneous knick-knacks, and there was no chest of drawers but only a couple of hatboxes. Lon squinted at a pair of baby-doll legs sticking out from behind one of them.

Carrying his investigation on to the kitchen, he saw it, too, was empty. A drying rack stood where a table should be in front of the window, and beside the counter was a wooden stool. Hardly a crumb could be found in the cabinets, and nothing in the way of crockery: only a half-empty bottle of lumpy milk and an ice bag occupied the icebox.

All that remained was the back door to the basement. It was unchained, and just when Lon gave its knob a twist and tug, the door opened to a young woman standing outside, her hand holding a skeleton key out to where the lock had just been, and a look of wide-eyed fright frozen on her face.

She didn't scream or even gasp. Just stood there stock-still and barely breathing.

Lon grabbed her outstretched wrist and yanked her into the kitchen, slamming the door behind her. At this, she did shriek and began to plead:

"Please, Lonnie, I'm sorry, I didn't mean it, it was an accident!"

As she paced and frantically pulled at her hair, it was Lon's turn to freeze as if he were seeing a ghost. Wasn't he? That couldn't be… *She* couldn't be…

"Ollie?" he whispered.

"Oh, Lonnie, if anything happens to her, I'll—"

She dropped the brown paper bag Lon hadn't realized she'd carried in with her and threw herself into him with a sob and tight embrace. Though still in shock, he instinctively wrapped his own arms around her to steady her convulsions. He raised a hand to her head, petting the strange hair, as black and bluntly cut as one of her old porcelain Chinese dolls.

"Oh, Lonnie," she cried into his shoulder, "it was an accident, I swear. She saw me, and she fell, and I tried to—but it was no use, and I only left her now so I could fetch some supplies from…from a friend. The blood, Lonnie. She's lost so much blood, I can't—" And once more, the girl lost herself to weeping.

Lon brought his lips to her quivering head to comfort her with a brotherly kiss. "Ollie," he whispered again, "I don't—I don't understand. You're here. You've been *here*, all this time?"

Sniffing as she nuzzled her nose into his collar, Ollie nodded and tightened her hold around his waist. In a calmer voice, she said, "Yes, I've been here…with you…all this time. I couldn't run away from you farther than that—I just couldn't. And yet I couldn't stay. Home, I mean. I woke in the middle of one night and saw all my dolls staring at me, watching me, and they started chanting rhymes at me, all at once…and I couldn't breathe…I was so suffocated and *watched*, always watched. I couldn't take it. I was all balled up."

She looked up at him. Tears stained her cheeks, but she wasn't crying anymore. An unfamiliar and unsettling reserve had settled in her eyes instead, and only now did Lon notice the young woman Ollie had become. So like Eva, yet so very, very different.

All this time.

As his eyes searched her face, he saw one corner of her lips twitch upward. She then removed her hands from his waist and brought them to his cheeks. Stroking them with her thumbs, she said, "No one else…no one took me seriously. But you, Lonnie, you always did."

Trying to gulp some saliva into his arid throat, Lon smoothed the bangs off Ollie's forehead and lightly pinched her chin to incline her face a little more. He inspected the cheeks that had grown more defined and less plumped with baby fat, then peered past the smudged makeup to look into eyes that hadn't changed—other than that unnerving quality they'd assumed since he'd last seen them.

They'd always possessed the shine of intelligence, but this, this was the hardened look of experience.

"Good God, Ollie," he spoke softly, bringing his other hand to her cheek so that they now both stood holding each other's faces. "What has life been like for you?"

He thought of the shoddy and revealing costumes hanging in her closet and lowered his gaze from the dark circles beneath her eyes to the torn stockings on her legs. The thin overcoat she wore could hardly brace her against winter, and had she not even worn a hat outside? Languidly drawing his line of sight back up the length of her form, he thought he might have embarrassed Ollie with his pitying appraisal—a blush reddened her cheeks.

She dipped her chin as though in modesty, but her steely green eyes stayed fixed on his, and the raised corner of her mouth spread into a smirk. "Worth it," she replied. "Life has been worth it to have this, right now."

As she pressed against his body, Lon swallowed again and gently wiped her face dry with his palms. "To have what?"

Despite her half-smile, she looked so sad, lost. Sixteen had not been sweet to her, and in good time, Lon would have to learn why she'd left and never come to him despite living right next door—how he'd never spotted her. But in this moment, all he wanted was to cushion her from the world's sorrows, the pain that had clearly cut its teeth on her young bones.

His vision dulled with tears as the blurred image of Ollie's face came closer to his own; he felt her hands draw his head down and heard the floor creak as she poised herself to meet him halfway.

"You," she sighed, before planting her mouth on his with a quick, tentative kiss.

When she released her lips, she as soon applied them again, and Lon met them voluntarily, again and again—but with the platonic kisses of a dear friend or family member. He never suspected he'd be encouraging her in any romantic fashion until Ollie's next kiss pressed harder and lingered longer. Her fingers slid back from his face to clutch his hair, and he was about to lower his hands to her shoulders and lightly push her away when her tongue penetrated his lips and so expertly—too expertly—engaged his own. She tasted of tobacco and stale gin and smelled of the same, mixed with that nauseous lilac. And yet, with his hands on her bony shoulders, her malnourished frame felt like Eva's in his arms. Eva, who he hadn't felt in this way for so long, who was the only one to quell his fire, after fanning his flames to begin with. Eva, whose bobbed hair he could now feel between his fingers and her hips thrust against his; Eva, for whom he'd yearned for so long but who had left him for Finlay and might now for…ever.

"Eva!" Lon broke away and shoved Ollie back in the process.

"But—"

"No, Ollie."

"*Yes*. Don't you feel it? Haven't you known?"

She approached him again and reached for his face, for his arms, anything she could grab on to as he continually backed away, unable to go farther than the rear door. There, Ollie had him cornered, and she continued her excited pleas as the knob jabbed into his tailbone.

"Lonnie, I…I'm stuck on you," she exclaimed with rapture, arching her back and grazing his chest with breasts much fuller than Eva's. "I've always been goofy for you, and now that I'm grown up, we can finally be together."

"My dear," Lon cried as he gently fended her off. "No, no, no. I cannot tell you the happiness this is to see you, that you haven't truly left us. But this—you and I—can never be. I love you as my sister, darling girl, but I'm *in* love with Eva. We're to be married."

"Married! Oh, Lonnie, are you off your nuts? Don't daydream like Eva does. She would never leave Finlay. Even if she wanted to, even if you're the one who knocked her up, she could never leave the high-hat life. She could never walk away like I did. She's not strong like I am. She lives in a fairy tale, but I…I'm real. You and me are the same, baby. You just told me so in your kiss." She pinned him to the door with her pelvis. "I don't fly with the fairies; I stand on the ground, flesh and blood. So stop looking up at castles in the sky. Be with me here, now."

When she reached again for his face, Lon gripped both her wrists and held them away. Ollie softened her expression and smiled. She was like an alley cat, and something in her demeanor told him she was used to men being rough with her.

"Oh, I don't doubt that you do love Eva," she said, "but even you must know she never really gave herself over to you. Not fully. You know that."

He loosened his grip on her slightly.

"And I don't expect you to fall out of love with her," she said. "Not right away, at least. For now, I'm content being the closest to Eva you can ever have. I'm not the bug-eyed Betty I used to be, and, in time, you'll see in me what you saw in her—but even more. You'll see I'm better for you, truer to you. Lonnie, you'll see!"

As a knot strangled his throat and pressure built in his chest, Lon felt his face break. To process everything happening in this instant was unbearable, and his emotions ricocheted off one another in overdrive—the joy at discovering Ollie, the horror of her seduction, the despair that the love of his life was possibly dying in the room next door. He couldn't deal with this now; he needed to get back to Eva's side.

Sputtering as moisture seeped out his eyes and nose, he firmed his grip on Ollie's wrists and gave her a violent shove. She slammed against the oven with a clang, her face twisting in anguish. Without another word, she clawed at a burner behind her back and threw her teakettle at Lon before fleeing the kitchen.

He'd deflected the metal pot with no injury, but on hearing the front door slam, Lon was seized with an irrational panic that she might have run next door to harm Eva. Pulling himself together, he chased after Ollie—but not without gathering Eva's clothing first.

A quick look into his room assured him Eva still lay alone in comatose peace; the essence of a smile graced her face. She already looked better than when he'd left her. He dumped her damp dress on the floor and hastily covered her with the fur—but not without pressing a soft kiss to her forehead. He was loath to leave her once more, yet he couldn't let Ollie get away, not again. Eva would never forgive him for it.

Leaping down the stairwell to the thumping sounds of New Year's revelry, he overtook Ollie at the courtyard gate. He was able to pry her fingers from the latch, but before his swiftly chilling fingers could clasp hers nimbly enough, she elbowed him in the stomach, kicked him in the shin, then the groin, and doubled back to a nondescript side door.

On reaching it after her, Lon descended stairs to find himself in a dank and dark utility room. A thundering clatter in the corner alerted him to Ollie's progress, and he followed the direction of the sound through an open doorway, tripping and jumping over fallen mops and brooms along the way. Entering the cavernous storage space of the basement, he sped after her clacking footfalls, out the open back door, and into the cold.

Staring out at nothing but an open lot, he searched ahead then left and right. He saw the lights along Clark Street and the occasional motorcar passing by, but no Ollie. Surely she couldn't have run out of sight so fast?

Hearing nothing but his own panting as the steam of his breath clouded his eyes, in time there was the telltale clank of metal overhead. He looked up to see a shuddering Ollie on the fire escape. She was clasping her thin coat close to her chin, and in the same hand she held one of her shoes. She'd likely removed them both to make it as far up as she had in silence, but the other one must have dropped, giving her position away. As she paused there, a couple of flights up, Lon could see her eyes glinting with tears. But she hadn't given up. Not yet.

He dodged the shoe as she threw it at him, then took the steps two and three at a time, pursuing Ollie as she resumed climbing up and up and up—until there was nowhere else for either of them to go but the roof.

"Ollie." Lon gasped on stepping over the shallow ledge and onto the gritty roof surface. The icy night air clenched his lungs, and he was already losing sensation in his ears and nose—he could only imagine how the barefooted little ragamuffin ahead of him must feel. "Please." He huffed and tried to catch his breath. "Please, come back with me. I'll take care of you." All he could see was her small silhouette huddled against the lamplight shining from the courtyard below. Her frosty breath rose from her head like a halo.

"No!"

"Yes. Please. Come now, that's a good girl."

"I'm not a girl, I'm not good, and I don't need taking care of!"

Taking slow, measured steps toward her, Lon endeavored to keep his voice sedate and not incite hers to become any more hysterical. Once his eyes adjusted to the contrast in light and dark, he could see how she stood with her calves flush to the opposite ledge. "No, no, of course not. It's only that…well, it's nice for us adults to have someone care for us, too, isn't it? Someone we can take care of as well? That's all I meant, Oll—Olive. Only that I want to be here for you now. As a man caring for a woman. A grown woman who can care for me, too."

She repeatedly shifted her weight from one foot to the other, which Lon hoped would rock her to a calmer state. He closed the gap between them by another few feet.

"You're so grown up," he soothed. "I look forward to getting to know you again. To be a part of each other's lives once more."

Stepping ever closer, he heard her mumble, "You want to be here for me now?"

"Yes," he exhaled. "Yes, precisely. Will you allow me?"

Her compulsive swaying slowed to a stop. "But…" Her chattering teeth were audible from where he now stood two yards away. "But why weren't you there for me *then?*"

"What?"

"You were always there for Eva. Why weren't you there fo-or me?" Her voice had risen to a higher pitch, and she started swaying again. "It's a-all your fault!" She cried with sniffling sobs, and Lon could hear her begin to hyperventilate. "A-As soon as—Eva go-ot married, you-oo only looked after me-hee to feel close to *her!*" Her volume reduced to a whimper. "On their wedding day, you-oo promised. You promised you'd ta-hake me to dinner. But you n-never did. And then you ne-ever came ba-hack."

"But, Ollie, I…" He raised his hands in supplication but realized she was right. Everything he'd done had been for Eva's sake, and everything she'd done had been for his. Had their vision really been so tunneled that they hadn't noticed the lonely girl struggling her way into adulthood?

He dropped his hands, which fell with a clap to his sides. He walked forward without hesitance now and drew Ollie to him in a protective hug. She cried into his shoulder as she'd done before, but it seemed with reluctance that she eventually wrapped her arms around him, too. Once there, though, they held him tightly, with tender feeling, Lon sensed, and they embraced each other this way for a long moment.

Resting his chin on her head to offer it warmth, he looked out across the courtyard. To the right, he could see the light on in Ollie's room, and the unit below his flickered with the shadows of its partygoers. But his own windows remained as dark as his heart. Where was that damn doctor? Lon didn't want to brush Ollie off again so quickly, but he knew he needed to get back to receive the physician—and hopefully, mercifully, please, dear God, deliver Eva back to health. He would hold Ollie a minute longer, but then they needed to climb back down.

It was too cold for clouds to cover the sky. As Lon stood there under the piercing stars, holding his lost-and-found little sister in his arms, he saw his future with a clarity he'd never had before. Yes, Eva would recover; she'd become healthy as a horse and bear their next child, then the next and the next. They'd raise a whole litter of them, living with Aunt Estella and rebuilding their lives in the wholesome environment of her estate, cultivating themselves mind, body, and soul with the aid of her library, her land, and her love.

And he would restore Ollie to her family. The Hugheses would have another chance at happiness, and the Redcliffes…well, the Redcliffes were resourceful. They'd do all right in the end, matching Finlay with the next debutante ready and willing to provide their heir.

Yes, all the loose ends of Lon's frayed life would tie up nicely, and for the first time, the world was open and glittering with possibility.

Just then he heard a window grind open, and the cacophony of the New Year's party grew louder. Looking over at it, he saw a couple of guests poke their heads out into the fresh air. At the same time, a growling engine rolled to a pause out on the street. The doctor had arrived.

Lon reasoned it was probably best to wait until the physician reached the gate. Then he could call down to him to stand by until Lon could get there to let him in. Otherwise, if he tried rushing down now, he not only risked Ollie's safety, but also might not reach the gate before the doctor would give up waiting without any response.

The party's chaotic chitter-chatter congealed into an organized countdown:

"*Ten…nine…*"

Clearing his throat to call out as he watched the doctor step out of the car, Lon gave Ollie's shoulders a last brisk, warming rub.

"*…seven…six…*"

He was about to let her go and yell to the doctor when he felt one of her hands suddenly slide around from his back to his front, grabbing him at the center.

Enveloped in Lon's embrace, Ollie had felt his pain seep into her own.

Despite her earnest efforts, she knew there was no saving her sister, and she already grieved for Eva. Lon would, too, obviously, but in his and Ollie's shared loss, there would be new hope. Life always grows from decay, and she knew — just knew — that no matter what Lon had said in her kitchen, he was meant for her. They were soul mates; he would realize that soon enough.

And yet Ollie couldn't wait. She'd already waited so, so long, and her words obviously hadn't worked. Nor had her kiss.

Which left her with the one surefire way she'd learned to make men aware of the woman she was. The trick of her trade. Lon would never view her as a lover until he felt the truth of their connection. And what better time for a fresh start than the New Year?

So, when Ollie heard the countdown begin, she seized her opportunity. She would show him, she would prove to him all she could offer.

Lon gasped, but the more he protested, the harder she stroked him in sync with the countdown.

"*…five…four…*"

And as she simultaneously sucked at his neck, he succeeded only in spinning them in a half-circle.

"*…three, two…*"

"Ollie, NO!"

At last he broke away from her hold. But so much momentum had gone into the effort that, as Ollie tumbled backward and onto her behind, Lon propelled the opposite way and fell over the ledge.

"*HAPPY NEW YEAR!*"

August 2000

The door to 4D creaked open on its hinges, but only after releasing a cracking sound as though a seal had been broken. The sharp, sour scent of fresh paint in the warm weather would have explained that, but the must and dust drifting to Kate's nostrils instead carried anything but new-apartment smell. Even in the pitch-blackness, she knew she was alone in there.

No farther than two steps in, her foot skidded on what sounded like paper. She stood still, one hand clasping the vintage knob and the other limp at her side. Whether it was the thickness in the air or her nerves, she kept her breathing shallow; the dank yet almost sweet smell gave her a tickle at the back of her throat. Old attics, neglected bookshelves at libraries, the century-old taxidermy at the Field Museum — all these settings projected inside her head as she tried to place the pervading sense of just…old. Had she walked into her neighbor's new studio flat or some ancient crypt, lost to time?

All Kate could make out was the dull, honey-colored hardwood flooring illuminated in a puddle of hallway light at her feet. Aiming a dry cough into the back of her hand, she then reached for the wall just inside of the doorframe and patted her palm against it for the switch. She only felt an uneven surface until the side of her palm scuffed against a ridge. Concentrating on that spot, she did trace the outline of something rectangular as if sculpted in bas-relief, but it was no light switch.

What the hell, she thought, continuing to feel around the pebbled and almost thorny wall.

A door slammed, and a peal of laughter erupted from below.

In a single bound, Kate hopped out onto the landing. She heard girlish giggling carry from the building entrance to the stairs, accompanied by the bass of a male voice. David's voice.

Oh, God. Retreating a few steps toward 4D, Kate stretched to grab its doorknob and swing it back to a slow, quiet close, twisting then releasing the skeleton key.

At least that's what she played out in her mind; her body was immobile to anything but shifting her eyes to the as-yet gaping door to 4D. The voices grew louder and closer.

Yet not close enough. They could have only climbed to the second-floor landing before their footsteps stopped and Kate heard a key grind into a lock. That broke the spell freezing her in place—she threw herself against the wooden railing to see long golden locks a couple of flights down. They brushed just above elbows that reclined on the railing below.

Kate heard David say, "C'mon in," and with a bubbling titter, his latest conquest slipped from sight as she did what she was told to the sound of lip smacks. Digging her fingernails into the banister's waxy coating, Kate looked back at 4D. This time, she entered it with moxie.

She snatched the piece of paper from the floor and walked deeper into the darkness, using her free hand to feverishly feel for a light switch along the textured wall, marveling she hadn't bumped into anything—furniture, or so much as a bag or box or shoe. In the silent stillness, she grew rigid once more, and became aware of the close air and stale feel of decay closing around her.

Seizing the quiet, she listened for any sound coming from David's actual apartment. On the second floor. So if it hadn't been him next door all this time, then who—

Tap tap, tap tap-tap, tap tap.

Kate spun and flattened her back against the wall, feeling the discomfort of its lumps and points snagging at her thin dress. The sound had come from the wall adjoining this unit to hers.

Christ. Is someone in my apartment?

The knocks sounded again, somewhat subdued yet clear as anything.

"Olive?" she whispered. Sniffing back her trepidation, she caught a trace of perfume that diffused into the air. David's ho-bag downstairs, perhaps, but definitely not Olive's lilac.

The cool, clean scent cut through the haze bogging Kate down, its freshness rejuvenating her thoughts a bit. Looking to the source of the taps and visualizing her own wall on the opposite side — her dear, sweet, yellowed Jaundice — she had a literal light-bulb moment of realization:

Leo had said most of these apartments still had their original fixtures, and if not, the management tried to replace them as closely as possible to preserve the building's historic charm. So this unit probably had wall sconces like hers. In which case, they could have rotary switches of their own.

She inched her way toward the shared wall, flailing her hands until she hit a solid surface. Patting around at the general height of her unit's lights, she found one on this side of the wall and pinched down its electric candle until she felt a little metal nub beneath. She twisted it.

Click.

And then there was light. She flicked on the second sconce and stepped back to take in what appeared to be a mural on the wall. Snowhills and the skyline, tall trees and the Water Tower. Kate looked down to see her dusty happy hour flyer in her hand and spun around to face an empty room.

Aside from the painting that transformed it into quite something else, straight ahead was a mirror image of her studio: the large door for the Murphy bed, the hallway next to it leading to the kitchen, windows draped in dark velvet, and across from them, the rough wall Kate had exfoliated her hands on.

"Oh, my God."

A muffled laugh rang out from somewhere off the stairwell, and the thumping bass of trance music began to vibrate the walls — Kate could venture a guess from where. On tiptoes, she stepped to close the door after retrieving her purse from the landing. Then, padding to the middle of the room, she spun around in place to see a white house and a great gray chimney, a pagoda and a koi pond, a lake, a lion, and music staffs dotted with half, whole, and quarter notes. But the longest stretch of wall that Kate stopped to face was the *pièce de résistance.*

"Oh, my God," she repeated. "Eva."

She sank to the hardwood floor. Setting the flyer down with Olive's bag, she adjusted into cross-legged position and just stared.

The vibrancy in color and pattern on all four walls evoked Henri Matisse, whose work Kate had seen at the Art Institute but never to this scale. The mural right in front of her stretched the length of the room and from floor to ceiling. The prevailing color was green: rolling emerald hills in the distance; dewy, mossy mounds of Kelly green and lime in the foreground. A ribbon of deep blue streaked with teal and jade angled down from the upper left corner, carrying a spectrum of flower petals on its current.

And green were the eyes of the chocolate-haired woman reclining alongside the stream. Her brown bob looked at once sleek and soft where it hugged her brow and nestled beneath her cheeks, and from her fine head to her toes was nothing but ivory flesh. She lay on what appeared to be a slim oriental rug of crimson tangled in mustard vines and rusted florals. Her shoulders were propped on an oversized pillow of gold swirled with beige, the cushion tilting her forward to reveal the pale pink buds of her breasts. From her tiny waist rose the curve of a slim hip, and one leg draped over the other to partially obscure a dark tuft in between. And while one arm was flung over her head in pleasurable abandon, the other lay lazily outstretched toward the river. Where her pale fingers tickled the waters, a sprinkling of sandy specks filtered into the current and eddied upstream to where the band of blue met the ceiling.

Kate's lungs emptied of air as she craned her neck to behold where the stream flowed into the darker blue abyss of a night sky.

"Lonnie," she whispered, "it's breathtaking."

She didn't question it was his work. She knew it; she felt it. And she knew well enough from Eva's wedding photo that this was her likeness, captured in a surreal yet earthy quality only love could render. Surely intended for his and her eyes only. But now Eva was still here, nearly a century later. *Now, she is for everyone.*

But no, Kate thought next. This art was clearly not on display for all. Management could have made it a miniature museum open to the building's tenants or public, rented it out for events or to tenants at a premium—or painted it over altogether and maintained business as usual. But they hadn't. They'd seemingly left it, just as it was, for all this time, across all the hands it must have changed between through the decades.

"An aunt of his, it turns out," Leo had said, *"donated a large sum to this building for its maintenance…An Estella Ashby."*

Was this why? With the stipulation that this unit remain private? Had she done it for Lonnie? Had she loved him that much? But then why wouldn't a proud aunt have made his talent known to the world, in honor of his memory?

Unless, of course, she'd wanted to hide it from Finlay. *Yes, of course.* A nude painting of Redcliffe's wife in another man's home, one she'd probably posed for in a post-coital glow, was not something to leak out.

A waft of the perfume from earlier drifted by. A second later came the familiar knocking, but this time near the door. When Kate looked to it, she remembered the rectangular protrusion from the wall by the doorframe. Nothing was readily visible, but a varying shade of green did show itself—a patch of pale jade within brighter emerald grasses. She stood to inspect it closer.

Running her hand along its relief, she felt the papery edge of what must have been a large flake of paint detaching from the wall. With age, moisture, and the building settling, it wasn't surprising the painting might crack or deteriorate in spots. Kate bent down and ran her fingertip along the edge, wondering if it was a sloppy repair-job. The lighter green paint was more matte, powdery, and lacking the flourish and texture of Lonnie's other brushstrokes. In fact, the piece now peeling away was thicker than paint; its underside had the golden tone of parchment, and the wall beneath it was the same emerald as the rest.

On a rush of instinct, Kate tore the patch from the wall. She flipped over what was indeed paper in her hand—an envelope. Still fairly crisp. Looking at the sconces, she noted the bulbs also had to be relatively new. For that matter, despite its musty smell, the room wasn't nearly as dusty or rotted as it could have been. Very little gray fuzz along the moldings, few cobwebs adorning the fixtures and corners.

So Olive probably did come here. But change the bulbs? Reach the corners of the ceiling? And while it didn't look recent, someone must have dusted and swept at least once after the woman's death.

Braving the dark of the hallway, Kate strode into the kitchen. She swatted at something that brushed her head and heard a light, metallic tapping overhead. She reached for the culprit and gave it a yank. Just as suspected, the pull cord illuminated a ceiling lamp.

"Wow." From the linoleum countertops to the wooden icebox to the tarnished iron and white porcelain stove, all of the fixtures looked original to the room.

Except for the Swiffer propped in the corner by the rear door. And a white handkerchief next to the sink that looked a lot like the kind Leo carried around in the pocket of his overalls.

What better project to occupy a volunteer handyman than a unit unavailable for rent? Why pay staff for the upkeep of some dead rich woman's wishes they couldn't make money on?

Huh. No wonder Leo had eyed Eva's wedding photo so gravely. He'd recognized her.

Kate slapped the painted paper against the palm of her other hand as she walked back into the main room. Peeling open the envelope, she proceeded to carefully pull out the folded sheets of thin paper inside. She glanced up at the mural one more time before looking down to read the pinched cursive writing.

April 2000

*If you have found this, then you have found my key
and my truth. Or maybe they have finally taken
a wrecking ball to this place, laid to rest the poor
souls who already had one taken to their lives. The
destructive force that was me.*

*But my arthritis aches and the seconds tick
ever closer to the midnight of my memory and my
life, so I had best get on with it. Take this as my
confession — may it absolve me of my sins. I killed
them, you see. I killed them both.*

Kate flipped through the pages and scanned the last one for a
signature. Sure enough, it was signed *Olive "Ollie" Hughes.*

*No, it was not directly at my hand, but it was me
who they both recoiled from and, in so doing, fell to
their deaths.*

Kate felt a heaviness in her gut as Olive first explained what had
really happened that New Year's night in 1926. How very much
in love she'd been with Lonnie, so one day soon after her sister's
wedding, she had discreetly followed him home to Camden Court,

where she'd learned of his secret life. How she'd taken to strolling past the courtyard building every day after school, lapping around onto Diversey and then onto Pine Grove to resume her way home.

How one day as she'd passed by the Lincoln Park Arms Hotel on Pine Grove, a man with glimmering diamonds on his fingers and lapel had caught her eye. How he'd smiled and tipped his hat to her. And how after future encounters like this, he'd eventually succeeded in luring her into his hotel room.

Child predator, Kate thought. *What scum.* But it got even worse, if that was possible. The man hadn't wanted Olive for himself, just any man in the city willing to pay.

We both knew I was terribly plain, but he told me a blank canvas has most potential for fine art. He charmed with all the promises any young woman would have fancied. I already had money and status, of course, but I desired more; what I didn't have was adventure, romance, rule-breaking. If life in my parents' house had stifled my breath, and my love for Lon had taken it away, this man, for the time being, helped me breathe again. Because he gave me a plan. I didn't have to do it alone, and I would have somewhere to go. He would help me become someone else. But first, he would capitalize on the fact that he knew exactly who I already was.

Kate's posture slumped as she read how "Diamond Mack" had ingratiated himself to Olive by being such a good listener. He would take her side on everything—grievances with her parents, jealousy of her sister, lovesickness over Lon. *Of course* she was right to feel how she'd felt; *of course* she had everything she'd wanted coming to her. And Mack would show her how. All Olive would owe in compensation was a pretty piece of jewelry from her momma's or her sister's stash. That gorgeous emerald engagement ring, for instance, that Mack had seen in all the papers. His sage advice had been to test her purloining prowess by starting small. Ollie'd decided to practice on Eva's favorite handbag.

I suppose in stealing that, I was almost looking to get caught. But no one noticed, as they usually didn't.

Doting on a child isn't the same as knowing a person. Fair enough, as I barely knew myself.

It was New Year's Eve 1926 when I escaped their notice for the last time. It was easy with the distractions of my parents' entertainment down below. I tiptoed down the staircase, out the side garden door and through the gate, carrying nothing but the little purse filled with my sister's rings and miscellaneous mementos. And my doll under my arm, of course. Otherwise I didn't bring so much as a coat: a frigid night to be sure, but I didn't have to go any farther than the Arms the next block over. Once there, I put on the dress and applied the makeup Mack had laid out for me. I'd been so cold and scared, but Mack's room and whiskey were so warm and comforting, I let him take Eva's rings and my virtue that night. He said it would prepare me for my future, for when Lon and I could finally be together. He said he had made me into the "new woman" of our time.

I suppose I was his little pet for the next few weeks. He set me up with the room here at Camden Court and subsidized my first month; I think someone was already living there at the time, but Mack pulled those wonderful strings he had, and somehow they got the boot. But after that first month, he said I'd have to pay my own way, stand on my own two feet. Only then would Lonnie respect me, and I believed him. But I had no resources of my own, no training, no connections that would keep me anonymous, so he promised he'd make the introductions. That was when I met Madam Mae.

I don't know what to say for myself. Why I trusted that man is beyond belief for you, I am sure, but at the time all I knew was he had all but delivered me to

*my dear Lonnie's door, and somehow delivering me to
that of Madam's seemed more honorable to me than
returning me home for reward. Surely his commissions
on me never reached the ransom my parents had posted,
but Diamond Mack worked in mysterious ways and
often with vendetta, and who am I to question that
now? Who am I but nothing less than a murderer.*

"And here it is," Kate whispered. Olive had finally led up to New Year's 1927 and her role in the demise of Evelyn Redcliffe and Alonzo Ashby. She explained Eva's tumble down the same stairs Kate had just climbed. How, following the miscarriage in the cold bath Ollie had frantically fixed for her, Eva had caught an infection.

"Miscarriage?" Kate hissed. Still holding the letter, she dropped her hands with a thud of her knuckles on the floor. *But that doesn't make sense.*

She read on as, panicked, Ollie had taken to the streets to find medicine and bandages that might comfort, if not cure, her big sister.

*He gave them to me, not Mack but the man who'd
by that time been giving me a lot of pretty things, but
most of all his attention. He could do no more for me,
though, than what I'd asked, not wanting to entangle
himself in the mess of my real life out from behind
the smoky curtains of Madam's. He was a good man
but a coward, and of course he never intended to leave
his wife for me. He thought me sweet, but I was a stain
now, and so I returned into the cold night alone.*

Kate read on to learn how a crestfallen Ollie had returned to her room only to find Eva gone and Lon in her stead. Of the words they'd exchanged and the horrible chase to the rooftop.

*I'd barely had time to process I was losing Eva
before I then lost Lon. I don't know why it wasn't my
life instead of his. I was blinded by love, by lust for a
reckless, irretrievable moment, but it was only affection
I'd wanted to show him when he'd stepped back to save
my dignity. And yet he couldn't save himself. And nor
could I.*

*Mack said he'd made me a new woman, but no.
I'd still been a child when I ran up to that roof and
Lon — my brother, not my lover — followed after. But
I climbed down that icy ladder an old woman who
no longer knew her mind. I was numb from the cold
of winter and shock of death before my eyes when I
walked back to Madam's and rocked myself to sleep in
one of her closets.*

Madam Mae, however, refused to offer safe harbor for very long
unless "Stella" got back to work, so Olive had dragged her feet back to
her room one night. Blank as a slate, she'd ambled into her bathroom and
pulled the door closed with such force that the glass knob had fallen out.
She'd stayed there for days, drinking at the tap but otherwise prepared
to starve on that cold tile floor; it was what she'd deserved, after all.

Olive had completely lost sense of time when a male voice asked
from the hall whether anyone was there. She didn't answer but heeded
his warning to move away from the door. Crawling into the bathtub,
she'd lain there as lifeless as Eva had until the door was kicked in.

*The gentleman at the door wasn't of the uniform I'd
expected. He wasn't a cop but an aged yet able chauffeur,
a man I recognized from when Lon's Aunt Estella
rode into town, after Eva had married and gone to the
country. She took us for a drive along the lakeshore
to see the turning leaves, then to Michigan Avenue for
dessert. She even encouraged Lon to purchase a sweet
doll I saw in a window there. Sure, I was too old for it,
but unknown to them, I thought it had Lon's eyes and
my skin; it's what I imagined his and my child would
look like one day. And of course, forever seeing me as a
little girl in braids, my parents were pleased by the gift.
But how Lonnie had loved his great-aunt, and I, too,
grew fond of her that autumn day, so I chose Stella for
my name when Mack checked me into this hotel.*

*And it was Stella Parker whom Estella Ashby
discovered at rock bottom. She gave me a sweet from*

*her purse and commanded her driver to fetch me some
nourishment at once. It wasn't until I had something
in my stomach that I even realized she was covered in
black crepe. And then I remembered, and then how I
cried. I wept into this old woman's shoulder and told
her everything.*

*She cried with me, but she did not blame me. She
was more relieved to know Lon had not taken his life
in hasty reaction to Eva losing hers. Who knows if
he would have, though. Had he lived, Lon would have
returned to a corpse. And demands for explanation.*

As it was, Estella took care of that.

Evidently, before the worst could be thought of Lon and posthumous accusations placed on his name, Estella had confessed his
and Eva's truth to the police and next of kin involved. The mural had
obviously helped reinforce that. The situation had also been handled
quietly on site thanks to the Redcliffe's and Hughes's joint influence.
Forensics, still in its infancy, ruled out foul play, and the sheer shock,
horror, and embarrassment of it all had been enough for both families
to call off any further search for the young woman next door who'd
evidently discovered Eva first and done what she could to help…

*…a Good Samaritan, clearly, but a marginal,
impoverished little flapper as ascertained from a quick,
sloppy scan of my lodgings. They thought perhaps
I'd fled for help or in fear; prints indicated I'd been
confronted by Lon. At any rate, I was assumed and
proven innocent on the spot. The discoveries in Lonnie's
room overshadowed everything.*

*If there was anything Finlay sought to avoid, it
was scandal, making it all the easier for Estella to get
her way New Year's Day 1928, when she called for a
private meeting in Father's study. She insisted Lon
be cleared of any association with Mrs. Redcliffe and
her death. The Redcliffes must have complied, though*

it didn't take long for rumors to circulate that Lon was otherwise inclined when it came to sexual relations anyway — eyewitnesses in the building had spotted Eva in her guise, and no doubt rather than feel the cuckold, Finlay would have encouraged any gossip that hurt Lon's reputation without reneging on Estella's wishes.

The rich and influential can be slaves to image, but I'd venture it was pure human sorrow — the keen heartache of losing a child — and the denial that sometimes salves it that compelled both families to decline comment on the baby. "Eva died in premature labor," was all they'd confirm, not how far along she was or if a preemie was now fighting for its life. And while gossips of course speculated, no one dared question the Hughes or Redcliffes again as they withdrew from public eye for an extended period of private mourning. Who would have guessed their unhealthy mixture of pride and grief would so greatly work to everyone's advantage in but a few months' time.

Kate puzzled over that last statement but nodded as the other pieces fit. Flipping to the next and second-to-last page, she read Olive's notation that it had taken her six days to write everything so far, whenever memory and arthritis would allow. On the seventh day, then, she'd vowed to conclude her morbid memoir:

Estella was satisfied with the families' wishes not to pursue Lon's neighbor for questioning, but she privately needed to meet the woman who could have been the last to see her nephew alive. She knew me instantly, of course, without having to even study me the few seconds Eva and Lonnie had required. I don't think even my parents could have done that, not right away. But Estella had a way of seeing people that reminded us we were alive. If ever there was an angel on this Earth, it was her. Predictably, she urged me to return home, threatening to take me there herself. But after some time, I think my inexplicable grief and guilt prevented her from pressing my fevered protests any further. She merely held my hand and told me what we would do.

She had already initiated the purchase of Lon's room as a private residence and would do the same for mine. I would then live with her in Wisconsin — in secrecy — for at least a year, where she would tutor me in that grand library of hers. I was to find proper employment as a secretary. In so doing, she would help hide my identity but lectured I would have to face the consequences if someday I got found out. It hadn't been a crime to kidnap myself, after all.

A phone ringing jarred Kate's concentration. The Nokia tune—coming from right where she'd left her cell on the side table next door. Probably Dexter checking if she'd made it back safely. She smiled at the courtesy and went back to the letter.

Naturally, I rebelled at first. But over the course of that year, she strengthened me in every way possible. Before I knew it and could even believe it for myself, I was eighteen and prepared for what could come next, and I would take it head-on. But by that time in 1929, Father and Mother in all their devastation had removed themselves to a ranch somewhere in Texas to start over in a life without their daughters. They also lost a good amount of their fortune later that year, but with money already in the land, they still weathered it all right not to be down and out. Father was always resilient like that, though I can't imagine how Mother fared. I was concerned for them, and I missed them. I truly did. And I mourned their loss even though they still lived. But I could have never faced them again, not with knowing what I'd done. So with their absence, I felt a little bolder about returning to Chicago. And really, I was simply so very much changed — in appearance <u>and</u> spirit. A new woman indeed.

Yes, I was changed beyond how time and training had developed me. Little had I known as I watched my sister lose her fetus that I'd already been carrying one myself to remember a client by. Soon enough, I was showing as much as Eva had been, and when my daughter arrived, it couldn't have been more than two, three months after my niece or nephew would have been due. Estella and her private physician cared for us both. And after countless long talks during that time in 1928 — on Estella's porch swing, in her parlor surrounded by Lonnie's lovely paintings, or in the room we'd temporarily made the baby's nursery — we reached a mutual decision of what I must do next.

Leaving that child, my child, on the steps of Finlay's country house was the most difficult experience of my life — and I say this after having brought two innocents to their untimely deaths. Three innocents, rather, lest we forget the unborn child I also killed that dreadful day. And so, eye for an eye, life for a life. I gave Finlay my baby to raise as Eva's — the "miracle" child the public would come to believe had been in an incubator at the Michael Reese Hospital all that time. And on the grace of Estella, my benefactor and my savior, I started my own life anew.

The rest is just details. Specks of sand in the grand scheme of the universe. Everything I have related here is everything I hid away in the corners of my mind that wouldn't fit in a couple of dusty shoeboxes. Until they came back. First my baby, my miracle child indeed. Nothing short of divine intervention returned her to me, though I did not deserve it and I cannot let her know. Not while I live. And now Lonnie and Eva. They've come back to me, too, and I need them to forgive. Please.

I will see you on the other side,
Olive "Ollie" Hughes

Kate folded the letter in half and brought it to her heart. Trying to find feeling in her legs again, she sniffed and looked up at Lon's painting of Eva.

"So it's been you two over here. This entire time." She wiped a tear and actually laughed that her imagination had taken the leap that someone would flirt with her through a wall—and someone like David at that. Wishful thinking, when given enough time, had become delusional believing.

Hey, desperate.

She started as this time a louder and more classic ring exclaimed from her next-door landline. If it was Dexter, she shouldn't worry him much longer.

On a deep inhale, she elongated her spine toward the ceiling, then slumped her shoulders and calmed herself with another moment's meditation. Romantic and tragic as the tale was, modern pragmatism told her that no way could Olive have pulled off any of what she did in this day and age, when private lives weren't so private anymore and police investigations were so much more sophisticated. Regardless, Kate and her new drinking buddy would have to have a good long heart-to-heart tomorrow. Hopefully Vera learning that she had, in fact, known her real mother and greatly helped her out in the last years of life would bring her some peace. Either way, Kate would be there for her.

After a while, she did find her legs again, and she used them to stand and walk out to her own apartment door. But not before returning Olive's letter to its envelope, shutting off the apartment lights, and locking the door behind her with the skeleton key—which, along with the letter, she tucked into Eva's favorite black beaded purse.

Pressing her palm to the lacquered door of 4D, she whispered, "Good night, Eva. Good night, Lon. Until we meet again."

On closing the door to apartment 4D, Kate retrieved her own modern-cut key from the bag and slipped it into her lock. In spite of herself, she wished she would find Dexter in there, waiting for her with the room filled with candles and his sundial indicating it was sex o'clock. *I could show him a thing or two with my astro-labia, too, Vicki.*

Instead, her door opened to a vacant room, its darkness reproaching her again for her stupid fantasies. She had half a mind to take it out on Olive. Yes, after all this, the old gal deserved quite the talking to.

But that would have to wait. For starters, the woman had already lived one hell of a punishing life. And in death, writing on the bathroom mirror and that eye-trick in the purse clear across town tonight must have wiped her out of a crapload of paranormal energy. Kate would be sure to switch on her lights and appliances all at once tomorrow to give the Phantom Flapper a good recharge before the fuse blew.

And then her heart leaped as she heard a voice breathlessly call, "Kate!" up the stairwell. She spun around.

"Dex! What are you doing here?"

Taking the steps two at a time, he fell into her with a hug. "I freaked when you didn't answer my calls. I just wanted to let you know I was on my way over. I don't mean to crowd you, but I'd crawled into my bed, and I—I just needed to hold you. You shouldn't be alone on your birthday."

"Well, technically it's not my birthday anymore, but…thanks." She pressed a kiss on his hot neck.

"But what are you still doing out here?" he asked. "You couldn't just be getting home now?"

Watching his eyes dart around her face as a crease worried itself into his brow, Kate opened her mouth to explain, then figured she could do one better. Closing and locking her door again, she switched keys and reopened 4D.

She extended her hand for Dexter to take.

Beneath the soft folds of green chenille, Kate turned her face from the sweet-smelling nook of Dex's neck to look up at Lon's starry night. The points of paint flickered in the golden light cast by tiny flames scattered across the floor. Even the emerald eyes of Eva's likeness seemed to dance.

Kate thrilled as the pads of Dexter's fingers traced along her bare arm. "Nice call on the candles," she whispered.

As soon as he'd seen Lon's studio and its impact on Kate, he'd suggested they stay the night there while she told him the rest of its story. Though maybe not on an eighty-year-old Murphy mattress; the frame was probably rusted in place in the closet anyway.

So, quietly and efficiently, they'd snuck back and forth between Kate's place and 4D to carry in her futon cushion, pillows, blankets, and every candle they could find on her shelves and in her cabinets—including an economy-sized bag of IKEA tea lights, which they'd high-fived as a great score.

As the dozens of little fire hazards lapped at the air, Dex replied, "The jazz music is a nice touch, too."

Kate's lips spread in a wide smile. "Yeah, that Lonnie knows how to woo a dame, all right."

He paused his caresses to give her a squeeze. "Best wing-man ever. Thanks, dude," he spoke out to the open room before rolling onto Kate to blanket her with his warm skin.

She eased her leg up and down his thigh and rocked her hips into place as he planted kisses along her clavicle and dipped below. Stretching her arms above her head with an arch of her back, she bit her lower lip and shut her eyes for a lingering, pleasing moment.

Reopening them to the ceiling, she sighed. "Oh. Look, Dex. He included them."

He kissed his way back up to her earlobe before twisting to see where she pointed.

"Ah, Pleiades. Your favorite." He grinned down at her, giving her a chance to enjoy the refreshing cool of his deep aqua eyes. Then, with a light peck at the tip of her nose, he resumed his efforts beneath the chenille.

Closing one eye, Kate counted up the star cluster's seven white dots, dedicating one to each of the special soul mates housed under Camden Court's roof:

Lon and Eva, Vera and Leo, Olive, me, and…

Wrapping her arms around lucky number seven, she lost focus on the ceiling as he took her to the stars.

Acknowledgments

This feels too much like an Oscar speech when there's no way I should be the only one on stage. So I've brought my own trophies to hand out (swiped from a little league team — just pretend the tiny player is a writer wielding a really big pen). Without further ado, the awards go to...

Omnific Publishing, for bringing this story from my Mac to the world. Special thanks to Elizabeth Harper, Lisa O'Hara, and Tracey Miller for seeing its potential and taking the chance. To CJ Creel and Sarah Allan, the dream team of editing whose brilliant insights have not only strengthened the story but made the process hugely enjoyable as well — you are absolute stars. To Kimberly Blythe and Coreen Montagna, for further polishing it up real pretty, and Traci Olsen and Micha Stone, for their marketing and design expertise — and patience with my over-excited fool self. And dearest Fred, who knows who she is and why I'm grateful.

Bev Nickelson, sister and author extraordinaire, for being a never-ending font of creative inspiration and encouragement — and forging the path to us becoming the next Brontës. I tip my best bonnet to you.

Ryan Wagner, for supporting my little literary hobbies until they weren't hobbies anymore but pipe dreams come true. Sorry the price has been coming home to a disheveled hag at the computer most days.

Joyce Keough, who lamented, "Where's my writer? Where's my poet?" when all four of her offspring pursued business degrees. Well, here ya go. Now it's Jeff's and Steve's turns to step up to the plate (which is a very appropriate metaphor, by the way, for this trophy I'm handing you).

Frank Keough, who won't want to read the saucy bits his little girl wrote (I'll paperclip those pages together) but should enjoy sneaking into the Aragon Ballroom and Green Mill with her all over again. I sent Lon and Kate there in homage to that enchanted Chicago afternoon with you.

And — really? The orchestra's starting the music on me? Fine. As I was saying…

To the Twenties and my twenties in Chicago. They were both roarin' times, and had the former been any less dodgy and the latter less douchie, I wouldn't have had so much material to work with.

About the Author

Rumer Haven is probably the most social recluse you could ever meet. When she's not babbling her fool head off among friends and family, she's pacified with a good story that she's reading, writing, or revising—or binge-watching something on Netflix. A former teacher hailing from Chicago, she presently lives in London with her husband and probably a ghost or two. Rumer has always had a penchant for the past and paranormal, which inspires her writing to explore dimensions of time, love, and the soul. *Seven for a Secret* is her debut novel.

www.rumerhaven.com
@RumerHaven

Young Adult Romance

The Ember series: *Ember & Iridescent* by Carol Oates
Breaking Point by Jess Bowen
Life, Liberty, and Pursuit by Susan Kaye Quinn
The Embrace series: *Embrace & Hold Tight* by Cherie Colyer
Destiny's Fire by Trisha Wolfe
The Reaper series: *Reaping Me Softly & UnReap My Heart* by Kate Evangelista
The Legendary Saga: *Legendary* by LH Nicole
Fatal by T.A. Brock
The Prometheus Order series: *Byronic* by Sandi Beth Jones
One Smart Cookie by Kym Brunner

Paranormal Romance

The Light series: *Seers of Light, Whisper of Light & Circle of Light* by Jennifer DeLucy
The Hanaford Park series: *Eve of Samhain & Pleasures Untold* by Lisa Sanchez
Immortal Awakening by KC Randall
The Seraphim series: *Crushed Seraphim & Bittersweet Seraphim* by Debra Anastasia
The Guardian's Wild Child by Feather Stone
Grave Refrain by Sarah M. Glover
Divinity by Patricia Leever
Blood Vine series: *Blood Vine, Blood Entangled & Blood Reunited* by Amber Belldene
Divine Temptation by Nicki Elson
Love in the Time of the Dead by Tera Shanley

Romantic Suspense

Whirlwind by Robin DeJarnett
The CONduct series: *With Good Behavior, Bad Behavior & On Best Behavior*
by Jennifer Lane
Indivisible by Jessica McQuinn
Between the Lies by Alison Oburia
Blind Man's Bargain by Tracy Winegar

Erotic Romance

The Keyhole series: *Becoming sage* (book 1) by Kasi Alexander
The Keyhole series: *Saving sunni* (book 2) by Kasi & Reggie Alexander
The Winemaker's Dinner: *Appetizers & Entrée* by Dr. Ivan Rusilko & Everly Drummond
The Winemaker's Dinner: *Dessert* by Dr. Ivan Rusilko
Client N° 5 by Joy Fulcher